MW01413626

Tomorrow Is Today

Tomorrow Is Today

David Fleming

Copyright © 2004 by David Fleming.

Library of Congress Number: 2004094998
ISBN: Hardcover 1-4134-6296-0
Softcover 1-4134-6295-2

All rights reserved. No part of this book may be reproduced or transmitted in any form or by any means, electronic or mechanical, including photocopying, recording, or by any information storage and retrieval system, without permission in writing from the copyright owner.

This is a work of fiction. Names, characters, places and incidents either are the product of the author's imagination or are used fictitiously, and any resemblance to any actual persons, living or dead, events, or locales is entirely coincidental.

This book was printed in the United States of America.

To order additional copies of this book, contact:
Xlibris Corporation
1-888-795-4274
www.Xlibris.com
Orders@Xlibris.com

23987

This book is dedicated to

Conspiracy Theorists EVERYWHERE!!

Preface

While the World held it's breath, December 31st, 1999 passed into history. The year 2000, the beginning of the 3rd millennium, descended upon the Earth minus much of its predicted hype. The hype, whether it was conveying the end of the end of the World, or the dawning of a new age, did not quite materialize as forecasted during the late nineties.

By the summer of 1997, the World began to witness and some even took notice of unprecedented worldwide events. Most did ignore the peculiar weather patterns, which caused floods in traditional barren regions, and at the same time caused droughts in the farmlands. Tropical cities as well as Northern ones have broken records by double digits. Safe drinking water is becoming as scarce as affordable as unleaded gasoline. Food supplies have become contaminated by various sources of insects, as well as microscopic organisms. Super strains of viruses are crippling vast numbers of people throughout the World, and are resistant to the last remaining antibodies available.

In America, though the politicians stress that crime is at an all time low, the fact is, it is not. The politicians stress that the country's economy is getting stronger. The fact is, it is not. Economists predict at the current rate of inflation, America will be in a state of hyperinflation by June 2001 perhaps even complete collapse by 2010.

By the close of 2007, it seemed that the American people had started waking up from their media induced comas. Early 2008 saw sporadic outbreaks of violence against the Government. More anti-government movements sprung up protesting the seemingly dictatorial stance of the Federal Government. When the President said in her speech before the United Nations concerning banning civilian firearm ownership, that the U.S. Constitution was a dead document, the effect was tantamount to a declaration of Martial Law. Immediately 13 states banned together and threatened cessation, as firearm and ammunition sales rocketed beyond the Y2K fright. With most of the U.S. Armed Forces still engaged in Middle Eastern conflict, she warns that she will use United Nation Forces to quell any unrest, as well as the enforcement of any gun bans. Her words ripped through America as if a hostile enemy has just threatened to invade the United States. The state of the Union was like a fine mist of gasoline hovering over an awakening volcano.

Meanwhile, elsewhere in the World, Britain finally abandons its sovereignty and joins the European Union. Construction has begun on a span connecting Spain with the African continent. The Central Intelligence Agency receives anonymous information that a weapon of massive destruction is positioned to depopulate the City of New York. A nuclear emergency search team was dispatched to New York's Central Park's great lawn. Since the anonymous tip failed to disclose where beneath the vast great lawn the lay, a search of the entire area commenced. An unsuspecting cover workers reseeding the lawn was released to an unsuspecting public.

The massive search soon located the radioactive bomb, otherwise known as a dirty bomb. Its potential range of destruction would of terminated hundreds of thousands of New Yorkers, and reduce Manhattan to an inhabitable wasteland for generations.

There were dozens of suspected factions but currently the U.S. is engaged in some type of military action against them. Then there was China and the Russians. Two forces America cannot afford to fight, without the very possible overcome of defeat. Some in the U.S. Intelligence community of planting the device had suspected Israel, tipping off the U.S. Government, all in an attempt to cause a U.S. led retaliatory nuclear strike against the Islamic nations. The President has completely isolated herself from the people of the United States, as well as most of her military leaders, which is par for the course since she desires to allow the U.N. to manage and control U.S. Forces.

More and more demands for an investigation into the President's alleged win considering the revealing malfunctions of the electronic voting machine that voters have been forced to use nation wide. She has been in office for only six months and she stands a very good chance of being recalled. She has accelerated the assault on the Middle Eastern Countries labeled as part of an axis of evil. She has reversed her promise to bring jobs back to America and has declared to erase the border between the U.S. and Mexico. Her distance for the law of the land has enraged Congress, the Senate and according to the last Fox News poll, 79% of the American people. The American economy, its government and its very survival is on the verge of collapse.

The New Agers are still proclaiming that a cleaner, safer World is still just around the corner. They state that the evildoers of the World will soon be snatched away. They stand firm on this notion for they insist they have been told by the spirit of the Earth that the evildoers will be snatched away if constant worshipping of the trees, rocks and wildlife continues.

Some within the New Age Movement point to the sudden

rash of Worldwide UFO reports as a sign of an Earthy renewal. Satanism has now become a recognized religion in America. On October 31st 2008, a 24-hour satanic channel went online capable of being received within any home in North America.

The churches of America screamed in protest, but it was all to no avail. The Christian churches did continue to drive their message of their soon returning, Lord Jesus Christ, but many Americans shouted back that they no longer believed in the Christian God. Even some of the leaders of the Catholic Church publicly stated that Jesus Christ was nothing more than a Martin Luther King of his day. Secular Humanist media godless scientist, and a pagan induced society bore havoc with the gospel.

Bibles and any other Christian related materials had been banned from public view. America has followed the Canadians lead and has considered these materials as works of hate. An internationally known American rock group burned Bibles while on stage, while proudly displaying a satanic Bible. Without warning over a three day holiday weekend, the President signed an order in January 2008, removing the tax-exempt status of the church. Church burnings have erupted once again, but this time it was not only the black churches targeted.

The ozone crisis has worsened. The southern hemisphere during daylight hours has become dangerous. The Australian government has limited beach goers to one hour, and school aged children must wear hats with brims wide enough to keep direct sunlight off their faces, sun screen and no daylight exposure beyond 30 minutes. For the fifth straight year temperatures in Alaska have failed to drop below freezing. Heat waves from Texas to Lake Michigan have killed close to five thousand people since the summer of 2005, while the East Coast has experienced super rainstorms packing winds well over 100 miles per hour. New York City, Boston and the New England states soared from summer like temperatures of upper eighties and lower nineties to 105 to experience a drop in temperature to 45 in 4 hours. Masses of migrating birds have been discovered dead all over the United States and Canada. Whales and dolphins have been breaching themselves to the point Green Peace advocates are predicting the marine life extinction in 5 years.

Network T.V. weather personalities and government scientists all appear on T.V., across America down playing the non-traditional weather patterns. They expel scientific terms to demonstrate Earth's normal 500 year cycles. There is nothing to be concerned about, they assure and then go on to compare the abnormal weather to the likes of an Indian summer.

Others loudly disagree. They are immediately and viciously attacked by not only the so-called experts, but by the mainstream media as crackpots, kooks, conspiracy nuts and alarmists. Some on the AM talk radio circuit have even called for such contradictory speak to be concerned terroristic and should be silenced by the Office of Homeland Security.

What the crackpot, conspiracy nuts and kooks disagree with is what is causing the strange occurrences on Earth as well in the heavens. They loudly and strongly state that the strange weather events upon the Earth in recent years are due to an object out in space. An object larger than the planet Jupiter, entering the Solar System, hidden by the shadow of the Sun.

There is some dispute if this object is a planet or a comet. Some even pose the idea of a large extra-terrestrial spaceship, but all agree its presence is real, and whatever it is, planet X, Nibiru, or an extra terrestrial spacecraft, it is causing massive sunspots upon the Star, thus causing it to release solar flares so intense, that life upon Earth can become prehistoric overnight, . . . literary!

Twenty years ago, the near invisible visitor made the press. The Russians, as well as the American scientific agencies including NASA confirmed its approaching trek. Then suddenly, just as darkness flees when light advances, all official discussions about planet X stopped, but then, the digging began.

American military analysts became concerned when it was discovered that the Russians were boroughing deep into their Ural Mountains. U.S. think tanks warned that the Russians are moving towards a first strike option, and are preparing to survive America's retaliatory nuclear response. Yet, at the very same time, various citizens living in Pennsylvania and the Virginia Mountains reported massive digging projects. Their demands to learn why such large scale projects were in progress clouded in such secrecy, and in some cases threats of arrest and physical harm if anyone approached the mining sites.

Perhaps preparations for a nuclear confrontation, or perhaps preparations for massive Earth changes brought on by a passing heavenly object many times the size of planet Earth, thus causing havoc unseen since the time of Noah.

One million people had gathered in New York's Times Square to welcome in the New Year. 2012 A.D. promises new beginnings for some and a beginning of the end for others. Madam President has managed to keep her position, surviving an impeachment attempt in March of 2009. Though she had publicly announced that she would never leave her office until she was no longer useful, many Americans wondered about her usefulness.

Useful to whom?

This mindset caused a concern that she might engineer a domestic crisis, which would justify her calling for martial law, thus shutting down the American people as well as the civilian control over the government. The end result of her action would translate into her being President for life, since no elections can be held. There is no law requiring civilian control returned to the people. America would then become, Amerika.

Nothing has really changed with the status of the World, except war, hunger, disease and the dwindling sources of drinking water had gotten worse. There is no Utopia of peace. There is no one-World government, for Russia and China are opposing the Europeans man's ideas of who shall rule the World, and how.

America is embroiled in another presidential election campaign. Though she had an administration most compared to Hitler's, she has won the Democratic nomination, and seeks re-election. The Republicans, still rattled by the controversy and fallout in 2000, has chosen the former governor of New York hoping to capitalize on his tough rolled up sleeve image. On the Independent ticket is the former Army General that is credited with saving America from a terrorist nuclear attack. His solid character, and larger than life persona bearing the strength of John Henry and the bravery of Hannibal delivers an aura of respectability to the race.

America needs a leader. No Magalia manic, or a puppet on a string, . . . or is it just too late to fix what ails the land of the free, and home of the brave?

The international joint manned mission to Mars launched in 2010, disappeared in the Martian orbit without a trace. As the joint American, Japanese, Chinese, Russian and E.U. 34 billion dollar spacecraft uneventfully slipped behind Mars' dark side. To this very day, it has not emerged from behind the red planet, as planned. Without a word spoken in distress, all communication links, radars, signals of any kind simply and suddenly ceased to emit from the historical craft.

As some mourned, others asked questions. Debates exploded into conspiracy theories. Was the mission to Mars necessary at the cost of 225 billion dollars? Was there even a mission to Mars, hinting at the disputed Apollo moon missions. Was the mission only a cover to evacuate the elite from Earth? Did the flight land on the dark side, where perhaps a base existed unseen from the eyes of Earth?

And what of Planet X and its now sometime visible companion satellite only from the most southern regions of the Earth at dawn? Such questions are hardly raised in public anymore. Astronomers not in line with the secrecy doctrine have been suicided, or are just simply missing. Public viewings from observations are either closed, or are off line due to so-called, mechanical malfunctions.

Internet web-masters have terminated any web sites regarding Planet X. They have been ordered to cancel such sites as per a diminutive unclear Patriot Act edict relating to terrorism in the form communications causing public alarm.

With all of these events, the World looks for relief. Wisdom knows, that before relief can come, a change must come first. The old must pass away before the new can begin. Experts on everything from Earth changes and astronomy to ancient civilizations, medical science, scholars of the World's religions and human behavior do agree . . . with the unprecedented weather, diseases, war and famine, . . . it does appear to be the beginning of the end. All of these events . . . past, presently and forecasted . . . collectively and indubitably point to a paramount climax, . . . *tomorrow* ***is*** *today*.

Happy New Year!

Chapter One

APRIL 26TH, 2012. 1451 HOURS
FEDERAL BUREAU OF INVESTIGATION
J EDGAR HOOVER BUILDING
WASHINGTON, D.C.

Special Agent Victoria Owens sits at her desk in a large office on the sixth floor of the Hoover Building. The office is an open space that consists of half the floor, with smaller cubicles throughout. Opposite her, sits Special Agent Michael Peterson at his desk. He sits quietly, watching Owens, as she reads an intelligent report. The report concerns a new and more hostile 'skin-head' like white supremacist group. This new hate group is based in New Jersey, and now has spread to New York's Staten Island, creating havoc on the city's isolated borough.

As she reads the report, Peterson watches, as she unconsciously runs her long slender fingers, slowly along her forehead, just above her left eyebrow. While he watches her, he begins to recall his feelings when he was first assigned to work with her, three years ago. He took one look at the attractive Afro-American Agent, and desired to return to the sleepy Boise office. Immediately he felt that she wasn't qualified for the Counter Terrorist assignment based here in Washington. He was appalled. He knew how hard he had to work to become accepted into this elite detail. He then became determined to stay in the unit. If anybody leaves, . . . it will be her. If she can't hack it, he was more than ready to show her the door. He vowed not to over look her shortcomings. He composed himself with the belief that she would not be around long.

Unfounded bitterness showed him to be a fool. His narrow minded up bringing instilled resentment to Victoria Owens mere presence in the unit, as well as the F.B.I. Without knowing the woman, or of her capabilities, but only evaluating the color of her skin, he had deduced that she was beneath him. The fat that she is also a woman placed her even lower.

Mike Peterson places his hand on his forehead. He slowly but firmly, drags his large hand downward, as he begins to feel embarrassed about the thoughts he once had for Victoria. He continues to recall when she first arrived, and he managed to get a hold of her personnel file. Her record shook the prehistoric belief system that he was raised on. His exposure to people of color, was very limited. His deep southern roots were that of segregation. When he joined the United States Marines, his outfit was almost completely devoid of Black men. Then shortly thereafter, when he joined the Recon Rangers, his unit had no blacks within its ranks. He never had any respect for Blacks. The Media helped to feed the racist fires, with their portrayals of criminals, welfare cheats, lazy husbandless, baby birthing, ignorant, drug taking people or simply niggers.

Peterson could not assign Victoria Owens to any of these categories, once he had completed reading her file. She is the opposite of all he was brainwashed to believe. It was from that moment on, he looked upon Victoria with a different pair of eyes. He became very curious about her. He wanted to know what made her tick. What made her what she is, and if she was as good as her impressive file said she was.

Victoria Owens' 35th birthday is in 17 days. She has been with the Bureau for 9 years. For the past 3 years, she has been assigned here in Washington, D.C. to the Anti-terrorism Office. Victoria is from Brooklyn, New York. She joined the United States Army 2 days after she graduated from high school. She had desired to see the World. Besides, she reasoned, the Army could not send her anywhere worse than the mean streets of Brooklyn. She has grown up in an environment of urban warfare. The streets of Bedrod-Styuyvesant had preconditioned her for whatever the U.S. Army could muster up.

After picking military police as her occupational specialty, she was then immediately shipped off to a simmering 'trouble spot' . . . the Korean Peninsula. During the two years that she was there, she managed to speak and understand the language well. She also learned the art of 'Wing Chun'. Wing Chun is an ancient Chinese martial art. She was taught the art of speed and simplicity, by an Army Interpreter who was born on Mainland China, but grew up in New York's Chinatown.

Upon the completion of her 'tour' in Korea, she was very skilled in the art of Wing Chun. She decided to remain in the Army. She applied, and was accepted into Army Intelligence. Victoria was then shipped off to Germany to join a task force investigating an item for sale on the 'black' market. The item, . . . a U.S. Army Electrode Magnetic Pulse device. Upon detonation, this device can blanket an entire area, the size of a small nation, like Israel rendering communications, machinery and even defensive weapons systems useless.

Being her Mother's only child, but one of many of her father's, whom she hasn't seen in decades, the relationship between Mother and daughter was very close. Victoria's Mother was completely behind her decision to join the Army. "Uncle Sam will pay you to see the World." Her Mother has said. "Then maybe you will meet a nice man, cuz' God knows, you ain't gonna meet none 'round her."

Victoria and her Mother spoke every Sunday morning, . . . until three months ago. Late one night, her Mother suffered a massive heart attack, while she slept. She never woke up again. Victoria now has an enormous void in her life. She has since completely immersed herself in her work. She still has not accepted her Mother's sudden, unexpected death. Victoria refuses to face it. She runs from it like a fugitive runs from justice.

Agent Owens looks up from the report, and then immediately speaks in an uninterested tone, "Mike, . . . why are you showing me a report on 'skin-heads' trying to stir up trouble on Staten Island?"

Without giving him a chance to answer, she adds, "They haven't graduated to our league, . . . yet." She hands him the sheet of paper, "The district office can handle this."

As he takes the report and places it on a far corner of his desk, Peterson, with his smooth southern pronunciation, begins, "I figured, . . . you being from New York and all, . . . that you might be interested on what was going on back at home."

Leaning slightly towards him, she informs flatly, "Mike, . . . New York City is a big place. I'm from Bed-Sty." She now motions toward the report, "That noise there, . . . is going down on Staten Island. Though they are in the same city, they are two totally different Worlds."

"Well, forgive me. I'm just a poor old country boy from Louisiana. What in the Hell do I know about New York City? The closest I've been there is you."

Victoria leans back in her cloth covered cushion office chair, and says, "Remember when you, and those other gallant Marines, landed in Columbia in 1990, to rescue that detachment of D.E.A. Agents being held captive by that drug cartel?"

Beaming with pride, he loudly answers, "Of course! . . . Oooh, rah!!" He now instantly recalls the mission.

"Bullets were flying through the air, as thick as mosquitoes in the Bayou." His facial expression now suddenly changes to one of dread. He looks the woman Agent directly in her eyes, and flatly admits, "I've never been so scared ever, . . . or since."

With the same soul stirring tone, Victoria returns, "Well, . . . that's New York. The only difference is the zip code." She ended sharply.

"So bad, they had to name it twice, huh?"

Victoria smiles slightly as she leans forward, resting her arms on the rear edge of her desk. She then glances up at the 24-hour wall clock.

"What time is it?"

"Ten minutes to go." She answered.

A beat of silence falls between the duo. Peterson suddenly, in an unemotional tone, speaks, "You know Vicki, . . . I've been monitoring the intelligence information concerning those skin-head-nazis types—"

"Found some old buddies?" She fires at him with a smile.

"Oh com'on now, . . . I'm serious." He returns sternly. "I think we ought to take a real close look at these people. Maybe we should go to the Boss, and get something cookin' to shut these people down."

Taken totally by surprise, Victoria automatically exclaims, "What!?"

Now with conviction, Peterson continues, "These people are soon to become a major National Security concern. They're organized with networks and everything. They have money, . . . their weapons are sophisticated, and they're out of the shadows, and no longer care about being seen." He ended strongly.

"Well, . . . when they show their faces on Eastern Parkway, then I'll be impressed." She said flippantly.

In a chilling tone, he responds, "By then, . . . it'll be too late

"Mike, . . ." She starts patiently, ". . . Hate groups have been around for hundreds of years."

Quickly responding, he firmly states, "Victoria don't you realize that the next war this country is involved in, will not be across the sea, . . . but right here within the United States. You heard of rumors of war? Well baby, . . . what we have here are rumblings." He takes a breath of air, and continues forcefully, as he strains to speak at almost a whisper, "A race war is coming."

"Oh Mike com'on. You know for years, I've heard everything from a meteor smashing into us to alien invasions."

Peterson continues his point.

"Victoria, you're not listening, . . . this war could lead to the fall of the United States."

In a cold tone she replies, "The United States has already fallen."

A dispersing clerk suddenly steps up to Victoria's desk, and flatly announces, "Agent Owens, . . . your orders, . . ." She pauses, as she hands Victoria a typewritten sheet of paper, with the bureau's letterhead affixed at the top of the page, ". . . To attend the Atlanta Conference, concerning the anti-terrorist procedures for the Pope's millennium mass. Your hotel reservation, and confirmation number, which is located at the bottom of the page."

Victoria looks up from the sheet of paper, as the clerk hands her a small vanilla envelope. The deadpan woman now continues, "Your round trip tickets. You depart from Washington National Airport, Monday morning at 8:45 a.m."

Not taking the envelope, Victoria politely informs the clerk, "I won't be needing those. I have my own transportation."

Dumbfounded, the clerk begins, "But, . . ."

Interrupting the clerk, the Agent explains her unusual action.

"After the two week conference, I'm going to start my vacation. I won't be returning to D.C. until after my two week vacation, so, . . . I won't be needing those." She ended motioning to the envelope.

Taking a moment for the information to settle in, the clerk gives a half hearted smile, and says, "I guess that'll be alright." Her smile now becomes more sincere, as she says, "Have a nice trip."

As she walks off, Victoria's eyes focus I on Peterson, as he turns and watches the shapely clerk lustfully. Victoria sits quietly, as he continues to take in an eyeful. Now satisfied, he turns back around wearing a devilish smirk, and locks eyes with his partner. Victoria begins to slowly shake her head disapprovingly. Peterson drops his smirk, and says, "Your not a man, you wouldn't understand these things."

"Anyway, . . . as to your after work invite, . . . I would like to, especially since you're buying, but I better pass. I want to get on the road tonight."

Dumbfounded, Peterson asks, "With what? That shitbox of yours will never make it to Atlanta."

Suddenly, as if a beam of light illuminated a revelation, a grin begins to spread across his wholesome, all American boyish face. Peterson's eyes are now twinkling, as though he is having a supernatural religious experience.

With concern, Victoria asks, "Mike, . . . are you alright?"

Now full of smiles, he answers with elation, "You got the car, didn't you?!"

Victoria beams a joyful smile, and nods in acknowledgement, "No shit Sherlock."

"Hot dang!! Com'on, . . . let's go and check it out." He said as he stood.

Victoria motions towards the clock, and flatly informs, "It's not quite quitin' time yet."

Leaning toward her, Peterson begins in a low tone, "Aww

com'on, . . . they won't notice, besides, . . ." He now stands up straight, ". . . We're the A-team. When the going gets tough, the bureau calls us."

Unhappily Victoria responds, "That's why they're sending me to Atlanta, and you, . . ."

She stops suddenly, realizing that she didn't know what his assignment was for the next two weeks. She stands, and with a suspicious tone, she asks, "Just what is your assignment?"

Trying his best to act annoyed, Mike begins to explain, "You know, I was pretty pissed off when they wouldn't send me to the Atlanta Conference with you. I went straight to the old man's office, and let him know that we are a team. I told him how disappointed I . . ."

"Stop right there." She said cutting him off.

Mike Peterson looks to her innocently. Victoria sees through her partner's act as if it was made of glass. "Don't go any further, I'm not wearing any boots." She smartly snapped.

Judging from her tone, he knows that he has failed to fool her. Like a child caught with its hand in the cookie jar, Mike looks away from her. Victoria steps from around her desk, and as she heads for the door, she grabs Mike by his forearm, and says, "Com'on, . . . I want to know every bit of the soft detail you managed to finagle."

The two left the office, and now stand at the elevator bay. Victoria stands in front of the eye contact evading Peterson, though his 6 foot 2 and a half-inch frame surpasses Victoria's by some almost 6 inches. After looking in all directions but hers, Peterson has finally looked into her eyes. Her brown hazel eyeballs seem to expel an irresistible compulsion to acknowledge her. Peterson refers to this stare as Victoria's demonic cast.

"Well Michael?" She asked in a tone that was gentle but yet firm.

"Vacation." He answered, bracing himself.

Just then the elevator announced itself. Without waiting for her to respond, he immediately departs from her, and swiftly approaches the elevator doorway marked with an illuminating softly glowing red arrow pointing downward. Victoria follows him. As she joins her partner at the arriving elevator, she clenches her teeth. "Vacation?"

The elevator doors part, revealing a brightly lit lift, with no one else aboard. As Mike steps into the elevator, he sighs. Victoria follows him on board. As Mike turns to face the closing doors, Victoria stands at his side, facing him. The descent to the ground floor, feels as if it is descending from the 400th floor. Now, somewhere between the 2nd and 3rd floors, Victoria's eyes seem to begin to burn into the side of Peterson's head, like two powerful sunlamps.

Victoria's stare continues as the two exit the elevator, then through the lobby, and then out of the building. As they walk through the parking lot, Mike Peterson can no longer stand his partner's non-verbal persistence. Like a walnut being squeezed in a vise, he finally cracks.

"Yes, yes, I'm going on vacation, while you're in Atlanta." Defensively he continues, "What's the big deal, . . . you're going on vacation once the conference is over right? Well, I'm just startin' mine two weeks before you do."

"I see." She said flatly.

"I have some extra time I want to burn up, . . . why not?"

A pause of silence falls over the two momentarily. With the lack of nothing else to say, Peterson asks, "So what are you going to do with your days off?"

"I don't really know, . . . perhaps a road trip. See America, . . . that kind of stuff."

Feeling guilty and not understanding why, he says, "Mary and I are going down to spend sometime at her fathers. You remember where he lives?"

Victoria responds, "Oh, I will never forget."

"Why don't you come down when you're finished in Atlanta? It's only about a day's ride."

"Mike, . . . that place is in the mist of swamp, and alligators."

Perking up, Mike smiles brightly as he explains, "Com'on, . . . we'll eat, drink, . . . Hell I can even get you laid."

Victoria stops with a shocked expression on her face, as Mike stops with her and adds, "Mary's brother digs you."

"Excuse me?!"

"What?" Mike innocently asked as he drops his smile.

"What makes you think I want to get laid by Mary's brother?" She asked sharply.

"Then I'll get you anybody you want." Mike responds unemotionally.

Still sedate, Victoria asks, "And what makes you think I want to get laid?"

"Com'on Vicki, . . . everybody needs to loosen up. And quite frankly I think it's time for you to do so."

"What?!!" She explodes.

In a calming tone, Mike explains himself, "Lookie here. You're my partner. I worry about your welfare, and I think your problem is that you're not get'in enough action. You seem all keyed up. Uptight."

"What?!! . . . And what draws you to that conclusion, Sherlock? It couldn't be the fact that I work with a man who was born 150 years too late?"

Waving his hand, as to wave her off, Mike begins, "No, no, no, . . . I'm talking about the fact that you have never mentioned him."

"Mentioned who?"

"Precisely he smiles.

Shaking her head slightly, and in a disgusted tone she says, "Mike, . . . go to Florida." She then begins to continue to walk.

Walking beside her, Mike asks, "Vicki you haven't, . . ." He is finding it awkward to say the words, ". . . You know, . . ."

She stops her walk, and faces the struggling man.

"What?" She asks coldly.

Shyly he continues, "You know, . . . switched sides?"

She steps up to him. They are now standing so close that light cannot pass between them. Through clenched teeth Victoria responds in a low tone that sounds as demonic as too her appearance.

"Switched sides?"

In almost a whisper, Mike responds, "Yeah, you know, . . . gay, lesbian or whatever the correct term is these days."

"You know, . . ." She began in the same low tone, but in her usual smooth, even sounding voice, ". . . You can be such an asshole sometimes." She then walks off.

Mike thought that he smelled a whiff of burning flesh, as Victoria departed.

"Oh don't get mad." Mike said in a winded tone, as he steps off after her.

"I'm not mad. I expect nothing less from you."

"Listen, . . . I'm worried about you. You work out as if you're on ESPN, and your body speaks for that, but it's your brain that need the R & R."

Victoria simply looks to him as if he's crazy, as he continues.

"That big beautiful sex organ needs that sexual spark now and then to fire life throughout the soul. Him, . . . her, whatever it . . ."

Stopping, Victoria responds sharply, "Now wait a minute, . . . before this gets out of hand. I like men okay. I just haven't found the man who can sex my brain, and cause that fire you speak of!"

Correcting her, Mike interjects, "No, . . . the brain needs a sexual spark to fire, . . ."

"Oh whatever!!" She erupted. "When I find the right man, . . . I will be sure to name an orgasm after you." She then walks off towards her parked car.

Mike Peterson watches the woman Agent as she walks towards the gleaming black sports car. In a trans-like state he begins to follow her.

"Wow." He mumbled to himself as he looks upon the black beauty. Sitting menacing in a corner parking space is a redesigned 2012 Nissan 400Z. 355 horses. All wheel drive. Solar sensitive glass. Heads up windshield display and a shape fitting a sci-fi movie set.

Victoria's car is covered in a triple metallic black pearl, giving the eye catching two seater the illusion that the surface would be wet to the touch. The fat sticky 45 series tires will hold the car on the road even while the g-forces begin to pull you apart. The car will launch from 0 to 60 in under five seconds, and as for top speed . . . ?"

"Faster than a speeding bullet." Victoria answers as she stands at the car with Mike at her side.

Mike gives the car a complete look over, nodding his head slightly expressing his approval. With a word, he suddenly extends his hand out towards her with his palm up. She looks to his open, waiting palm, but remains still. Mike snaps his fingers, as he says, "The keys, woman."

"What keys?" she returns with a restraining smile.

He now notices the lack of door handles.

"Hey, how do you get into this thing?"

As she approaches nearer to her car, she casually states, "You have to have the *right* touch."

Standing next to him, Victoria places her hand gently upon the glass of the driver's door. Mike watches her, and witnesses the driver's door suddenly become ajar, and instantly begins to rise on a 45 degree angle, exposing the sports car's interior.

As Mike stands in awe, Victoria continues, "Bio-metrics baby." She said with a smile. "No keys, no remote key transmitters. Its all touch and voice. My left or right hand allows me, and only me access, and my voice and only me voice will start it. All of that input is downloaded on a chip, and stored in the car's CPU."

"And if you should get a cold one day, or HAL here goes haywire?" he asked as he peers the inside of the 400Z.

"There is a 24-7, eight hundred number, a series of questions and answers, and remote access is gained via satellite." She answered promptly.

"Vicki, you have definitely been watching too many James Bond movies." Mike said as he slides his hands over the gray leather driver's seat, and inhales deeply. "Ahh, . . . I love the smell of a new car."

He now stands erect, and looks to Victoria with a big smile.

"This is all the sex, I need." She said with a smile of satisfaction, as she's looking over the car.

"Yeah, well, . . . since you don't have a man or any children, . . . you can name me as your beneficiary." He said, dropping his smile from his face, and continues in a serious tone, "I could use the money after you kill yourself in this thing. Girl, . . ." He starts with his tone now fatherly, ". . . Have you gone major league crazy?" He looks to the car, and quickly adds, "This is not healthy." He looks back at her. "How much did this thing cost you?"

"Who the Hell are you, the I.R.S.?"

"Hell, I bet you coulda bought a house with that money."

"And what would I do with a house?"

"Maybe settle down."

"Look Daddy, . . . unlike you, I haven't found a man like Mary. Just because I have one of these, . . ." She pointed toward her groin, ". . . I am *not just*, going to have a child. I cannot subscribe to that abnormal plan of putting the cart before the horse. I'll wait and he'll find me. THEN, we will get married, and THEN I will get pregnant, and that child will have a Mother, *and* a father. That is the way Nature planned it, from Almighty's blueprint."

"Oh here we go, . . . you're getting political again."

Correcting him, she flatly informs, "I'm not getting political, . . . perhaps biblical, . . . and these days, it's needed." She ended solemnly.

Michael Peterson turns and looks the car over once again.

"I'm really worried about you in this thing. This is not a normal car. This thing looks like something the Anti-Christ would drive around on the weekends."

"Still associating black, with evil, huh?"

"Oh don't start with that crap." He snapped, but then immediately changes his tone to one of sincerity, "Hey listen, . . . I did try to go along with you to Atlanta, but 'upstairs' only wanted to send one Agent, and they made it very clear that they wanted you, and only you to do this. That's no bullshit."

Victoria looks away from him in thought. Peterson sees the questions forming in her head. He then gently offers, "I think it has something to do with the new image of the Bureau. You know, . . . changing times."

"You mean the changing faces of the Bureau." She said sharply.

Becoming defensive, Peterson flatly responds, "Hey, . . . if you or anybody else can do the job, then they should have the job, . . . no special treatment because of something that happened hundreds of years ago."

"First of all, it's still happening today, and second of all, . . . I damn sure did earn . . ."

"I know you did!" He returned loudly. "I'm not talking about you, . . . Hell. I'm not really concerned about all that. What is really bothering me is out there." He motioned outward. "I'm talking about terrorism on the shores of America. The nuclear threat is greater today than during the cold war. America faces bankruptcy. Weird diseases eating the flesh off of people. 10 year olds packin' guns in schools, killing raping . . ." He looks to Victoria with a seriousness that made her focus completely on him.

She has never seen him so passionate on such issues. She does know his position on such issues as capital punishment, civil rights, welfare and women's rights. These topics have sparked a number of verbal confrontations between the partners in the past. She now notices that he has evolved into a person that doesn't simply sit around and voice an opinion of ignorance, which implies that if the minorities were removed from the American scene, then all would be right.

Peterson has continued talking while Victoria was side tracked in thought.

". . . World Trade Center in New York was a test run. The gas attacks in London, and Paris subways last year that killed close to 500 people could have been New York, Washington or L.A. Imagine that?"

Victoria sees the look of concern on Mike Peterson's face, as a pause of silence falls between them.

"And the Mass in Atlanta?" Victoria smoothly asked, recovering from the silence of deep thought.

Peterson responds immediately, "It's like a fat juicy worm to a trout." He pauses for a beat, and then asks matter of factly, "Why is he going to Atlanta anyway?"

"The new Pope is on a World tour in an attempt to spread the word of peace, hope and the return of Jesus Christ."

"In America's most bloodiest city?" He asked smartly.

"Can you think of a better place for the word to be heard?" She answered sharply.

Waving his hand at her, Peterson then says, "You know there are groups out there that want to pop him. There is a determined bunch out there that believes the pope is the anti-christ and seek to assassinate him to stop the end of the world, and then there are others who believe his death is necessary to fulfill some prophecy. Doing it here in America during this three day revival, in front of an international audience of millions, perhaps billions, . . . is a temptation that no true terrorist can resist."

The response causes Victoria to swallow hard. Mike continues his thoughts, "You know I've been thinking, . . ."

Victoria wants to comment on his opening statement, but she's too curious to hear what he has to say.

". . . If General Armstrong gets elected, and the polls do indicate that he has a shot, we're going to be busy as a bunch of beavers."

Now with an idea of the direction his thoughts are headed, she says, "The Middle Eastern Alliance threat against him?"

Nodding in agreement, Mike Peterson says, "Yeah, . . . those crazy bastards held a trial over there. They found the General guilty of war crimes, and passed a death sentence."

Becoming slightly resentful to the Alliance's action, Victoria begins, "But *they* assembled a few weapons of mass destruction. The Mosodd discovers the Alliance is in possession of operational intercontinental ballistic missiles. Israel freaks out and readies its nuclear forces. Meanwhile the British, . . . while spying on the Chinese, back up the C.I.A.'s suspicion that the missiles are targeted on cities, and military installations within the continental United States, which is possible due to the discovered deal between the Alliance and the North Koreans.

"Yeah, it was October, 1962 all over again." Peterson recalled bleakly.

"Yes, . . . but then, the Russians backed down. This Alliance has demonstrated that it would risk total annihilation, just to strike at us, or Israel."

"They might have bloodied our nose, but we would of killed them." Mike said strongly.

"That doesn't matter to them, Mike. Look, . . . even after General Armstrong led the combined U.S. Forces to cut the nuclear balls off the Alliance, and in the mean time he destroyed their war making capabilities, . . . they are still not afraid. Their country is in ruin, and they still threatened to strike out at the U.S. with terrorism."

A pause of silence passes between them, as their thoughts continue to process.

"I'm just glad that the Russians or the Chinese didn't step in, . . . you do realize, it would have been World war three." Peterson stated.

"Honey, World war three already went down from 1950 to 1953 in Korea. You are talking thermo-nuclear warfare. Billions dead and the rest dying"

Peterson gently says to her, "and what about the next time?"

"Well, . . . I do know that the Russians and the Alliance have signed an agreement. They vowed that they will help the Alliance to combat any aggressor in their next conflict." She continues regrettably, "This old World of ours is getting to be a very dangerous place to live. The tension and fear during the October, '62 incident was only a drill. The next time, . . . well, . . . that maybe if they decide to take Israel, . . . and then, . . . I think, . . . it's gonna be, . . . mushroom cloud city."

"That's really raw, Vicki." Mike responded in a low tone.

In a tone of abandonment, Victoria continues, "Mike, as you well know, we are not the America of old. We are now a broken nation." She pauses for a short thought, "I think we are finished. Just like it all came to a close for the Romans, . . . it's now our turn up at bat. Perhaps, . . . one day the White House will get a telegram that'll simply say surrender. Or we'll be held at bay by nuclear gunpoint. Then there is the old Pearl Harbor tactic, . . . they'll just sneak us. One day we'll look up to the sky, just in time to see one of their ICBMs go, . . . BOOM!" She ended loudly.

With his mind in the distance thinking about the doomsday that can befall the World, Mike Peterson hauntingly comments, "Once again the World holds its breath." He now takes a deep breath, and flatly says, "Well, . . . if Armstrong does become President, maybe he can strengthen us again."

Filled with conviction Victoria announces, "Jonathan Taylor Armstrong, will become President of these United States. I can feel it."

"Well Victoria, . . ." He begins with doubt, ". . . I don't know about that. I don't know if folks are ready to have a Blackman as President."

She narrows her eyes, and then coldly asks, "The country or the likes of you?"

"Oh low Vicki, . . . low"

"I remember when David Dinkins became the Mayor of the city of New York. Somebody said that they didn't want to live in a city where the niggers were running things."

"You hold on there Missy, . . ." He begins sounding severe, "These days when most of us are only one paycheck away from poverty, . . . and sick and tired of the murder and mayhem on the streets. Then there are those of us that remember when this land was considered the land of milk and honey. Now morality is gone, . . . new and younger hate groups, are emerging, that makes the 'Klan' seem like a bunch of juvenile delinquents." He now is becoming slightly emotional, as his voice becomes harsher, "Do you realize that the American farmer is going the way of train travel? Where in the Hell is America going to get its food from in 15 years, huh?" He pauses now only to take a breath, "Chemically fed cows, and test tube chickens. We gave up on the drug war, and now these idiots are giving out condoms, and banning bullets." He moves closer to her, and continues in a sincere tone, "This country is in real serious trouble. It's in critical condition, and it looks like it is going to die. There are things happening today that has folks really scared."

"You mean, . . . the feeling that something big is about to happen. Like a big balloon, . . . it's all going to pop very soon?"

Peterson takes a step away from the woman Agent as his mind processes her last statement. Victoria sees the bewilderment on his face. As she starts to clear her point, Peterson says, Mary's preacher pappy says that these days in which we live are those of the 'end time'. Do you buy that jazz?"

"The Bible is filled with many warnings, foretold thousands of years ago. Not only do they describe an end time, or last days, but the Creator's wrath which is to be witnessed by the Earth."

"Oh com'on, you don't believe in all that jazz do ya? God, . . . which God? What God?"

Sharply Victoria says, "Look Mike, . . . you or nobody else has to be a God fearing, Jesus lovin' Christian to believe that our days are short. Simply look at the headlines, . . . look at the state of the World. Only a fool can believe that America at this rate, will celebrate a tri-centennial." She now changes her tone, and adds, "Mike we are getting a little too heavy to be so sober. So what's the matter, what's really bothering you?"

"I don't know." He said automatically, "I am sick and tired of watching this country going to Hell in a hand basket. Then there's Armstrong, . . . forget the fact about the race thing, I'm just worried that if he becomes President he'll make us all walk around with Bibles in our pockets. I just don't want his beliefs jammed down my throat."

"The country that you are clearly concerned about was based, and built on the words of the Bible."

Snapping he replies, "There's nothing in there that can be proven."

Just as forceful, Victoria answers, "Oh no, read the book. Then you compare the text with the headlines of today."

"Random chance." He fired back. "But I will agree with you that Armstrong may be the way to go. It is time for a change in America. The Hippies of the free love, Age of Aquarius, flower children era, have had their run. They have single handedly ruined this country."

"And don't forget about the disconnected multi-millionaires,. businessmen and lawyers and fascist minded men." She interjected quickly.

Not derailed by her comment, Mike continues firmly, "Morality, family values and secured constitutional rights are being challenged by this nitwit we have for President. She wants to BUY peace in the inner cities, by paying off the gang leaders, but sits down and discusses plans to ban firearms from squared away citizens. Police departments across this country, have been reduced to powerless tax burdens, meanwhile, . . . the hardcore criminals are having a field day." He now becomes stern in speech, "All the bans, taxes and laws are NOT going to stop the scum."

"So your point to all this?"

Peterson draws in a lung full of air, and states, "All I'm saying is, if Armstrong can keep this country from going to Hell, then I couldn't give a good God-damn if he's black, brown, yellow, red or Martian green."

"A-men to that." She said softly.

Peterson looks skyward. Victoria stands silently as her partner peers at the heavens. He looks back upon her, and smiles. Seeing him in such rare form, Victoria is amazed by his passionate position. She has been noticing a progression in him. He's not the same man she met three years ago.

"Have you been struck by lightening, lately?" She asked in search for an explanation, regarding his behavior.

"What?"

"Are you alright? What brought all that on? I'm impressed."

Peterson gives her a slight grin. Then in an upbeat tone he asks, "Going anyplace special on your vacation?"

"No, . . . I'm going to go as far as a week will take me, and then spend the remaining week, making my way back."

He smiles warmly at her. She returns the expression, and then starts getting into her car.

"Hey, . . ." Mike called out to her.

Victoria stops herself, just before she sits upon the grey leather driver's seat.

". . . Are you sure you don't want to have that farewell drink?"

Regrettably she says, I'll have to pass, Mikey. If I start drinking with you, the next thing I'll know, it'll be Monday morning."

"So, you'll roll out of bed onto that big old silver bird, and you'll be in Atlanta in time for lunch."

Motioning towards the car, she says, "I've made other travel plans, remember?"

"Yeah alright, . . . so you won't leave till Sunday, Sunday night, right?"

"No I'm leaving tonight. I'm going to go home, take a shower, and a nap, then head south."

"Why tonight?" He asked with surprise, "You don't have to be there till Monday."

"I want to have a look around first. You know, familiarize myself with the locations. Collect a little intell of what's going on around town."

"They'll brief you on all that on Monday."

"I don't like to depend on only one source of intelligence."

Michael reacts with a cynical facial expression. Victoria then adds, "Hey, . . . you taught me that, Mister Recon, . . . forgot?"

Peterson smiles at that, and confesses, "Yeah, yeah you're right."

Victoria sits behind the wheel of her 400Z.

"Engage." She commanded.

In an immediate response, a digital recording of a proper English bulter announces, "Good afternoon mad'dam."

The sudden ground shaking rumble of the Nissan coming to life, causes Peterson to look upon the idling, super high performance car as though a man-eating predator cornered him. Victoria notices his reaction. "Relax, . . ." She begins, smoothly, ". . . It doesn't bite."

"Engaged, Victoria? Engaged? How star trek can you get?"

Mike continues in a fatherly tone as he cautions, "You watch your ass riding around these United States. There are a lot of 'hayseeds' who think black folks are in season, you hear?"

With a southern draw, Victoria answers mocking him, "Don't fret now." She then continues in her normal voice as she orders, "Don't end up as gator bait playing around in the swamps, making that stuff."

"Ahh shucks girl, . . ." He starts, ". . . Listen hear, . . . I'm gonna bring us back a batch, and it'll be me and you, swappin' stories."

"Hell no. I'm not drinking any of that liquid 'crack'." She said firmly.

"Ahh com'on Vicki, . . . I got all the bugs ironed out of this recipe." He said with a reassuring tone.

"Goodbye Michael." Victoria announced, as she pushed a button on the steering wheel, which activates the closing door mechanism.

"Alright, . . . so you got a little sick, . . ." He now raises his voice to be heard through the lightly tinted window. As Victoria begins to drive away, he adds, ". . . But that was because you tried to drink your body weight!!"

He now smiles as he watches the shadowy 400Z drive out of sight.

Chapter Two

9:43 P.M.

Victoria arrived home a few minutes to six. Since all of her clothes were packed for her Atlanta trip, she decided to take a nap. After about an hour and a half, she couldn't sleep anymore. She switched on her T.V. and channel surfed, until she came upon the Weather Channel. She was just in time to catch Atlanta on the list of cities for tomorrow's weather conditions.

82, partly cloudy, she mumbled to herself. Then a commercial began. Victoria muted the sound, and laid back, looking up toward the ceiling. The soft illumination from the streetlights outside, reflected the gently swaying trees to appear to dance for her on the ceiling. The hypnotic moments of the shadowy figures caused Victoria's mind to drift. At first, she rechecked her mental checklist, for anything she could of possibly forgotten. Not hardly. She is too regimental in planning. Victoria is a firm believer in the six 'P' rule. Proper Planning, Prevents, Piss Poor, Performance.

Her mind then focused on her heavy conversation with Mike in the parking lot. She shivered at the thought of it all.

18 months ago, most thought that the crisis in the Middle East, would without a doubt, lead to nuclear warfare. Israel was facing down the barrels of an Arab Alliance. Rumors of imminent nuclear war placed a cloud of fear over the United States that it almost caused complete anarchy in the streets.

A lot of what Mike Peterson stated in the parking lot, Victoria remembered her Mother speaking of during the crisis. Ma knew it was not the time of Armageddon. Despite all that proclaimed it was truly the end of time, Ma knew without a doubt that this wasn't. As she lies on her queen sized bed, her thoughts are now completely on her Mother. Simultaneously her mind fills with various moments of her life with her Mother. When she started to remember her Mother lying in her wedding gown, while engaged in an eternal sleep peacefully in an alluring rosewood casket, Victoria immediately sat up quickly, as if to force the memory from her mind. Now sitting on the edge of the bed, the still morning daughter, dismisses the recall in an attempt to try and block the event from existence.

Victoria looks to the T.V. in time to view a weather map of the eastern portion of the United States. The satellite image is showing a rainstorm moving across the region. Without needing the volume, Victoria could understand from the various colors displayed, that the storm though violent, was indeed all rain. The heavier shaded areas Victoria knew meant heavier rainfall. As the muted weather person explained, Victoria mentally notes that the worse part of the storm is tracking an east, northeasterly direction. The weather map suddenly changes, and now show the projected weather conditions for tomorrow. Victoria looks closely and sees that the Atlanta area was free of wet weather.

As the weather map changed to project Sunday, Monday, and so on, Victoria calculated, if she departed now, . . . she looks to her alarm clock, and reads the bright red L.E.D. numbers, . . . 9:47, . . . it should take her ten hours to get to

Atlanta. Satisfied with the idea, Victoria bounces to her feet. She begins to strip off her panties and bra, as she walks towards her bathroom.

10:53 P.M.

Victoria exits the elevator, and begins to walk through the sub-terrain, florescent lit parking garage. Her white high top padded sneakers didn't report her steps as she walked across the concrete floor towards her car. Victoria eyeballs the shadows, bearing in mind what a juicy target she would make for a robber. The weight of her clothing in her garment bag, slung over her shoulder has begun to irritate her. The bag's thick hanger hook has begun to bear down upon the three fingers supporting it, causing them to ache. With her other hand, Victoria pulls a luggage cart containing a large, and smaller suitcase. The small wheels of the cart squeak slightly echoing within the garage sounding as if several mice trailed behind her. The small wheels of the cart, as it is pulled along, rolls over bits of grit, sounding as if an old record is about to play.

Victoria steps up to the rear of her menacing black sports car. With her hand that pulled her luggage cart, she places it upon a small palm sized area beneath the Nissan badge on the hatch lid. Instantly the rear lid released, and enables Victoria to effortlessly raise it. A whiff of the new car aroma fills her nose. She then slings the heavy garment bag from her shoulder, into the empty cargo area. She promptly examines her fingers. The hanger of the heavy bag left a clear red swollen impression across the inside of her three fingers.

Victoria dismissed the slight affliction, as she began removing the stretch cords from the luggage cart. She then lifted the small case and places it in the car, beneath the garment bag. Victoria then picks up the larger suitcase, and manipulates it underneath the garment bag also. With a pull on a lever, the luggage cart collapses, folding itself down to the size of a briefcase.

Victoria places the cart in a corner of the cargo area, and pulls down the trunk lid. The solid thud of the lid locking close, echoed throughout the garage like a cannon shot.

. She places her hand upon the glass to gain entry. She slides in behind the wheel, and commands her car to start. The procedure is still very alien to her, but it is so cool. Her on-board 'Butler' greeted her. The security system has accepted Victoria's bio-system clues, and the 'Butler' will now execute all of Victoria's commands. The bullying 'Z's engine cranks, and then suddenly explodes to life. The car's power plant shatters the death-like silence of the garage.

Already on the passenger seat sits a roadmap of the eastern portion of the United States. Lying besides that is a block-by-block street map of the City of Atlanta. Despite the navigational system on-board the Z, Victoria does not want to rely on satellite fed systems considering the increased solar flare activity, and their related black outs. She withdraws her cellular from her jacket pocket, and places it on top of the maps.

Though the air is cool, Victoria decides that her jacket is not needed while she drives. She exits the car, sliding her lean 5' 6 and a half inch frame from behind the steering wheel. She then sheds her black nylon windbreaker from her well developed torso, exposing her grey sweatshirt emblazoned with 'ARMY' along with the Army's seal, across her full chest.

She then removes two wallets from her jacket pocket. One she tosses into the passenger's seat. The other, she drops onto the driver's seat. Then, she tosses the jacket onto the passenger seat. She now begins to wrestle her shoulder holster off. She places the holster with her semi-automatic pistol, along with the wallet on the driver's seat which contains her work I.D. inside a storage compartment centered between the driver and passenger seats.

Victoria now climbs back into her black beauty, and adjusts herself for comfortability. She inhales a lung full of the new car aroma, and grins as she visually takes in the cockpits surroundings. She 'guns' the engine. The car responds like a savage, bloodthirsty beast. An absolute sense of power now passes over Victoria like a fever. She 'guns' the engine once again. The finely tuned Nissan muscle is starting to arouse her. She figures that if she is starting to feel aroused at idle, then when she gets the car up to about 90, turning around 3,600 R.P.M.s, she just might embody a sexual experience uncharted by Masters and Johnson.

She chuckles to herself at the thought, as she vocally activates the Xenon high intensity discharge headlights. The dashboard and console explodes into a brilliance of light that resembles downtown Las Vegas. Victoria dims the green, red and neon orange radio and instrumentation lights to a soft barely visible glow. She steps on the brake, while shifting the vibrating six speed gear selector into first gear. She pauses momentarily as her mind confirms, the door to her condo is locked. Everything is turned off within, and she has everything she needs for the conference is packed. Satisfied that all is complete, Victoria guides the car out of the garage. Like a F-14 Tomcat positioning itself on a carrier's flight deck for take off, the 400Z slowly turns onto the traffic free street. The traffic signal light at the head of the block, seemed to convey a little more when it, seemingly on cue, displayed it's green bulb. Like a fighter launching from the deck, Victoria's Z would have been airbourne, if it had wings.

Victoria left her Oxon Hill, Maryland neighborhood, crossing the Woodrow Wilson Memorial Bridge, into the State of Virginia at a respectable subsonic speed. By the time

Victoria reached Petersburg, leaving I-95, for Interstate 85, she had become very pleased with her new purchase. As an early 60's Motown hit filled the cockpit, Victoria effortlessly plotted the Nissan over the flawless roadway as she sang along.

The last thing Victoria remembered seeing was a road sign advising that the North Carolina State line was 12 miles away, before the rains came. Without warning, raindrops the size of golf balls suddenly burst upon her windshield only moments before the rain completely blinded her.

Now with her windshield wipers at maximum, and her speed down around 40, Victoria recalls that she has never experienced such fury. Only the faint marker lights of an 18-wheeler a few yards ahead, guided a determined Victoria through the deluge.

Victoria turns down the stereo music. Only a whisper sounds from the system, as she concentrates on the road, that is quickly turning into a stream. As she passes through the City of Durham, the little voice of logic, suggested that she stop and wait the storm out. Victoria was almost swayed by the little voice within her head, but saw the truck still rolling on. Taking an 'if he can do it, so can I', attitude, she too continued onward.

Outside Greensboro, the rain suddenly stopped it's crushing downpour. It was as if someone had just turned off their shower. The road spray created by the truck, continues to hamper Victoria's vision. She signals the trucker by flashing her high beams, indicating that she is about to pass. Immediately the trucker signals back, flickering his marker lights, and then off she went.

SERVICE STATION 5 MILES
NEXT STATION 33 MILES

Victoria looks down to her fuel gauge. It reads a little more than a quarter of a tank remaining. She decides to stop at the next station. Unbeknown to the traveling Agent, a tanker truck, carrying hazardous waste material, lays on its side across the southbound lanes of I-85 like a dead dinosaur.

The hazardous chemical waste oozes out of the bright silver tanker like blood from a wounded beast. Motorist traveling in both directions along the Interstate stopped to render aid to the truck driver, but immediately fell victim to the foul smelling, clear, gelatin substance. The cool springtime rain drops of the storm struck the substance, and instantaneously, a white cloud began to rise, and engulf the area like a fog.

Highway patrolmen, with their cars blocking the southbound lanes of I-85, have enough flares lit, that undoubtedly could be seen by orbiting spacecraft. They are giving the sporadic arriving motorist an option, . . . either pull off the roadway and wait, or U-turn to a route around the sealed area.

Immediately upon arriving at the roadblock, Victoria thought it is a D.W.I. checkpoint. Then just as quickly she dismisses the thought. An escaped prisoner? Now she sees a car crossing the grassy median and headed northward. As she brakes, she wonders aloud, "What the Hell, . . . ?"

There are just tow cars in front of Victoria's as she slowed her Z to a stop. The first car has just pulled away, making a U-turn across the grass now turning muddy median. Victoria stabs the button to lower her window with the red glossy polished nail of her index finger.

Now the car in front of hers pulls away from the Troopers. Victoria allows her car to creep up to the waiting Lawman. She looks to the uniformed figure. Though he stands two feet away, she cannot see any of his features. His wide brim, Smokey the bear type hat seems to cover his eyes. The high collar of his overcoat, and the wet outer garment, distorts his form. The glare of the flares, and high intensity of the 'take down' lights, along with the door mounted spotlights, painted the Trooper in a shadowy cast.

"Ma'am' . . . there's a wreak up ahead." The Trooper began in an authoritative tone, "We have been forced to shut down the Interstate."

"For how long?"

"Don't rightly know Ma'am'. The wreak involves hazardous waste material. Could take 6 to 8 hours to clean that stuff up. Where are you headed?"

"Atlanta." She answers automatically, while dreading the idea of a deviation in her travel plan. "Is there a way I can get around the wreak?"

"Well actually, you are in the middle of nowhere. In order to detour around the wreak, you're going to have to U-turn here, . . . go back up the Interstate, until you hit 64 East. Stay on 64 till you get to 49. Hang a right, and stay on 49, . . . it runs right back into 85."

"That sounds pretty easy." She says lightly.

"That'll take you some time to cover, but I guess it'll be better than watching us all night."

With a smile Victoria says, "Yeah, . . . I'll give it a shot. Thanks."

"Good luck." He returns as he stands back, slightly away from the car.

Victoria eases away from the Trooper. She then guides her car across the median, and slowly accelerates to the posted speed limit as she now heads north.

Thirty miles later, Victoria reaches route 64. She turns onto the thoroughfare, and begins heading eastward. It now suddenly dawns on her to check the route the Trooper gave, against her road map. Victoria pulls off the roadway, stopping her car in a brightly lit parking lot of a transformed mobile home, now a 24-hour dinner.

After tracing the Trooper's route, Victoria reveals in a dissatisfied tone, "Jesus, . . . that'll take me forever." She continues to peer at the map. Looking like someone in a desperate search, she mumbles, "There has to be a shorter route."

A light rain begins to fall, as Victoria sits in her car, scanning the multi colored road map of the State of North

Carolina. Her eyes suddenly lock onto a route. She smiles once the feasibility of the route, confirms cutting off more than half of the Trooper's course.

"109 to 49." She said, as she places the map on the passenger seat and switches off the overhead map light. Victoria looks out through the rain-covered windshield. As she activates the wipers, she comments to herself, how dark it really is out there. The wipers responded immediately, clearing the sheet of precipitation away, enhancing Victoria's visibility. With her wipers set for 'mist', causing them to activate once every 15 seconds or so, she watches the rainfall accumulate on the windshield between wiper wipes.

That little voice of logic, in the back of her head, suggests perhaps driving along unknown roads in the dark, and during a storm is unwise. If I was wise, she answers herself, I would be in a desert on a camel, following a star to Bethlehem. She then takes her foot off the brake pedal, engaged the clutch, while placing the car in first. She gives the car some gas, and drives out of the parking lot, eastward on 64.

Victoria has forgotten about her vehicle's need for fuel. She has become sidetracked with concern that she is lost, somewhere in North Carolina. According to the road map, the first intersection she was to encounter, should have been route 109. When she arrived at that intersection, which was more like a country cross road, she paused. No traffic was behind her, nor has she seen any traffic since she has been on 64.

"What did you expect, . . . an Interstate?" She quipped to herself, as she turned onto the dark and solitary two laned blacktop.

2:43 P.M.

The rain has now since stopped. Victoria nervously wonders if she had turned onto the correct road. It has been annoying her that since route markers weren't posted at the intersection, she could possibility be headed for who knows where. Then suddenly like a lightening bolt streaking across the sky, she remembers about the gas. The illuminated needle lies flat on 'E'.

"Oh shit." She mumbles to herself, as she looks back to the road, feeling completely empty herself. With a nauseated feeling beginning to surmount her, a small green sign begins illuminating in the beams of her headlights.

MADISON 6 MILES

Where there is a town, there has to be gas, . . . she reasoned, and then begins to beseech her car to make it to town.

2:47 A.M.

A lone Madison, North Carolina patrol car sits at the side of the road. It's overhead blue lights revolve smartly, engulfing the immediate darkness in a soft blue blaze. Four flares lay across the town bound lane. As Victoria rounds a blind curve, which peeks while cresting the horizon, a lone Madison Police Officer stands leaning against his idling white patrol car. As he takes a drag on his cigarette, he notices the soft bluish glow of Victoria's headlights radiating the shadowy curve.

The weathered Officer watches the enlarging headlights, as he exhales releasing the cigarette smoke through his nostrils. As Victoria's car emerges from the curve, the Officer drops the remaining portion of his cigarette to the damp asphalt. He begins to slowly walk away from his car towards the double yellow road markings in the center of the road.

The flashing blue lights immediately catch Victoria's attention. As she instinctively begins to slow down, her attention to detail picks up on the patrol car, the flares across the road, and a figure, obviously a police officer, stepping out towards the middle of the road. A sinking feeling comes over her, as she deducts another road closing.

The Madison Officer activates his flashlight, and now begins to wave it slowly from side to side. Victoria mumbles curse words under her breath, as she gently brings her car to a stop at the Officer. The powerful Mag-lite, blinds her. She activates her power window switch, and as soon as the window separates from its seal, the Madison Officer sharply announces, "You can't get through here, . . . go back the way you came, and find another route."

Lightly without tone of confrontation, Victoria asks, "Is there a traffic accident up ahead?"

"Go back the way you came, and find another route." He said harshly. "Do you understand?"

Trying to remain cordial, Victoria explains, "Officer listen, . . . I can't go back. I'll never make it. I'm on fumes now."

In a condescending tone, the Officer returns, "Well, . . . you sure in Hell can't go this way." He said motioning towards town. "The road is closed."

"There's no way I'm going to make it anywhere, in *that* direction." She said as she motions with her head towards the way she came. "I'm just going to have wait here until the road opens."

Quickly and sternly, the Officer says, "Hell no, . . . that's not an option."

Innocently Victoria explains, "I'll pull over there, . . ." She points to a small clearing along the side of the road as she continues, ". . . Off the road. I'll be out of the way."

Victoria has surrendered the idea of traveling any further tonight. So much for best made plans.

"No, . . ." The Officer said with a bark, ". . . Now turn this vehicle around and 'git'."

Total disbelief engulfs her. She couldn't believe the unreasonable actions of the Officer. "I can't, . . ." She now imitates the way, and tone he said 'git'. ". . . I have no gas left."

"Well that's your problem, now ain't it."

His response is like a match to a gasoline soaked fuse.

"Just what the Hell is your problem?"

Exploding in anger, the Officer shouts, "Don't you *sass me*!! I'm the law here, girly. This is the way we run things down here. I say, you do, . . . or you will spend sometime in my jail!" He ended sharply.

As he spoke, Victoria sat and felt her heart rate increase. Her breathing quickened, and became deeper. She no longer heard him shouting at her, but she did see the hate in his bulging blood shot eyes, as well as veins protruding from his neck and forehead. She watched his tight, thin-lipped mouth spew his words. She resisted the mighty temptation to snatch his tongue from him. The desire not to cause the Bureau any embarrassment, or herself with an assaulting a police officer rap. She calmed herself with a few deep breaths, and then flatly informed the Officer as non-threatening as she could.

"Look, I didn't come here to piss you off."

"Too damn late now girly."

That's it, she thought to herself upon his response. He's looking for a fight and I'm not going to give him one. Understanding that he may be a little nuts, Victoria surrenders and announces, "I'm out." She then began to prepare her car for motion when the Officer slams his metal flashlight hard upon the open window frame.

Startled by the loud metal-to-metal contact, Victoria immediately looks to the Mag-lite resting in a shallow dent on the frame. Then in a low slow eerie tone the Officer said, "You get your ever loving black ass outa that car."

Victoria raises her eyes from the flashlight to the Officer's blood shot peepers. After peering into the dark, cold orbs, and seeing his empty soul, she now becomes frightened, . . . very frightened. She thought about staying in the car, but quickly rejected that idea. This psycho will bust the car up.

She thought about reaching for her gun, but then she reasons he will have shot her to pieces.

"Whatever you're thinking about ferget it. You *will die* tryin'." He ended reassuringly.

She now thinks about identifying herself, as a Federal Agent of the F.B.I., but she reasons that he is so out of control, that it is unpredictable what his reaction might be. Though she has ruled out an apology, and an extension of police assistance.

The Madison Police Officer has now taken a step away from her car door. He motions for her to exit, as he slid his long stem metal Mag-lite to it's holder on his gun belt. Victoria reluctantly began to comply with his order. She has decided to build a civil rights case against this madman. As she climbs out of the car, her mind is checking for all the elements needed to bring charges.

"Face the car, and presume the position, you know how, I'm sure you've done this before."

The order was like a splash of cold water on an unsuspecting face.

"What?" She responds in disbelief.

In a stern voice the Officer replies, "Put your hands on the car, feet back and spread 'em!!"

In a total disbelief that this entire situation is unfolding as is, Victoria displays a nervous smile and says, "You've got to be kidding."

"We can do this here and now, or after you get out of the hospital." He responds coldly.

Realizing that this nightmare is getting out of hand, Victoria drops the weak smile, and sternly says, "Enough is enough. I work for the . . ."

Like a wild bull storming out of the gate, the Officer suddenly rushes her shouting, "I told you to turn around, . . ." He now has reached her, and pushes her towards the car, as he spins her around, ". . . And spread 'em!!!"

His sudden rush caught Victoria completely by surprise. Within a blink of an eye, he moved from a few feet away from her to the position they now stand in. Victoria didn't realize as she spoke, his Hell forged temper boiled into a blinding rage. He now stands with Victoria pinned against the car. He holds her by the back of her neck, standing behind her. She's still dazed by the swiftness of the attack. She now realizes that she has lost control of a situation that she admits she never really had

He kicks her feet apart, and rearward. He then states, "You do know how to spread 'em, huh? Isn't it true that black women spread their legs like peanut butter?"

"Get the Hell off me!! What in the Hell do you think you're doin'!!" She said full of fear and anger.

"I'm gonna search you for contraband." He said, and then instantly slams his open hand up against her crotch, and squeezes.

Immediately Victoria detonated. As she attempts to react against his action, the Lawman counters by managing to sweep one of her legs from under her. Victoria crashes to one knee. Pinning her torso to the side of the car, he says, "You niggas from up north need learnin'."

With the side of her face pressed against the cool damp sheet metal of her car, rage boils within her veins like molten hot lava. His body against hers, and sensing his drawn kips inches from her ear, made Victoria's skin crawl. Instinctively, she moves to remove him from her.

The Officer never saw her left elbow coming. He did feel the sledgehammer like impact against the side of his head. He automatically stands straight up, as the blow momentarily stuns him. Victoria proceeds to follow through by extending her leg and sweeping it with the force of a mule. Her leg strikes the surprised Officer low, at about ankle height. As he hit the asphalt buttocks first, Victoria is up on her feet.

The Agent is now trying to think rationally, but no clear

thought can be processed. Her initial response is to finish him off, as he wallows on the roadway. As he begins to rise, she is trying to convince herself to what is happening is real. This has to be a dream, she thinks to herself. A very, very bad dream.

The Madison Officer is now on his feet, and facing her. Victoria is having a hard time combating a uniformed Officer. She was raised to respect and obey authority. The United States Army, and the Federal Bureau of Investigation trained her that way, but her Mother backed by the word of the Almighty also taught her self-preservation.

The Lawman withdraws his eighteen-inch metal flashlight from its holder. Victoria sees the anger in his eyes. He says something to her, but between the heavy southern draw, spoken through his clenched teeth, she could not understand him. But she does know from the inflection that it was now time to fight. The entire Universe seemed to become non-existent. All Victoria could see is the Lawman and the five yards that separates them. The distance seems only to be about five inches. The Cop seems to have grown ten feet tall, and the flashlight he holds in his hand, is a big as a sewer pipe. The scene seems to slow to a speed where Victoria can observe every minute detail. Her mind is now no longer cluttered with conflicting data.

She continues to project the helpless field mouse cornered by the hungry cat. The Officer begins his attack with his flashlight, and the little field mouse now turns into a vicious King Cobra. A forward kick to the center of his chest stops him dead in his tracks. She then immediately delivers a spinning kick, which connects with the hand holding the light. As the Mag-lite flies through the sky like a guided missile, Victoria's athletic leg is once again impacting on his legs, at about the ankles. While the flashlight sails through the crisp night air, the Officer, defying gravity only for a moment, finally crashed upon the blacktop upon his back.

The confrontation has now escalated.

As she recovers from her sweeping maneuver, her back is to the Officer. She rises to her feet in this position because, she know he was not an immediate threat because she heard him fall upon the ground. So, as she rose, and began to face him, the Officer, while flat on his back, has started to go for his sidearm.

Her eyes lock on his action, just as his hand reaches the weapon. Without hesitation, she began to step towards him. Like a clap of thunder, the snap locking the gun in the holster opens. Victoria now leaps upon him. They struggle feverishly. He's trying to withdraw the semi-automatic pistol, and she's trying to keep it in the holster.

Victoria is preventing the weapon from being drawn with all of her adrenaline boosted strength. The Officer is cursing loudly at her as he struggles to free his weapon. Victoria knows this cannot continue for much longer. Though reluctantly, she now accepts the notion of ceasing his function. Victoria reasons that her campaign must be decisive and immediate. She looks to his face as he screams racial insults, and establishes that driving his nose bone into his brain will be her course of action. Just as she swallows the lump in her throat, and prepares to strike, she is suddenly struck by lightening.

What Victoria experienced was man made lightening. Realizing that the battle for his Beretta 96 was incurable, the struggling Officer reached with his free hand for his Nova stun gun. He then applied the non-lethal weapon, and then in a quick stabbing motion, he jams it into Victoria's side, activating it.

Victoria's body stiffened, and as the 40,000 volts of electricity surges through her body, she immediately took on the appearance of a freshly captured fish, dancing helplessly on the shore.

The Madison Officer stops injecting Victoria with the paralyzing stun. As he rises to his feet, he keeps his eyes on the downed woman. He slips the device back into its small holder on his gun belt. Victoria is now positioned on her back. Her eyes are open, and are wide enough to seem as if they were about to pop out. It is clear that she is not dead. The Officer is watching her closely enough to see her chest slightly heave, and then deflate. Though she lies motionless in a dream like state, she can still see and hear.

The Officer now unholsters his semi-automatic pistol. He then stands over Victoria, straddling her body. He leans slightly forward and points the .40 caliber pistol, less than an inch from Victoria's right eye. Movement for Victoria is impossible at the moment. She sees from the expression on his face, and the crazed look in his eyes, that her death will happen here and now. She predicts that his course of action is to pop her, and then dump her. She reasons along the fact, that with all of the woodland around the area, nobody would find her until she started stinking up the countryside.

She is more angry than frightened now. To go out like this, unable to avoid it, fight back or scream out. This son of a bitch, is going to take me out cold. Sensing that only moments remain, she out of defiance, screams at him mentally, . . . fuck you!!!

Suddenly flashing lights, immediately followed by the roar of a car's engine, causes the crazed Cop to quickly lower his weapon, and look towards the direction of the rapidly approaching car. The Officer pauses as he sees another Madison police car pulling along side of his cruiser, and stop. He now looks down at Victoria and through clenched teeth says, "You lucked out, Nigga'." He then begins to stand as he discreetly reholsters his weapon.

Captain Christopher Preston is now exiting his car. Captain Preston is second in command of the Madison Police Department. The Officer takes a step away from the still floored Victoria, she is now starting to sense her extremities once again, as the tall, well fit Captain starts his way over towards them.

"Just what in the Hell goes on here, Jack?" The Captain asked firmly.

The Officer displays a bright smile, and responds flippantly, "N.W.A. Captain." He then looks down toward Victoria.

The Captain now reaches them. He looks down at the woman and remarks, "I see you've adjusted said attitude, huh?"

Victoria is now fighting hard to regain the function of her motor skills.

"Who is she?"

"Probably some whore from up north." The Officer replies.

Looking over at her car, the Captain says, "Whores don't drive cars like that." He then looks back towards the Officer and adds, "Run a check on that 'rig'."

As Jack goes over to her car, Captain Preston lights a cigar, and squats down next to Victoria. He firmly takes a hold of Victoria's face and comments, "Pretty little thing."

"She's a panther, she tried to take my head off!" The Officer shouts from the car.

"Sounds like you are in a whole heap of trouble, Missy." Preston said.

Then letting go of her face, he orders, "Com'on, . . . get up." As he stood he brought the still groggy Victoria up with him. Captain Preston now catches the sight of another Madison Police cruiser, as it comes to a stop next to the other two patrol cars. As he helps Victoria to remain steady on her feet, he watches the young patrol Officer Stephen Davis, exit his marked patrol car. The Captain mumbles a few curse words under his breath. He then bites down on the cigar and angrily commands, "Jack, . . . get over here."

As Officer Davis begins walking towards the gathered, Jack reaches the Captain. As Captain Preston watches the Rookie approach, Jack, in a low hostile tone questions, "What in the Hell is he doin' here?"

Quickly Preston asks low enough so only Jack could hear him, "What have you found out, . . . anything?"

Immediately the Officer responds, "No record. It has temporary tags, though. Its probably not in the NCIC system yet."

"Cuff her." The Captain orders, as he places Victoria in an arm lock.

Jack quickly stuffs Victoria's personal items into his pants pocket, as he begins to remove his handcuffs from his gun belt. Davis steps up to the gathered, as Jack places his cuffs on the still stunned Victoria. The Captain places his hands on his hips, and begins to bark at the newly arrived Officer.

"Just what in the Hell are you doin' here, boy?!!"

Startled by the unexpected brutal inquiry, the Officer takes a few steps rearward, as his facial expression takes on a look of anxiety. As the Captain stands with his hands on his hips, his middle-aged face of stone gives him the appearance of a man with no soul.

Captain Preston's six foot, four-inch frame, is topped off with a crew cut. A permanent scar runs from just above his left eye, rearward along the side of his head, passing his ear. The path of the Iraqi sniper's bullet, fired on the closing day of the 1991 war, is reflecting brightly amidst the flashing lights. No hair has ever grown back to fill in the path of the bullet that creased his head. Needless to say, the man's Frankenstein appearance is intimidating.

Stepping towards him, and closing the gap between in one step, Captain Preston shouts, "Where are you suppose to be now?!!"

"There was no traffic. Everyone is stayin' inside because of the storm and all." He now motions towards Jack Hayford, and his disheveled uniform, and adds, "I'm sorry I missed the show."

"Oh I bet you would of loved helping her to kick his ass, huh?" He responded coldly.

"You bet cha." Davis answered firmly.

"Yeah well, . . . even with two *bitches*, . . ." He pauses for a beat for his message to sink in, ". . . On his back, . . . he would of still came out on top. He's been policin' before your Mama knew how to make you." The angry Captain slightly turns his head towards Jack, and the now almost completely revived Victoria. "Officer Hayford!!"

"Yes Sir!" Jack returned sharply.

"Get your prisoner in your car, and then get on your radio and tell Millard to get down here with his flatbed truck on the double."

"Yes Sir."

As Jack Hayford callously hustled a shackled Victoria off towards his car, Captain Preston looks to his watch. He then directs his attention to Officer Davis. In a lower tone, but with one still filled with hostility, the Captain says, "Boy, . . . I ought to bust your ass for this. Failure to obey an order, and being outside of an assigned patrol area."

"Captain, . . ."

Becoming even more enraged, Preston responds, "Don't Captain me, Boy!!"

"Listen, . . ." Davis begins strongly, ". . . Doin' radar on a stormy night, like tonight is dumb, . . . besides, who in the Hells out on a night like this?"

"That ain't the point. You were given orders!!" He now continues in a lower but firmer tone, "Isn't that what gotten' you thrown off the Highway Patrol?"

The young Officer looks away devalued, but then responds bitterly, "No, it was because I took a dump in my egotistical Captain's car."

Coldly, the Captain replies, "I don't like you Boy. The Chief, well he thinks you are some kind of hero, because you took out three bank robbin' scumbags all by yourself. Well get this, Sergeant York, . . . you fuck with me, and I'll fuck you. Now get where you belong." He ended sharply.

Officer Davis pauses, looking the Captain in his dark hollow eyes. The Officer is now remembering the fatherly advice Chief Hill gave him on his first day concerning Captain Preston. 'Give the Captain a wide berth'. Davis now looks away from the Captain, and starts walking off towards his car. Preston also starts towards the parked vehicles, but at a much slower pace.

Officer Jack Hayford pushes Victoria into the back seat of his caged patrol car. The unexpected shove causes her to fall rearward, onto the seat. With her wrist cuffed behind her, she lands on them, thus causing them to tighten. She then adjusts herself, and sits upright on the cool vinyl seat. She refuses to scream out or complain about the nerve tearing pain. Unemotionlessly Victoria asks, "What am I being arrested for?"

Leaning inward from the outside, and speaking only loud enough for her to hear, Hayford responds, "Hey girly, you better be glad you *are* being arrested and not tagged."

"Hayford!!!"

The Captain's voice exploded in the stillness, as if Goliath had called out. Preston watches Davis get into his cruiser as Hayford approaches. The Captain stops his slow walk, but continues to puff on his now half chewed cigar. As Hayford steps within earshot for a low tone discussion, the Captain begins in an aggravated resonance.

"You just couldn't stand here and keep this damn road closed, huh?" The Captain asked as he continues to watch the Rookie, now making a U-turn and driving away.

"She pissed me off. She was just askin' for it." He returns flatly.

"So what are you going to do with her now?"

Hayford looks back towards his cruiser and responds in a sinister tone, "I'll take care of her."

"No good." The Captain immediately returns. "The Kid has seen her."

"Fuck him. It would be my pleasure to pop him too."

"Listen to me, you blood thirsty son of a bitch, . . . unless you want out of this thing, then nobody but that bastard coming through tomorrow gets popped. Unless you like kill'in more than money."

"Say no more, I get the drift."

Smiling, the Captain says, "Good. Now listen here, . . . you take the girl on in. There's some confiscated cocaine in the property room. Stuff some up her nose, and then 'book' her on driving while impaired, resisting arrest, assaulting a police officer with the intent to injure and possession. Judge Graham won't question this, and any tales she has to tell will fall on deaf ears. She'd be another monkey busted for runnin' drugs."

"Say Boss, . . . why go through all this trouble?"

"First of all she has been seen, so she can't be dumped. I don't want anybody asking questions now."

"So, we'll just leave her in the lock up. By noon, it ain't gonna matter no how. She ain't local. Nobody is gonna` track her here, before we do what we are fixin` to do."

The Captain nods in agreement.

"So, what about the people I was waiting for?" Jack asked.

Through clenched teeth, Preston angrily says, "You shoulda thought about that before you got involved with her." He then pauses momentarily, and then adds, "I'm not going to worry about them, they'll find their way to the Station. Get her squared away."

Jack starts to walk off, but then the Captain stops him by taking a hold of the Officer's forearm. The Officer looks to the stern faced Captain with bewilderment.

"And Jack, . . ." Preston starts lightly, ". . . The girl gets to the station. No escape attempts, no D.O.A. and no trying to make her swallow your baton. You keep it in your pants. There is no time for fun and games, you hear?"

"Damn Captain, . . . I can't screw her, . . . I can't kill her, . . ."

Captain Preston removes his cigar as he leans into Hayford's ear, and interrupts his complaining. "Five million dollars."

Hayford's face starts walking towards his car, the yellow flashing lights of the tow truck brightens the darkness, as it approaches from town. The Captain returns the cigar to his mouth, and then begins to walk slowly towards his car, with a smile.

Chapter Three

Madison North Carolina is a small out of the way town, not far from Healing Springs, and only 45 minutes from UnWharrie National Forest. Only the very old or the very young live in Madison. Madison is a town 40% black and 50% white. The rest of the population are American Natives and Asians. The people here get along. Outsiders bring and produce trouble. The Madison police force is very quick to deliver enforcement, jail or even expel troublemakers. Civil rights do not apply here.

Madison is a town known to the locals for it's roadside markets, it's hospitality and speed traps. Madison is also the hometown of former Lieutenant General Jonathon Taylor Armstrong, a strong black American candidate for the Office of President of the United States.

The Madison police force is a small detachment consisting of a Chief, a second in command, which is Captain Preston and six full time officers. No minority members or women are officers. The Chief claims none from these groups are interested in joining, though the ones that are always seem to develop some type of disqualification.

Housed in the rear of the station, which is the size of an

average two story house, are two 8' by 12' jail cells containing 8 brawlers. Despite the stormy rainfall, barroom brawls, especially on Friday nights are standard. The two jail cells are side by side, with a column of standard iron bars between them. Both cells open out to a 10-foot wide passageway, that leads out into the operation are of the station.

Also on the first floor of the station, is the communication center, which is only a desk with a base radio upon it. The officer's locker room, which is about the size of a large walk in closet. The weapons storage room, that has the same protection as a bank. There is also a bathroom, small kitchen, the Captain's office and the reception area.

On the level above the first floor, is the Chief's office, which faces the front of the building, over looking Main Street. Next to his office is the conference room. Then there is a storage room, and an empty room designated for the use by outside agencies, like the State Police, the American Red Cross and recently it has been used by the United States Secret Service, when the General is in town.

It is nearly 3:30 when Victoria arrived at the station without any further physical incident, but she was subjected to brutal verbal abuse by Officer Hayford. Her body slightly aches but her mind and wits are once again as sharp as a tack. She has decided not to divulge her identity until she has made her telephone call. Right now she wants to play it cool until she is able to let somebody know where she is. She then looks upon Jack Hayford. She restrains herself with the determined desire to see Officer Hayford in cuffs, facing Federal jail time.

Like a thorn in her side, she remembers about her gun and her Federal I.D. beneath her driver's seat. She worries about how they would react upon discovering it. She wonders if they already found them. She then tries to delude herself into believing that, if they are discovered, they won't hurt her position any more than what it is now.

In the back of her mind, plays the worse case scenario.

They panic when they find the I.D. They then decide to bury it, along with her car, and her body out in the middle of nowhere. It would be as if she just disappeared. This very possible scenario causes a chill to discharge throughout her body.

Victoria is led into the brightly lit station. Inside is an Officer busily typing, and a very well dressed, rugged looking, very German appearing, middle-aged man standing very disciplined in the reception area. He immediately catches Victoria's detail attentive eye, because he seemed so out of place among these Hillbillies she thought. Just before she was pushed towards a small opening in the chest high reception counter, she notices the distinguishing earpiece worn by the protection teams of the Secret Service.

As she is shoved towards the cell area, she ponders the presence of the Agent. Then she thought, maybe he isn't an Agent, but then that thought is immediately dismissed. That man has Federal Government written all over him. What have I stumbled into, she wonders internally.

Officer Hayford unlocks the thick gauge steel door which leads to the two-cell area. He swings the door wide and shoves Victoria inside the dimly lit passageway. The momentum causes her to stumble down the passageway now in full view of the cell's occupants. Hayford struts toward her. Victoria stands facing him defiantly. He then suddenly backhands Victoria across the face. The sudden powerful blow causes her to turn away from him, as she drops down to one knee. Cheers and comments explode from some of the detainees.

"When I take these cuffs off you, I don't want none of your shit." He said harshly, and then began removing the cuffs.

Victoria looks into the cells she now faces. Most of the bar brawls are at the round iron bars, looking at her. She sees that some appear to be dumbfounded, while others are amused. Then suddenly her eyes lock onto the man with the crazy eyes. He unemotionally peers at her. He then hauntally says, “Hey Jack, . . . she’s a problem? Put her in here.”

Just then Victoria’s swollen wrists are freed from the handcuffs. She now slowly rises to her feet, as Hayford responds back to the man with the crazy eyes.

“She thinks she’s a bad ass.” Hayford said, as he unlocks the cell. He then grabs Victoria by the shoulder, and slings her inside the cell. “Here you go boys, . . . fresh meat.”

“When do I get my phone call?” Victoria asked sternly.

Hayford laughs heartily, as he walks out of the cellblock, and closes the heavy steel door behind him. Victoria now turns from the departed Hayford, and faces her cellmates. They all stand silently, staring at her. Victoria glances to the right and to the left at the peering roughnecks. She sees the stainless steel bench bolted to the rear wall of the cell. As all eyes watch her, she walks over to the empty bench, and then sits upon it. She looks at each and everyone. A death like silence fills the cellblock. Victoria feels her heart pounding against her ribs like a kettledrum. As the men continue to look upon her, she sits primed to leap upon the first one that advances towards her. Though she is terrified within, she dares not reveal that emotion.

Officer Jack Hayford swaggers from the heavy door, giggling like a schoolboy. He stops at the Officer typing on the computer, and in an dominating tone says, “What in the Hell are you still doing here?”

“I was nearing the end of my shift, when the bar called to report a fight that was getting out of hand. They really messed the place up this time.”

“Oh, they’re just some good ole’ boys lettin’ off some steam.”

“You put a woman back there, Jack???”

Stopping and slightly turning towards him, Jack disparaging replies, “Don’t you go worrin’ about, none of your business.”

Intimidated by him, the Officer returns to the keyboard and then smartly says, "Well, . . . it's your ass."

Unbeknown to Hayford, the well-dressed gentleman, now stands directly to his rear. Having the need to have the last word, Hayford replies to the concerned cop, "I recommend you have those knuckleheads outa here by the time the Captain gets here."

Hayford turns around, and is clearly startled by the man's seemingly sudden appearance. "Jesus Christ, . . . what are you tryin' to do, . . . give me a stroke!?"

Smoothly the man asks, "Why did you bring her here?"

Jack Hayford then takes a step back, and states, "Police business." The man peers, as if he's looking through the arrogant, redneck momentarily, before he politely asks, "Where is Captain Preston?"

"He'll be in shortly."

"Shortly?"

"Yeah, . . . like in *soon.*"

"You must reach out to him at once. If any further delays are met, then the entire action will be terminated." The man ends sharply, showing the first signs of emotion.

"Oh yeah, . . . well we're here. Fuck the rest of them. Whata you say, . . . me and you, fifty-fifty."

Through his earpiece, the debonair gentleman receives word that the Captain is pulling up in front of the station. As Hayford waits for a response, the mysterious man turns his back on the Officer and faces the entranceway. Hayford clenches his teeth at the unfriendly gesture. He starts to spin the spit and polished stranger on his heels, but now the Captain enters.

Preston stops just inside the station house, surprised to see the man standing with Officer Hayford, apparently waiting for him. Another man, neatly dressed in business attire, and wearing the identifiable earpiece, now enters the station. Entering with him are two men dressed in North Carolina State Police uniforms. Behind them is a bearded, olive complexion man, with cold dark eyes.

"We have had to accelerate the timetable, since you were gone, Captain." The German begins urgently, and then lowers his voice and continues sternly, "This place is like Times Square. Captain, this operation is starting to become an abortion."

"Everything is under control." The Captain returns in the same low tone, and then firmly orders in a normal tone, "Jack, . . . show these people up to the conference room, . . . then you come back down here, and attend to what you have to do, and get back out there and await our friends." He then looks to the German and says, "I'm going to get the Chief down here right now."

As Hayford starts up the stairs, the German looks from the Captain, and then motions for the trio of men to follow, as he starts up the stairs behind the cop. Captain Preston looks to his watch. He now looks to the Officer typing on the computer in the operations area and sharply says, "Boy, . . . I want them brawlers outa my jail, and your ass home. I need you fresh in a couple of hours. Let's go!!"

"Almost done, Captain."

As he heads up the stairs, Preston firmly commands, "Move it Officer, move it!!"

There are five men locked in the cell with Victoria. They are all still staring at her, including the three men in the adjoining cell. Victoria has determined that 'Crazy eyes' is the ringleader. She is also sure that two of the five cellmates don't want any trouble. They have spectator eyes. Their eyes are moving back and forth from 'Crazy eyes' and his two cohorts to her. The three men in the other cell are standing at the separating wall of prison bars, peering in, as if Victoria is some sort of zoo animal. She slowly turns towards them. One man immediately looks away. The man next to him, continues staring blankly. The last man places his face between the bars, and extends his tongue suggestively at her. Victoria now looks away from them, and directs her attention back to 'Crazy eyes'.

"Hey Jimbo, . . . !" The man with the wiggling tongue suddenly shouts, ". . . She don't like that!" He starts to laugh while adding, "What's the matter Mama, you ain't never had your tweeter tickled?"

Now 'Crazy eyes', and company join in the laughter. She looks to the other two young men in the cell. They look away from her.

"We know you ain't no virgin."

Victoria immediately looks to see who said that. 'Crazy eyes' and his two friends continue to laugh. She looks to the other cell. The man with the tongue displays it once again. She then looks to the other men in the adjoining cell. Once continues to stare. Victoria figures that the lights are on, but nobody's home. He is not going to be a problem. The other man has moved. He now sits on their stainless steel bench. Victoria now slowly turns her attention to the three problems in her cell.

They, and the man with the tongue, continue to joke about her. As their sense of humor becomes more and more vulgar, Victoria begins to think about her road trip to Atlanta thus far. Hand to hand combat with a K.K.K. cop. Arrested, assaulted, sexually abused and now she stands in a cell with some good ole' boys, with pussy on their minds.

The thoughts now enrage her. If you boys want my pussy, she says to herself, you're gonna have to take it, but then, . . . you're gonna have to fuck me dead. She coolly sits back on the cold bench defiantly. As she continues to eyeball the men in her cell, she has finally decided that enough is enough.

4:00 A.M.

As Victoria sits in the cell, her cramps are making her feel mean. Pit bull crazy mean. Her thoughts are that either the cops will discover her Federal identity, or these hillbillies are going to make her squeal, like that poor man in 'Deliverance'.

Meanwhile upstairs in the station's conference room, a meeting is in progress. In the conference room are Captain Preston, the mysterious German, his Aide and the bearded man. The two Troopers are standing outside, in the hallway, guarding the conference room door.

". . . And the status of the town?" The mysterious German asked.

Sitting at the head of the table, with the German to his right, Preston begins, "The phone lines have been cut, as well as the cable T.V. line. People around here will simply think that the outages are due to the storm, . . . which wouldn't be unusual. There is only one road in and out of town. That is not going to be much of a worry. This storm came in handy. It'll keep these folks indoors. I say we are now in complete control of Madison."

"But what of the Chief, . . . he's one loose end that need to be tied." The other well dressed man comments.

Captain Preston turns to his left, and addresses the man, "Don't you worry about him, Mister Smith, . . ."

"I'm Mister Smith." The German announces.

Captain Preston then automatically looks to Mister Smith, as the other man identifies himself, "I'm Mister Jones."

Preston now looks to him and smartly comments, "You guys are going pretty heavy with this cloak and dagger shit, aren't ya? Well anyway, . . . I've taken care of the loose end. The Chief will be here any minute, now."

The bearded man nervously announces, "I do not like this." He begins with a heavy Middle Eastern accent. "Too many delays. The weather, . . . the timetable changing . . ."

Interrupting, Mister Smith snaps, "You listen to me. This operation *will* proceed. You just worry about your task."

The bearded man did not respond in words. He continues to look upon Mister Smith with contempt. Interrupting the staring contest between the two men, Captain Preston asks, "Do we have an E.T.A. on the delivery?"

Mister Smith then looks to Mister Jones, and then nods slightly. Mister Jones then addresses himself to the Captain, "As we awaited your return to the station, we received a communiqué." He now pauses momentarily to look at his watch. "At approximately 0433 hours the delivery is due to arrive at the farm."

"That's only 30 minutes from now, and we still do not have all that needs to be completed *here*." The bearded man frantically interjects.

Sternly, but smoothly, Mister Smith glances towards the man, and says, "What did I tell you?"

"Don't worry, . . ." The Captain starts at the concerned man, ". . . The Chief will be here in any minute. Relax partner."

With total disgust, the bearded man replies, "You Americans are so reckless. Nothing has been to plan or to timetable since inception. The matter is becoming most heedless."

Mister Smith looks to the Caption and asks, "And how do you feel about this Mister Preston? Do you feel that aborting our plans is necessary?"

"Hell no, . . . I think we've come too far to stop now." He answers solidly.

"I too feel we have reached the point of no turning back." Mister Smith said. He turns to the bearded man and compassionately says, "My friend, . . ."

The bearded man looks to Mister Smith. The German reared man then narrows his eyes, and sharply says, ". . . Shut the fuck up. Do I make myself clear?"

The bearded man sees the icy blue eyes of Mister Smith peering at him. They seem to burn right through him. The sight causes an uneasy wave of fear to pass over him. The bearded man started to protest the man's harsh statement, but the threatening posture of the unknown Mister Smith, suspends his rebuttal.

Just as the bearded man swallows the lump in his throat, Victoria is approached by 'Crazy eyes'. She is watching him intensely, as he strolls up to her with a wide smile, looking like an alley cat that swallowed the mouse. He stops and now stands about three feet in front of the still sitting Agent. Victoria sits up straight. With a hard facial expression, she looks to the space-intruding roughneck, while primed for battle.

'Crazy eyes' drops his smile, and then begins to grab at his crotch. Unmoved by his action, Victoria, while looking directly into his eyes reveals, "I warn you, . . . I'm in a real BITCHY MOOD."

Snickers, and chuckles rip throughout the cellblock. The inmate with the crazy eyes, now unbuckles his huge brass 'USA' belt buckle, and proceeds to display his hardened man sex.

"Merry Christmas, baby." He said as he held his sex before her.

Instantly Victoria launches a swift kick to 'Crazy eyes' groin, with such force, that it lifted the surprised man inches off the cool concrete floor. Before 'Crazy eye's' brain can realize the attack, Victoria is on her feet.

Witnessing her strike, one of 'Crazy eyes' friends rushes the Agent. With the same lightening fast, and just as damaging strike, Victoria kicks the advancing friend's right knee. Within a blink of an eye, Victoria has T.K.oed' one man, and dislocated the right knee joint of another.

Cries of agony echo within the cellblock, as the now crippled attacker wallows on the floor. A semi-conscience

'Crazy eyes', staggers on his feet while holding his swollen purple toned sex organ. He falls over his wallowing friend, onto the floor. He then silently curls into a ball.

'Crazy eye's' other friend, Jimbo only remain. He looks up from his two floored friends to Victoria. The woman's eyes were waiting to meet his. The man in the other cell begins verbally attacking Jimbo. His teasing attack on Jimbo's manhood, engages the man.

"Why don't you shut the Hell up Tommy." He shouts to the agitator. He then turns and points to Victoria, and assures her, "I'm gonna rip your head off!!"

Victoria does not reply. She remains steadfast in her consideration. Jimbo steps toward her in a boxing stance. With his head tucked in, his hands protecting his chin, and his elbows guarding his ribs, he moves in the kill.

Just as she was about to kick, the man with the knee that now bends in the opposite direction, throws himself across her feet. Jimbo moves in, and throws a series of punches that Victoria skillfully dodges and ducks. Victoria then immediately returns with a fury of counter punches, which cause Jimbo to back off a step or two. Victoria meanwhile attempts to kick herself free, but the lock upon them is too strong.

Jimbo now steps in with a powerful roundhouse swing. Victoria ducks, and Jimbo's fist just brushes the top of her head. As Victoria pulls herself downward, out of the path, of what is a sure knock out punch, she targets the side of man's head that is binding her feet. With her weight behind her downward driving knee, she attempts to drive the joint into his ear.

With a shout he releases her legs, but Jimbo snatches her by the hair, and forces her to stand. He now takes a hold of her throat and squeezes. Victoria immediately breaks his chokehold, and throws a punch to his face. Her jab to his mouth breaks his lip. Jimbo violently reacts by tossing her away like a child would a doll.

Victoria stumbles, and then finally falls with her back against the bars separating the adjoining cell. Tommy, the man with the gifted tongue, grabs Victoria across her body, pinning her to the bars. With a sinister chuckle, he says into her ear, "Got cha."

Jimbo swipes the small amount of blood escaping from his swollen lip, and then smiles.

"Oooowee!!" Tommy exclaims, "She's a Hellcat, ain't she?" He said to Jimbo, and then adds, "Whata you say, . . . you from the front, and me from behind?" He said with a smile, and then he turns towards Victoria's ear, and asks, "What do you say?"

Victoria does not struggle with Tommy, his hold upon her is solid. She remains still and silent, as she watches Jimbo, as he looks over his downed friends.

"You sure do smell pretty." Tommy says, as he sniffs about her.

Jimbo looks towards them in time to see Tommy start feeling Victoria's breast. Tommy with glee announces, "She likes this man, she ain't even fighin' it."

Victoria is now looking upon Jimbo amorously. His lust driven desires lock onto Victoria. He moves towards the object of his desire like a nomad to water. Victoria waits until she could almost feel Jimbo's breath upon her, before she high kicks him in his chest. The unsuspecting man stumbles rearward, tripping over his accomplices, before landing hard onto the floor. Now Victoria continues her attack on the surprised Tommy. She grabs the hand that is draped around her body, and bends the fingers back until they snap like twigs on a tree branch. Tommy releases her screaming in pain. Before the injured man could retract his arm back into his cell, Victoria snatches the limb, and pulls it towards her as far as she could. As if she is snapping a two-foot long wooden stick in half, she breaks his arm at the elbow.

Just as she releases Tommy's broken arm, and he continues to scream in pain, Jimbo grabs Victoria, spins her around and lands a punch to her jaw. The sudden attack stuns her as she goes with the momentum of the blow. Jimbo follows through. As he grabs her to steady his target, while cocking his arm to deliver another punch, Victoria counters with an over the top punch that impacts hard on Jimbo's nose. He releases his hold of her as blood begins to pour from his broken nose. Victoria changes her position, as she prepares to follow through. She has targeted his head for a brain jarring kick that's sure to turn his lights out.

"You black bitch, . . . !!" He starts as he begins to recover from the nose breaking blow, "I'm gonna . . . . !"

Victoria powerful kick interrupts him. The angry kick catches the gutter mouth man on his chin, causing him to bite off an inch of his tongue. The portion of his lick flies through the air, as Jimbo falls rearward. His head, like a soccer ball and the iron bars like a goal post, Jimbo's head falls rearward with enough force to cause it to be driven between the bars. Victoria: 4, Malcontents: 0.

Victoria now looks to the remaining two occupants in her cell. The two men standing in separate spots of the iron cage are no threat to the Agent. An expression of shock and dismay adorns their faces. She now relaxes, and assesses her inflicted damage. 'Crazy eyes' has passed out. His still exposed purple, and swollen penis is evident that he won't be using his broken member no time soon. Victoria looks to the man with the dislocated knee, as she mentally notes that 'Crazy eyes' will remember her every time he goes to take a piss. The man with the future knee problem, is too, out cold. As she looks to her last combatant, she now just notices that his head, did in fact pass through the tight space between the iron bars. She has to do a double take to confirm what she sees. Victoria then chuckles to herself, over the sight.

Tommy's agony filled cries are heard by the Officers out in the operation area. Jack Hayford enters the cellblock, expecting Victoria Owens to be in pieces. He becomes dumbfounded very quickly as soon as he realized Tommy's cries are those of agony. Hayford now sees Tommy wallowing on the floor, holding his arm which looks like a limp noodle. Hayford looks into the cell containing Victoria. His brain cannot at first believe what his eyes are seeing. The Madison cop rushes to the cell door, and continues to look in disbelief. He throws his eyes over to the man still standing in dismay, and then desperately asks, "What in the Hell happened?"

The astonished man in the cell flatly responds, "The Lady got pissed."

Hayford looks at the still screaming Tommy, and the prisoner adds, "I was here, and what I saw her do, I still don't believe." He said, as he looked from the bewildered cop to Victoria.

Officer Hayford now looks to a seated and cool Victoria. She returns the emotionless stare.

"Jack, . . . hey JACK, ... !!!!" The arresting Officer of the bar brawlers shouts from the cellblock door, ". . . What in the Hell is all the shoutin' about?!"

Without taking his eyes off Victoria, Hayford answers loud enough to be heard over the misery filled wails, "Better get an ambulance here, J.T.!!"

"Is somebody hurt!?"

"Well no shit, son!" Hayford fires back, as he now looks towards the Officer's direction.

Captain Preston now enters the cellblock, and rushes over to Hayford. Looking into the cell at the injured, the Captain sternly states, "Jack, . . . you're just plum mean."

"I didn't do all this Captain." He then continues as he looks upon Victoria, "She did."

The Captain looks back to Hayford, and in a flat, unimpressed tone he says, "Well, . . . if she could knock you on your ass, . . ." He pauses momentarily to allow the point to carry on.

"She ain't nobody, the boys are all drunk."

Preston now steps closer toward Hayford, and in a low tone announces, "Time is very short. Get the wounded outa here, and release the rest."

"Including her?"

The Captain pauses in thought.

"Don't you want your dessert?"

With a smile he responds, "You bet your bars."

"Then fuck plan 'A'. After these people get the fuck outa here, . . . take her for a ride. She ain't no typical jig. She is the last thing we need here and now. In the mean time, isolate her. Put her in the holding cage." He ended and then begun to walk off.

Hayford looks back at Victoria. Their eyes meet. The Officer then opens the cell door. He removes his handcuffs from his gun belt, and tosses the restraints at the seated Agent. The bright silver tone steel shackles land on the concrete floor. They slide the rest of the distance, coming to a stop at her feet.

Hayford takes his pistol from its holster and holds his semi-automatic at his side.

"Put them on." He coldly orders.

Victoria looks from him, to the cuffs. She then looks back towards him. Instantly she thinks about the fact that they don't know she's a Federal Agent. Well, the little voice in the back of her head starts, maybe now they do.

"Now!" Hayford says through clenched teeth. "Right the fuck now!!"

Victoria looks to the gun in Hayford's hand. She looks back to him, and sees in his eyes the blood lust. She then slowly picks up the cuffs. To die in a cell in the middle of nowhere North Carolina at the hands of this bastard, enrages her soul. Just to piss him off, she complies with his order. As she affixed the cuffs to her wrist, she looks at Hayford. I'm not going to make it easy for you, her smirked expression projected towards Hayford. As she looks into his now lightly disappointed eyes, she knew if and when the time came, . . .

she is going to have to kill him. She has dropped her smirked expression, as her mind realizes Hayford's demise. It is nothing personal, . . . it's only about survival.

4:26 A.M.

Distant rumbles of thunder are within the fast moving clouds racing overhead. Strong gusts of wind are blowing hard enough to hauntly howl among the dark town's square buildings. Chief E.V. Hill arrives at the police station as angry as a bunch of African killer bees. As he stomps into the station, Tommy and the prisoner whose head was knocked between the bars, are being helped out of the station by E.M.S. personnel, and followed by their arresting Officer.

The Chief stops and views the whimpering Tommy and the swollen head, and broken nosed man, as they are helped in an ambulance, as another ambulance pulls away from the station. Assuming a jailhouse fight is what the Captain has called him out of his bed in the middle of the night for, enrages the 32-year veteran. The Chief now continues his march into the station. As soon as the Madison top cop crosses the station's threshold, he bellows for the Captain.

Captain Preston along with Mister Smith are standing together in the control area, when the Chief entered. The tough older cop marches towards his Captain, as he speaks loudly and in a tone full of authority.

"What in the name of Stonewall Jackson goes on here Captain?! What happened to those men?!" He adds as he motions towards the departing wounded. "Did Hayford have anything to do with this?! Where is he?!"

"Sir, come with me. I'll brief you on the details." Reston said as he attempts to guide the Chief towards his nearby office.

The Chief looks to Mister Smith and then rudely asks, "Who are you?'

Mister Smith produces his hand and announces, "Smith, United States Secret Service."

Disregarding Mister Smith's handshake, the Chief turns to Preston and loudly whines, "You didn't call me down here about that darn fool?"

The German man quickly speaks, "I determined it necessary."

The Chief slowly turns to the dapper Agent, and looks at him as if he is crazy. Mister Smith now adds in a professional manner, "It is a matter of security, Sir." He then graciously gestures towards the Captain's office.

"I thought this visit is supposed to be low key." The Chief begins, "No big deals, no press corps, and shit. The Boy is supposed to be coming home for a rest."

"This is only going to take a matter of minutes." Mister Smith charms with a smile while still motioning towards the Captain's office.

"No, after you, . . . Mister Secret Service." The Chief said with a false smile.

As the Agent walks towards the office, the Chief's eyes fall upon Victoria standing in the rear corner of the holding cell. Chief Hill turns to the Captain, and simply points to Victoria. The Captain starts explaining sounding like a child tattle telling, "That is the root of all the trouble we have been having around here."

The Chief looks back to Victoria, and then back to the Captain.

"That pretty little thing?" He said in wonderment.

"A real she-devil, Chief. Drug possession, resisting arrest. She attacked Hayford, . . . she is the one that did all that damage to those other prisoners."

Looking back at her now, Chief Hill evaluated the Captain's information and remarks, "Well Hayford needs his ass kicked, . . ." He now becomes irritated when he asks, ". . . But why was she in contact with male prisoners. Preston, you're slippin' boy. I should kick your ass for that." He then walks off towards the office.

Preston begins to follow the Chief. As he begins to walk,

he glances at the front handcuffed woman prisoner, standing within the small steel mesh cage. Victoria maintains eye contact with all who look upon her. Though, she doesn't project the fact, that she is scared to death, she remains faithful that her prayers of liberation will be answered.

Aside from that, she wonders what is going on. When Mister Smith identified himself as a Secret Service Agent, and the Chief made his remark about a darn fool arriving, . . . she thinks, and then Presidential Candidate General Jonathan Taylor Armstrong came to mind. She now remembers that the General is from a small North Carolina town, . . . Madison, bingo. She thought that she should reveal her identity to the Chief, but then that little voice in the back of her head protested the idea.

In Captain Preston's office, standing against the wall, unseen by the entering parties is Mister Jones. Victoria watches the Chief enter the office with the Captain a few steps behind him. Mister Smith stands in the center of the office, facing the doorway. The chief enters the office loudly, demanding to know why in the Hell his Captain wasn't good enough to be informed of a security matter. ". . . Hell he is able to talk very well, . . ." The Chief continues now inside the office, facing Mister Smith. ". . . He could of briefed me later on. Hell, . . . this Boy ain't the dang-blasted President!!" He ended shouting.

Not yet, Victoria mumbles as she overhears the Chief's ranting. From her position she now notices that she can see into the Captain's office via a reflection displaying the activity onto a large glass showcase. The image is faint, but is enough for the Agent to monitor. As the Chief yells at the Secret Service Advance man, the undetected Mister Jones, steps up behind the brash Chief of Police.

"So speak boy, . . . what's so dog-gone important?!"

Mister Smith smiles at the wrinkled face Chief. As a dazzled expression blankets the Chief's face, Jones grabs the Chief's head, and mercilessly breaks his neck. Instantly, without an uttered word, the Chief was dead. Victoria is startled by the sight she has just witnessed. As Jones places the Chief in a chair, Mister Smith speaks into his communicator, “Are we clear?”

A voice immediately answers in the affirmative.

“Very well, come in here at once.” Smith said into his radio device. He now turns to Mister Jones, “Go upstairs, and inform our bearded friend, we’re going to set up camp in here."

With a nod, Mister Jones departs from the office. Seeing Jones approach, Victoria acts as if she is unaware of what has just occurred. She quickly turns her back towards the office. Joes walks by her while on route towards the stairway. Entering the front doors are two North Carolina State Patrolmen. Victoria sees them enter. She becomes alarmed to the fact, that these two Officers are unaware of the dangerous situation they have just walked into. Watching carefully as Jones, and the Troopers meet. Victoria could not believe her eyes, when Jones points towards the Captain’s office.

As the Troopers approach her on their way to the office, the hairs on the back of her neck rose, as if she is about to be struck by lightening. She caught herself staring at the approaching men. She then quickly looks away from them. As they pass without saying a word, Victoria cannot shake the feeling that something was very wrong about them.

Victoria has started to question what she had witnessed previously in that office. She slowly looks to the reflection, and watches. Deep down she knew her questions about her observations were unfounded. She knows her eyes and conclusions are not wrong.

“What about the woman?” Mister Smith questions the Captain.

“She’s gonna be taken out for a ride in the woods, and in about a thousand years, she’ll be a fossil.” The Captain answers.

Mister Smith now directs his attention to the two Troopers who have just entered the office. He looks to the dead Chief, and says, “Take him, along with his car, and drive them off the road.” He ends coldly.

As the Troopers gather the limp body, Mister Smith speaks into his hidden microphone, which is on the inside, just below his sleeve cuff. “Status on the outside?”

An instant response of all’s clear, convinces the regimented suit wearing man, that the removal of the Chief’s body will proceed covertly. As a Trooper leads the other, who has the Chief’s body draped over in a ‘fireman’s carry’, out of the office, Mister Smith approaches Captain Preston. As he stands face to face with the emotionless supervisor, he gently remarks, “Nobody will question a traffic accident on a night like this.” He ends with a sinister grin.

Victoria cannot believe her eyes at the sight of the murdered Chief’s body being taken out like the garbage. She looks back towards the office, and then glances to the reflection. She could see the mysterious Mister Smith and the Captain engaged in conversation. She could only guess to what they were saying. She did know that since the Chief’s dead body was brought out in front of her, that she too was dead already.

Captain Preston suddenly emerges from the office, and stands at the caged door. Victoria and he lock eyeballs. A lump develops in her throat that prevented her from swallowing. She just can’t believe that this entire episode is occurring.

“Hayford!!” The Captain suddenly barks causing Victoria to jump.

Mister Smith departs from the office as he smoothly speaks into his microphone, “Instruct them to return to the station and wait, once they have completed their task.” He ended as he exits the control area, and heads out of the door.

Victoria watched the mystery man as he passed on his

way out of the station. Once he has departed, she returns her attention to the Captain. His stare seems to violate her soul. An uncontrollable shiver engulfs her body making the bewildered woman tremble. Trying to maintain her mask of valorous, Victoria flatly asks, "Just what goes on around here, Captain?"

As Hayford emerges from the nearby bathroom, the Captain displays a sincere smile and replies, "A new World order."

Officer Jack Hayford steps up to the Captain and surrenders, "I had to take a wicked dump. No more barbeque pig's feet and greens."

Disregarding the Officer's comment, Preston flatly advises, "It is time."

Hayford looks to Victoria as the Captain continues, "When you're done, return here to the station."

"Got cha."

Captain Preston looks off in the wake of Mister Smith. Hayford unlocks the steel cage, and opens the door.

"Where are we going?"

"You'll find out when we get there." He answers smartly as he displays his handcuff key. "Come here."

Suspiciously Victoria says, "Oh what's this, . . . you let me go, and I get shot in the back trying to escape?"

She has now begun to move away from him until her back strikes the cage's rear wall. Hayford snatches his pistol from its holster, and points it at her face. Angrily he says, "I could blow your fuckin' brains out right now!"

Victoria stops breathing, as she now expects the largest and shortest headache of her life.

"Get over here." He instructs.

Victoria approaches him slowly. "Come on, com'on, . . . take it like a woman." He said.

Hayford inserts the cuff key into the handcuff's keyhole. As he releases her, he says, "You try any of that Bruce Lee shit, . . . I'm gonna ventilate your head."

Once the cuffs were free from her wrist, Hayford shouts

for her to turn around. She turns slowly as he continues, "Yeah, yeah, . . . you just forget about it." He waits until she is completely turned around before he continues, "Now, . . . put your hands behind your back!"

Victoria does as told, and Hayford immediately cuffs her wrist. He then pushes her hard against the wall. Standing directly against her, he positions his lips inches from her ear, and gently says, "You had your chance. What's the matter, . . . you don't want to hurt ole Jack, huh?"

His body pressing against her's enrages the frightened woman. Through clenched teeth she replies, "No, . . . I'm just not in the mood to have my head vented."

Hayford smiles, and then gently suggests, "It's such a beautiful night, . . . whata you say we take a drive in the country?"

"Why don't you just kill me here, and save the gas." She returns flatly.

Hayford sucks on her ear. Victoria cringes as he releases her ear, from his mouth with a loud smack.

"Too messy." He answers, as he steps back away from her, and then adds as he smacks his lips, "Definitely as sweet as chocolate."

Victoria slowly turns around and faces him. The moisture from his mouth feels cool on her ear. She desires greatly to pull the extremity off her body.

"Com'on." Hayford said to her, motioning the numb Agent out of the cage. Trans-like, she obeys. As she approaches the repulsive man, he takes her by her firm upper arm, and guides her out of the building, picking her jacket up along the way.

Victoria reasons that even if she had told the Chief who she was, he would have still been killed. She sums up that her plight would of not changed. The voice is still urging her to play this out. She just hopes it's the voice of her Guardian Angel, and not the voice of an inpatient Angel of Death.

Victoria notices as soon as she steps out into the early morning stillness, that the temperature has dropped. A brisk breeze rustles through the full trees. As she is led to the only remaining car parked in front of the station, she notices downtown Madison looks like a well-kept ghost town.

Officer Jack Hayford places her in the rear seat of his patrol car, and throws her jacket in after her. He slams the self-locking rear door, and then quickly climbs behind the steering wheel. He then promptly drives off along Main Street, into the darkness.

"What are you bastards up to?"

Hayford looks back at her via the rearview mirror. Victoria sees his dark evil eyes in the mirror. She then says, "What's the big secret? Who am I going to tell?"

"Nigger Armstrong." Hayford finally said.

"General Armstrong?" She asked in a confirming tone.

"How *many* of *those* bastards runnin' around?"

"Is something going to happen to the General?"

"What are you doin', . . . writin' a book?"

A pause of silence falls between the two. Victoria then weakly asks, "Are you going to kill me?"

"Babe, you're already dead." He answers unemotionally.

Victoria tries to swallow, but her mouth is just too dry. She has to continue talking or panic will set in. "So, why was the Chief murdered?"

"Hey, . . . !! What's with the fuckin' questions?" Jack snaps as he looks to her via the rearview mirror.

"Well, what in the Hell do you want from *me*?! It's not like I get *driven* to *my death* everyday. At least *I want* to know why I'm going to be murdered!! Not too many murder victims are given that *courtesy*!!!" She fired at him like a machine gun.

Jack responds by simply turning on the F.M. radio. Country western music erupts from the car's speaker system. Victoria now thinks about her plan. What plan? The mental debate begins. Then the soothing, soft tone of the voice speaks to her. Again it assures her to just sit and wait. An opportunity to escape will come. Despite protest from fear and logic, Victoria decides to take the recommendation of the voice. She then sits back and listens to the belly aching of some cowboy moaning the lost of his faithful hound dog.

Rookie Officer Stephen Davis has positioned his patrol car off the road, along side a blind curve. He has set up his radar equipment as per orders from Captain Preston earlier this evening. The eager Officer is still fussing, mumbling about the stupidity of his fixed assignment. Davis knows this stretch of two laned black top. He reasons that on a nice dry night at this hour, no traffic runs at this hour. Why in the World does that Frankenstein lookin' bastard want traffic control done her, on the post midnight shift, on the stormiest night of recent memory. I'm being kept away from somethin' he thinks to himself.

Suddenly his radar alarm goes off. Reacting to is slowly, figuring that it was just another bat, he looks to the L.E.D. readout.

75

That ain't no bat, he mumbles as he adjusts himself, while preparing to engage the speeder. Davis watches the L.E.D. as the 75 miles per hour speed of the rearward approaching vehicle begins to slow as it approaches the 90-degree turn.

73
72
70
68
65

The rain has now stopped for sometime. The road is no longer rain slick, but it is still pretty damp. Taking this curve at 60, 65 is pretty risky.

"This boy is haulin' ass." Davis mumbles as he yanks the gear level downward.

As the readout displays 63, the approaching headlights begin to illuminate the darkness. Like a predator awaiting an unsuspecting prey, Davis waits for the motorist to pass his position. Then like a flash Jack Hayford drives by.

Taking a split second for his mind to register the unexpecting sight of the Madison police car, speeding by. Davis froze momentarily as he watched the blurring white sedan drive by. Slamming the gear selector upward in disappointment, a now frustrated Davis picks up the microphone of his police radio. As Jack begins accelerating along the flawless country road, Davis's voice announces, "Jack, . . ."

The veteran Officer turns down the F.M. radio, and listens.

". . . Just when I thought I had me a speeder to keep me awake, . . . here you come along."

Victoria's ears perk up, as Davis continues, "Just where in the Hell are you off to? You need a back up?"

Jack snatches up the microphone, and sternly says, "Never you mind boy. You stay put as ordered."

"Well, . . . you better take it easy . . ."

Jack interrupts him, "Boy, . . . I've been runnin' this here road, while you were shitin' in your 'p.j.'s'!" He then throws the microphone onto the seat beside him, and then mumbles, "This kid is too nosey, . . . he don't mind his business." He now speaks for Victoria to hear him clearly, ". . . After I do you, I'm gonna pop him before he fucks things up."

Hayford slams his foot down on the accelerator, causing the sedan to speed up. Victoria can see the speedometer reaching the 100 miles per hour mark. She looks to the crazed cop, and calmly states, "If you are trying to *scare* me to death . . ."

"Shut the fuck up!!" He returns angrily.

"You know, if a deer, . . ." She starts to continue calmly.

"Fuck the deer!!"

"But I . . ."

"Fuck you!!!"

Immediately with the sharpness of a razor, she firmly responds, "I bet you couldn't, even if you wanted to."

"You keep runnin' your fuckin' mouth!" He warns.

"How long have you been a closet fag?"

Jack looks back at her through the rearview mirror. Appearing the devil himself, Victoria looks at him in the mirror. She now knows she has struck a nerve.

"I'm sorry if I can't give you what you want. I'm just not equipped for that kind of action."

Just as she spoke, a lonely off road trail leading from the two laned highway, catches Jack's eye. He slams on the brakes. The fast traveling patrol car slides to a stop. Immediately Jack puts the tire-smoking sedan into reverse. He backs the rear wheel-spinning vehicle to the trail's entrance.

As he plots the car onto the unpaved trail, Jack begins in an agitated tone, "I'm gonna really enjoy doin' you!"

He's no longer talking to her through the rearview mirror. He has now turned his head completely around to face her. Victoria is alarmed by the demonic appearing cast on his face.

"You cunts make me sick. Yous' bitch about everything, and yous' want everything." He begins to rant as it is clear that he is now over the edge. "You were probably one of those bitches that cheered when that worthless whore, cut her husband's pecker off, huh?! Well I tell you something missy, before I die I will see that cunt's head on a stick!! Now, you enjoy your last minutes on Earth, you worthless black bitch!!!"

Victoria did not respond. She looks from him, to the darkness before them. Jack effortlessly wrestles with the steering wheel, as the V-8 powered sedan fish tails along the rain soaked trail.

Suddenly a clearing emerges. Jack stops the patrol car abruptly, in the barren patch of land.

"I'll give you a few minutes to look around." He started now in a much calmer tone. He takes a breath, and then continues in a relaxed and confident tone, "Pray, . . ." He says as he turns to look, ". . . Cause you are going to die here."

With her mouth as dry as a hot wasteland wind, Victoria responds on the verge of dismay, "And how are you going to account for me when I start stinking up the countryside?"

"I'm not concerned." Hayford answers flatly.

"Well, my presence is expected. They will come looking for me. They'll figure that I was located here."

"So what, . . . anybody that comes looking for you, will end up like you."

"Oh, . . . so your bad enough to take on the entire F.B.I.?" She said firmly.

Hayford turns and faces her. Victoria met his cold eyes. His glare seems to pierce her soul. She sits firmly, returning his look with her own crippling peer. Breaking the silence, Hayford flippantly responds as he turns away, "Ain't no F.B.I. gonna come lookin' for you, girl."

"You want to bet your life on that, numbnuts?"

"I'm a Federal Agent. F.B.I." She returns.

Hayford starts out of the car while completely unconvinced says, "Yeah, . . . right."

Victoria watches him exit the car, and snatches open the rear car door.

"Get the fuck out. It's time to die." He announces coldly.

"Listen to me, you bastard, . . ." She begins smartly, ". . . Dead bodies tell tales. The Bureau's lab is the best in the World. You won't get away with this."

Hayford reaches in and grabs Victoria by her sweatshirt. He then pulls on Victoria with such great force, that the 134-pound woman is extracted from the car like a rag doll. Still maintaining his hold on her, she stands on her feet, face to face with the homicidal man. Only inches from her face, Hayford speaks softly, "It does not matter who you are, or how you will now die." He then releases his hold and continues, "By noon, . . . nobody will *ever* give a rat's ass about you."

Hayford grabs her sweatshirt at the shoulder, and begins to pull her away from the patrol car. Victoria takes a few steps and in an act of total desperation for survival she spins, breaking his hold and delivers a power kick to the Officer's chest. He stumbles rearward, falling against the side of the patrol car. Hayford recovers immediately, throwing a punch at the bound, and now approaching woman advancing aggressively.

The punch from Hayford misses her as she sidesteps, and delivers another power kick, connecting along Hayford's jawbone. He immediately falls to his knees. Victoria, without hesitating, kicks the man against the side of his head, about the temple, as if it is a soccer ball and she is kicking the winning goal for the World Cup.

Flat on his back, Hayford lies unconscious. As she begins to bring her heavy, chest heaving breathing under control, she stands over the defeated. Without further delay, she squats over him. She feels along his gun belt for the handcuff key. As she feels for the key, she prays for thanks and the ability to recover the needed key.

With the cuff key now in hand, Victoria falls onto her back besides the now reviving Hayford. Knowing that he is now coming around, she begins to work feverishly. Victoria curses her B.W.A. as she strains to get her handcuffed wrist over her well-rounded derriere. She feels the hardened stainless steel restraints cutting into her wrist. The pain feels as if her hands are being ripped from her wrist.

Victoria rises to her feet as she looks upon Hayford just in time to see him awake and looking upon her. She now notices him unholstering his sidearm. Before she can react to the impending danger, Hayford has his weapon clear of the holster. She leaps toward the aligning weapon, as he raises it to firing position. Expecting to be shot this time, she is quite surprised when her hand manages to grip the frame of the semi-automatic before it fires.

Though they now face each other, with mutual expressions of amazement, the mutual surprised only lasts for a nanosecond. Now fully about his senses, Hayford becomes enraged. Victoria sees his eyes, the window to one's soul, transform from amazement to rage. Preemptively she strikes.

Just as Hayford's brain impulses are on route to his left arm, with orders to strike Victoria, she spits into his face. Hayford flinches and Victoria feels his gun hand, ease slightly. She follows through, wrenching the weapon from his hand. Hayford yells out in disgust as he instinctively reacts to the wad of saliva clinging to his face and eyes.

He takes a wild swing at the woman. The powerful, winding cutting blow, misses the Agent as she moves away from him. Curse words fly from his mouth like automatic gunfire, but they are obscured by his slurred engaged speech. Victoria has now maneuvered the .40 caliber semi-automatic pistol within her hands so that she has control over the weapon. Peering through his one widened, saliva free, blood shot eye, Hayford sees his weapon pointing directly at him. The sight makes the mean man abruptly stop cursing. Victoria is close enough to see his eyeballs darting back and forth. She sees the desperation in his eyes as they move from her and the gun. She knows he is contemplating an attempt to pounce upon her.

With her finger on the trigger, and mentally prepared to pull it, Victoria unemotionally advises, "Just freeze."

Hayford's eyes stop measuring the distance, and now looks upon her.

"Alright, . . ." He now relaxes and continues, ". . . Now what?"

"Suppose you start telling me, what in the Hell's going on?!" She answered in a demanding tone.

Hayford chuckles a bit, as he begins to wipe his face with

his hand. He then replies, "Oh what, . . . now that you have the gun, I'm supposed to be frightened like a little pussy, and tell you everything? Well, fuck you!! I ain't tellin' you a damn thing! So now what?!!"

Instantly Victoria fires a shot. The .40 caliber hollow-pointed bullet, rockets past Hayford's head, inches from his left ear. The woman's action, catches the hard man by complete surprise. He had figured Victoria wrong.

He now chuckles. While he wears his smile, he thinks. Though he is surprised that she fired the shot, he now reasons that Victoria is not a cold-blooded killer. Her bark is bigger than her bite, he presumes. He knows that if the shoe was on the other foot, Victoria would now have a .40 caliber headache.

"Talk to me, or talk to God."

"Fuck you, and your God."

Victoria now knows that Hayford is a nonsensical madman. There is not going to be any negotiations with him. As she aligns the sights of the weapon for a kill shot, she concludes that he leaves her no other choice. As she tightens her finger around the trigger, her eyes suddenly notices the stun-gun attached to his gun belt.

A new idea emerges. She relaxes the pressure on the trigger, and orders, "Toss me your cuff key."

"What do you have in mind?" He begins, and then sarcastically adds, "Oh that's right, . . . you are some kind of Fed. Whatcha gonna do Missy, . . . take me into custody?" He mocked, as he begins to do as told.

He tosses the keys to her. She catches them, and continues to take the gun trained on him. She then takes a few steps away. With a safe distance between her and the madman, she begins to release herself from the handcuffs. Hayford cheerfully announces, "So, . . . you are going to try and take me in, huh? This is goin' to be good. Hey, . . . you know what, . . ." He started lightly, ". . . I'm goin' give you a fightin' chance. I'm gonna put my hands behind my back, for ya."

Victoria, now free of the cuffs, commands, "Get on your knees!"

"Whatever you say, . . ." Hayford starts lightly, and as he begins to do as instructed, his tone changes into a grim warning, ". . . But I warn you. You best shoot me now, cuz, . . . I'm going to get that pistol from you, . . ." He now turns his head slightly towards her, ". . . And then I'm gonna kill you." He ended chillingly.

Victoria believes every word he has said, and she knows he means it. She also believes he is a part of a huge conspiracy. She knows he is a hardcase, and attempts to make him talk have been useless, perhaps until now. If this new idea doesn't work, she will have no other choice but to dispatch him here and now.

Victoria figures the likes of Hayford are just too dangerous to allow to walk and live among us. He is the type of man that sat in on the plans to kill JFK, or Martin Luther King Junior. He is the type of man that would pull the trigger on such men, and consider it a duty.

As she continues her thought, Victoria wonders if he murdered noncombatants while he was in Vietnam, killing old men, women and children for sport. He probably would led the lynching parties, hanging scores of blackmen, and then partaking in the brutal raping and slaughtering of their helpless wives. He would be the type of man that would plan, approve and or detonate a nuclear device over an American city to boost funds for S.T.I. or sparking a frightened Congress to outlaw liberties to the point of tyranny, under the guise of National Security.

Victoria figures that the death of the Chief of Police, the presence of the shady characters at the station, her one way ride out into the countryside, and the pact that the General is due to arrive in town later today, suggests one thing, . . . assassination!

As she marches towards the kneeing Hayford, he verbally

taunts her. Victoria is no longer hearing him. Her thoughts have consumed her.

Hayford figures he will launch his attack, when she begins applying the handcuffs to him. He visualizes the scene in mind. As soon as she is within range, he will launch his vicious attack, like a great white shark, leaving only pieces of her for the worms.

As Victoria approaches, Hayford calculates her steps. Four more steps, he figures, as he prepares to attack. He becomes excited by the thoughts of his surprise attack. The expression of her face when she realizes, she's gonna die, as she feels me slowly crushing her fuckin' neck, he thinks to himself.

As Victoria reaches the halfway point of his projected attack range, she delivers a straight forward kick. Her foot contacted Hayford directly below his chin. The tremendous impact slams his lower jaw upward, sandwiching a few millimeters of his tongue between his teeth, thus severing his lick. He didn't see the kick that seemed to stretch his neck a few inches, before it carried him rearward onto the rain softened ground.

Victoria immediately moves in and lands upon his chest with her knee. She places the pistol, hard in his nostril. She grabs him by his stringy hair, and forces his head slightly upward, and then announces through clenched teeth. "I'm not your average, . . . everyday, . . . F.B.I. Agent. I will kill you. I know how to deal withy murderous scum, like you. There are no negotiations, . . . no deals. I do believe in fighting fire with fire."

She removes the gun from his face, and releases his hair. Still dazed, Hayford attempts to grab at her. Victoria puts the gun in her waistband, and snatches the stun-gun from his belt, as she fends off his grabbing attempts. Without any hesitation, Victoria places the electronic device directly between his legs, and then activates it. Like the Frankenstein monster receiving an awakening charge, Hayford's body reacts violently, as he screams through clenched teeth.

As Victoria continues to apply the hair raising charge, Hayford screams suddenly begins to diminish. Not wanting to roast his nuts, she releases her finger from the switch. Sternly, she now speaks to him, "Who else is involved in the assassination plot? Why do you people want to kill Armstrong? Just how do you people plan to pull this thing off?!"

With his breath short, and his heart feeling as though it is about to explode, Hayford labors to speak. "You really think this is gonna make me talk? You dumb bitch, . . . I've been interrogated by the best. I was tortured by the masters. If I didn't talk for the NVA, the Russians, or the Chinese, what makes your black ass think I'm gonna talk for you?" He ended firmly.

Victoria depresses the stun-gun switch, and responds harshly, "Bullshit, . . . you probably squealed like a pig! Now tell me, . . . who, why, where and how?!!"

Unbeknown to the Agent, as she spoke, the batteries that power the stun-gun are rapidly discharging. The current to Hayford's groin, is no longer paralyzing him.

"And if this doesn't work, . . ." She continues as she is applying the fading voltage, ". . . I'll lay some Bed-Sty' shit on ya, that no NVA or Russian has ever heard of." She ended sharply.

Hayford's jab to Victoria's chin is delivered with the speed of light, and the force of a wrecking ball. Before Victoria can process any conscious thought, she was landing hard on her back. As she lies momentarily dazed and disorientated, Hayford stands to his feet.

Victoria automatically looks to the stun-gun, as if she wants an explanation from the device as to what had just occurred. She squeezes the switch and the electrical arch performs weakly as if illuminates between the two contact posts. Hayford now stands laughing. Victoria looks to him, standing only a few feet away. She drops the stun-gun, and immediately reaches for the pistol in her waistband.

"Your ass, is now mine." Hayford coldly informs.

Frantically Victoria searches her waistband for the weapon. Hayford takes a step toward her. She now realizes that the short flight she took, propelled by his punch, or the impact of the crash landing, dislodged the gun from her waistband. Victoria immediately flips over onto her fours, and begins a frantic search. Perhaps the weapon is close by.

Hayford now reaches her. Concentrating heavily on the finding of the gun, she doesn't sense the man behind her. Hayford throws his arm around her throat and neck, forcing the woman onto her belly. Victoria claws at the stone hard limb as it squeezes her neck like a vise. Breathing is now becoming difficult.

"I'm going to kill you slow." Hayford said as he applies a steady amount of pressure, thus slowly choking the woman. "You thought you could fuck wit' me, huh?" He continues as Victoria begins to fling her arms and legs wildly.

Her actions are now starting to become comical to him. Chuckling he says, "You're flappin' around like a big catfish I caught last summer."

Victoria feels as if her eyeballs are bulging from their sockets. She feels her lungs expanding to draw the slightest amount of oxygen that might sweep past the choke point.

"If it makes you feel better, . . . I mean if it makes it easier for you to die, . . . you or nobody else woulda prevented Armstrong from dyin' tomorrow morning. There is too much money involved. You see, . . . money busy the right people. The proper talent."

Victoria's wild thrashing has now dwindled to weakening movements. Just as the darkness seems to close in, Victoria's left hand finally strikes the gun.

"You know, . . ." Hayford calmly continues, ". . . Even his own Secret Service people are involved, and so are some crazy, don't give a fuck 'Towel Heads' from . . ."

Hayford never finishes his sentence. While he spoke to Victoria, she in a last ditch effort maneuvered the pistol to stop her slow death. Quickly raising the pistol up, and pointing it to the rear and just past her head, she open fired. Hayford never saw the matted black pistol rise from the grass in the darkness. His attention was strictly on providing Victoria with an agonizing death.

Officer Stephen Davis has just switched off his radar unit in disgust. He is frustrated and fed up with the way he is treated by the Captain. Why am I being assigned to all of these meaningless tasks of late, he wonders. I'm tired of being treated like an outcast, he continues. "Enough of this shit, . . ." He says. I'm going to see the Chief about this in the morning, he continued the thought to himself.

As Davis now entertains a thought about quitting all together, Victoria is pushing Hayford's dead body from off hers. She then stands, coughing and hacking, as she keeps an eye on the fatally wounded man. Her last ditch maneuver paid off. Though most of the half dozen shots missed, the ones that struck their mark assure Hayford's demise. As she looks down upon his lifeless body, she reasons that the bullet wound to his neck, face and head offer enough evidence for no need to check him for any vital signs. She reaches down and removes the two loaded magazines from their pouches on his gun belt. She then stands up straight and looks around the area, as she begins to plan her next move. She has immediately begun to omit what she has just done to Hayford from her mind. She fights to keep her mind clear. Though he was in the process of killing her she feels somewhat sorry of what she did to him. She glances down at him. His wide-open eyes expresses the surprise he must of felt as the spray of bullets struck him. She has never sent a man to Hell before, but in Hayford's case, she sends him with her blessing.

She looks away from the dead man, and begins to ponder what she is up against. She figures that she cannot trust the local law enforcement. She remembers what Hayford said about the members of Armstrong's Secret Service protection team. She wonders who else in the government is involved. Who can she trust?

As she depresses the magazine release button, and allows the magazine to fall to the dark grassy ground, she inserts a fully loaded one. A light breeze begins to blow, causing the leaves on the surrounding trees to rustle. Now the little voice in her head says, that she must derail the assassination plot. She walks over to the gently idling police sedan, and enters it. She slams her foot down on the accelerator. The rear wheels spin. Hayford in his rage, had stopped the car hard on the wet earth, causing the front wheels to dig into the rain soaked dirt. Victoria, slamming down on the gas pedal, caused the rear wheels to spin, thus digging the drive wheels into the ground.

Victoria gets out of the car, and views the problem. No time to ponder, she thinks. I have to get back to town, now.

Officer Davis, now bored silly, decides to take a ride along the two laned county highway. He does not head towards town, but further outward, in the direction Hayford was last seen heading in. He humored himself with the idea of driving out to the shore, and plowing the car into the Atlantic Ocean. He now chuckles to himself as he guides the cruiser along the unlit highway at about 5 miles per hour.

Victoria has jogged from the clearing to the highway. As she stands at the roadway's edge, she catches her breath, looking in the direction of Madison. As she starts walking towards the town, the illumination of a car's headlights, begin to brighten the night. The voice in the Agent's head told her not to panic, play it cool.

As Officer Davis slowly drives up and crests the hill, he immediately notices a shadowy figure walking toward him on the opposite side of the road. When Victoria sees beyond the bright lights, and notes the silhouette of the police car, she prepares herself. In her right hand is the .40 caliber pistol. It's concealed by her black nylon windbreaker. As the

Madison police car slows to a stop, Victoria tightens her grip on the weapon.

Officer Davis illuminates Victoria with his door-mounted spotlight. Victoria freezes in the light, like an exposed animal. She immediately closes an eye to preserve her night vision. This action was automatic from her Army training.

"Hey lady, what cha walkin' out here all alone fer?" Davis asked.

Surprised by the routine inquiry, Victoria stumbles to answer. In a phony southern accent, she begins, "I'm headed to town, . . ." She said while turning her head slightly towards the voice. ". . . My car broke down a ways back." She said confidently that the cop would buy the answer and now leave her alone.

Reserved in the back of her mind is the fact, that she is prepared to kill the inquiring Cop if she has to.

"Com'on, . . ." The Officer begins, ". . . I'll give you a lift."

With a phony smile, she quickly returns, "That's okay, . . . the walk will do me some good."

In a sincere tone, and adding an unseen smile, Davis jokingly returns, "Com'on, . . . it's no charge."

"I'll be fine."

"Com'on now, . . . I can't have you walkin' around here in the dark. Com'on." He insists.

Victoria, not wanting to raise suspicion while in her tactically bad position, starts walking over to the police car.

"That's a girl." Davis said, as she began crossing the road. "How far down the road is your car?"

Victoria begins pointing with her left hand as she approaches his side of the car.

"Oh, I would say about a mile or so."

"I'll call you a wrecker." He said as he looks away from her, and reaches for his radio microphone.

Now standing at his door, Victoria smoothly raises the .40, and places the cool barrel in his ear. "You will do no such thing." She said softly but firmly.

Davis freezes, with an expression of horror on his face.

"What in the Hell you do'in?"

"Shut up!! You keep those hands on the steering wheel, and listen to me!" She replies sharply.

"You got my full attention, lady."

"What are you do'in out here?"

"What?" He asked in confusion.

Pressing the gun harder against his head, "What are you doing out here? What did they send you out here for?"

Pausing for a second, because he fails to understand Victoria's line of questioning. He senses that he better answer with something and quick.

"Patrol."

"Patrolling for what?"

"Speeders, Jesus Christ lady, what do you want?" He ended pleading.

She sees the fright on his face, and hears it in his voice. Victoria now wonders if he doesn't have anything to do with what was happening. What Hayford said earlier about a nosey cop replays in her mind. Maybe this is the Officer he was talking about.

In a light tone, she asks, "Were you the one who spoke to Hayford as he drove along this road?"

"How'd you know about that?" He asked in a surprised tone.

"Cause I was in his car."

Now enlightened, he says, "Then you're the one he collared. How did you get away from him?"

Flatly she answers, "I had to kill him."

Despite the fact that the gun is still at his head, Davis starts to turn toward the Agent. Shocked by her revelation, he erupts, "What, . . . Jack?!!"

Raising her voice over his, she returns, "Jack was trying to plant me in the woods!"

"What?" He dumbfoundedly asked.

"He was trying to take me out."

Snapping, he states, "And I'm supposed to believe that?!"

"Frankly my dear, I don't give a damn." She returned with no emotion.

Davis takes a breath. He looks straight down the road that lies ahead of him. Then he solemnly asks, "So, are you gonna kill me too?"

"Listen to me. I'm a Federal Agent." She said, and then removes the gun from his head.

Davis looks to her with confusion, as she starts to explain.

"I've got news for you my friend. Jack, . . . after he killed me, was coming to do you in. He mentioned how much of a pain in the ass you are."

She now sees the young Officer's facial expression change. Before her eyes his complexion turned a ghostly white. Victoria stands in silence, giving the Officer a moment to absorb the truth. As he turned slightly to look out before him, he thought about the information from the mysterious woman.

In a mumble, he asks, "What in the Hell is going on around here?"

"That's what I want to know. I've stumbled into this mess. Is there anything you can tell me?"

Looking at her, he asks in a sincere tone, "Are you really a Fed?"

"Honest to goodness."

"Bullshit, then why did he collar, ya?!" He snapped.

Sternly she responds, "Listen Toto, . . . you're not in Kansas anymore. The collar and the charges were bullshit. I'm sure you are not that green to law enforcement. Ole' Jack and I had a personality conflict from minute one."

Quickly he says, "Law enforcement doesn't kill, law enforcement!!"

"Oh, and the fact that he was trying to kill me doesn't mean a damn thing, huh?!!" She exploded.

"We will never know that, now will we? Dead men tell no tales!!"

"I witnessed them kill your Chief."

"And who might that have been?" He asked angrily.

"Your Captain was there along with a guy who had G-Man written all over him. There were also some state guys, and our friend Jack."

Davis gently rests his head against the headrest. "This ain't makin' no sense."

"Well no shit." She remarked softly.

"Unless it has something to do wit' the Armstrong visit."

"It does. I believe there is a plan to kill him this morning. That is all I got from Jack." She said.

"This is too much."

"Look, . . . I don't know who I can trust, or who I can turn to. So, that brings me to you."

A brief pause of silence falls over the two. Then in a weak, but firm voice Davis says, "Lady, I believe you. Something very wrong is going down here, and has been for awhile." He then turns to her and continues, "Jack has been outa control. The Captain is not wrapped too tightly either, and you, . . . I guess if you were really dirty you would of blown my brains out long ago." He now swallows hard and then sincerely says, "What do you want from me?"

Victoria sees the honesty in his eyes. She removes the gun from him. He looks away from her and admits, "I don't believe this. The shit has finally hit the fan." He turns back towards her and asks, weakly, "Are you sure about the Chief?"

Victoria silently nods yes. As she answers him, she sees the pain in his eyes. The Officer starts to get out of the car. Victoria stands, out of the way so he can exit. The six-foot Officer now stands facing Victoria. She looks over his hulking linebacker body, and is impressed with the sight.

"I've been kept away from somethin'. You say it's an assassination plot. Shit, . . . the Captain's involved along with Jack Hayford, but neither one is smart enough to pull something like killing a Presidential Candidate . . . . Especially one as popular as General Armstrong."

"I don't think they are the master mind either. My money is on the G-Man. Jack mentioned something about the General's assigned Secret Service Security being involved." She then continues the thought in almost a whisper, "Perhaps that G-Man is a part of the General's Advance Team."

Thinking, Officer Davis asks, "That G-Man, . . . is he tall, German, blonde?"

"That's him."

"Yeah, . . . he came into town, with some other guys, about a week ago. They said that they were Secret Service. That's all I know, the Captain dealt with them mostly."

"Then that clinches it." Victoria said firmly.

"So now what? Shouldn't we notify someone?"

The Agent looks to him and flatly returns, "Who do we trust? I don't know how high up this thing goes."

"So what, . . . are you hinting that it is up to us? I mean what can we do? We're totally out numbered." He said in a tone of desperation.

"Well, . . . they think I'm being murdered. So they won't be expecting me. I guess I will have to sneak up behind them, and bite them on their asses." She said.

Taking a moment of silence, Davis realized his desired action has finally arrived. Victoria's attitude motivates him to say, "Well seein' that I am the only local law available, you're gonna need me for some assistance."

Victoria looks to the Officer and smiles, as he adds, "I guess due to the nature of this event, it makes it a Federal matter. That makes you in charge."

"We don't have to be formal about this Officer Davis . . ." She then places the .40 in her left hand as she extends her right. "I'm Victoria Owens, F.B.I."

"Hot dang, I've only seen you guys on T.V. you were probably aware of the bullshit goin' on down here already, huh?" He asked full of spark.

"Let's just say I've been forced into this."

"Well do you have any idea of what they are up to now?"

"I don't know, when we left town, there was nobody around."

Smiling, Officer Davis says, "Well, . . . whata you say we go on in and find out?"

"So what are we kinda like, . . . joining forces?"

"You bet cha. This is great, . . . I just saw the 'F.B.I. Story' with Jimmy Stewart last night on T.V." He said filled with glee as he starts to get back into the car.

Victoria leans toward him and flatly says, "You know, Jimmy Stewart didn't get killed in that movie."

Davis looks to her, and she adds, "We very well might."

He drops his smile, and swallows the lump in his throat. He responds faithfully, "We are American law enforcement Officers. The possibility of death does not affect our duties."

Victoria stands upright. She has no words, or comments to his statement. As she now walks around to the passenger side and gets into the car, all she can do is pray. Davis immediately turns the patrol car around, and heads off for town.

The ride into town was completed in silence. Once Davis reached the empty streets of downtown Madison, he cautiously pilots the patrol car, towards the police station. Victoria senses are on maximum alert. Her hands begin to sweat. She adjusts her grip on the semi-automatic she holds, as it rests on her thigh. Her eyes seem to stretch ahead of the windshield, like feeler antennas.

She has made up her mind. She will take out any and all who are involved in this plot. She knows that the stakes are high. Her mind is clear, and she ahs no second thoughts. Tactically, what they are about to do, is suicide. Two against an undetermined number. Their weapons and capabilities are unknown.

Victoria looks upon Officer Davis. Even in the soft illumination of the sporadic lights of the town, she can see how youthful this man of no more than 29 really looks. As she looks away from him, she says silently to herself, it's me and Rambo. Her mind now focuses on her vacationing partner. She would feel more secure if Michael Peterson was sitting next to her now. Mike 'P' could probably take all of these guys out, with a butter knife, she thinks, reflecting on his Marine Corps Recon Ranger training and experience.

"There is a state car in front of the station." Davis announced as he brings the cruiser to a stop.

His statement snaps her from her thoughts. She then looks up and studies the scene that lays three blocks ahead.

"Is it possible that they could be real?" She asked in almost a whisper as she turns to him.

Davis displays a confused look on his face. Victoria realizing what she has just said didn't convey her thought.

"I mean, . . . do they normally come and visit at this time of night?"

"They could be here for any reason. A V.I.P. is coming tomorrow." He said trying to answer the Agent's question as completely as possible.

Victoria looks down the street towards the station in silence. Davis's eagerness gets the best of him during her silence. As he is about to speak, Victoria announces, "Check this out, . . ." She begins as she turns towards him, ". . . We go in. I'm your prisoner. If they are friendlies, then fine, . . ."

"And if not?"

In a serious no nonsense tone, she answers, "We then better take them down, or they'll take us out." She allowed the impact of her statement to settle in his head. She then adds flatly, "Now are you in or out?"

Davis looks towards the station in silent thought. A small grin begins to spread across his face. He looks to the Agent and says, "Are you kiddin', . . . I live for this kinda stuff." He said as the gung-ho grin now glazes over his entire face.

She looks upon the rookie. She's seen that expression before.

"Have you been in the military?" She gently asked.

"The Guard." He proudly says, and then continues, "Just

before I got out, we got activated for 'Desert Shield'. I was discharged January 3rd, three weeks before the shootin' war broke out. I couldn't believe it." He said in frustration, "I missed the only war I coulda been in."

Victoria looks away from him and wonders if everyone in this town is completely nuts. She quickly dismisses the thought. She's happy to have the gutsy back up, though she wonders if after the first shot is fired, will he go running off to his Mama. She now looks towards the station. She takes a hard swallow, and then commands, "Let's go, . . . it's show time."

Davis resumes the drive slowly towards the station. Victoria's eyes scan the area. She feels confident about her plan, but uneasy about Officer Davis's capabilities. She glances over and looks suspiciously at the jaw tight cop.

"We just might have to kill some people in there. They might be wearing police uniforms, ..." She continued as her mind instantly flashes to Officer Hayford, ". . . Can you handle that?"

"My Daddy raised no coward." He returns flatly, "Don't you worry none, . . . I'm with you now." He ended with a swollen chest.

Victoria looks away from him, as Davis pulls the car into an empty angled parking space in front of the station.

"You know, . . ." He starts, as he stops the car, ". . . If this is some sort of plan to kill the General, where is everybody?"

Gripped with tension, and watching the front door of the station, Victoria snaps, "What?"

"I mean, . . . why aren't they waitin' to hit him here, . . . in town?" He turns to her and says, in hope, "Maybe they've called it off."

Victoria looks from her forward view of the station's entranceway to him. "Let's go in and find out, . . . just like the way we've discussed, . . . just in case." She said worried.

Davis gives her a quick nod, as he exits the car. Victoria does not like the direction that his mind was thinking. She watches him and the entrance, as he walks around the front of the patrol car and opens her door. Quickly the Agent places the .40 cal behind her in her waistband, and then exits the car, masquerading as a rear cuffed arrestee.

As the pair walks side by side towards the station's entranceway, Victoria thinks about the Officer beside her. She wonders about his worth. If this hillbilly folds up on me, he is on his own, she settles in her mind.

One of the two well-groomed North Carolina State Patrolmen, sits in the operation area of the station with his feet up on the desk. He's flipping through an old issue of Hustler Magazine. His partner emerges from the nearby bathroom, just as Davis and Victoria enter the station. The two state Officers freeze, as their eyes fix on the entering pair.

Davis leads Victoria in her upper right arm. The man reading the colorful Hustler Magazine, tosses the publication onto the desk and slowly stands. A silence that can only be compared to death, settles over the scene. As Davis, leading Victoria, continues to walk towards the reception desk, the young Officer nervously asks, "Hey fellas, where is everybody?" He ends with a phony smile.

The 'hair' on the back of Victoria's neck begins to rise. She inconspicuously wraps her right hand around the grip of her appropriated pistol. She now recognizes the patrolmen as the pair that carried the body of the Chief out of the station.

Suddenly the Hustler reading cop past draws his pistol. Victoria's reaction is to also to go for her gun, but Davis reacted to the Officer's action by tensing up on Victoria's arm, preventing the Agent from executing her surprise attack. She snaps her eyes and head to the Madison Patrolman. Davis stands stunned by the state cop's action of pointing his weapon at them. Victoria sees the shock and apprehension on the young cop's face. I knew it!! She shouts within herself.

"Cover 'em!!" The state cop shouts to his partner emerging from the bathroom. "It's the bitch that was in the cell!"

The partner now pulls his gun from it's holster and points it at the pair.

Victoria stops trying to smoothly break fee from the Officer's hold. She relaxes, reserve with the thought, that she is still armed, and capable of taking company with her to the grave.

"Hey, . . . !" Davis begins protesting, ". . . What the fuck goes on here?!"

"Shut up cop!!" The once Hustler glancing cop orders.

The state cop now motions towards his partner, while his gun is pointing at the pair. The partner now commands in a firm voice, "Cop, . . . get over here!!" He then addresses his accomplice, "You better get Mister Smith on the horn."

Davis releases Victoria's arm, and begins to walk toward the state Officer, as the other impersonator heads for Victoria, as he spouts, "You stupid black bitch, . . . why did you let him bring you back here alive, you know now we are gonna have to kill you."

Never judge a book by its cover. It has the same consequences as when someone assumes something about someone else. It is obvious the state patrolmen have forgotten these words of wisdom.

Though his .40 caliber pistol is out and ready to fire, his reflexes are not able to react fast enough. His mind cannot overcome the assumed reality that Victoria is handcuffed. Her movement, as fast as the twinkling of an eye, is much too fast for the state Officer to respond. He does not see the semi-automatic pistol, but does see the bluish white muzzle flashes. He also sees the first, second and third shots explode from the gun, as Victoria fires from her hip. The multiple shots find their mark, fatally.

Victoria's surprised attack, not only catches her target off guard, but it also catches the other masquerading patrolman. Davis is standing near enough to the second man to grab his extended weapon. The two men now wrestle feverishly over the gun. The state cop manages to pin Davis to the wall. The fight has now turned into an arm wrestle, and Davis is losing. The young cop is applying all of his strength, but the gun is still steadily turning towards him. His eyes are locked on the gun pointing towards his direction. He is no longer aware of anything else. He sees only the gun, and struggles for his life.

Victoria steps up behind the state Officer, and presses the hot barrel of her gun, hard against the side of his face, as she grabs the back of his collar. The fake cop now freezes.

"I give, I give." He surrenders pleading.

Davis snaps out of his tunnel vision mode, and sees Victoria holding the gun to the man's head. He snatches the gun from the surrendering man's hand.

"Don't kill me." He continues to plead.

Davis delivers a punch to the man's stomach. The unsuspecting blow, causes the man to fold inward. Victoria immediately counters by sweeping his feet from under him, causing the counterfeit cop to fall rearward onto his back. Instantly Victoria stands over him. She points her gun at the downed man, as she quickly speaks to Davis, "Better check and make sure they were alone."

"Right." Davis returns, pumped with adrenaline.

She rips the transmitter from under the cop's sleeve, as Davis practically trips over the other dead body. He looks upon the multitude of the bullet wounds, oozing blood momentarily before he moves on.

"What are you gonna do to me?" The imposter asked as he looked towards his dead associate.

"You wanta live?"

Now looking back towards her, he nods yes.

"Then I want to know, what you know."

Frightened, he licks his lips and begins to speak, "But there's nothing you can do about it."

"Why don't you let me decide that. Where are your friends now?"

He swallows hard, and then answers weakly, "Picking up a delivery."

"Don't riddle me. Speak clear English." She said firmly. "Are you talking about the General?"

"No, . . . he's not due in 'till about six. We are to be cleared out by then."

"So what are they picking up then?"

"I don't know what it is."

Sternly she warns, "Don't bullshit me man, I'm not in the mood."

"All I know is that whatever, or whoever it is, it's pretty damn important. It's gonna make this thing work."

Out of breath, Davis returns, "We're not alone."

Acknowledging the Officer with a nod of her head, Victoria continues questioning.

"How many of them are out there?"

"I didn't count heads."

Angrily, she thunders, "About?!"

"A dozen, maybe."

In a calmer tone she asks, "Who is backing you guys?"

"I don't know all that shit, . . . I'm just in it for the money." He said desperately.

"When are your friends due back here?"

"I don't know."

"You don't know where they are, . . . how many they are, . . . or where they went to do whatever?"

"Hey I'm just security. I dress up like a cop, in case anything unexpected pops up." He strongly informed.

"Well I guess you've fucked up. Cuff his worthless ass." She said sternly.

Davis hands her the floored man's gun. He then forces the man to roll over onto his stomach. Snatching a pair of handcuffs from his gun belt, the young Officer says to his prisoner, “Com’on, . . . I’ve got a nice cool cell waitin’ for ya.”

Victoria removes the extra ammo magazines from the cuffed man’s gun belt, and puts them in her jacket pocket.

“You’re gonna need more than that, little lady.”

Davis snatches him off toward the cellblock. While departing Davis informs Victoria, “In the Captain’s office, . . .” He motions towards the office near the detention cage. “. . . There’s some maps and papers. They might have some answers.”

Victoria nods in acknowledgment. She starts off towards the office, as the pair disappears into the cellblock. She steps over the dead man, and stops to look down upon him. She pauses long enough to eject the magazine from her weapon, allowing it to fall onto his body. The hardened Agent squats, and relieves him of his two extra ammo magazines. She inserts one into her gun, and then places the other in her pocket. Nearby is his .40 caliber semi-automatic. Victoria picks it up, and places it in her waistband, as she stands.

Sensing an urgency now, she quickly steps to the scene where she had witnessed the Chief’s murder. She enters the well-kept office, and immediately notices the county map opened on the desk. Victoria’s curiosity peeks. She walks around the desk, as she looks upon the map.

A large ‘X’ stands out on the map. Another mark consisting of a red circle is also on the map not too far from the ‘X’. A grease pencil line is drawn from the local airfield to the red circle, is traced by Victoria’s finger. Puzzled, she looks over the map for other markings.

Davis returns from locking up the imposter. As he appears in the doorway, Victoria visually acknowledges him.

“He’s all tucked away.”

“How much did he offer you to blow my brains out?” She asked flatly.

Startled at first by her insight, Davis shamefully admits, "Half his cut, . . . two hundred and fifty thousand dollars."

Maintaining an unemotional expression she says, "One hundred and twenty-five grand, . . . I'm not cheap huh?"

"No, you don't understand." Davis says as he begins to explain, "He offered me two hundred and fifty. He's due five hundred thousand for his part in all this. I can't believe it."

Victoria flatly informs the Officer, "There is a 100 million dollar reward, or contract if you will, for General Armstrong. A fraternity of Islamic nations want to try him for war crimes."

Davis is standing before Victoria with his mouth open in disbelief.

"So, what did you tell him?" Victoria asked with suspicion.

Davis takes a moment to allow all the information to sink in. He then answers smartly, "I told him no deal. It would put me in a higher tax bracket, . . . lucky for you huh?"

Victoria allows a small smile to overthrow her hardened facial expression. Davis sees her facial refashion, and now smiles himself. Victoria exhales in relief, and says, "Come over here, wise guy." She then motions towards the map before her, "See if this makes any sense to you."

Davis joins the Federal Agent, and looks over her shoulder at the map. He instantly identifies the locations of the markings.

"The 'X' is in the middle of old man Miller's farm, . . . what's left of it." He adds as an after thought. "It's now a big open field, with dried up vegetation on it." He explains as he looks to the 'red circle'. "The red circle, . . ." He begins as he pauses momentarily, while he takes a closer look, ". . . That is the General's residence."

"Residence?" She questions as she thinks, "Does he have any family there?"

"Oh no, . . . his folks are all gone. He has no kin around these parts anymore."

Victoria, while looking at the line from the airfield to the General's house, now deducts, that this is the route the general will be using from the airfield. She reasons the assassination attempt will go down somewhere along the route. Where the 'X' is marked on the map, is where she thinks is a gathering point for the assassins, since it is not close to the route. There is where they must be polishing up the final details. If they are there, she continues to think in silence, then there I should be also.

"I guess for a hundred million, . . ." Davis started, as he breaks Victoria's thoughts, ". . . Would be worth for them to take a chance, and kill the General. I figure they'll try and do this somewhere between the airfield and the General's house." He ended, as he continued to look upon the map. "Hell, why don't we go to the airfield and warn, . . ."

Interrupting him, Victoria says, "We don't know who's who. That's why it is really just up to us."

Sadly Davis states, "That man prevented nuclear Hell from rainin' down upon American cities, and we can't trust fellow Americans to prevent his death." He takes a breath, and then adds, "I ain't too proud of being an American, right now." He ended in disgust.

Lightly Victoria asks, "Are you ready to go, and crash a party?"

"I'm ready to go and kick some ass!" He answered in an angered tone, and then explains, "As far as I'm concerned, these son-of-a-bitches are traders to this here country. They are commitin' acts of treason, and those who commit such acts against the United States should be hung, . . . or a fact similarly there of." He swallows, and then in a softer, but stern voice, he continues, looking to her with committed eyes. "I ain't takin' no prisoners. This man may be the next President of the United States. I aim to send a message back to those, anti-American bastards, . . . fuck wit' us and die."

"Pretty speech kid, . . . but if we are not smart, and don't do this right, it won't mean a damn thing. We are going to have to do our jobs, minus the emotions."

Davis takes a deep breath, and now asks, "Alright, . . . what's our next move?"

"The 'X' marks the spot."

Davis looks to the wall clock over the doorway. "We better move. We have about another hour before first light." He notes.

The Officer opens the center drawer of the Captain's desk. He removes a key ring containing only two keys. "Come wit' me." He tells the Agent as he starts out of the office.

Victoria follows the Officer out of the office. Davis quickly walks to and unlocks a door marked storage. Once inside, he flicks on the light switch, and immediately begins unlocking a solid steel security door. As Victoria enters the storage room, she finds herself surrounded with office supplies and files. She is now complexed.

Davis now pushes open the heavy steel door. As it swings open he flips up a light switch. He now steps into the secured room. Victoria stands with an unobstructed view of the armory. She then steps forward, and as she steps across the threshold, Victoria softly asks, "Who's your purchasing Officer, . . . the Terminator?"

She looks over the room with her eyes opened wide, as they tried to absorb all the equipment that is stored within. Shotguns, rifles, sub-machine guns, stun grenades, crates of ammunition, gas masks, body armor, helmets and a rack of black military styled jumpsuits. The climate-controlled room causes Victoria to quake as a cold chill engulfs her.

"It'll make no sense engaging in a shootin' war with the peashooters we have now." Davis said, as he picks up two heavy-duty bullet resistance vests.

"A-Men." Victoria mumbles as she looks around at the weapons. Her eyes fall on an 'H & K' MP-5.

Davis hands her a vest. Victoria takes the garment into

her arms. The Officer begins to put his vest on and snap it closed. Victoria walks over to the rack of jumpsuits. She quickly looks them over as she scans for her size. Finally she finds her size. She puts the vest on top of a crate of ammo. She pulls her jacket off, and then takes the one-piece garment off the rack. She unzips the rugged cotton military wear. She now figures, due to the weight of the jumpsuit, combined with the vest, that she will be too warm wearing all these things atop her street clothes. Victoria turns towards Davis, and orders, "Turn your back."

He momentarily looks to her with confusion, but then immediately he complies to her instruction. He turns his back as he continues to adjust himself in the vest. Victoria immediately pulls her 'Army' sweatshirt from her well-developed torso, and allows it to fall to the fall. She now strips her grass and dirt stained sweatpants from her body. Without hesitation she steps into the never worn before jumpsuit.

"Okay." She said to Davis as she zips up the garment.

Davis turns to her and sees that she has changed clothes.

"What are you doin', . . . tryin' on clothes?" He said in an alarmed tone. "We are not going to some 'Ebony' Fashion Fair. We are going into battle."

As she prepares to put on the vest, she returns, "Yes, and I'm dressing for the part."

Victoria slips the vest over the jumpsuit. She immediately notices the weight not to be as heavy as she expected. The super tough vest is able to withstand a pointblank shotgun blast. As she snaps the protecting garment closed, she notices a load bearing vest. She takes the load bearing vest, and slings it on. She snaps it closed and then begins to insert the fully loaded pistol magazines into the bearing vest's pockets.

Davis has moved to the heavy weapons in their racks. As Victoria begins to unload the many handguns she has acquired, Davis asks, "Do you have a preference?"

Looking over to him, she sees he is standing near some 'H & K' MP-5's.

"The MP-5." She said, as she now notices a stack of special operation type thigh holsters.

"Good choice." Davis returns, as he snatches one from the rack.

With all of the magazines stored away in her load bearing pockets, Victoria takes Hayford's .40 pistol and places it in the thigh pocket of the jumpsuit, leaving the rest of the empty pistols on top of the ammo crate. She now walks over towards Davis. While on her way she stops at the stack of thigh holsters. Davis has also grabbed a load-bearing vest, and as he closes it up, Victoria is adjusting the thigh holster to her liking. The two move swiftly and silently. As Davis moved toward a crate of ammo, Victoria takes the pistol from her pocket, and places it in the holster. She then picks up the sub-machine gun Davis pulled out for her. She begins to examine the weapon. She releases the magazine, and glances at the bullets loaded within it.

"What type of ammo is in here?"

"Golden Sabers. Jacketed hollow-points."

Victoria reloads the weapon. Davis has opened an ammunition crate, and as he moves away, he says to her, "That is ammo for the MP-5, you better take as much as you can carry."

Victoria walks over to the open crate. She knows that once the shooting begins, it won't belong before it stops. Davis has walked over to a large metal cabinet. With his back to her, she becomes curious to what he is doing. She grabs a couple of the loaded magazines out of the crate, and starts putting them into her load bearing vest pockets as she continues to watch the Officer. Once finished she starts over to Davis with her MP-5 in hand.

Inside the cabinet are two Remington Sniper Rifles, each with a massive night vision device mounted upon them. Next to the sniper rifles is a compact Browning Automatic Rifle. It is outfitted with a low light scope, and a laser dot aiming system. As Victoria steps up next to him, he looks to the Agent with a smile. He then grabs the B.A.R. and states, "We're gonna need all the firepower we can get."

Sarcastically she asks, "Do you people have a tank out back?"

As he looks over the B.A.R., his eyes sparkle, as he grins like a kid on Christmas morning, "I've been dying to use this baby." He then looks to the Agent and says, "Com'on, we better get a move on."

As he steps away, Victoria notices an open box on the floor of the cabinet. She peeks inside, and discovers a dozen neatly packaged hand grenades. The Agent reaches in and withdraws one of the explosive devices. As she examines it, she recalls her Army knowledge of the weapon. She knows that this is no training tool. Victoria puts it into her vest pocket and then begins to withdraw three more, mumbling, "We need all the firepower we can get."

The two exit the armory and start out of the building. When they come across the body of the dead imposter, Davis stops. Victoria watches the Officer, as he looks upon the dead man. She sees in his blank, vacant expression the uncertainty.

"Yo, . . ." She unemotionally begins, ". . . Don't dwell on it, or you will end up just like him."

Davis looks to her. She then motions toward the door firmly. The Officer glances back towards the body, and then starts out for the door. He and Victoria walk silently towards the Main Street exit.

"Watch it, . . ." She warns. ". . . We don't know who may be out there."

Coldly Davis responds, "My, my, . . . won't they be surprised."

Chapter Four

At the spot on the map marked with an 'X', is Mister Smith, Captain Preston, Mister Jones, the bearded Middle Eastern man and a dozen of cohorts waiting in the barren field. They sit in the dark, among half a dozen vehicles, including two Madison police cars and a police van.

"Tell me something, . . ." Mister Jones begins directing his question to the Captain, ". . . How in the Hell did you ever end up here?"

With a slight smile, the Captain returns, "You haven't fished in the waters around here."

"Fish?" Jones asked with surprise. "You set up here for the fishing?"

"I'm getting too old to globe hop for the company, and do dirty deeds."

Now joining in the conversation, Mister Smith adds, "Besides, . . . no agency mission had rewards as beneficial as this mission." He continues with a smile. "When this sun sets, . . ." He said as he looks up to the pre-dawn sky, ". . . We all shall be wealthy beyond our dreams."

"Yeah, well so long as we don't end up like those guys who did Kennedy." Mister Jones voiced with concern.

Mister Smith and Captain Preston look to one another and begin to chuckle like a pair of schoolboys with a shared secret. Mister Jones looks to them with a complexed expression.

Suddenly Mister Smith ceases his merriment. His facial expression becomes firm, as he listens to the information that is coming over his earpiece. A distant thumping begins to approach from the sky, becoming louder by the second.

"Quickly the flares!!!" Mister Smith roars to the milling around men.

Mister Jones, along with Captain Preston look skyward towards the direction of the approaching helicopter. Preston looks to his watch, and then states, "This is startin' to cut it really close."

"We're fine now." The sky watching Jones returns.

"I don't see why we have to wait around for this shit." Preston protested. "We could blow Armstrong's escort to Hell, and deliver that nigga's ass to those towel heads, and then collect."

Addressing himself to the soul-less man, Mister Smith sharply says, "Armstrong is only one part, of the sum. Our comrades want to project a yet stronger message."

"Snatching Armstrong within the U.S. ain't strong enough?" Preston asked sarcastically.

"Armstrong is not going to be delivered to them. His sentence is to be carried out here in America." Jones flatly informed. "Captain, we are standing at the inaugural of World changing history." Jones ended as he looks up to the now visible helicopter.

Flying low over the not too distant tree line, a blacked out Huey helicopter, thunders towards the illuminating flares. Suddenly, a sun bright light fires from the aircraft to the ground, engulfing the makeshift landing zone in artificial daylight. The unmarked helicopter touches down near the awaiting men. The hurricane like updrafts cause dirt and dried vegetation to swirl about.

The pilot immediately shuts down the engine causing the mighty twirling rotors to begin slowing to a halt. The first man out of the helicopter is Alaa. The Syrian born native, views America as a godless devil. He feels that the United States should be destroyed, or brought under the rule of Allah. This Islamic fundamentalist is here on American soil, with the backing of a coalition of Islamic Nations. The middle aged man scans the scene. His eyes finally come to rest on his group of American contacts.

"You know him?" Mister Jones asked, looking to Mister Smith.

"Yes, . . . he's our boss." He answers flatly, and then begins to walk over towards the newly arrived.

As Smith crosses the few yards that separate them, Alaa's party begins to unload the helicopter. Four heavily armed men, dressed in black battle dress uniforms, deplane. They exit the craft carrying two, three foot tall silver canisters, and another canister about the same size as the others, but much wider. The green painted cylinder is a compressed air canister, but it has been cut down to only half its usual height.

Sternly, and in a heavy Middle Eastern accent, Alaa speaks to Mister Smith, "Is this field secured? How much longer to Armstrong's arrival?"

Nodding his head smoothly in response to the first question, Smith then says, "A little more than an hour."

Smith is watching the four men, with the canisters. He sees the men are armed with AK-74's, and have ammunition belts across their bodies. With their faces covered, they appear to be like shadows. Smith now remarks, "You keep very menacing company."

"These men are for insurance." Alaa said flatly.

Mister Smith now directs his attention to the canisters. As he studies them, he is joined by the bearded man.

"There isn't a chance of them detonating now, is there?" Smith directed his concerned question to Alaa.

Quickly the bearded man interjects, "No, . . ."

Smith turns toward the man, and then he continues, ". . . They first must be combined, . . . to mix, . . . before they can release their death." The bearded man explained.

Mister Smith's mouth becomes slightly dry as he thinks of the once described effects of what lies within the steel canisters. He looks to the bearded man and says, "Lead them to the van, . . ." Started, dismissing the horrifying thought, ". . . and let's get out of here."

Turning toward the men in black, Alaa instructs them to follow the 'bearded one'. As the instructed men begin to follow, Mister Smith and Alaa begin to walk behind them, side by side.

"I'm surprised to see you here." Smith said to Alaa.

"My presence is to ensure flawless execution of this plan."

"Flawless plan, flawless execution." Smith responded positively.

Displaying a slight smile of approval, Alaa firmly says, "Very well, then we shall return here to this very spot once all is in place. Together we shall fly to New York, and await the news of our victory at the consulate."

"And when do we receive payment?"

"Your money awaits in Belgium, as instructed. It will be released to you once the American News Media announces the devastation done here."

Special Agent Victoria Owens and Madison, North Carolina Police Officer Stephan Davis, reached his police car unmolested. The death still streets of Madison gave the pair a feeling than, they were the last man and woman on the face of the Earth. They rode in silence, as Davis raced the high output V-8 sedan toward old man Miller's Farm. Victoria prayed silently for their protection. She wondered if this was to be her end. She feels positive about the action she's about to engage in. She is being driven to stop this assassination. She cannot explain it. Perhaps only another law enforcement office, or patriot soldier can. She does not want to die. She does not want to be a hero. This is just simply another battle between the forces of good and evil. She has left the welfare of her soul to Jesus. Fear no longer grips her. What happens now, must happen.

Miller's Farm is located 9 miles from the police station. Davis drove along route 208, which must have been planned by men who build roller coasters, or were intoxicated. The entrance to the abandoned farm is a dirt and gravel road. It's a wide road, that travels at a steady upgrade into the thick tree line, that borders route 208. The road then curves to the right as it peeks. It then levels out, passing the uncared 103 acres to a grand farmhouse, that is now nothing more than a weather beaten shack.

Davis stops the car on route 208, at the entranceway to Miller's Farm Road. He looks to Victoria, and announces calmly, "This is the road that leads to the 'X' on the map." He then activates the left side spotlight, located on the overhead light bar.

Victoria is surprised by the location. She begins visually looking around the area. She had expected to run into the terrorist. Davis now explains, "That road goes up to the fields." He started as he looked upon the road. "They are up there." He ended in a confident tone.

Frustrated and bewildered, Victoria returns, "You sound sure." Before he can respond, she adds, "I've got a feeling, we've missed them, and they are either on their way to the airfield or to the General's home."

"Well, they didn't go to the airfield, besides it's too busy there. Too many people around."

Firmly Victoria informs, "Terrorists like a public audience."

"That may be, but they are still up there." He reinforces

sternly as he turns towards her. Seeing that she is about to explode like a volcano, he quickly adds, "Look at the road, do you see any tracks?" He asked as he points to the roadway.

Victoria leans over in order to see out of his window.

"What tracks?"

"See, if they woulda left from the farm, there would be muddy tire tracks all over the black top." Davis reasoned.

Victoria looks to him, as she settles back in her seat. Valid point she notes. She looks at the road leading into the darkness, and softly says, "Let's go."

Davis switches off the vehicle's lighting, and then proceeds onto Miller's Farm Road. As Officer Davis and Agent Owens venture slowly up the rough road, the mercenary convoy has begun to drive off. The leading vehicle, a Madison marked patrol car, is being driven by Captain Preston. Behind him is an unmarked sedan with Mister Jones, and an Aide who is driving. Mister Smith and Alaa are sitting in the rear. Following them is the police van containing the four men in black, along with the canisters. Behind them, is another Madison police car loaded with men dressed as police officers.

The storm clouds have drifted completely out of the area's skies. A quarter moon hangs low over the distant horizon. The eastern sky has begun to lighten, with the hint of daybreak. Davis steadily guides the police sedan along the unpaved grade.

"Hey Owens, . . . you married?" He asked to ease the tension.

"No, . . . you?"

"No." He answered, pausing before he asks, "Did you ever want to be?"

Now dazed by his line of questioning, Victoria answers lightly, "Yes, . . . but Mister Right hasn't shown up yet."

Smoothly, Davis responds, "I've found Mister Right, but we couldn't get married."

Victoria snaps her head towards him with a boggled

expression. Her silent response prompts the Officer to continue, "The state of North Carolina frowns on alternative lifestyles."

Wowed, Victoria now responds, "You're gay?"

Davis glances at her, and asks, "Surprised?"

"Frankly, . . . yes."

"Yeah well, since Marty died, I don't feel much for anything." He stated joylessly.

His tone causes the woman's heart to sadden. Her mind instantly recalls her mother. Immediately dismissing the recall, Victoria fires back.

"Aids?"

Restrained, Davis returns, "Not all gay men die of Aids."

Now feeling as if she is only two feet tall, she looks away from him. She sees herself, in her mind as the cartoon character that turns into an ass.

"He was shot through the head, at close range." Davis suddenly revealed.

Shocked by the revelation, she turns to him and probes, "Murdered?"

Davis does not respond to the question. He continues to talk, as if he is in a trans-like state.

"He was found in his car, in front of our place. He would of never killed himself. He was too high on life. Things were good between us. We were happy." He ended flatly, then taking a breath and continuing, "They tried to sell me that it was suicide, . . ." He stopped, and then looks to her with tear filled eyes, ". . . You're damn right it was murder. Murder committed by an evil, in this here town, . . . and its name is Preston."

He turns and looks outward through the windshield, and then over to the road that leads to the farm.

"Preston, . . . the Captain?" Victoria asked softly.

"He did it. I know it." He answered in a haunting tone. "The Captain tried like Hell to get me thrown off the force, but the Chief ignored his rhetoric."

"Why, . . . because you are gay?" She probed tenderly.

"You got it."

"But then, . . . why kill your friend?" She asked, confused by his statement.

"To fuck wit' me, I guess."

Suddenly the reflection of headlights grew larger, as the Officers approached the curve.

"Showtime." Victoria mumbles, as she chambers a round into her MP-5.

Davis also sees the lights, and then immediately stops the car. By the time Davis has gotten the car stopped, they are engulfed in the bright lights of Captain Preston's car. As the pair got out of their patrol car and behind the doors for cover, Preston begins slowing his car to a stop.

Davis reaches in and activates all of the car's exterior lights, including the overhead flashing lights. He then rests the B.A.R. on the doorsill, aiming in the Captain's shadowy, but visible outline. Captain Preston has no idea as of yet that something is amiss. He exits his auto, with a cigar butt clenched in his teeth, and yells toward the blocking police car.

"Jack let's go!! Get that damn thing outa the way!! There's no time for games!! And turn those fuckin' lights off, what's the matter wit' you?!!!!"

As he aligns the sights of the B.A.R. on the Captain, Davis yells back, "Sorry Captain, but Jack can't hear ya!!!"

Preston pauses momentarily in thought, as he is joined by Mister Jones.

"Who is that?" He asked in an alarmed tone.

Now realizing who it is, Preston shouts, "Davis!!! What the fuck do you think you're doin', boy?!!"

"Davis, . . ." Jones begins worried, ". . . Who's Davis? How did he know where to find us?" He ended frantically.

"Where is Jack?!!" Preston shouts with concern.

Speaking up, Victoria announces herself, "No, your boy

Jack failed the task you gave him, Captain. He is now worm food by now!!"

"Who the fuck is that?!!" Jones asked now sounding like he is on the verge of a breakdown.

Calmly the Captain explains, "Davis is one of my officers, but he is not apart of our little party. The woman is some black bitch Hayford stumbled over earlier." He ended quickly and then returned his attention to the pair. "What goes on here, Davis?!" He shouts with anger.

As the hostile Captain spoke, so too did Mister Jones into his communicator. Davis strongly announced as he activates the laser aiming system. "We've got you covered, and now your busted!!"

"We?!" The Captain questioned, while not realizing a red laser dot is projected on his chest.

Now advancing from the cover of the police car, Victoria approaches the men. The Captain stands with the persona of ice, and Mister Jones is clearly shaken by the encounter. Victoria emerges without her MP-5, or her pistol in hand. The men stand quietly as she approaches.

Now standing about five yards apart, and halfway between them and the B.A.R. bearing Officer, Captain Preston smartly remarks, "What are you made up for, Halloween?"

Mister Jones nervously lets out a chuckle. He then looks to the Captain, he has now begun to also chuckle. Victoria joins in with a laugh, and then says lightly, "Hey fellas, . . . see, see if you want to laugh at this, . . ." She then drops her smiling face, and sternly announces, "I'm Victoria Owens, Special Agent of the Federal Bureau of Investigation."

Immediately Mister Jones, stops his laughing, and drops his smile. He looks to the Captain, as well as Victoria. She continues bitterly, "You see, Captain, . . . you never know who you're foolin' with."

"What's to stop me from blowing you away?!!" Mister Jones shouts as he reaches for his gun.

"Perhaps *you* should look to the Captain's chest."

Jones, stops his action, and looks. Victoria continues, "You may not care, but I'm sure the Captain now has something to say."

Mister Jones as well as the Captain look to the glowing cherry sized illumination, projected over the center of Preston's chest. Victoria smugly adds, "I understand the rounds from that weapon Davis has pointing at you, can penetrate cinderblock, car bodies and steel doors, . . ." She pauses momentarily to allow the information to sink into their heads. She then continues, ". . . And if you think you're macho enough to handle that, . . ." She now produces a hand grenade, and pulls the pin, ". . . Then we will *all* surely die, . . . right here, and right now."

Entering on the scene is Mister Smith. Smoothly he comments, "There's no need for anyone to die here."

Immediately remembering him from the station, Victoria sternly addresses the mysterious man.

"Who are you, . . . the brains of the outfit?"

Modestly, Mister Smith begins to explain, "I'm just a link in a very short chain, Miss, . . . ?" He ended pausing for her to disclose her name.

Preston quickly fills in the pause of silence, "Fuck this bitch."

Smith looks to Mister Jones. The nervous man relates, "Owen, . . . she says she's F.B.I."

Perking up, Smith turns toward Victoria with a smile and says in an impressive tone, "Well, well, well."

Smith now steps towards the Agent.

Alaa gets out of the car, and watches closely.

As Smith takes a few steps towards the Agent he begins kindly, "Agent Owens, . . . this is the bottom line. I've got firepower behind me you wouldn't believe. In ten seconds, you could be history."

"Then I'll tell you what, . . ." She begins unintimidated, ". . . Why don't we just get it on. I am not going to just simply step aside, and let you assassinate Armstrong, but just tell me one thing, before the party begins, . . . who's also behind this operation, . . . the K.K.K., . . . the Neo-Nazis Party?"

Mister Smith begins laughing. His hearty outburst unnerves Victoria, as she looks over the others.

"Did I say something funny?" She asked sharply, filled with tension.

Undetected, Alaa slips away towards the rear of the convoy. Now regained control of himself, Mister Smith suddenly changes emotions, and snaps at the grenade holding woman.

"Is that what you think this is all about?! You think a conspiracy has formed, because a black man is running for the Presidency?! Allow me to inform you of something Miss, . . . this matter is beyond race." He now lowers his voice, but remains firm, "You see, if the General is elected, he will definitely prevent the changes that are needed to complete a one World Government, thus crushing the only hope mankind has for Heaven on Earth."

"The New World Order?" Victoria gently asked.

Now demonstrating a broad smile, Mister Smith answers yes.

"For decades, former Presidents have enacted a lot of initiatives, bringing this country in line with the New World Order. The President has picked up where other Presidents have left off, but, . . . her continued service is required to deliver America into the hands of Global Rulership!"

Gently, the Agent remarks, "It doesn't look good for her re-election."

"Hopeless."

"So, . . . why such an elaborate plan?"

"The plan is designed to bring America to its knees. The assassination of Armstrong, along with the deaths of multitudes of American citizens, will be the first major terrorist strike, within the United States of this magnitude. The Twin Towers in New York will pale in comparison. A national emergency will be declared and the President, through Executive Orders, will suspend the Constitution, as well as the Bill of Rights." He then smiles, and adds, "But you know, Miss Owens, . . . there are no provisions requiring the President to reactivate the Constitution. This elaborate plan, as you call it, will change everything."

Unbeknown to Davis and Owens, Alaa has instructed the heavily armed impostor officers, to go around, and out flank the duo. As Mister Smith lays out the New World Order for Victoria, the fake Officers reach their objective.

Davis's position is very well protected. His car is between him, and the undetected killers dressed as police officers. One of the impostors, aligns his sights on Davis. The only possible target, is the unsuspecting Officer's head. It is a shot that is going to have to be made on an angle, through the rolled up window of the patrol car's rear door.

"Who's Armstrong's advance man?" Victoria asked sternly.

"That would be Mister Jones." Smith reveals, pointing the man out to her.

Victoria looks to the man and proclaims, "You Sir, are a traitor to the Service, as well as your Country."

As her disapproving glare pans from Jones, onto Smith, she questions, "Are you Secret Service, as well?"

"Central Intelligence Agency."

Surprised by his response, but did not allow the emotion to show, Victoria immediately asks, "Is this what you Spooks call a 'black' operation?"

"It would be, Agent Owens, but you see, . . . the Company has nothing to do with this. We are all freelancing."

"So what do you mean, . . . all you people believe this New World Order bullshit?"

"No, not at all."

"Then what is it? You all had nothing to do this weekend?"

"Do you want all 100 million reasons why?"

Now a light bulb sparks to life within Victoria's head.

Mister Smith further explains, "You see, . . . there is no reason for you or us to die here, and now. Perhaps, . . . shall we say, five million dollars. Five million reasons for you to step over onto this side of the line."

"What are you fuckin' crazy?!!" Preston exploded.

Smith begins to defend his proposal, "She would be an asset. She took on those men in your jail. I believe she could have killed every single one of them. She has escaped from your psycho cop, and has probably killed him. I am not looking forward to engage the grenade she's holding."

"I am not going to turn my back, and close my eyes to this." Victoria responded to Smith's offer.

Preston says to Smith, "Yeah well, she may be tough, but she sure is stupid."

"I took an oath to protect this country from all enemies, . . . foreign or domestic!" She added strongly.

Smith turns to her, and snaps, "Why are you so damn loyal to a country that disrespects, dishonors and lies to you? You still haven't gotten your promised 40 acres and a mule, while war enemies that have killed America's sons and husbands have been compensated. It's the year 2012, and you are still being referred to as nigger." He ended sharply. "So tell me, . . . why so loyal?"

As they spoke, the impostor is sighting his weapon on Davis. Via a radio link, they inform that only Davis, and the woman exist. There are no further opposes. Upon hearing the report from the hidden gunman, Mister Jones begins shouting, "Take them out!!" As he reaches for his concealed gun.

Instantly a shot rings out from behind her. Instinctively, Victoria begins to turn towards the shot's report. Captain Preston begins pulling his gun from it's holster. A bullet smashed into the rear door's window, deflected, and then struck the patrol car's windshield, missing the intended target. Mister Jones begins firing at the Agent. A bullet strikes Victoria on her left side, causing her to turn 180 degrees.

Immediately, Preston fires a volley of rapid shots, which impact on her upper, and mid back.

Davis recovers from the near miss, and directs his 7.62 caliber, semi-automatic rifle into the trees, from which the shot came. The mighty weapon sheds the timber, and the impostors as well.

The .40 caliber rounds, striking Victoria in the back like sledgehammers, force the Agent towards the ground. As she falls, Preston and Jones continue to fire upon her. Victoria, as soon as she fell to the ground, immediately rolled into the darkness of a swallow roadside depression. As she disappears from view, the grenade she was holding, comes bouncing back into sight. It skips upon the ground towards the still firing, free lancing terrorist. Taking only a split second to comment to herself about the effectiveness of the vest, she waits for the grenade to explode. Preston, Jones and Smith all see the baseball-sized bomb bouncing toward them.

They all scatter. Then with a thunderous, earth quaking blast, the small anti-personal device reports. With her Army training now fresh in her mind, she immediately throws another grenade toward the Terrorists. She then pulls another from her vest pocket, pulling the pin, and tossing it towards the remaining imposters in the tree thick darkness. The second grenade goes off with the same, thunderous boom, as did the first. The third followed as well, but it is accompanied by a chorus of screams. Victoria spouts from the roadside crevice, as the explosions still echo, and debris shower upon the area. As she darts across the road, she fires her pistol toward the stunned Terrorists. Captain Preston is quick to recover from the blast, and begins firing on the quick moving Agent. As she slides into a crevice near by Davis, Alaa calls to his men.

Officer Davis has just loaded a fresh magazine into his weapon. Captain Preston is now joined by Mister Jones, as they both fire at the Officer's positions. Victoria returns a volley of shots, and then informs Davis that they better move to another location. Davis takes a quick look towards the woods. He then jumps into the ditch with Victoria, and says, "Cover me, and when you hear me open up, follow!"

"Wait!!" She said as she loads a fresh magazine into her pistol.

When she releases the slide, Davis takes off into the woods. Victoria immediately fires on the Terrorists as fast as she could pull the trigger. She completely covers the disorganized group with gunfire. While under fire, Alaa shouts instructions to his men, but all orders suddenly stop when Davis open fires with the B.A.R's devastating firepower.

Victoria reaches Davis as he delivers accurate fire upon the Terrorists. She instantly releases her now empty magazine, and reloads a fresh one. Davis once again runs off, further into the woods and Victoria follows. As she runs she looks back, and promptly notices that they have stopped shooting. As she follows Davis through the underbrush, leaves and dodges trees, she realizes that they must be in close pursuit. So right she is.

Captain Preston stands at the edge of the tree line where Davis and The Agent have entered the woods. He stands enraged in his once clean, razor sharp, pressed uniform that is now dirty and torn. His chest heaves from his rapid, heavy breathing. He's watching the four men in black, ascending into the darkness of the woods, in the fleeing duo's wake.

Victoria looks to her rear in time to see figures of men pursuing them. Their images are clear against the small bush fire, which one of the grenades caused. Preston turns to Smith and says, "I'm going with the hounds. I know these woods."

Smith nods to him, and as the Captain takes off after the men in black, Smith starts walking over towards Mister Jones, who is yelling for his Aide to hurry. Smith is joined along the way by Alaa. In his heavy Middle Eastern accent, the man asks, "Shall he correct the disarray he has created?"

"That he shall." Smith answers coldly.

Mister Jones is watching his Aide attempt to push the Captain's heavily damaged patrol car clear of the road. As Mister Jones's unmarked sedan begins effortlessly pushing the patrol car off the road, the men now stand all together. Mister Jones informs flatly, "There's nobody left alive on the hill." He ended motioning towards the position where the impostors were. "That grenade took them all out." He said unemotionally, and then realized Preston's absence, "Where's Frankenstein?"

"Hunting." Smith replies, and then says, "As soon as he clears the road we're off."

"Thirty minutes before Armstrong arrives." Jones stresses.

Smith turns to the man and says, "You better go now, and meet the man."

"Will you be in position, and vacated in time?" Jones asked with concern.

"After you deliver Armstrong to his residence, get yourselves back here."

"Save me a window seat." Jones said.

Approaching Madison at about 500 miles per hour, is the small chartered jet carrying General Jonathan Taylor Armstrong, and a small band of Secret Service Agents, along with his Aide. The chartered jet's cabin is configured unlike a passenger airliner. Onboard is a seated briefing area, a few lounges, that can transform into sleeping quarters. An office and private sleeping area for the candidate. A galley, and several bathrooms. This aircraft is not Air Force One, but is a red eye traveler's dream.

It is very quiet aboard the jet now. The General and his Aide, have succumbed to a needed sleep. With his leather high backed chair tilted slightly rearward, and beads of perspiration forming along his close cropped hairline, he dreams. His Aide, surrounded by papers, charts and a cold cup of coffee, is balancing in his chair, as he sleeps as he holds onto a stack of papers. As if in slow motion, the Aide's body begins to lean forward. Like a mighty tree in the forest, his torso picks up momentum as it begins to fall. As his body continues it's crash landing, the papers on his lap too begin to fall floorward.

Suddenly the Aide catches himself, and stops his sure collision with the General's metal desk, but then like a paper avalanche, the mountain of files, begins showering the floor. The splashing of paper onto the thinly carpeted floor, startles the Aide from his dozing state.

"Sorry, General." He apologizes automatically, now just realizing the General was asleep.

It is apparent that the General was engaged in a nightmare. The Aide and close friend of the General's looks upon the sleeping man. Immediately the Aide knows the General is in a sleeping Hell. Just then a passing Steward stops at the open doorway, and gently announces, "Gentlemen, . . ."

The Aide spins around, and now faces the slim middle-aged man.

". . . Please prepare for landing." The Steward ended, but now notices the General traumatic conduct.

The Aide notices the sudden expressional changes in the Steward's face.

"What is wrong?" The Steward asked with concern, as he slowly begins to enter the office.

The Aide at a loss for words, looks to the sweating, slightly flinching man who seems to be in agony. The Aide looks back to the Steward, who is now standing next to him. The bewildered Aide then looks back at the General, as the Steward says, "Is he dreaming?"

In a low tone, the older Aide answers, "I think so."

"Well he sure in Hell doesn't look as if he's having a good time."

Nodding his head in agreement, the Aide approaches the seated General. In a firm tone, the Aide addresses the dreaming man, "J.T., . . . General, . . . com'on, . . . we've arrived, General."

Armstrong's eyes exploded open. The sudden awaking startles his former military Aide. As the General sits straight up in his chair, his Aide asks with concern, "Are you okay?"

He takes a deep breath, and then answers somewhat winded, "Duke, . . . we were back in the desert."

With surprise, Duke responds, "The desert?"

The General stands and continues with a grim tone, "Yeah, . . . but this time it was different, . . ." He starts as he is looking Duke directly into his eyes, ". . . We were at ground zero. Operation Apache had failed." He then looks away from the salt and pepper haired right hand man. He looks upon the floor, and in a trans-like stare continues, "I saw the nuclear strikes. I tasted the dirt and sand, . . . and I felt the heat from the blast melting my flesh." He ended, looking upward to him.

Duke starts to slowly nod his head. After a brief pause of silence, Duke says softly but strongly, "No doubt General, . . . if Apache did fail, your dream just now, would have been a reality. You, me, and tens of million Americans would now be nothing more than radioactive dust."

"Gentlemen, . . ." The Steward politely intrudes, ". . . I must ask you to prepare for a landing."

"How long before we touch down?" Armstrong asked in a strong upbeat tone.

"Roughly ten minutes, Sir."

The General announces, "I'm gonna make myself pretty." He jokes as he starts out of the office. He then glances back towards Duke and asks, "Duke, will you stand-by?"

"Sure General." He answered, as the man exits.

The Steward looks upon Duke, and says, "That was one Hellava dream."

Duke begins to pick up the papers, as he comments, "Down right spooky, if you ask me."

The Steward kneels, and begins helping the Aide.

"I didn't know you were with the General when he blew up the missiles in the desert."

"We've been side by side for years."

In a serious tone, the Steward asks, "What really happened in the desert. I mean, we weren't getting any straight news from the media here in America, but other news sources, from other countries were painting a pretty gloomy picture. Then suddenly the crisis was all over, the troops started coming home. The media, the White House, everybody began downplaying the entire incident. The President says we were never in any real danger. I mean, there was so much bullshit, I don't believe any of what that slick witch says anyhow."

Duke stops his action, and looks to the Steward. He begins in a low tone, "Israel was about to be invaded without a doubt. We were ordered to reinforce the Golan Heights. You didn't know this back home, but an unofficial shooting war had broken out in the Heights. I think that was down played as reports of sniper strikes. Anyway, . . . I think Syria froze when they saw our forces in the Heights. Then our spy satellites located a hidden missile installation, out in the desert. Now things start turning into a James Bond story." He pauses to take a breath, "British Intelligence had been listening in on the Chinese. They discover that four operational, long range I.C.B.Ms. are in the desert. A 99 percent confidence factor was given that the missiles were targeted for strikes within the continental United States. The General was constantly bumping heads with the U.N. Commander. The U.N. wanted to utilize negotiations, and ordered the General not to take action on the missiles."

Shocked by the information, the Steward interrupts, "Since when does the U.N. dictate to American Forces?" The Steward asked with a ring of objection.

Firmly Duke responds, "1993, by Presidential Order." Duke allows the answer to settle momentarily before he continues, "The General smelled a rat. Here a minimum of four nukes in the control of American and Israeli hating madmen, and all the U.N. wants to do is talk."

"Bullshit."

"No shit, . . ." Duke returns, and then continues, "Fearing that nuclear warheads can rain upon American cities, the General led two platoons of Army Rangers on a night-time raid into the desert. Eight hours later, the nuclear threat no longer existed, nor did the missile installation. It is nothing more than a big hole in the sand. That my friend was Operation Apache."

The Steward swallows hard, and says helplessly, "Needless to say that it is insane to have non American military leaders, in command over U.S. Troops. So are all the other new age ideas the government is implementing. It's like they are giving America away, . . . slowly but surely." He pauses in thought, as he gathers up the remaining papers, and says, "I think it's time for another Boston Tea Party."

Duke now stands with papers in his hands, and says, "You are probably right."

Duke now sees the General engaging in conversation with one of the Secret Service Agents. Then as an after thought he adds firmly, "Perhaps with the help of God, . . . starting January 22nd, 2013, we can begin the process to take America back."

After running for what seems like five miles, Davis stops to catch his breath. Directly behind him, Victoria stops with him, and immediately studies their rear for the men in black. The early morning light has brightened the sky, but among the trees, the light is still gloomy. Victoria no longer sees the followers, but senses them. The shadows, and the trees can hide an army out there she notices.

"Davis, . . ." She begins as she breathes hard, ". . . We better keep moving. They're on our trail" She said softly with urgency, between gasps for air.

The Officer looks to their rear. In a desperate tone, he quietly asks, where the trailing men are. Victoria then sharply replies, "If we stay here much longer, they'll be in our face."

Understanding her response, Davis quietly asks, "How much ammo do you have left?"

"Not much, . . . how much further to the house?"

"Bout' two more miles."

"You ready?"

"Yeah."

"You lead, I'll follow."

Davis begins through the bush at a trot, with Victoria following behind, constantly watching their rear. The men in black are combat veterans. Unbeknown to the Officers, the men in black, know exactly where they are. The Terrorists, flanking their targets, are now ready to strike. Victoria is expecting if any shooting to begin, it will come from their rear. She continuously watches for any sign of the approaching men. Suddenly, like a downpour of rain, the Terrorists fire upon them.

The General's jet touches down as hails of bullets approach the Officers. The aircraft taxis off the runway, as the first ray of sunlight, acts as a spotlight on the airport. Mister Jones, and his Aide are standing on the apron with their sedan, which is parked in front of the waiting limousine.

Immediately when the Terrorists open fired, Davis and Owens, threw themselves to the ground. They scramble for cover among the wood's natural protection. Victoria simply places her .40 over a fallen tree, which she is using for cover and fires wildly. Despite Victoria's fire, a man in black begins to advance outside of her lines of gunfire. Davis is just in time to see the advancing man stop, and aim at Victoria on her exposed flank. As she stops to reload, and the other men begin to advance towards them, Davis sparks into action. He aims and dispatches the aiming man. He now evacuates his position, just as the other men pulverize it with bullets.

Like a baseball player sliding into home, Davis now shares the downed tree with the Federal Agent. Simultaneously they expose themselves slightly, as they commence to open fire on the attacking Terrorists. The Officer's combined firepower forces the advancing killer to seek cover. They now momentarily cease their automatic fire.

While maintaining an observation position, with his weapon at the ready, resting it on the downed tree, Davis quietly speaks to Victoria.

"Get outa here."

"What?" She said as she looked to him.

Keeping his eyes locked in the direction of the Terrorists, he explains, "Look, if we both stay here, and get killed, it would have all been for nothing. We are not preventing them from still gettin' to Armstrong."

Victoria replies sternly, "I can't leave you here."

"Listen, . . ." He starts in an aggressive tone, ". . . Those bastards are on their way to murder the General."

Suddenly from not too far away, Captain Preston shouts, "Hey Boy, . . . whata you say, we chew this over?!"

"You can't fight these bastards alone." She said to Davis through clenched teeth.

"I can hold them here. You slip down the hill. Then go up and over the big hill with the power lines. The General's place is about another mile on the left." He said in a rush.

"Boy, . . . don't let that girl get you into deep shit!! You hear me Boy!!"

"Let's go." She said to Davis in a determined voice.

Davis snaps back at her, "Damn it, No, . . . now git'" He then adds in a calmer tone, "Get your ass outa here."

Victoria looks to him with pleading eyes. Davis feels her emotion, but dismisses her, and then addresses the Captain.

"Captain, . . . !!" He begins as he places his last two

remaining B.A.R. magazines beside him. "... Why don't you just kiss my ass!!" He then glances over towards Victoria and smiles.

She wants to cry. As she fights the tears from forming, she reaches into her vest pocket and withdraws her last grenade. She places the device in his hand, and regrettably says, "When all else fails."

Suddenly a fierce eruption of gunfire reports from the Terrorists. Davis immediately returns fire, as bullets eat away at the wooden cover. Victoria knows he is correct. Though she desperately wants to stay, she knows she must go. As she slithers away amidst the intense firefight, her eyes begin to fill with tears. She mumbles a prayer for Officer Davis.

Agent Owens followed Officer Davis's directions. A light fog engulfs the low lying land bordering the clear water stream. As the sun slowly climbs into a cloudless sky, it's bright light also brings a soothing warmth. All during her fast moving trek, Victoria has heard the battle of one against so many. With great discipline, she fights the compulsion to return and aid the Madison Officer.

What Officer Davis said was true. If they were to defeat the evil forces in the woods, valuable time would have been lost. By the time they would of reached the General's house, it would have been too late. They may have won the battle, but they would of lost the war. Without Davis staying behind, and occupying the Terrorists, an attempt to stop the rest would not be possible. In war, sacrifices are always made. Agent Owens knows this. Officer Davis knows this also.

As she climbs the hill with the power lines overhead, she no longer hears the distant gunshots. She stops and turns toward the direction of the battle site. A queasy feeling introduces itself in the pit of her stomach. She cursed the Captain and his goons, as she continues onward with her mission.

At the battle scene, the guns are now silent. A delicate cloud of gun smoke hangs low over the scene. Officer Davis has spent all of the ammunition for his B.A.R., and his semi-automatic pistol. He has announced his surrender, has thrown his weapons out toward the Captain and his forces. Davis now stands facing them with his hands behind his head.

"Where's your girlfriend?!" The Captain shouts, while still concealed in the bushes.

Directing his answer towards the Captain's voice, Davis defeatedly answers, "She high tailed outa here, long ago."

Snapping twigs, and crushing dried leaves began to sound all around him. Davis's right leg begins to tremble slightly, as the still unseen Terrorists advance toward him. The scene unfolding before the Officer, seems so unreal. It is also dream-like.

Davis's heart is pounding so hard, that he can hear the organ, as clearly as though it is in his head. Though fear has captured him, and it is causing him to tremble, he is still in control of his thoughts. He is still focused on his mission to delay or stop these murderous madmen.

Simultaneously, on his extreme left and right, a man in black, emerges from the cover of the brush, and trees. Another appears from the woods, and they approach the Officer swiftly, with their guns pointed and ready. The man from the left, aims his AK-47 at Davis's face. Davis can smell the gunpowder, and the warmth from the hot barrel. The other man begins a visual search of the area behind the captured cop. The man sees noting as he looks down the hill. Victoria has left no traces of her departure.

Captain Preston now emerges from his concealed position with the last member of the men in black. Davis watches the emergence.

"No, . . ." The Captain starts, as he approaches the Officer, ". . . You didn't want to listen. What, . . . you wanted to be some sort of hero?"

"I was just doin' my job." Davis answered firmly.

Preston stops at about five feet from Davis. He looks into the scared young man's eyes. He points his handgun at the

Officer's face. The two men in black, at the Officer's side, back away from him. The men in black and Preston have now formed a semi-circle in front of the doomed Officer.

"I'll make sure that it's written on your tombstone." Preston coldly remarks.

Suddenly a rumble of mumbling erupts from the men in black, as they begin pointing their AK's at the Officer. Then one of them speaks in broken English, laced in a heavy accent, "He kills our Comrade, . . . we too shoot him."

Lowering his gun, Preston says, "Be my guest."

Just then, the unique sound of a grenade's safety pin, ejecting away, rings in Preston's ears. He immediately looks to Davis. Their eyes meet. Preston no longer sees the Officer's eyes filled with fear. He now sees vengeance.

All at once, Davis launches the grenade from behind his head, just as the men in black prepare to fire. Preston, seeing the final seconds of his World coming to an end, screams out, and begins firing at the Officer. The other men open fire as well, as the grenade descends upon them, and explodes.

Chapter Five

The home of the deceased parents of retired General Jonathan Taylor Armstrong, sits isolated on a knoll, overlooking its 60 acres. The huge 4600 square foot country house was built solidly in the mid-80's as the dream home his mother had always desired.

Victoria has now reached the stately home. She climbs low over an unkempt chicken wire fence. Remaining low, she advances towards the house. She stops amidst an old rusted tractor, and then visually, begins to examine the setting.

Analyzing the lack of activity, she reasons that the General has not yet arrived. Then the thought of the Terrorists changing their plans, suddenly dawns on her. Suppose the Terrorist's plot has been discovered, and the General has been diverted?

While looking over the two story wooden framed house, she decides that the only way to know for sure, is to probe into the house. She squats to check her weapon. She unloads the magazine from her pistol. She checks the number of rounds remaining, and then re-inserts it. Victoria checks the pockets of her vest. As she goes through them, she places the useless MP-5 magazines in a pile at her feet. Now, discovering that she has no more extra ammunition left for her pistol, she becomes worrisome.

She now remembers her partner's recon tales. When low on ammo, . . . one shot, one kill. Priority target selection. The pawns become unimportant. The important targets, leaders and decision makers, she thought over to herself. As she looks to the house, she can see a highway patrol car, parked in the driveway. Her first instinct was, 'phony cops' were about. The thought was re-enforced as she also notices a Madison Police Department van. She recognizes the van as the same one that was at the farm.

With the few remaining rounds she has left, she names them for the men she has encountered at the farm, and any other key player, . . . and possibly, . . . if all else fails, . . . the last one for herself.

Victoria silently darts over to the side of the house, which is actually an attached, four-car garage. She peeks into a window. What appears to be a vehicle enclosed in a cover, is the only thing inside the structure. Victoria, gripping the pistol in her hand, ventures to the front corner of the house, where the elevated porch begins. As she nears, she can hear a conversation concerning women, from at least two male voices.

Fearing that the men are on the porch, and will, without warning peer out and discover her, Victoria retreats towards the rear of the six-bedroom home. As she rounds the car garage, and comes upon a basement window, she looks inward. Seeing nothing, she now moves to the next window. Before she looks inward, she checks her rear, and also takes a good look around her surroundings. Satisfied that no one has discovered her, she continues onward. As she looks into this window, she sees a faint light, and distorted shadows moving about. Her curiosity heightens. Cautiously, she moves around the corner, and peeks into the very next window. Her view is the same as the last. Frustrated, she curses under her breath.

In the basement, the bearded man is completing the timer's adjustment. The crude sinister device sits snugly within the sheet metal housing of the home's heating and cooling system. Mister Smith, along with Alaa, stand watching the evil technician. Alaa suddenly broke his stance, and walks over to the nearest window. He opens it, now exposing only the window's screen.

Victoria practically jumps out of her skin when the sudden noise of the opening window jolts her. Her finger tightens on the trigger, as she aims her weapon towards the noise. She unconscientiously holds her breath, as she awaits a target. Alaa turns to Mister Smith, as he moves away from the window, and says, "To expedite the biological agent." He ended with a grin.

"That is good." The bearded man said.

Mister Smith looks to his watch, as the unseen Victoria peeks in from the window. Suddenly Mister Jones's voice broadcasts from a portable radio, "Exect One to Exect Base, . . . be advised we are about ten minutes out."

Mister Smith looks over to the bearded man and asks, "Present status?"

Now standing over the lethal apparatus like the proud creator he is, the bearded man looks to Mister Smith. He then depresses the single black button on a palm sized wireless remote transmitter. The red digital display now illuminates a 40 minute countdown.

"Operational."

Alaa now walks over to the bearded man, displaying a proud smile.

Like a national hero, the bearded man hands Alaa the remote. Beaming with pride he instructs, "To activate the fail-safe, . . . simply press the button once more."

Swooping through the screened window, feet first, Victoria lands on the cement basement floor on her feet in a squat, like an old scene from a 60's super hero T.V. show.

"Federal Agent, . . . get those hands up and freeze!!!" She announced with authority, as she pointed her gun at the stunned group.

Alaa stands shocked, not believing his eyes. The bearded man stands with his hands, looking as though he is trying to reach the ceiling. Mister Smith, is not showing any emotion. He remains cool with his hands at only chest level.

"Disarm yourselves now!!"

Protesting her presence, as he carries out her commands, Smith shouts, "It is *impossible* that you survived!"

"Shut up!!!"

Like rumbling thunder, rushing footsteps are now heard overhead. As she sees Mister Smith placing his pistol on the dusty rough floor, she watches him start to stand up straight. She now looks to her left, and sees the stairway. The now pounding footsteps have approached the top of the stairs. Victoria's heart and mind has now reached beyond their capable capacity. As the heavy footsteps begin to descend down the stairs, Victoria now knows it's decision time. She glances at her captives, in time to see Mister Smith's slowly spreading grin. The bearded man suddenly now begins to frantically yell, "Here, . . . here, . . . !!!" As he waves pointing towards the overwhelmed Agent. ". . . Here, here!!"

The mass of charging feet are now about midway down the stairs. Victoria stands, turns, and now faces the back side of the aged wooden stairs. She immediately fires, sweeping the stairs with .40 caliber hollow pointed bullets. Mister Smith quickly bends over and reaches for his pistol. Victoria sees his movement out of the corner of her eye. As he gathers the weapon in his hand, several bullets strike his body.

Alaa watches as Mister Smith's body is propelled rearward from the momentum of the projectiles. He now adjusts his vision to witness the bodies of the two Terrorists dressed as highway patrolmen, come to rest, entangled together at the foot of the stairs.

"Oh please, . . . mercy!!" The bearded man exclaims, as he drops to his knees with his hands pressed together.

Alaa looks to the begging man, and then over to the Agent. Victoria aims her weapon at them, while in a classic Weaver stance. Alaa grabs the man by the back of his collar. While forcing the man to his feet, the black fatigues wearing terrorist, disgustedly says, "To your feet!! We do not beg for life!! Our only reason for life is to serve and please Allah! Our mission is now complete, . . . !" He then looks to Victoria, and through clenched teeth adds, ". . . There is nothing that this American Scum can do, but die, . . . and be eaten by the hounds of hell."

The bearded man looks to Alaa with frightened eyes, and says, "I do not want to die, Alaa." He then looks to the Agent, and asks sincerely, "You F.B.I. yes, . . . then arrest me. I will cooperate. I throw myself on your mercy."

Becoming enraged Alaa pulls the man rearward against his bosom, and scrams at him, "You demon dog!!!"

"Shut up, and release him now!!" Victoria commanded.

Fearful, the bearded man pleas to Victoria, "Save me from this madman. I will disarm the device. I will reveal to you all you desire to know!"

Victoria looks to the device. Immediately she discerns that the bomb like device is beyond the ordinary. Nuclear has come to her mind. All the elements are present for that thing to be a small nuclear device.

"Curse your tongue!!"

Stepping slowly toward them, Victoria commands, "Release him at once!!" She said with her throat dry from fear.

Victoria is pointing her gun towards them, but the close proximity of the desperate man's body to Alaa's makes a shot too risky. She begins to advance on them, closing the distance. Victoria is prepared to deliver a pointblank slug to Alaa. As the Agent moves towards them, Alaa ferociously addresses the bearded man, "You knew this task was to deliver you to Allah's breast!" He begins.

Unseen by Victoria due to the bearded man's body blocking her view, Alaa withdraws a 6-inch twin edged scalpel sharp dagger from his waistband.

"You are a coward, . . . !!" He shouts as he prepares to knife the unsuspecting man," . . . Wicked, like the American disgorge you seek sanctuary from!!"

Alaa executes two hard deep thrusts into the man's back. From the bearded man's mouth, Victoria suddenly sees blood begin to emerge from the now gagging man. She immediately stops her advance, as she looks to the dying man in dismay.

Smiling, Alaa flings the dying man's body aside. The bearded man's body falls towards the floor. Alaa's strike has taken the Agent totally by surprise. Awed by the undetected stabbing, Victoria glances upon the bleeding man's body momentarily, and then looks back upon Alaa. The murderer stands with the bloody knife at his side. Aiming her pistol at him, she mournfully says, "My God."

"My actions here are sanctioned by Allah." Alaa said firmly.

Questioning his statement, Victoria starts, "Your God approves of terrorist acts?" She now continues with bitterness, "Your God approves of you to come to America, and attempt murder, and to commit murder?"

Unemotionally he answers, "Yes, . . . you Americans are a cancer that needs to be controlled. Your President even understands that." He now continues with conviction, "But if you people of America cannot be controlled, . . . then extermination is the only recourse."

Coldly, she comments, "Then, . . . your God is the devil."

"Curse your tongue, demon dog!!" He responds with fire. "The wrath of Allah shall be felt in your land, . . ." He said as he motions towards the two canisters, ". . . And there is nothing you can do to stop it!" He ended sharply.

As Victoria glances to acknowledge the device, Alaa speaks in an unaffected tone, "You have won, . . . nothing, . . . not even me."

As she looks back to him, she is in time to witness him plunge the bloody knife into his heart. She stands amazed, as his aorta immediately begins to spurt blood outward past the deeply inserted knife. She lowers her gun slowly, as she unconsciously takes a step from him.

With his eyes fixed on her's, Alaa staggers for a step and a half. He then falls to one knee, and then onto the other. His movements appear as if he's moving in slow motion. With his eyes still focused on her's, Victoria witnesses them begin to roll upward. His body begins to tilt forward, like a falling tree in a forest. As his dead body falls forward, his shoulder strikes a wooden support beam. It is in this position, supported by the load-bearing beam, Alaa's dead body comes to rest. Victoria pauses for a beat to gather her thoughts, as she looks upon Alaa. With blood now oozing from his mouth, and a puddle forming, and rapidly becoming a pond, Victoria is sure of his demise.

"Shit." She mumbles in amazement as she looks over the entire scene. The bodies at the bottom of the stairs, Mister Smith, Alaa, and finally the bearded man. Satisfied that no immediate threats are present, she now holsters her weapon. She now walks over and begins to examine the crude looking device, as the General's small convoy enters onto the property.

In the leading sedan are Mister Jones, and his trusted Aide. Also in the car, are two Agents that were on the plane with the General. Upon driving up to the house, Mister Jones immediately sees the Madison police van and the other vehicles. He snaps his head toward his Aide. His Aide also sees the vehicles, and looks to Jones. They both share the same thought without saying a word. A lump forms in the men's throats. Jones sees the concern in his Aide's eyes. He looks away from the man, as he worries about why they were still in the house. Jones begins to radio Smith, but has decided that it might tip off the two Agents in the back seat. He's decided to hang loose, and be prepared for anything.

Victoria looks the device over. What in the Hell, she thought to herself, as she looks over the primitive appearing thing. As she scanned the mysterious instrument, she quickly accused its properties. Suddenly, her ankle is seized. The death grip arresting her ankle startles her. She immediately looks down to her ankle. She sees the hand of the bearded man wrapped around the joint. She now looks to the bearded man, and sees that he is still alive, though just barely.

Weakly, he pleads, "Help me, . . . you must, . . . help me."

Instantly Victoria sees his wound is a fatal one, and he's on his way to meet Allah.

Squatting just above the floor, Victoria sternly says, "Tell me how to shut this damn thing off!!"

"Help me!"

Coldly she returns, "No, . . ."

His eyes widen in surprise.

". . . You help me first." She ends sharply.

He only has a few remaining breaths of life. He rolls his eyes from the Agent, and looks towards the device. He releases her ankle, and then points towards the bomb. Victoria deducts that his trembling index finger is aimed at the bomb. In a rush, with her voice indicating that she is on the verge of panic, she asks, "Yes, yes, . . . but now what?!!!"

He makes a stabbing motion with his index finger. The man's arm falls limp, and he becomes lifeless. In Arabic he says in his last seconds of life. "—"

"—" Victoria remarks in a desperate tone as she looks to the device with trepidation.

Outside, the General has stepped out of the limousine. The advance men, Mister Jones and his Aide, have exited their auto along with the two Secret Service Agents. An

Agent from the limousine has begun walking towards the house, as the others now begin to exit the limousine. The two Agents that rode with Mister Jones start walking towards the limo. They join with an Agent that is carrying a case the size of a businessman's briefcase, but this one is twice as thick.

Looking to his watch, Duke informs the General, "You can grab a couple of hours of decent shut eye before the parade."

"What time is the parade?" The General pondered.

"It kicks off at noon."

General Armstrong inhales a lung full of air, as he looks around at the hilly, green scenery. Armstrong refreshingly comments, "The hills haven't lost that fresh, clean aroma."

Mister Jones's Aide turns to Jones, and in a tone that is low and nervous, he asks, "So what do we do now?"

Watching the now housebound group, led by the General, Jones answers, "We just cool it for now."

"There's something very wrong here. I think we have been left out to dry. We've been fucked. They gonna kill us with that nigga' and collect our cut." The Aide ended in alarm.

The Agent that had approached the house first, is now in the hallway leading from the entranceway, by passing the large living room, and an upper level stairway. He continues along the hall towards the kitchen, and the rear of the house. He passes the open door, which leads down a flight of stairs to the basement.

As the Agent passes the door, a whiff of gun smoke is captured by his nose. The distinct odor of the pungent burnt gun smoke immediately stops the Agent in his tracks. He takes another sniff. He then turns to the basement door. His suspicions now rise. His sense of danger is now triggered by the circumstances. There is the gun smoke, and the lack of the police personal, but their vehicles parked outside.

The Agent looks onto the basement's stairway, as he reaches for his gun. It only takes a moment for the Agent's brain to confirm what his eyes are seeing. The crumbled bodies of what appears to be police officers, lying dead at the bottom of the stairs.

The General and the others, have just entered the house, when the Agent sounds the alarm into his communicator, “Condition Red!! Condition Red!!”

Within a blink of an eye, an Agent grabs the General, while he produces an Uzi submachine gun. Simultaneously, another Agent pushes Duke clear of the General, while whipping his Uzi from beneath his trench coat. The two Uzi toting Agents bring Armstrong over to a wall, opposite the entranceway, before anyone else had time to think. Startled by the sudden outburst, and being practically plowed over by the Agent, Duke shouts a protest, as he lies prone on the hardwood floor, landing this way as a result of the Agent’s push.

“Quiet!!” The third Agent with the case yells, as he trains his semi-automatic pistol on the front door.

Duke does so. From his worm eye view of the tense scene, he sees an also stunned General, closely flanked by the two heavily armed Agents. One has his weapon aimed at the stairway, and is also covering the hallway. The other has his weapon pointing outward, covering everything, and everyone. His orders are to kill *anyone*, approaching the General, while the ‘Condition Red’ is in effect.

Agent Owens is feverishly attempting to unlock the key to disconnect the timer, and/or the triggering device. She is busily tracing wires, as the Secret Service Agent begins his descent into the basement. Victoria has not concerned herself with the previous noise from above. She figured it was the General’s party arriving. The now sudden stillness, and the obviously descending Agent, caused paranoid thoughts to flood her logic.

Victoria stops her visual study of the device, and quickly pulls her pistol from its holster. She ejects the magazine into her hand. She sees it’s empty, and the realization that one round remains in the chamber, resigns her with the thought, that if any firefight begins, her participation will be quite stint.

She looks toward the stairway, and waits for the descender to appear. Victoria slowly returns the weapon to its holster. The Secret Service Agent, steps over the bodies, and comes into view. Victoria slowly rises, from the device, and now stands erect. The Agent immediately spots her. Victoria raises her hands chest high. The Agent goes into a combat stance. With his pistol pointing at her, he shouts, "Don't you move!! Don't even breath!!" The tense Agent advised.

Into his communicator, the ready to shoot Agent reports, "I have a contact."

In a calm, and gentle tone, Victoria speaks, "I'm Special Agent Victoria Owens of the Federal Bureau of Investigation, . . . Washington D.C."

The Agent looks upon Victoria with bewilderment. Victoria sees his facial expression transform into one of disbelief as he flatly returns, "And I'm suppose to take your word for that, huh?"

Sternly snapping, Victoria responds, "I suggest you get on the horn, and I.D. me, and then get yourselves some heavy duty back up here, right now!" She ended sharply. "My friend, there is an assassination plot in progress on the General."

The confrontating Agent, maintains his eyes and gun on the woman Agent, as he speaks into his mouthpiece, "Jake, you read, . . . it's a bloodbath down here. Tell Ray to get on the horn, and bring in some help. I have a woman contact here who claims to be F.B.I. Have Ray check on a Victoria Owens, . . . out of D.C."

Outside, and looking toward the house, Mister Jones, upon hearing the Agent's transmission via his radio earpiece, mumbles, "How can that be? How could that bitch be in there?"

Grabbing the stunned babbling man by the lapels, the Aide shouts, "Com'on, . . . it's over!!" He ended as he begins to pull Jones toward the car.

Ray, the Agent that carried the oversized case into the house, upon hearing the transmission, immediately opens the metal grip. The case houses a direct satellite uplink scrambled telephone, a video monitor, and keyboard. Jake, the Agent with the General, covering the stairway and the hall, shouts over to Ray, "Did you get all that?"

"Got it!"

As Jake communicates with the Agent in the basement, the other Agent with the Uzi informs, "Sir, we are at 'Condition Red'. There is an immediate, armed, hostile threat to you, . . . but it is now unclear of their location or strength. There is however a woman in the basement, claiming to be a Federal Agent."

Standing, General Armstrong sternly suggests, "I think we should go below, and determine what's what."

As he stands, the Uzi toting Agent voices, "Sir, that might be very unwise."

"I think we can whip a single woman."

Jake now stands, and adds with concern, "Sir, she could be apart of what the C.I.A. has warned us about concerning an assassination or kidnap plot."

"I didn't think they would have the balls to show up here." Duke said.

The General looks to the two Agents and firmly says, "Gentlemen, . . . perhaps I've been an American fighting man too long, but the idea of being terrorized on my own soil infuriates me." The man then turns and starts towards the basements door.

Jake quickly stands in front of the General, blocking his advancement. The Agent says, "Sir if you must, then I insist that you are injected with the B.E.A.S.T."

The General is puzzled by the Agent's statement. Jake

looks to Ray, and firmly says, "Ray, . . ." He then looks back to the General and continues, ". . . Prepare the B.E.A.S.T. for injection."

"Right, . . ." The Agent answers, ". . . All dispatches have been sent, . . ." He continues as he looks at the video screens, as he reaches into the case, ". . . The Crisis Desk, and the F.B.I. have acknowledged our request."

The General and Duke, who is now slowly beginning to rise from the floor, exchange a glance. Armstrong sees the dumbfounded expression on his Aides' face. Without any words needed to be exchanged, the General knows Duke does not know anything about the B.E.A.S.T.

"Just what in the Hell is this 'beast' thing that you want to inject in me?" Armstrong asked.

Ray walks up to the General while discarding the sterile wrapping from a simple injector. Jake gently says, "That's the 'beast'. In case this situation is the execution of the threatened kidnap plot the C.I.A. uncovered, and we cannot stop them from said action, then this device will be able to help Special Operations to track, and execute a rescue."

"You mean this 'beast' is like a homing device?"

Ray returns, "In a way, but this is much more flawless. The bio, electronic, allocation, satellite and transmitter are undetectable. We will know within 12 feet of where you are, . . . anywhere in the World. You see, . . . this is the next generation of tracking devices. This is definitely not like the ones infants are now being implanted with. This little baby can able an intelligence satellite to also *see* where you are. Like your environment. Not only will we know *where* you are but also how many cockroaches are in the room with you. Welcome to the 21st century."

"And just where are you going to put that thing?" The General asked with concern.

Motioning toward the area, Ray says, "The inside of your right upper arm."

The General starts to remove his garment, but Ray

immediately says, "No Sir, . . . that won't be necessary." He then moves in, and as he reaches for the General's upper right arm, he politely says, "If you'll allow me, . . ." The Agent begins as he raises the man's arm, gathers firmly a small amount of fleshy tissue, and clamps it between his fingers, ". . . You will feel just a slight pinch." He advises, as he brings the injector up to the captured piece of flesh.

The General looks to the simple design of the injector. The device looks like a skeleton of a small water pistol. A piece of plastic forms the handle, and a trigger. A small cylinder, about the size of a tube of lipstick, sits atop a stainless steel, straw like tube. Housed inside of the tube is the 'beast'. The 'beast' is about the size, and shape of a grain of rice.

Mister Jones, and his Aide have reached their sedan. Mister Jones now grabs his Aide and resigns, "Chester, . . . its no use. We've had it."

In a panic, Chester, . . . the Aide explodes, "Are you mad?!! We can still get away!!"

"No Chester, . . . there's nowhere to run." Jones said flatly.

"We can't just give up! Do you know what they will do to us? I can't deal with that!!" He now continues in a tone of desperation, "We can join their side." He said with a forced smile. "We have no choice." He reasoned.

"No one defects from the United States." Jones said unemotionally.

"We're outa here, . . . let's go!!"

Becoming excited Jones says, "Man, . . . *they* are going to kill us! We failed. They do not like that. They do not need us now. I'm stayin' right here!!"

With suspicion, Chester looks to his cohort, and sneers, "You ball-less bastard, . . . I leave you here, and your ass will start blabbing, and I'll be picked up or picked off before I can leave U.S. airspace."

"Ahhh fuck you!!" He snapped. "The ball game is over!!! I rather rot in jail in the U.S. then take one in the head by those crazy bastards over there!!!"

"I leave you here alive, . . . they'll kill me for doing so. That was the deal." He said coldly.

"Tough shit."

Now enraged, Chester screams, "You're killing me!!!!!"

Meanwhile, . . . in the basement, Victoria is still being held at gunpoint. The now transmitting General, and Jake come down the stairs. Armstrong pauses, as he begins to cross over the bodies of the fake uniformed officers. Armstrong now approaches the battle weary Owens. Along the way, he first looks upon the dead bodies of the Arab terrorist Alaa, Mister Smith, and the bearded man.

The no nonsense man, now stands halfway between Victoria, and the pistol covering Agent. He looks the hand raised woman over. She reminds him of battle. Her worn, scuffed, torn, blood splattered clothing, her dirty face and tired eyes. Victoria looks upon him and notices, that he seems much smaller than his larger than life reputation. The tales of General J.T. Armstrong, seemed to have been accomplished by a man 7 feet tall and made of iron. Victoria also notices that he is a handsome, and rugged man. Much more so than when she has seen him on T.V. even though he is just shy of 6 feet tall.

"Are you with the F.B.I." Armstrong asked sharply in a tone filled with authority.

"Yes Sir." She responded instantly, as trained by the U.S. Army.

Interjecting, the Agent with his pistol pointing at her states, "That is still yet to be confirmed."

Nodding in acknowledgment, Armstrong continues, "What happened here?"

Taking a deep breath, Victoria answers flatly, "In short, . . ."

She motions to the dead, ". . . They were or are apart of an assassination plot to kill you, Sir."

Just then a distant series of gunshots erupt. Jake immediately speaks into his communicator, "Talk to me Ray!!"

Looking out of the window with Duke at his side, Ray reports, as he watches Mister Jones lying on the ground dead, and Chester stumbling, trying to get into the sedan. The Aide then finally succumbs to his gunshot wounds and falls to the ground dead.

In disbelief, Jake repeats Ray's report aloud.

"And they were also apart of the plot." Victoria announced. "Those two over there with the uniforms, are undoubtedly fakes, or have turned for the money. I've been encountering them all night." She now points to Mister Smith, "He's C.I.A. and he's a representative of the Islamic Consolidation, . . ." She continues, as she now points to Alaa, ". . . that you pissed off."

As the Secret Servicemen listen to their earpieces, the one holding the gun on Victoria, lowers is suddenly. Armstrong notices the Agent's action. Directing his question to the Agent he asks, "Confirmation on the young lady?"

Flatly the Agent responds, "Yes Sir."

"Why aren't you in Atlanta?" Jake asked sternly.

Lightly Victoria responds, "A wreck out on the interstate last night, and then I ran out of gas, and the local law enforcement decided to keep me around for a few laughs."

Armstrong eyes now fall on the device. As he moves over to it, Victoria continues, "Tell your man on the horn that there is a farm about 3 or 4 clicks from here. They used it as a drop point last night. Someone might still be there waiting to 'e-vac' these guys outa here." She said in an authoritative tone.

The Agent looks to Jake. Jake nods to him, and then the Agent goes upstairs. Victoria has turned, and now sees the General examining the device. She goes over to him, as Jake slowly follows her.

"Sir, . . ." Victoria starts, ". . . May I suggest that you clear out. I have a nasty feeling that this thing might be some sort of bomb. Judging from all the fuss they've invested, . . . I won't be surprised if it's some sort of a mass destruction device."

Now looking to the bomb, Jake very worried asks, "A weapon of mass destruction? What, . . . like perhaps, nuclear?"

Victoria turns to him and says, "My money is banking on a biological agent." she begins to explain, as Armstrong begins to tinker with the bomb's wiring, ". . . , but either way, . . ." She stops, seeing the man tinkering. She immediately takes a hold of his hand, stopping him.

Instantly he looks up to her. An electrical current is now complete. As she, and he looked into each other eyes, it was as if a mutual detonation exploded within them. In the few seconds that her hand was in contact with his, and their eyes discloses immediate attraction. Victoria feels her celibate body begin to spark to life. She politely, but firmly says, "Sir, . . . you can cause a detonation."

Sharply the General responds, "Agent Owens have your eyes ever seen a device of this nature?!"

Defensively she replies, "I've been trained in the explosive field."

Like a razor, the General continues, "*Your* tampering would of induced an explosion *akin* to nuclear proportions."

"Akin?" She repeats in a questioning tone.

Becoming very firm, Jake says, "Alright that's it, . . . what ever this thing is I don't like it. No wonder the bastards haven't tried to take the house." He looks to the General and says, "Sir, I must insist that you 'e-vac' immediately."

"I'm not leaving. I can't leave." Armstrong begins and then looks away from the concerned Agent. "I've seen this thing before. It's a poor-man's nuclear weapon, but with biological fallout. These things were their failsafe devices. We came upon them in the desert, . . . thank God they did fail." He points to the metal canisters, "In here is some nasty, 100 percent fatal, state of the art germ warfare. Its airborne spread like a flu, and just as contagious. In short, . . . it causes your body's insides to turn into jelly. Death comes calling in less than 36 hours, . . . and that's the good news." He looks at the canisters and then grimly adds, "Yup, . . . I'm afraid there is enough here to wipeout most of the eastern seaboard."

"Jesus Christ." Jake mumbles

Armstrong turns towards him and says, "The only saving grace is that, it cannot survive long in the atmosphere. Within 12 hours it will dissipate." He then lowers his head, and continues sadly, "And now because of me, a few million lives are in jeopardy." He now becomes angry. "These bastards are too cowardly to bring their fight to me."

"Sir, . . ." Victoria gently begins, ". . . They said something about how their plan will not only remove you from the picture, but it will also cause a major change, within this country. Something referring to a New World Order." she reported the best she could from memory.

The General pauses in thought. Now the pieces fit into place. His assassination would ensure the trailing President's re-election. If the President is re-elected her deceitful, ominous, secretive plans of a liberty-less, 'Big Brother' America, will become a reality. If this plan of a biological terrorist attack is carried out, it will cause an outcry from the American people for Federal protection, . . . even if it means surrendering constitutional liberties. Then what? The President will have a country controlled by the government. No longer will the American people control it's government. All remaining liberties will be outlawed under a guised of security. Then what? Will she then hand the United States over to a foreign power, the New World Order, thus making Americans slaves beneath the thumbs of a World wide government, controlled by people who consider Americans devils?

For General Armstrong, the realization that his enemies are now here from abroad, and that they also might be native born Americans, has finally sunk in. It can now no longer be explained away, or ignored. Even if he is to survive this planned biological strike, his one nation under God theme, will be struck down by the fearful masses, and a hostile un-Godly media. It's all or nothing, and it comes down to this Hellish device before him.

In a low, strong tone, he says, "Jake, . . . get on the phone to the Defense Department. Let them know what's sitting here in my basement."

"Yes Sir." He returned, and started to walk off.

"Take the pretty lady with you, and then all of y'all clear outa here." He ended forcefully.

Surprised by his statement, Victoria and Jake look to one another, as Armstrong resumes examining the device.

"Sir, . . ." The S.S. man begins adamantly, ". . . The men upstairs, and I are United States Secret Service Agents, . . . and we do not abandon our duties."

Armstrong looks from the Agent to Victoria. She takes a deep breath, releases it, and then flatly says, "I'm just too damn tired to move."

The General now looks to them both with disgust, as Jake informs, "I'll go now and make the notifications to the Defense Department." As he departs, Victoria begins to pull the heavy vest from her sore, bruised body. She allows the worn vest to drop to the floor. She now squats down beside the man, at the device. The General looks to her with a frowned expression. As if to read his mind, she sternly responds to his expression, "No, . . . I'm not leaving, . . ." She then adds lightly but firmly, ". . . so forget it."

A pause of silence falls between them, as they look upon one another. The General softens his expression, and then says, "You look as though you've been through Hell."

Flatly she returns, "It's been a long night Sir."

"Drop the Sir, . . . my name is Jonathan. My friends call

me J.T. I would like for you to do the same, . . . Miss, . . ." He pauses for her to answer.

With a soft smile, she reveals, "Victoria, . . . Victoria Owens."

"I must say, Victoria, . . . you are the stuff which action hero's are made of. Taking on these men single handedly, . . . what are you, . . . an F.B.I. secret weapon?"

Dropping her slight smile, and pausing momentarily while reflecting, she says, "I had help. A local cop by the name of Davis." She ended sadly as her eyes began to fill with tears.

Gently the General asks, "Where is he now?"

"Dead." She now takes a swallow, and continues, "We had to split up in the woods outside of Miller's farm. He stayed behind to keep them off my ass, while I made it here to stop them." She now looks away from him and adds, "I'm going to have nightmares about this for quite sometime."

"Bravery and beauty. Not a combination I personally would look for in a commando." He ended while looking into her brown eyes.

Looking into his eyes, she feels a sense of security. Beyond his lean, mean fighting machine exterior, his eyes reveal a kind, gentleman. Suddenly she remembers. While watching his farewell ceremonies, his righteousness beams from him like a lighthouse beacon in a storm. It strikes you and then immediately warms your heart. The weeping by most in attendance is evident of his projection.

"Are you ready to do or die?" He asked.

"In for a penny, . . ." She began, ending the saying at that point.

Armstrong now visually studies the bomb. He sees the digital timer counting backwards atop of the crude weapon. From the timer, an 8 and a half inch piece of metal conduit, leads to an electrical junction box. Out of the other side of the box, is another short length of conduit, which leads to, and connects the two metal canisters. The same short piece of conduit connects to a larger third canister. The General's mind replays the scene of the discovering dozens of these lethal monsters in the desert, surrounding the Alliance's stronghold.

Seeing the distant 1000-yard stare upon his face, Victoria is prompted to ask, "You've seen these before?"

"This is a bio-chemical bomb. An experimental device, rumored to have been developed by the Lybians." He now looks to her and continues to explain, "We ran into a few of these things in the deserts." He looks back to the device and adds, "Depending on the size, . . . one of these things can kill all life, within an area the size of Texas." His eyes continue to study the bomb, "When the timer reaches zero, . . ."

Victoria looks to her watch.

". . . It'll complete the circuit, and cause the chemical and biological agents to mix, . . . thus causing the deadly reaction."

Victoria looks from her watch to the downward counting bomb, and announces, "I figure 18 minutes to detonation." She now looks to Armstrong, "I would feel a lot better if we shut this thing down now, and then discuss it's capabilities."

"So would I, but there might be a problem that might prevent us from doing just that." He said grimly.

Victoria looks to him with a braced expression, as she flatly says, "And what's that?"

"This thing might be booby trapped."

Starting to become unglued, Victoria sharply says, "So now what? The Explosive Ordinance Division is God knows, how far away." She quickly looks to her watch, and adds, "We don't have that much time left." She pauses for a beat, "What about an air strike?" She poses as an afterthought.

Armstrong shakes his head no, and says, "It would be a gamble, but the odds would not be in our favor."

"What in the Hell would we, or anybody else at that matter, have to lose? Doomsday is only a few minutes away."

"Victoria, . . ." The General firmly begins, ". . . Waiting

for the E.O.D. would not be wise at this time. Though they are damn good, I'm sure they have never seen a device such as this. Waiting for the E.O.D. will be nothing more than a waste of time, and lives, when this thing detonates." He stops as he looks upon her.

Her eyes are locked with his when suddenly it dawns on her. Perking up, she says, "General, . . . there aren't any booby traps."

The General's facial expression displays doubt. As if his expression was verbal, she answers him, "I figure they would of skipped the installation of booby traps. They never figured anyone would have foiled their plans."

"What about you and the officer giving them Hell all night?"

"I surprised the Hell outa them when I came through the window. I bet, . . . they were sure we would have been whacked in the woods. With your advance man in their pocket, . . . it was perfect." She ended with a smile.

The General thinks over her reasoning. In a moment he then nods in agreement.

"Then, . . . it's going to have to be you and I. With your training and my exposure, we can conquer this device."

Victoria looks away from the confident man to the bomb. She takes a silent pause, as she thinks about what the General has just said. She then looks to him, and swallows hard. She knows that the General's logic is correct. His idea is the only acceptable course of action.

"I guess it's show time then, . . . what do we do first?"

The General takes a few seconds before he responds. He continues to look the woman Agent in the eyes. He wants to make sure, she has what it takes to complete the assignment before them. Impressed with the guts that she has already displayed, and the valor that seems to be a second nature, he finally answers her. "We have to pry off that junction box."

Victoria grabs a small open tool bag and drags it over.

As the Presidential hopeful, and Special Agent began working on the mysterious weapon of mass destruction, the 'hot phone' at Joint Special Operations Command Headquarters, in North Carolina, erupts to life. Within minutes of receiving the relayed emergency call, the J.S.O.'s Commanding General activates Special Forces Detachment: Delta.

Thirty minutes later, two 12 man detachments, armed with everything from .50 caliber rifles, AK-74's, M-16A2 with .40mm grenade launchers, and M-24 Sniper Systems, containing laser aiming device, and thermal sight aids, board an all weather Chinook helicopter.

Flying in an air support role is an AC-130U Spector gunship, which is now turning onto the runway, with a green light for take off. The AC-130's 105mm Howitzer, and it's two lesser cannons can fire on ground targets, with sniper-like accuracy. Delta Forces E.T.A. from Pope Air Force Base to Madison is 45 minutes.

Ray is in constant contact with the U.S.S.S. Crisis Desk. He is now informed that Delta Force is airborne, and enroute. Armstrong and Owens have now exposed the spaghetti thin wires within the electrical junction box. This is the same type of bomb encountered in the Syrian Desert, he thought to himself. If it was defeated once, it can happen again.

Victoria looks to the mass of jumbled wires. In a panicked tone she reveals, "They're all the same. Same color, same thickness. How are we going to know which one to cut?!"

Armstrong reaches into the box with his fingers, and begins to lift and separate the wires. Victoria looks to her watch, and then back to the cool general. He sees the desperation in her eyes. He breaks the eye contact. He cannot answer her question. There is no way of telling, and there is just not enough time to disassemble the conduit.

Armstrong now swallows a lump in his throat the size of an eggplant. He begins to entertain that death is just . . . he peeks to the counter . . . .

05:37

"General if we cut the wrong wire, . . . we could cause a detonation."

Armstrong gently takes the unraveled wires, and spreads them apart from one another. Victoria stares at the three wires, which now look as large as cables. Armstrong remains silent, as he nurses the wires.

Detail leader Jake descends the basement stairs undetected by the duo. His sudden appearance in their presence startles them.

"Sir, . . . ?"

Not as jumpy as the woman Agent, Armstrong answers calmly.

"A Delta Force Unit is about 20 minutes out."

Immediately the General barks, "Turn those boys around. We don't have a handle on this thing yet!"

Victoria mumbles in almost a whisper, "They're going to be 15 minutes too late."

Armstrong looks to Jake, and bleakly says, "Listen Jake, . . ." As he stands he puts his large bear claw sized hand on his protector's shoulder, and continues, ". . . Get on the horn and alert those boys that this will be a hot 'LZ'. They're going to need their N.B.C. gear."

Jake stands up straight as he maintains eye contact with the careworn man. He glances over to Victoria. Her eyes meet his. He sees that her's are distressed, and her expression is uneasy. The veteran Secret Service man swallows hard, and robotically replies, "Will do General."

As he starts off, he then immediately stops and faces the duo. In a fearful, stiff tone, Jake asks, "If this thing goes, will we go quick, or, . . . ?"

The General begins to slowly shake his head no. Armstrong's action causes the inquiring Agent to stop talking. The General softly but bluntly adds, "And it's not going to be pretty."

With that the Agent turns and rushes off.

"You know, . . ." Victoria starts gently, ". . . It's times like this I wish I could undo the things . . ."

Abruptly Armstrong interrupts her and snaps at her, "Victoria, this is not the time to hold your eulogy!"

Victoria looks at him surprised by his outburst, as he continues, "It won't be up to Delta Force, or the E.O.D. There is no time to wait and hope. The question before us is, . . . do we sit her, and cry in defeat, allowing this thing to spit it's poison, and kill millions!"

Fueled by fear, she snaps back at him, "Either way General, . . . they win!"

With his voice sounding like thunder, he replies, "Bullshit!!" As he wraps a finger around the white thin bell wire furthest from him, he continues, "We have at least a one in three chance!"

Victoria's eyes are locked on the man's thick index finger hooked around the wire. She then firmly yet gently grasps the General's forearm with both of her hands. She looks from the device, to the candidate.

Her eyes meet his, as he says in a gentler, but potent tone, "I'm sorry that you had to be here."

Softly she responds, "I guess it was meant to be."

She smiles softly. Her sudden emotion dazzles Armstrong, as well as it did herself. Fear no longer engulfs her, as she says, "I know all that I endured last night was not meant for us to die, here and now."

She now looks to where his finger rests upon the wire.

"Pull it, Jonathon." She said in almost a whisper.

Her soft words soothe his soul. Without any hesitation, the General plucks the wire, thus breaking it's connection. Victoria instantly looks to the clock.

23:03

She pauses breathless, as she watches to make sure the countdown has stopped.

Filled with excitement, she shouts, "I think that was it!!" She displays a big smile, and hugs him while she says, "Good choice General."

Suddenly a clap of plastic dropping onto cement, sounds out. The Agent, and the General immediately direct their attention to the direction on the noise. They are just in time to see Alaa's body dislodge from the beam, and finally crash upon the cool floor.

"Sore loser." Armstrong smirks.

His eyes now lock onto the unidentified black, palm-sized object, as Victoria chuckles in relief. As the General approaches the fallen object, Victoria happens to glance at the digital display.

01:00

She blinks her eyes in disbelief, and focuses her eyes upon the readout once again.

00:94

Her blood instantly turns to ice water, as sheer terror hits her with the crippling effect of a shotgun.

"My dear God."

Armstrong felt the emotion from her voice strike him like a bolt of lightening. He seemed to have taken only one step to reach her.

"What happened?" He voiced with desperation.

"I don't know, . . ." She begins frantically, ". . . But it will be all over in a little more than a minute!" She ended, as she just notices the transmitter, "The bastard struck from the grave. The fall probably activated a back up system. In case their plan was uncovered at the last minute, they would have a fail safe, . . . even if it meant for them to go down with the ship."

The General positions the remote in order to press the button again. Moving quicker than an eye can see, Victoria arrests the hand with the index finger ready to strike.

"Wait, Jonathan, . . . one button." She said as she looked upon the remote. "This is set up to push once to arm, and again to activate the secondary system, period." She ended sharply.

She looks to the timer.

00:37

"But, . . . if we can stop the countdown, . . ." She looks to him, ". . . It will never know when it's suppose to blow."

Victoria becomes frantic, as she looks over the sealed device for a button, switch, or anything.

The General looks upon the countdown.

00:27

As Victoria continues her frantic search, and now has begun to try and detach the conduit from the timer, the countdown rapidly continues to approach zero. The General's attention is suddenly distracted. His eyes fall upon the man with the dagger sticking out of his chest.

Calmly Armstrong stands, and begins moving towards the dead man. Victoria stops and watches him. In one smooth swift movement, the General snatches the knife from the man's chest, and with a war cry, plunges the knife downward. The adrenaline induced strike forced the double edge bloody blade to penetrate the timer's display, and travel ¾ of its length, thus impaling the timer. Both sets of eyes are upon the timer. The blood which remained upon the blade now gives the inanimate object, the effect of a bleeding wound. Victoria freezes, as she watches the counter. Her eyes are locked on the 0000 display. Armstrong mumbles prayer, as he watches. His chest slightly heaves, as his adrenaline levels begin returning to normal.

Seconds of silence pass. The countdown displays holds at 0000.

"Don't tell me that this thing was a dud." Victoria said with a shortness of breath.

"No baby, . . . I doubt it." As he looks down upon the readout, "This was a case of Divine Intervention."

Victoria sighs with relief.

"Amen."

The General now squats down besides the sleeping mass destruction device. "They could have a couple of these things across the U.S."

Victoria places her hand tenderly upon his shoulder and says, "No, . . ."

As she shakes her head, he looks up to her. She then continues, ". . . From the discussion I had with him, . . ." She motions towards the dead Mister Smith, ". . . This one was the only one they needed to overthrow the U.S. government, and all the liberties we citizen's enjoy."

His expression now transforms into one of bewilderment. Victoria smiles warmly and continues, "He mentioned a New World Order. Your death, resulting from a terrorist attack would have generated a change in the way the government does business." Armstrong gives an approving grin. He now stands. He and Victoria are only inches from one another, when he says, "And that change would bring a military dictatorship within a year. Oh yes, . . . that's the direction they want to take the U.S. in. Our liberty, finances, and laws brought about by foreign powers."

"And their laws will be enforced in this country by their troops on our soil." She looks to the device, and then to the dead men. Her eyes finally return to Armstrong's. "If you win General, . . . could you change things?" She begins compassionately, "I mean, . . . there's so many of them. Will we, . . . as a nation, survive? Will you as a man?"

Moved by her true sincerity, he pauses for a moment in thought.

"Whatever the Almighty wills, . . . it will be done. All I can do, is hope and pray."

Victoria feels as if her body has just turned into one giant goose pimple, as she is engulfed in a warm wave that seems to lift her six feet off the ground.

They continue to look upon one another as millions of thoughts and desires circulate throughout their minds. Then suddenly Victoria's eyes drop from his sight. As if a storm cloud consumed the sun, she painfully says, "I've got to get outa her." With distress in her eyes, she looks to the General and adds, "I don't feel too good."

Her back feels as if a mule wearing a red 'S' and a cape, kicked her. The effects from the bullets fired from Captain Preston, and Mister Jones outside of Miller's farm is causing her increased discomfort. Now also her cramps, which have been plaguing her since the beginning of this ordeal, seemed to have just multiplied to the point she has never experienced before.

The adrenaline high that she has been on all night, has left her. All the pain she had experienced earlier, but did not feel has now suddenly attacked her with fury. She looks to the inactive bio-chem bomb, as she turns to exit the cool damp basement. Armstrong watches her, as she walks slowly past the dead. Victoria's last look at the conspirators is done in silence.

As she slowly climbs the bullet hole riddled wooden stairs, Armstrong glances over and looks at the device. He then swings his head and eyes over to Alaa. The General steps over to the very dead man. As he stands over Alaa, he looks over to Mister Smith's body. The stone-faced man slowly begins to shake his head. "Nice try guys." He said softly.

As Victoria reaches the top of the stairs, a simultaneous roar, and a house shaking rumble, suddenly explodes through the stillness. Duke, Jake, and his Uzi toting partner, are looking upward through the windows. Victoria emerges from the stairway and exclaims, “My God!!”

Ray, with the cell phone pressed to his ear, turns to her and responds calmly to the shocked Agent, “F-16’s out of Pope.”

“What?!” She returned confused, and suffering from the loud, low flying warbird’s engines, still rumbling in her ears.

General Armstrong now appears behind the Agent, as Jake turns and faces them. Ray adds, “Delta Force is very close behind.”

Victoria turns to the General and says, “I have to go back up into the woods.”

From the look in her eyes, he knows exactly why she wants to.

“The Officer?”

Victoria nods her head yes.

“Officer?” Jake questioned.

Armstrong explains to the Secret Service Agent, “A Madison Police Officer. They were a team. He laid down cover fire, as she made her way here.”

Jake looks to Victoria and asks, “Where is he??”

“Somewhere between here, and Miller’s Farm. I know exactly where.” She responded sadly as she looked away from the Agent.

Jake looks to the General. Armstrong slowly shakes his in return. Jake now understands that there isn’t a need to rush to the Officer’s position. He takes a breath, and then offers, “Sir, . . . I suggest we wait until Delta is on the ground, and briefed of the current situation before we or anyone else leaves the premises.”

Firmly Victoria says, “I have to get him down off that hill.”

Jake responds, "We will Agent Owens, we will."

Suddenly her knees buckle. As she begins to collapse, General Armstrong catches her. The sudden weakness catches the tired Agent by complete surprise. Armstrong sees the distress in her eyes.

"Com'on." He gently says as he gathers her into his arms, and walks her over to a cloth covered sofa in the living room. Duke rushes over to assist the couple.

"I'll get her a glass of water." He said after he took a quick look at the woman.

Now in the distance, the heavy thumping of helicopter blades, come into earshot. Victoria sits on the sofa with her head rearward, and her eyes closed. Armstrong watches over her, as she speaks.

"I, . . . I got so dizzy, and weak."

"You're coming down off your adrenaline high. It's all starting to catch up to you." The General said gently.

Jake and Duke join the couple at the sofa. As Duke sits next to her, he places the cool glass of water in her hand. Jake softly addresses Armstrong, "How did you two make out downstairs?"

All heads in the house are now looking at the General. Unknowing to one another, they all were holding their breath to hear the General's answer. Armstrong looks the worried Agent in his eyes, and says, "Jake, . . . you are going to live to see another day." He then broke out in a smile.

There are sighs of relief and even a few chuckles of nervous laughter. Victoria is smiling at Duke as she begins, "Thank you." Now referring to the glass of water. "I don't think I have the strength to lift this." She adds lightly.

With sincerity Duke responds, "Miss, . . . you're just plumb tired." As he departs her, so does Jake, and the General starts in a sincere, caring tone, "As soon as everything settles down, we are going to get you to a hospital. I mean so you can be checked out."

"Don't worry, I'll live. I just need a hot bath, and some

sleep." She pauses momentarily in thought. Her expression becomes solemn, "But before I do that, I want to get Davis off that hill."

"Where you two close?"

"Not even buddies, . . . but he trusted me. Why, . . . I don't know, but by him doing so saved my life, . . . and yours too." She pauses and then continues, as she moves closer to him. In a direct tone she says, "General, . . . you better know who your friends are. Your enemies are numerous."

General Armstrong looks away from her in thought, as she continues to look upon him. Both of their minds filled with many continuous thoughts. This attempt on his life has brought a stalk of reality to the candidate. He has heard of the threats of what could happen to a blackman, if he got too close to sitting in the chair in the Oval Office. Armstrong was expecting a problem from the small-minded bigots, Americas has produced. He expected the hate mail, threats, and even an attempt by a brainwashed Neo-Nazis, . . . but this, ...

He smiles at the thought. The thought that he must be closer than he thinks, for unknown forces to plot and attempt to kill him, makes him feel euphoric. Do or die, he says to himself. He then looks upon the quiet, tired, cramping but still attractive F.B.I. Agent. Victoria is wondering if he is going to live long enough for the voters to make a choice in November. Then the voice in the back of her head reminds her of all that she has endured to ensure his survival of this attempt. No, she reasons with herself, it wasn't for naught. Now the thought that she may very well be sitting beside the next President of the United States, cause a chill to race through her body. She smiles, as goose-bumps, explode all over her body. Though she is in pain, fatigued, and only has the strength of a new born kitten, her mind now wonders what he is like. Not the candidate, but the man. Despite all she has encountered, and her present condition, she is still after all, a woman.

Minutes later, the Delta Force arrived, and secured the area. Medics attached to the Delta's detachment, examined Agent Owens. They had diagnosed her with exhaustion, and dehydration. Though she insisted on joining the recon team that was sent to search the woods, she was instead sedated. A temporary I.V. with Ringers, and D-5-W was applied. She will now sleep for the next 19 hours.

The biological warfare device is removed from the General's residence, and escorted by armed guards to Fort Detrick, Maryland.

Chapter Six

SUNDAY 12:04 P.M.

A well-rested Victoria is now standing in the back lot of the Madison police station. She shields her eyes from the bright sunlight with a dark pair of glasses. Covering her slightly sore body is a stone colored long cardigan, with a short sleeve top, and a pair of black stirrup pants.

She stands patiently, as a road serviceman completes filling her car with gas.

"Try it now, Miss, . . ." The man begins, ". . . Let's see if she'll catch."

Victoria hops inside of the car, and starts it.

"Ooo-wee, . . . !" The man said as Victoria exits the idling 400Z, that's purring like a saber tooth tiger. "Ifin' my great grand pappy had one of these here, he wouldn't never gottin' nabbed runnin' shine!"

Victoria smiles as the admiring man hands her his clipboard. As Victoria signs, the man looks to her car, grinning at it lustfully. When she finishes, Victoria gives him back his clipboard. The man takes the battered clipboard, and tears off her receipt. Taking her copy, Victoria gives the man a sincere thank you.

"Take it easy, Miss." He said as he walks off.

Victoria gets back into her car. Just as she closes the door behind her, the cellular phone rings. Pausing momentarily in wonderment, as the second ring now sounds. She picks up the communicator.

"Yes?"

"One moment for Assistant Director Skinnermen." A polite feminine voice gently announced.

Victoria's eyes widened with surprise at the announcement. Before she could draw any thoughts, the authoritative, but smooth voice of the F.B.I.'s number two man begins, "Special Agent Owens, . . . Assistant Director Skinnermen."

"Yes Sir." Victoria replied.

"I want to voice to you a job well done."

"Thank you Sir."

"Positive words of your performance has reached the ears of the Director's as well as my own. Now listen to me Agent Owens, you are now hereby given a change of orders. You are to immediately start your two-week leave. Once that has been completed, you are to report to my office, . . . understand, Agent Owens?"

Surprised, and slightly disappointed, she returns, "Completely Sir."

"Very well. Again, . . . you've done one Hell of a job. You have represented the F.B.I. with Fidelity, Bravery, and Integrity. Enjoy your leave."

"Thank you Sir."

The call from Washington terminated. As Victoria hung up the phone, she beams with pride. Though slightly disappointed about the Atlanta trip, that emotion rapidly began to fade, as the personal 'at-a-boy' from the Assistant Director of the Federal Bureau of Investigation sunk in. As she settles back into the car seat, the General stands at her door.

Startled by his seemingly sudden appearance, Victoria jumps, and grabs the center of her chest.

"Easy, I'm one of the good guys." The General said with a smile.

Returning a smile, Victoria surrenders, "I guess I'm still a little jumpy."

Dropping his smile, and in a gentle tone he asks, "Were you going to leave town without saying goodbye?"

Slightly blushing, and about to melt like butter left out in the summer sun, Victoria answers, shyly, "I, . . . I called the house. They said you had gone to church. It was getting late, and I had to start getting on the road, . . . but, . . ." She continues, as she motions towards the cell phone, ". . . I have just received new orders."

"Which are?"

"Well, . . . Atlanta is aborted, . . . I've been put on leave as of now. The Assistant Director just phoned me, himself."

Flatly Armstrong asks, "So, what are your plans now?"

"I plan to take this black beauty for a two week ride." She said looking away from him.

Not taking his eyes off of her, he responds, "Sounds like you are looking for something."

Victoria turns to him, and answers, "Just some peace. I need a break from things."

"Ever thought about fishing. It works for me."

"What I know about fishing, could fit on the head of a pin."

Motioning towards the not too distant mountains, he begins, "There's a stream up there in those hills. It's peaceful, isolated, and some mighty good eatin' come from its crystal clear waters." He ended with a smile.

Exploding in an uncontrollable smile, Victoria says, "I love fish."

"I bet you have never had anything like what comes from out of that stream."

"I'm a city girl, General. That's quite possible."

"Well we all can't be perfect." He smiles, and then adds, "I'm going up there tomorrow morning, . . . why don't you come along. I would be honored."

Victoria pauses as she looks away from him like a shy little schoolgirl. The little voice in the back of her head shouts for her to accept. You haven't been wrong all night she reasoned with the voice. She faces the General and says, "I would really like that." She then displayed a smile.

The General returns a bright smile, and offers, "What would you say to lunch, as we discuss the details about tomorrow?"

"Sounds good." She returned cheerfully.

Armstrong opens her car door, and as Victoria reaches to switch the car off, the cellular phone rings. She answers, and a very familiar voice begins, "Yee-ha!!, . . . you go girl!!" Michael Peterson's intoxicated voice explodes from the receiver.

Victoria snatches the telephone from her ear as he begins his loud comment.

"I heard in detail, about your little adventure. Fuck Rambo!" He said proudly.

Victoria motions to Armstrong, indicating a moment. The understanding General nods in acknowledgment, and moves away from the door.

"Michael, there was, and will never be any media coverage about this, . . . how did you find out about it?"

"Com'on Vicky, you know the Bureau has it's own information network."

"Oh yeah, . . . the gossip hotline." She comments defeatedly.

With concern he asks, "Hey Babe, . . . you alright?"

"Yes, I'm still in one piece."

"I hear the shit was pretty deep, and you pulled it off. Hell, I wish I was there wit' cha, sounds as if it would have been my kind of party."

"Mikie, . . ." She started solemnly, as she was about to tell him about the brave young Madison Officer Davis, ". . . I'll fill you in when we get back to Washington."

"To Hell wit' Washington!" He fires at her. "I heard Skinnermen gave you your two weeks commencing now, . . . so get down here. Forget driving around the country like some damn nomad."

Victoria looks towards the General, who is standing out of earshot, with his back to her.

"Ahh, . . ." She starts as she thought. ". . . My wondering tour of the U.S. is nixed for now."

"Good, when can we expect you?"

"I'll give you a call if I do head your way."

"If, . . ." He shouts back, "What are you talkin' 'bout Victoria? What are you gonna do? What are you up to?" He ended in a harmless frenzy.

She smiles at her partner's thirst for information. The woman Agent then answers smoothly, "I'm going fishing, kisses."

As she moves the phone from her ear, she can hear his rapid firing questions. She hangs up the telephone, as she switches the idling muscle car off, and then she steps out. She looks to her rear, out of the lot towards the street entrance. Two black full sized Chevy Suburbans sit idling. One loaded with Secret Service types. The other is empty. Victoria notices men and women standing about. Two Agents stand in the driveway, halfway between Victoria and the street. Their unyielding stare gives Victoria the feeling of being a small creature being stalked by meat eaters. Presidential candidate Armstrong approaches her. His approach catches her attention. She faces him, "I see they have beefed up your security."

They now stand face to face.

"Yes, they did." He returned as he looked out towards the street.

Sharply Victoria says, "You know, . . . I hope you fail."

The General looks to her. Though he is surprised by the Agent's abrupt statement, he remains steadfast.

"And why is that?"

Continuing in the same tone, Victoria answers, "It just seems, . . . that every time a man stands to lead the people, whether he's J.F.K., Martin Luther King Jr., or Gandhi, . . . he ends up murdered." She takes a breath, and compassionately adds, "Just look how close they came to do the same to you. Look how much they are willing to sacrifice, in order to kill you. They would of murdered hundreds of thousands, perhaps millions."

"Listen to me, . . ." The General began sincerely, as he looked the concerned Agent in the eyes, ". . . I came into this Presidential Candidacy with a lot of baggage. Yes, . . . there are factions within the United States, that don't want to see me as President. There are those overseas Fundamentalists, that don't want to see me as the President either. I have pledged an allegiance to the United States, and not to the United Nations. Yes, . . . I have made some enemies, . . . even some, that I would have never suspected." He stopped in a downcast tone.

Armstrong takes in a lung full of fresh, Carolina air, and continues to explain.

"You see, . . . what happened here in Madison, . . . and what you risked your life for, involved much more than a plot to prevent a blackman from becoming President. It was also much more than a 100 million dollar bounty on my head." He now pauses momentarily for Victoria to absorb the information. "You see, . . . all this was about fear. A level of fear that no homebound American has ever experienced, Terrorism." He said with the effect of a knock out punch.

"Our entire way of life would of changed, if these people were successful. In a months time, a vast majority of the liberties, we Americans enjoy right now, would have been outlawed. As sure as the Almighty, this nation would have no longer been a government for the people, by the people. The United Nations would TOTALLY control our military, and our people. The Office of the President, would surely be forced to take orders from others than congress." He now continues with a determined voice, as he speaks with a strong heartfelt conviction, "No Victoria, no, . . . not in my lifetime. If it cost me my life to prevent such a 'New World Order', then very well. I'm too much of a God fearing, country loving patriot, to live in America that is FORCED to pledge allegiances to the U.N."

Sincerely Victoria says to him, "I'm so afraid for you."

"Don't be." He now smiles slightly, and continues, "Some things are not in our control. The time for me to become President of these United States has arrived. Yes, . . . my fate may be the same as those I follow, but my trust is with God, . . . and professionals like yourself."

From her heart, she reveals her honesty, as she softly says to him, "I want to be there for you, but I don't have a red 'S' on my chest."

He chuckles a little at her comment, and then says, "No, you don't need that. You possess something much more powerful that that."

They both share an admiring look at one another, as they stand facing each other in silence. Then gently he asks, "Do you understand where I'm coming from now?"

"Yes, I do." She returned in a whisper.

"This is OUR country too. We earned that by the blood we've shed on the battlefields. This is also OUR home. We earned that claim by the sweat of OUR forefather's brow, during its construction. I intend to lead it and the people on a road to recovery. Back to the days of when America was one Nation under God, indivisible, . . . with liberty, and justice for all. I will not let this country down, . . . and I will not let YOU down."

With tears of compassion forming in her eyes, Victoria says, "You have to be very careful."

He feels her heart sent advice. He takes her by the hand, and raises it up to his mouth, kissing it tenderly. As he embraces her hand with his thick, manly hands, he says, "I stand within the hands of God. He IS in control of my destiny, . . . NOT my enemies."

With that said, they both begin to smile brightly at one another. Their smiles soon give way to chuckles, which transforms into spirit filled laughter. As Armstrong leads her toward the street, he puts his arm round her shoulders, while she simultaneously slings her arm across his waist. Fear no longer shadows the woman Agent. As she continues to laugh with the General she can feel the bondage departing from her.

'But thou, oh Lord, shall laugh at them. Thou shall have all the Heathens in derision.'

The forces of darkness were delivered a major setback by the unknowing hands of a single F.B.I. Agent. The sole actions of Victoria Owens have without a doubt, changed history.

For the time being.

Chapter Seven

A lot of the World's affairs grinded to an almost complete halt, as the scientific community spoke before the U.N. concerning an unparalleled gravitational pull upon the Earth. It is agreed that on the 27 of December 2012, a large heavenly body will pass the Earth. This passing which they insist is just a passing and in no uncertain terms will strike the Earth.

The passing planet sized satellite is many times the size of Earth and is the cause for the Sun's violent discharges which in turn has caused the non-traditional weather as well as planetary upheavals. The Worldwide debates have been raging for weeks, about the gravitational effects on the Earth.

Without question, there will be some global flooding, but some experts are projecting massive Earth changes. Island nations might disappear beneath roaring seas. Entire continents could shift, or break apart. Worldwide earthquakes, volcanic eruptions, even polar ice caps melting, all could result during this unimaginable chaos.

Meanwhile, the American media is down playing all reference connected to the event. Late night talk show hosts joke feverishly about October 5th being doomsday, while others begin to gather in prayer.

MAY 4TH 2012 A.D.

For weeks now, the World has been experiencing unusually potent storms. The United States is currently experiencing strong winds, and rising coastal waters. Manhattan's subway lines, are all shut down due to flooding, as well as the island's coastal roadways. Flood waters in the low-lying regions of the Mid-West, have just about divided the U.S. in two. London has taken on the appearance of Venice. Yesterday, four major quakes were reported in Russia, South America, China, as well as in Mississippi. All resulting over 6.5.

Madison, North Carolina is presently engulfed in a rainstorm with winds approaching 60 miles an hour. The property around Armstrong's home, is scattered with motor homes, and doublewide trailers, in use by the members of the United States Secret Service. To aid the protectors, a satellite uplink provides them with a bird's eye view of the entire property. Electronic sensors guard the perimeter, along with subterranean sensors to detect human footsteps. To complete the security package, a team consisting of a heavily armed man and a strictly trained dog patrol the property on foot. Their movements are monitored by the low orbiting satellite. The eye in the sky can also monitor all air traffic in a 350-mile radius. This ability allows for missile warning, or any other air threat.

Day, night, all weather radar is used for ground contacts. Agents are armed with small arms, as well as ground to air Stinger Missiles. Armstrong's motorcade is traditional, consisting of armored limousines, but it also includes two Raptor Gunships. These vehicles make this motorcade quite unique. The Raptures are cosmetically a typical full sized

Suburban, outfitted with a 500 horse powered full-blown 454, supercharged V-8. The Rapture is manned by a two-man crew, a driver and a gunner. The vehicles are equipped with radios, G.P.S. guidance, ammunition and a six barrel 7.65 caliber mini gun. The Raptor's primary mission is to provide the motorcade with effective and decisive firepower, and if necessary, Armstrong's escape vehicle from an overwhelming armed confrontation. The Raptors were a gift from a Saudi Prince for saving his oil rich nation.

Except for those who are on patrol with their four legged partners, and the personnel manning the various monitors, just about everyone else are huddled around TV's. Several channels are broadcasting live coverage of up to the minute analysis of the current weather effects all around the World.

Experts from all nations agree that the weather will calm down, but expressed real concern about what lies ahead, after the passage of the dark star. The Russians firmly state that the passage can cause the Earth to flip over, shifting its axis. Others voice a concern of the Earth being pulled out of its orbit. The United Nations insist on no such major events. They claim only massive flooding and a slight increase in earthquakes and perhaps even some volcanic eruptions. They conclude that there will be a Worldwide death toll of no more than 200 thousand. The prophecy community blasts the scientific and charges it with lies and deception. They base their findings with two articles of proof. One, something that dwarfs Jupiter is going to speed by the Earth. It is there. It can be seen, and no longer denied. Second, ancient writings of the Sumerians, the prophecies of the Holy Bible, to the Hope Indians and others who have been given sight beyond sight all agree . . . this passing will hark the end of the beginning.

Special Agent Victoria Owens and J.T. Armstrong are the only other people not watching the events unfolding on the T.V. They are alone in Armstrong's upstairs study. The study is actually in the sturdy home's attic. Some time ago, the General had it converted into a library study. It is here, that he enjoys some quiet time.

The rain outside falls with the force of stones. Armstrong stares into the rain splattered window, only to look out into the late afternoon's darkness, while Victoria busies herself looking over the bookcases lining the study's walls. Only the sound of rain is present, as the rain continues to beat on the solid house.

Victoria continues admiring in silence the written knowledge collected in the room. As she turns towards the silent man, and in an upbeat tone asks, "When do you ever have the time to read all of this?"

Seeing that her sudden outburst interrupted his deep thoughts, Victoria humbly apologizes.

"No, forgive me, . . ." Armstrong replied sincerely.

He now motions for her to sit in the chair in front of the large wooden desk, in which he sits behind. As she approaches, he says, "I guess I zoned out on you, huh?"

As she sits, she smiles nervously, and answers, "The rain can be hypnotic."

Armstrong's tone instantly changes to one of concern as he looks back towards the window.

"Have you ever seen rain like this?"

Immediately she answers, "Yes Sir, . . . Korea."

Armstrong sits back in his chair as a arm smile begins to display itself. Victoria assumes she caused the former Army General to reminisce fond thoughts of his times on the troubled peninsula.

"That's right, . . . you too, did some time over there. Yeah, . . . the rainy season is much like this, . . ." He started lightly, ". . . But its been raining like this for most of the last couple of weeks." He looks to the Agent and adds grimly, "This is North Carolina, and not Korea. You are going to have to swim back to D.C. I'm afraid."

"You might be right. The Weather Channel is reporting no breaks in the storm pattern until maybe next week."

"Then stay."

"I can't General, . . . my 'leave' is up in three days."

"So."

"I have orders to report. I do have a job, remember?" She said smartly with a smile.

"Then take a leave of absence." He responded firmly looking directly into her eyes.

The impact of his statement caught Victoria completely unprepared. As she pauses momentarily to recover, Armstrong adds, "Come work for me. I would like for you to be my Security Liaison."

He now pauses briefly to view her reaction. Victoria's pose of surprise, hasn't altered. Her blank expression, and non-blinking eyes, at first appeared to Armstrong that she was comatose. Foresight permits his continuance.

"I would like for you to oversee all of my security arrangements."

Gently Victoria interjects, "General, ..."

"The job pays very well." He interrupted, "Very well." He ended with an alluring tone.

Victoria wasn't comatose. She has absorbed every word, and sensed his sincerity. She has enjoyed her two weeks in his company. The idea to return to the Bureau excites her, but she questions if it is excitement or simply habit.

She wonders now, if her desire to remain with Armstrong is more than an exciting, challenging, occupational calling. These past couple of weeks she has gotten to know the larger than life legend. She has been able to interact with the man. Not the Candidate, or the national hero, and she has discovered that she has grown very fond of the man.

Mendacious, she weakly announces, "Sir, . . . I cannot do that."

She looks away from him, unconscientiously to hide her dishonesty.

Sternly he replies, "There's not a damn thing for you back there."

She looks to him, jumbled by his statement. Now, eye-to-eye Armstrong continues, "I cashed in a favor, and I had your 'jacket' pulled. You have smarts, guts, and most important, . . . I trust you. Hell, . . . I knew you coulda high tailed it outa Madison as soon as you were clear, . . . but you stayed." His tone now changes to a softer one, as he continues, "Bottom line, Victoria, . . . I need you to watch my back. The alliances that have formed to take me out concern me. I had no idea then, nor do I now know, how intricate the corroborators are. I don't know who I can trust anymore, . . . so I have to start all over again, and your name is number one on a very short list."

Victoria leans forward on her chair. Armstrong sees the intense thoughts, as her facial expression tightens, and displays dour. Frustration engulfs Victoria's soul. An emotional civil war has peeked within her. Her logic is insisting on the return to Washington, D.C. while her desire is to remain with the General.

Rage now surmounts her frustration. She stands, folding her arms, and begins to pace before Armstrong's desk.

"Victoria?" The General calls out tenderly.

Instantly she stops and faces the seated gentleman. His voice is the spark that detonates her volatile mood.

"Why must you be so stubborn?!" She asked sharply.

Dumbfounded, the General sits forward, and says, "Pardon me?"

Victoria commences pacing, as she speaks, "I don't really see why you still want to become President, when so many out there don't want you to be. You have a good life now. You're not out there ducking bullets and sucking sand. You're retired. Publishers are giving you millions for your life story, and millions more for your victory story in the Middle East. You can go anywhere, and enjoy what you have missed in your life, . . . but noooooo, . . . you want to be President."

She stops pacing, and faces Armstrong. She places her hands about shoulder width apart, on his aged, solid oak desk. She lowers herself, as she leans slightly towards him until her eyes are level with his. Armstrong sees the intensity within her pretty hazel brown eyes. Her stern cast is captivating, while mysterious, and enchanting capable of disarming any man that peers into them. Many dead men know now, that behind these bewitching eyes can lie a rage that is quite unearthly.

The two continue their silent, up close, eye-to-eye glaze. Victoria's deep penetrating eyes seem to be able to look upon a man's soul. Victoria is well inside of Armstrong's personal zone. The sweet perfumed traces emitting from her shapely person, soothes Armstrong's inner man, like a relaxing whirlpool bath.

In the theater of his mind, this scene becomes very dramatic. He suddenly, with a mighty pull of his one hand, slides the heavy vintage desk away. Then he, in one fluid movement, stands while scooping Victoria within his arms, and brings her body tight against his.

"Damn it J.T., ..." Victoria begins at a tone that's almost a whisper.

Her sudden address snaps the daydreamer instantly back to reality.

". . . These people don't deserve you as President."

"I haven't won Victoria." He returned flatly.

"You will, . . . and for what? Six months later they will be calling for your head." She ended with disgust.

"The people want me."

"Oh, . . . bullshit."

She stands up straight, and motions towards the outside.

"Those people out there, are just fed up with this current Administration's lies, upon lies."

She sits down, folding her hands, and holding them in her lap. She takes a deep breath, and then continues with her voice now revealing distress, "America doesn't believe in what you believe anymore." She ended, and then looked away from him.

"What about you?"

Victoria brings her eyes off the unwaxed hardwood floor, and looks the handsome man directly in his eyes. Armstrong sees the sincerity, and compassion, but turns away, and looks out at the bombarding rainfall.

"I believe in you. I know you are dedicated. I know you are capable to lead this country. And I also know that you are a good man. There are people, in fact, . . . entire nations out there that want to kill you, . . . and why? Because you want to fix a mess that someone else created. You want to fix a mess that they don't want fixed. You are a Blackman in America. A country that the demonic head of racism is still alive and well. So lets see, . . . the crazy Crackers hate you. Some black folks don't like you, because you are not capitalizing on your blackness, and the crazy Allah seeking bastards over there would love to kill you, at least twice."

"And it's for all those reasons I need you." He said flatly as he continued to look through the rain soaked window.

Victoria looks upon him, as he views the storm. Her mind replays his request for his assistance. Her eyes slowly drift from him, as she begins to question her imminent future. Silence invades the scene, but for the furious downpour of the rain pounding upon the roof above them.

Victoria now thinks about leaving the Bureau. She has never given this a thought before. She has no agenda to rise to the rank of Assistant Director, nor does she plan to become a life long active Agent, retiring at the maximum age, is she survived. Now she thinks over the possibility of coming to work for the General.

To protect him from forces that if they truly desire, WILL kill him. I could not stand to see him hurt, she confessed to herself, as she glanced over towards him to see him still looking outward. Her thoughts began to overwhelm her ability to process them. Some thoughts loudly argued for her to resign her position with the F.B.I., while another volley of voices chastised her for even thinking about discarding a secure, and elevating career. Yet there is a faint, but clear utterance. Returning to Washington does not have to be.

She is suddenly confronted with her emotions, and deep regard for this man. She looks upon him and does not see a Presidential Candidate, a best selling author or a war hero. She sees a man. A strong handsome, unattached, intelligent and compassionate man that is also in procession of a nice posterior. She now recalls the last two weeks with Armstrong. She is sure that he has sparked life back into an area she had shrouded from her emotions.

Suddenly Armstrong turns to her. His sudden attention, with his eyes meeting hers, unglues the deep thinking Agent. Though his tranquil look caused no alarm, Victoria reacted like a child caught committing a 'no-no'. Clearly becoming uneasy, Victoria adjusts her seated position, and now sits erect.

Armstrong eyes the abrupt change in her poise. Her facial expression displays contention, as her lack of eye contact, confirms his observation.

"I'll tell you what, . . ." He began forcefully, and intentionally to break her concentration. He pauses for a beat, and when her eyes automatically came upon his, he lowers his tone and continues, ". . . Why don't you get some rest. Sleep on my proposal." He ended with a smile, besieged by sadness.

Victoria nods, as she rises to her feet.

"I'll do that, . . ." She starts in a soft, downcasted tone, ". . . But I honestly doubt that I will be able to accept your offer."

Now looking upward at her, Armstrong gently returns, "You said you would sleep on it."

"Yes, . . ." She replied, and then forces a half hearted smile which lasted no longer than a flash of lightening, ". . . Goodnight General."

Before he could respond, Victoria has turned, and began walking toward the door. Armstrong watches, as she departs. He wonders why she doesn't accept his offer a little more positively. As he turns to look out upon the raging storm, he begins to accept the likelihood that she is going to return to Washington. He glances at the spot where she had just moments ago occupied. Her presence has left a lasting impression, and will continue to do so for quite sometime. He looks back out through the window. His heart is heavy, and his spirit feels as gloomy, as the weather. General Armstrong has grown fond of Victoria, and he misses her already.

The melancholy man sits back in his comfortable leather chair, as he continues to stare outward. Allowing his body to relax, and his mind to unwind, he sits silently. Her words of concern echo throughout the corridors of his active mind. He questions if it is true destiny to pursue, and capture the Presidency. He wonders if there would be an Office of President in the near future, with all the chaos in the World, and in America.

His thoughts suddenly sprung to Victoria Owens. He didn't fight the strong images of her consuming his thoughts. The memories of her being around will never fade. In such a short time, she has energized his drive.

He has now allowed fear to grip him. He's let the voices of dread speak. He let them blare, to the point that their voices drowned out the fierce storm. Though he sits as if his mind is in neutral, another utterance began. Like the soothing touch of a loved one, a presence begins to descend upon him. The apprehensive voices of doubt receded like an ocean at low tide. No longer do doubts of his destiny exist. He thinks of Victoria Owens now. Strong images of her consume his thoughts. He will miss her. He now smiles recalling the number of sunny, recreated adventures they have shared during the past two weeks. In this very short time, he has become very fond of the woman Agent.

Damn, he thinks to himself as he looks over to the door where Victoria departed, . . . if I ever get another opportunity, I will not allow it to remain as an aspiration.

Chapter Eight

MAY 6TH, 2012 A.D.

All in all, the World survived May 5th, 2012 pretty much intact. Though a record number of floods have occurred Worldwide, and the abnormal weather occurrence still continues, planet Earth continues to support life.

The rain has now stopped plummeting upon Madison. The morning sun is still blocked by an overcast, since dawn. It's 9:13 a.m., and the outside air temperature is a mild, windless 55 degrees. Victoria is already up, and dressed. Today she is due to return to Washington.

As she is packing her belongings, she is listening and sometimes glancing at the T.V. She has it tuned to a national morning news show. A lot of coastal cities, and low-lying areas are flooded. A minor earthquake along the Mississippi River was recorded overnight. This morning's weather forecast has just concluded with positive news for Victoria. The eastcoast storm is now out to sea. Washington's forecast today is sunny, and in the 50's.

Satisfied with the report, Victoria glances out of her

assigned 2nd floor bedroom window. The sight of Armstrong walking alone, causes her to pause at the window. She watched the slow strolling man, as he ventures away from the house. As a report from a noted scientist begins his warning pertaining to the abrupt changing weather patterns, and it's effect on the polar ice caps, Victoria begins to focus in on the General. She moves closer to the window, and immediately scanned well out ahead of his walk. She exhales, when she finally spots a security patrol team.

She now refocuses her eyes upon him. She is standing as close to the window as she can, as if she could listen in on his thoughts. She looks to his right flank, which a dozen motorhomes occupied by Secret Service Members, are a make shift field office. She looks to his left, but her sight is limited, because of the house's design. His concern for his safety, she remembers well. Like a haunting chorus his tone replays in her head.

She continues to watch him stroll. It disturbs her to see him without any immediate cover. She wonders what it would be like in Armstrong's place. The World seems so big, and he's so small. He exists with the knowledge that many would love to see his head on a stick. He can't even trust his government, or his security. Instantly, she now recalls his revelation of his trust in her.

"Damn it." She says softly through clenched teeth, cursing her flawless recall.

She turns her back on the window, as if this would silence her thoughts. While she stands with her back to the window, her eyes are attracted towards the T.V. She is not tuned into its function. Her silent pause is brief. She slowly turns and faces the window once again. Armstrong has strolled much further away now. She continues to watch him in silence. Her mind is processing a multitude of messages between her emotional side and the logical. As the mental debate endures, she continues to watch him.

General Armstrong has returned to the house from his late morning stroll. As he steps up onto the wooden porch, he is greeted by his old friend, and Personal Aide.

"Good morning, General." Duke conveyed formally.

The General extended his hand, and as both men shook, he returned the greeting.

"How do things look, out there?" Duke asked, as he looked outward, upon the scenic acreage.

Standing next to him, Armstrong turns and looks outward.

"I believe we came through the past few days of monsoons, pretty much intact." He now looks to his long time Assistant, and lightly enquires, "You weren't worried were you?"

"Com'on General, . . . I've stood with you in battle, staring death right in the face, unmoved by the possibilities of dying." Duke ended gloriously.

Armstrong places his hand upon Duke's shoulder and states, "Then, my friend, . . . we faced the wrath of man. These days, . . ." He then looks skyward, ". . . We are facing the wrath of the Creator."

A beat of silence passes between the two. Armstrong now gently continues, "Com'on old man, . . . we have only about a week remaining before we hit the trail again. Whata you say we start planning my up coming moves."

"Right." Duke answered automatically, while still pondering the General's prior statement.

Duke turns and as he starts to lead Armstrong into the house, he begins, "Well Sir, . . . one main issue is where are you going to make an Memorial Day appearance? Washington, or small-town America?"

As both men step into the house, Victoria is descending on the staircase. All three make eye contact. Armstrong stops walking as he looks upon her. Duke acknowledges with a smiling greeting, and continues to inform the General about the pros and cons of his choices.

Victoria has stopped her descent, as she looks upon the General with a blank expression. As they look upon each other during their momentary pause, Armstrong begins to witness Victoria's expression soften. Her budding smile seems to brighten the shadows of the day. Instantly Armstrong knew that this smile wasn't a simple expression of amusement. Combined with her foretelling eyes, she was expressing approval. Armstrong's broad smile confirmed to Victoria that her message was received.

"Duke listen, . . ." Armstrong began, interrupting the speaking man.

As Victoria descends the last few remaining stairs Armstrong continues in an authoritative tone, "Effective tomorrow morning, . . . Miss Owens will be a part of my staff."

Surprised, Duke looks from the speaking headman to Victoria.

As Duke gives Victoria an approving smile, Armstrong continues, "Her position will be that of; Personal Security Liaison. I will need you to make all of the proper notifications."

A smiling Duke looks to Armstrong and responds, "Yes Sir. I'll get on that right away."

Duke faces Victoria and extends his hand, "Welcome aboard."

"Thank you." Victoria replied, as she shakes his hand.

Duke gives her a wink and then walks off. Victoria steps nearing to the General.

"I'm glad you changed your mind, Victoria."

"How do you know that I have?" She teased.

Like a shy, innocent young boy, Armstrong shrugs his shoulders.

"Did you follow my suggestion?" He asked.

"Yes, . . . and by the way, they didn't seem too surprised." She answered with a suspicious tone.

With a smile, Armstrong says, "So, . . . there's no problem then."

"I don't like to be predictable."

"Miss Owens, . . . you are intelligent, resourceful, tough yet a beautiful woman, therefore you ARE predictable."

Accepting his statement with humor, she smiles and replies, "Oh really?"

"I think so."

"Well, . . . now that you have me, . . ." She said flirtatiously, ". . . Just what am I to do as your Personal Security Liaison?"

"Come with me, Miss Owens." He said invitingly, as he puts his solid as steel arm around her shoulder, and begins to lead her off. As they enter into the hallway, Armstrong calls out, "Duke, . . . prepare another briefing position!"

Chapter Nine

At the same moment, a half a World away, an Air India passenger jet liner is being surrounded by a half a dozen balls of light. Panic has seized the Air Bus as the various color, and sized flying objects paces, and buzzes the jet.

An N.A.S.A. SR-71 flying high over North America during a high altitude weather assessment, also encounters the phenomena of the balls of light. The pilot fights to control his craft, while his instruments become unreliable. This encounter lasted 2 to 3 minutes, then they suddenly peeled away and accelerated spaceward so fast, that they seemed to blink away. During the incident, the SR-71 fell from its cruising altitude of 80,000 feet, to a little above 10,000 above the frozen Canadian wilderness.

Reports from around the World begun to surface concerning the balls of flying light. Not since W.W. II, have balls of light, or then known as Foo Fighters, arouse. By nightfall, the skies high above were filled with military aircraft, searching out the Foo Fighters.

03:48
MAY 7TH, 2012 A.D.
NEBRASKA
MINUTE MAN 3 LAUNCH FACILITY
K-06

Alerted by the Intrusion Detection System, a squad of heavily armed U.S. Air Force Security Police Officers, race to a Minute Man 3, Intercontinental Ballistic Missile Silo. Patches of ground hugging fog, seem to transform the massive wheatfield, into an eerie alien landscape.

"With the crazy weather lately, the radar is just probably stressing out." A cocky Airman from Boston said.

A nervous Rookie from Jacksonville Florida, searching for reassurance, rations, "Just another drill, huh?"

"More like another malfunction." The cocky one instantly responds.

"My God, . . ." The driver suddenly mumbles.

"Shit, . . ." The Tech Sergeant exclaimed, as he peered up ahead at the fog, at the silo. ". . . Get on the horn and advise the MAF that we might have a fire situation here!"

As they rapidly close the thousand yards remaining to the missile site, bright, red and yellow lights appear as smoke in the fog, giving the silo the appearance that it is ablaze. As the heavily armored vehicle continues toward the site, the Airmen receive additional information.

"Fire?" The cocky Airman questions, "There's nothing there to burn."

Frantically, the communication Officer announces, "Sarge, I got a 'hot message' from Operations. They state, a controlled craft IS out there! It is reflecting good, solid returns on the radar. They are also picking up slight radiation emissions!"

The Tech Sergeant swallows hard, and then shouts out, "Alright people, . . . we are now at 'Hot Pistol!!"

"Hostile attack?!" The Rookie nervously uttered.

The cocky Airman turns to the 19 year old Rookie, and informs, "Looks like some son-of-a-bitch managed to sneak in and compromise a 'bird'."

"Who? How?"

"That ain't our concern. Right now, it's all 'bout Delay and Denial." The Airman ended grimly.

A chain-linked fence topped with barbed wire, surrounds the structure-less launch site. Hovering silently about ten feet above the hardened missile silo's massive sliding door, is an object, pulsating red, to a brilliant yellow.

As the Security Squad disembarked from their vehicle, with their weapons at the ready, the object begins a transformation. It changes to a gentle, almost soothing white.

Mechanically, the squad takes up tactical positions. As the driver mans the turret mounted M-60 machine gun, he mumbles a prayer.

The squad, with clearance to use physical deadly force against any unauthorized presence, stands in awe at the soundless object hovering before them. Suddenly, the object, some 50 feet in diameter, begins to increase in brilliance, as it menacingly approaches the tense squad. The object's advancement, like a gunfighter during a showdown, causes the squad to unconsciously step rearward with each 'step' forward it took.

Though no heat is felt from the brightness, it has become bright enough now to appear to be daylight. The electrical circuits and equipment in and around the armored vehicle suddenly erupts giving the vehicle a look of a roman candle on the 4th of July.

Though not injured, the driver begins to scream out in fear. Assessing that they were under attack, the Sergeant gives the order to open fire. The well-aimed firepower of M16A2s, M249 automatics, 50 cals. and a M203 40 millimeter grenade launcher, rips through the serene, predawn surroundings, like a mid-September tornado. As if someone flicked off alight switch, the object was gone. At speeds measured at over 6000 miles an hour, the object sped away.

Victoria awakes this day, minutes before 6 a.m. Her night was horrible. She tossed and turned, only succumbing to sleep intermittently throughout the night. This morning the sky seems to be ablaze from the sunrise. Thoughts about General Armstrong filled her mind all night, and now continue this morning. She cursed the circumstances under her breath. She knows she can do the job, but it would be a lot easier, if it wasn't involving Armstrong. Not because he's a Presidential Candidate, or because he's a national hero, or even the fact that factions seek to kill him.

Victoria recognizes that her feelings, . . . her deep personal concerns and desires, . . . might prohibit her from executing her task effectively and professionally. I can't walk around here as if it is just business, she thinks to herself. Each day, my feelings for this man grows. I can't do anything but think of him. Get a grip Victoria, she chastises herself. You are starting to sound like a love struck 17 year old. I do know one thing, . . . you can't continue on much longer like this. Tell the man how you feel.

"Are you crazy?" She mumbles in a whisper.

He's larger than life. He can have any woman in the World, . . . they all love him.

You're a coward, the voice within her head said.

Shut-up, and get off my back.

Look how he looks at you, stupid. And do you see any other woman up here as his guest???

Maybe he's not into women.

Now you're being an ass.

Well, . . . maybe he doesn't have the time, or the room in his life. He is on a mission. Maybe he doesn't need a woman in his life.

Then forget him.

I could never forget him.

Then leave him. Leave his side. Resign your position since you're so personally involved.

"Then I guess that's it then." She whispers gentle in a defeated tone.

All day Victoria remained quiet, and withdrawn. She avoided Armstrong, and retreated to the acreage of the grounds, with the pretense of a security survey. By early afternoon she had strolled the massive grounds, twice. When she returned to the house, she discovered Armstrong in a meeting with his Campaign Manager. After a small bite to eat, Victoria went up to her room, closed the door, and laid across the bed in thought.

Suddenly she awakens. Her room is now engulfed in complete darkness. Victoria quickly sits up and looks to her wristwatch, as she activates the watch's night-light.

20:48

"Damn." She mumbles in surprisement.

She doesn't even remember falling off to sleep. Victoria now gets up, and carefully walks over to the still uncovered window. As she approaches the window, the crystal clear black sky sparkles with stars, like diamonds on a dark velvet surface. She stops at the window, and looks out over the landscape. All is quiet she deducts as she observes a roving security team. Satisfied that all is well with them, she then glances over to the collected assortment of motorhomes, and double wide mobile trailers, grouped together forming a small village.

A gentle, soothing breeze blows through the screened window. The air smells good, crisp and clean. Her mind is clearer now than most of the day. She has decided to leave this assignment, and return to Washington. Victoria has decided that her personal feelings for Armstrong, and the inability of not being able to suppress them much longer could be too much of a distraction and perhaps, . . . an embarrassment.

Tomorrow morning I will inform him of my decision, she thinks to herself. She then lowers the window blind, and pulls the curtains closed. Then, she carefully makes her way over to the nightstand, and feels for the short chain on the bedside lamp.

The snake like chain eludes her fumbling fingers momentarily, as she tries to grip the light activating chain. Then finally, with a quick tug, the small bedroom explodes into brilliance. She reasons that the return of her appetite was due to her finally deciding what she is going to do about her plight with Armstrong. She looks to her multi-function timepiece, and figures she will have to stroll over to the Secret Service's makeshift kitchen, to grab some chow.

Immediately the thought impulse for her to change her clothes, flashed within her brain. Victoria immediately begins to disrobe, as she wonders what the Feds have on the menu tonight. As she stripped off her blouse, and laid it across the foot of the bed, she turns towards the dresser. She pulls open the wooden drawer, and withdraws an oversized jet-black sweatshirt. She then reaches rearward, and unfastens her white cotton bra. She slides the support off, and places it upon her stale blouse. Victoria sighs from the relief, as she closes on drawer, and opens an adjacent drawer. She picks up a floral printed pair of panties. Using her hip to close the drawer, Victoria unfastens her button fly jeans, leans against the solid wooden dresser, and begins to pull the stonewashed trousers off her body. Neatly she places her jeans atop of her clothing, and then heads off towards the bathroom for a quick shower.

The evening air is quite exhilarating. As Victoria inhaled deeply, she feels her body burst with energy. As she walks away from the S.S. Chow trailer, she is looking skyward at the twinkling stars above. She now decides to take a short stroll to help digest the tasty, but heavy slice of meatloaf, and thick as cement mashed potatoes and green peas, along with butter soaked dinner rolls.

The sky truly looks beautiful tonight. The stars look so close, that if someone stood on their tippy-toes, they would reach them. Victoria has wandered some 50 yards from the lights of the house, and now stands in the shadows. She continues to marvel at the heavens. As she pans the seller masterpiece, she humbly mumbles, "My God."

A chill engulfs her body as she absorbs the unquestionable design of an unquestionable Designer. More people should see this. More people should experience this, enlightening moment. Standing naked before God. Hiding behind nothing. No large buildings, or immersed in a sea of people.

Her mind now ponders about the star filled skies, eons ago. The great minds of long ago that were motivated by looking upon such great scenes. What great secrets do they know, she wonders as she marvels at the stars. Victoria questions if she will ever know the answers to the mysteries. Hell, her though begins as she depressively looks over the moonlight landscape, I don't even know the right answers for my life.

Like a lightening bolt, an image of Armstrong flashed across her mind. She immediately dismissed his image from her mind. She had locked him in a vault in the deepest recessions of her mind, . . . but he keeps escaping. She looks back towards the star filled sky, and then silently prays, Dear Lord, I need your help. Show me the way. Help me, . . . I don't know what I should do or which way I should go.

"In about 20 years."

Quickly spinning around to face the gentle voice, Victoria faces the shadowy figure. While she stands glaring, Armstrong steps toward her, looking skyward saying, "In about 20 years, we will be traveling out there."

Shaken by his sudden appearance, her heart is still beating rapidly as her brain registers his presence. She remains quiet while she keeps her eyes upon him. After a momentary pause, Armstrong slowly lowers his head, and now looks upon Victoria's face.

A million messages are racing through her mind. Like a tug of war, she feels her emotions starting to tear at the seam. While she wants so badly to rush into his arms, she restrains herself, citing protocol.

In a soothing tone, the General begins, "You know, . . . on nights like this, like to come out here under all these stars, and think."

Another beat of silence passes. Victoria remains silent. Armstrong then continues, "What are you out here thinking about Victoria?"

His compassion filled voice causes the emotional woman to want to cry. She turns away from him. He then gently probes, "Perhaps you wish to be alone. I'm sorry to disturb you." He ended wounded.

Turning her head slightly towards him, she firmly responds, "No, . . . please don't go."

"Victoria, . . . is there something I've said or done to offend you?" He asked desperately.

Hearing the pain in his voice, causes her to spin around, and immediately speak to him, "No J.T., . . ." She started, but then suddenly becomes at a loss for words. She then turns away from him and awkwardly continues, "I, . . . I think it would be in the best interest of you and I, . . . that I quit."

"Why?" He asked sternly.

Feeling hollow, and cold inside, as if her soul has just departed from her, she pleads, "Oh please just say okay, or something like, . . . it's been nice knowing you, and leave it at that."

Still stern, and unbending, Armstrong pressure her. "Why do you want to quit?"

"It's difficult to explain." She weakly responds.

"Difficult, . . ." He firmly returns as he steps closer towards her back, ". . . Don't hand me that. You obviously don't even know the meaning of that word. You're no quitter."

She spins around and faces him. On the verge of tears she states, "Maybe, but I am still a woman, damn it. I have feelings, . . . I'm a human being. You think I'm some sort of damn super woman. You want to know why I'm quitting General, well it's because of you."

As he closes the gap between them he gently says, "I don't want you to leave, Victoria."

Looking into his eyes comforted her.

"Why?" She asked in a soft voice.

"You're my Security Liaison."

"Is that all?" She probed, gambling all of the marbles.

"No." He answered sincerely, as his eyes stayed with hers.

His response surprises her. Now caught in a whirlwind of emotion, Victoria flatly says, "Convince me."

With their mouths only inches apart, they simultaneously move, meeting at mid-distance. At the first impulse of impact, their tongues engage each other's. At first their kiss is like a flash of lightening, but then the thunder followed. The intensity of their shared kiss, rumbled throughout their bodies. There is now, no more conflict within Victoria's emotions.

Victoria is standing at Armstrong's bedroom window, just as the first light of the dawn breaks over the horizon. She's wearing only his thick terry cloth robe. Her body quakes as she recalls the passion of their intimacy during the past darkened hours. Last night they exchanged submersed feelings. Last night, revelations were discovered. Last night, a climax of wanton desire detonated between them like a 100-megaton hydrogen bomb. She now glances over and looks upon the still sleeping man. Then without a though of regret, she surrenders her emotion of love.

Just what is love? She IS honestly concerned for his well being. Her thoughts ARE mostly of him. She desires not to be anywhere but with him. Feeling him deep inside of her touched her soul. There is no mountain too high, or valley too low. She gave him her body, and he has already captured her heart, as well as her mind.

Then, like a slap across her face, skepticism strikes her. Am I crazy, . . . how could I be in love? I bust BE crazy. She turns from him, and looks upon the illuminating landscape. I wonder if he meant what he said, or was last night only an act of mutual lust?

The debate within her begins.

No, . . . no not the way he made me feel, last night. He made LOVE to me. He was gentle, caring and kind. WE were LOVERS last night, she ended her argument, strongly.

Then doubt returned.

Man is logical, as opposed to the woman, which is emotional. Does he love you? Did you touch HIS soul? Would HE sacrifice himself for you? Will he awaken shortly, and regard last night as a lust induced action, completely devoid of sentiment?

A whirlwind of emotion swirls within her. Her thoughts have so consumed her senses, that her physical being seems to no longer exist, within the expansive master bedroom.

General Armstrong, and his Security Liaison didn't get much time alone during most of the day. They didn't have much of an opportunity to engage in a heartfelt conversation either. The morning began with a hectic pace of telephone calls, meetings, fax transmissions and tactical planning. A last minute invitation from the Governor of North Carolina was accepted by the General at 9 a.m. for a lunch engagement.

Immediately Victoria, and the Supervising Agent of the Secret Service began planning and plotting the 90 miles to Raleigh. Due to the abnormal atmospheric conditions caused by preternatural solar flares disrupting the Earth's magnetic fields, the General's trek to the State's Capital, will have to be made by ground transportation. The large scaled solar flares are not the only unnatural phenomena plaguing the U.S. as well as the World. Ozone depletion areas are widening. Floods in the Mississippi Valley have just about divided the country in two. A series of tornadoes have swept through L.A. County. Unseasonable temperatures in Alaska are making Fairbanks warmer than Miami by 20 degrees.

It is late afternoon when the four-vehicle convoy returns to Madison. Victoria has remained silent throughout the trip, as she sits across from the General, as he endlessly conversed with his Aide, and Secretary. The telephone calls to his limo seemed to never cease, though most of the calls were recalls, due to the atmospheric conditions, causing havoc to communications.

Victoria has been waiting for some sort of acknowledgment from him all day long. My God, she thinks as she looks upon him from across the stretched out limousine, did what we did last night mean anything? She has to look away as the sight of him, almost brings her to tears. She can't shake the emotion she possesses for this man. Why hasn't he acknowledged my presence today? Hey, remember me??? We possessed one another, practically all of last night! The thought that he was shunning her made her furious. She fought the impulse to clutch his neck, and bring him to retort.

Victoria is suddenly snatched from her realm of figment, when the limousine halted. The S.S. Agent, sitting next to the driver, exited the auto, and quickly opens the rear door for the General. The earpiece fastened to Victoria's ear, suddenly begins to confabulate about the General's arrival at the house.

The General's Secretary is the first to step out from the limousine. Victoria watches the woman exit. Her eyes then pan onto Duke, as he prepares to depart in the Secretary's wake. Victoria's eyes then pan over to the General, and meet his eyes.

Duke has now left the vehicle. A pause of unusual silence, and stillness is present in the stretched sedan. Victoria senses Duke and the S.S. Agent lingering about for the General's emergence from the car.

Suddenly the General slides towards the exit.

"General, . . ." She sharply begins.

The Presidential Candidate stops and looks upon her.

". . . One moment of your time, please."

Armstrong looks from the woman and then to his Aide. When the men make eye contact, the General firmly states, "Duke, . . . I'll see you inside shortly, . . . would you hold my calls."

"Yes Sir."

Armstrong closes the door, and then sits back onto the grey leather seating. Immediately a transmission to Victoria broadcasted into her ear.

"Guardian, . . . is there a problem?"

Victoria instinctively looked outward through the one-way black tinted door window. She sees the solitary S.S. Man speaking into his cuff microphone. As Victoria raised her cuff towards her mouth, the Security Phone, within the limo sounds. Armstrong immediately lifts the receiver, as Victoria calmly conversed with the concerned Secret Service Man.

"No Jay, . . ." The General said into the mouthpiece. ". . . Proceed to the barn. Miss Owens and I will be going along for the ride, we'll walk back to the house afterwards."

The General hangs up the telephone. It immediately sounds. Before the ring completes its cycle, Armstrong picks up the receiver.

"Yes, . . ." He flatly said.

The Supervising Agent, that was sitting in the front seat, is now on the phone. Armstrong now looks to Victoria. She once again meets his eyes. The General, while eyeing the visibly uneasy, and clearly annoyed woman, nonchalantly says into the phone, "No, . . . everything is just fine. We're just having a confidential word. We will return shortly." He ended cagily, and as he returned the phone to its cradle, he adds. "That should be all the security checks."

"At least they're not allowing any deviations go on unchecked, . . . even if you are with your own personal security." She said awkwardly, as she continues to look upon the man. She is distracted slightly by the transmission in her ear to the limo driver to proceed onward to the limo's secured parking shelter.

As the limo creeps slowly towards it's assigned area, Victoria returns her attention to Armstrong. His cast seems to be devoid of expression. Though the driver was not within earshot, Victoria feels uncomfortable discussing what's on her mind. She now tactfully stalls until the driver leaves the car.

"I think today's outing went very well."

"I agree."

"We haven't been able to talk much, today."

Armstrong nods in agreement. A moment of silence follows, as Victoria swallows hard, looking into the handsome man's warm eyes. She then glances out of the limo's door window, as it began it's backing into it's makeshift shelter.

"Just what is on your mind Victoria?"

She looks hard into his eyes, and sharply answers, "I just want to know, . . ." She pauses for a second, to ensure his full attention, ". . . What we shared last night, . . . was it just lust, . . . or . . . ?"

"Love?" He responds immediately.

"Love?"

The limousine comes to a stop. Victoria then hears the muffled thud of the driver's door close.

"Was that an answer or a question?" Armstrong asked.

As if someone pulled a plug from her body, Victoria suddenly loses her desire to get to the bottom of things with the General. I've musta been crazy to think such thoughts about this man. I'm going home, she painfully decides. She slides forward, toward the seat's edge, as she reaches for the door handle she flatly says, "I think I better return to Washington before I embarrass US."

"Victoria."

The impact of his voice caused her to freeze. As he slides towards the edge of his seat, she releases the door handle. With their eyes now positioned on each other's, Armstrong begins, "Though you have been in my life for only a short period, you have affected it greatly. You have touched me, . . . and though it was very passionate, I felt the love from you."

"Oh really?" She responded weakly, but tried to maintain strength. "And what about you?" She asked now leaning slightly toward him.

"You are constantly on my mind. When I see you, I feel really good. When you're not with me, . . . I feel naked, . . . cold and alone. When I close my eyes at night, I dream of a life with you."

Victoria unconsciously raised an eyebrow. Armstrong sees her reaction, and then says, "Surprised?"

"Astonished."

Surprised by her answer, he questions it. Victoria then explains, "Last night you said things to me, but this morning, I didn't know if you still meant those words."

"Victoria, . . . you question the integrity of the words I said to you?" He said in a disappointed tone.

"Talk is cheap, J.T."

Solemnly he declares, "You mean the World to me. I want you apart of my life."

The impact of his emotion upon her almost made Victoria cry. Her eyes begun to tear as she looked Armstrong in his eyes. Her heart is wide open for him. He has become as important to her as one of her life supporting organs. After a declaration like that there is only one fitting course of action to take. Victoria reaches outward and gathers the lapels of his suit jacket, and pulls the willing man towards her. As she brought him forward, she places her lips tenderly upon his. It wasn't long before their tender kiss evolved into a passionate deed. A declaration like that there is only one fitting course of action to take. Victoria reaches outward and gathers the lapels of his suit jacket, and pulls the willing man towards her. As she brought him forward, she places her lips tenderly upon his. It wasn't long before their tender kiss evolved into a passionate deed.

The summer months that followed, Armstrong's campaign rolled along, despite the security concerns over his public appearances. The weather seemed to be more of a threat to him than anything else. The untraditional weather patterns plagued the campaign schedule. The summer of 2012 broke high temperature records all over the World. London experienced temperatures of near 100 degrees for 34 straight days. Fairbanks, Alaska, Chicago, Seattle and the Nations Breadbasket boiled. Las Vegas and Phoenix were ghost towns by day. California's timberland burned constantly. Severe rainstorms flood the southeast. New Orleans looked like Venice. Heavy flooding in Mississippi, Kentucky, Alabama, Georgia and Ohio. Australia imposes a full daytime ban on school children outdoors, unless all exposed skin is covered.

The 'Black' press has come out against Armstrong. It is cited that, "He is out of touch with the African American community, and will not be sensitive to the needs of Afro Americans in the 21st century." Most of the hostility stemmed from Armstrong's interview on 60 Minutes. He corrected the Afro-American label addressed to him, and stated that he is, “An American that happens to be black.” The media begins to notice, and questions Victoria’s presence. They become crazed, like a pack of hungry wild dogs when it was leaked that she quit the F.B.I. to be with Armstrong. Who is this mystery woman???

Chapter Ten

September saw peaceful protesting suddenly sparked riots and bombings throughout France, when the French government refused to reduce its nuclear stockpiles. Civil war erupted in Mexico. A Japanese Defense Force's naval ship and a Chinese Destroyer exchanged gunfire. The month also brought relief from the heat, but not before violence erupted as well on the streets of America. In Miami, 15 days or urban warfare erupted when the city's police executed arrest warrants on suspected drug dealers. Three people were killed by the police during the raid. It was then disclosed that the police forcefully entered the wrong house. In Brooklyn, New York a Korean storeowner was acquitted for the death of a 13-year-old black youth, who the storeowner said was shoplifting. A week of sporadic rioting crippled the city. Los Angeles police captured a group of 'vampires' who were kidnapping citizens, in order to drain them of their desired blood.

September 9th the campaigning former U.S. Army General, and his party returned to Madison. That night, a tabloid news show 'revealed' Victoria so called life story. The very next morning, CNN was the first to report an airborne lung disease, known as Legionella, was rampaging through Atlanta. CNN also disclosed that the Center of Disease Control was very concerned about the whopping increase in Tuberculosis being reported by New York City Hospitals. From early samples, the C.D.C. has just discovered this strain of T.B. is highly communicable, and very resistant to known combating antibiotics. In the 19th century, 25 percent of the European population, was killed by this very same disease.

What CNN, or any other news service didn't know, was the fact that, a C.D.C. Strike Force was presently in N.Y.C. After conferring with the U.S. Military's germ warfare specialist in Maryland, a plan to quarantine the City of New York was under way. This is the first time in U.S. history, that an Outbreak Order was dispatched on such a massive scale. The White House Chief of Staff, after the meeting declared grimly, "Billions spent to divert a chemical or nuclear attack upon an American city, and now we're about to lose one to a lousy bug. Go figure."

The curiosity regarding Victoria abruptly stopped when the U.S. news media became busy with more headline grabbing items. UPI reported all out street fighting in Paris. Scores of civilians fighting with police, and now military forces, had entered its third day. Tension mounting between Mexico and the U.S. over trade, had reached an explosive level. Mexican leaders called out for Mexicans in America to protest, . . ."Bring America to its knees!!!"

Japan braces for war with China, as tensions between the two countries continue to grow worse. American cities suffering from viral infection and possible quarantine are not alone any longer. World News in now confirming that Hong Kong is sealed off due to a Dengue epidemic, racing through the island nation. The epidemic, caused by the Asian Tiger mosquito has infected well over 100,000 residents with an unconfirmed dead of 5 to 10 thousand with that number due to rise rapidly.

For the rest of the month, General Armstrong stayed at his Madison home. He made various appearances electronically on news shows. His novel, encapsulating his experiences in the Middle East leading American Forces to victory and eliminating the nuclear threat to America, was released on the 11th. Its debut on the bestseller's list at number one got Hollywood's attention and he has since been approached by major studios to recreate the battle for the big screen. Win or lose, Armstrong's publisher has begged the Candidate for his story on his Presidential race to the White House. His publisher sweetens the request by promising at least a 10 million dollar advance.

September 13th will be a day Victoria will never forget. After breakfast, she went over to trailer 5, which the Secret Service uses as a tactical briefing room. Victoria has just received the General's 10-city itinerary for next month's campaign drive. Just as she sits at the long rectangle shaped table to examine the lengthy, multi paged, detailed schedule that packs a 1-city visit in 14 days the dozen evenly spaced telephones on the table ring like a chorus. Victoria disregards the first ring. Upon the second she looks to see if there are any S.S. Agents around, figuring it would be for them. Midway through the 3rd ring, she picks up the phone.

"Hello, . . ." She then things professionalism, and instantly adds, ". . . Tactical briefing."

The unmistaken speech of Armstrong's Secretary's perfect diction begins to emphatically inform Victoria.

"Miss Owens, . . . ?"

Surprised that anyone knew she was in trailer 5, Victoria responds instinctively.

"Yes."

"Mister Armstrong requests your immediate presence in his study."

"Alright, . . . tell 'em I'm on my way."

Victoria slowly places the phone upon its cradle as she wonders what's up with the General's urgent request. A nooner, her mind devilishly ponders as she stands. While she exits the 40-foot doublewide trailer she chuckles to herself at the thought, and then dismisses it.

Armstrong slowly paces the study's floor. His facial expression displays concern as he awaits Victoria's arrival. Many matters are on the occupied man's mind. Today' polls show him 10 points behind the Incumbent. In a few days he is going to embark on a 10-city assault. These 6 states he must carry in order to win in November. He began to recall highlights of his two-hour telephone conversation with his Pastor. The review caused him to stop pacing. Suddenly, three knocks report clearly. The raps seem to explode within the silent room. Reflectively, Armstrong looks to the door. His thoughts instantly conceive Victoria. First clearing his throat, Armstrong firmly responds, "Come in."

Victoria opens the simple wooden door and partially enters. Concerned by the urgency that the message conveyed, she shoots her speech.

"Are you alright?"

She instantly sees the preoccupation upon him. His weak smile greeting her appearance, fails to hide his bearing.

"Yes, . . ." As He motions for her to enter, ". . . Come in, . . . I would like to talk to you."

Victoria complies. As she walks towards him, she lightly says, "So this is where you've been all morning, I assume."

"Yes." He returned in a tone, heavy with concern.

Victoria walks right up to him. Their eyes haven't deviated from one another's, since Victoria's appearance at the door. As soon as she stepped into his personal zone, Armstrong takes her into his strong arms, and kisses her. The kiss is brief but tender.

"What's wrong, J.T.?" She whispers with concern.

"Please sit down."

As he guides her to the side chair at his desk, he then steps around to take his seat.

"J.T., . . . what is it?"

He pauses briefly to collect his thoughts, and then begins.

"What are your plans, for the near future?"

Without needing time to ponder, Victoria answers right away, "To stay on her until you are elected President of the United States."

Armstrong begins to shake his head no. He then moves forward on his chair towards Victoria and says, "I'm not going to become President."

Victoria narrows he eyes and leans toward him, and firmly replies, "Nonsense. You are going to be the next President of these United States."

Again, he slowly shakes his head no.

Responding to the shaking of his head, Victoria firmly says, "There's no way he's going to be re-elected."

Armstrong sits back in his chair, and flatly says, "Oh yes he is."

As she stands, and begins to walk around his desk toward him, she sharply begins, "Why so J.T.?"

"Honey, just look at the state of the World." He answered in a defeatist tone.

Now sitting on the edge of his desk, only inches from him, Victoria responds, "Yes I know, chaos."

"And this country is going to Hell in a hand basket."

"But you can fix it."

"I can't fix America. I am only a mortal man. America needs a superman with Divine powers. This is now at the point where our Savior is our salvation."

"So what are you saying, . . . you're quitting the race?"

"The Book of Revelation foretells the state of the World before the second coming."

Interjecting her thought, Victoria interrupts, "Yes Sweetheart, . . . but that can be years, . . . even decades away."

"Several books in the Holy Bible, foretell signs of the

end of the World, as we know it. Disease, famine, earthquakes, floods, droughts, ware and bizarre weather, . . . but what makes these days fit the End Times signs is when the Messiah said, . . . when you see all these things, know that the end is near."

"So what do we do, . . . just give up and let the mutants have it all?"

"They already have it. Com'on, stand back and look at the entire picture. This country embraces evil. In the sixties, this country began turning it's back on the Almighty. This nation and it's laws are, . . . well, . . . were biblically based. Now public display can bring you a lawsuit." As he takes a breath, he slowly shakes his head, and then looks to Victoria and continues in a committed tone, "Victoria, . . . I'm a warrior. I do not quit in the face of battle, and I do not surrender. I will continue toward victory in this race, . . . but I do believe that our Savior will snatch us away before that objective is completed."

A silent pause falls between them as they ponder matters.

Suddenly, Victoria softly speaks, "You know, . . . my mother was a saint. When I was a little girl, we went to church every Sunday." She now slightly adjusts her position on the desk and then continues, "After I joined the Army, I started slacking off from church, but it never left my heart." She pauses for a beat, and then states, "As we approached the year 2000, a lot of people began talking about the end of the World. Some proclaimed, that May 5th, 2000, was going to be doomsday. Others projected a 3rd World War in 2007. All along the preachers, preached the return of the Savior, . . . but, we are still here. Don't misunderstand me, . . . I don't think anyone was wrong, . . . I just think they are off the mark a little. Something *is* going to pop, . . . there's no question about that."

In a soothing voice, Armstrong says, "If a man can look up and determine the weather by the signs in the sky, then why does he refuse to acknowledge the signs of the end of the age?"

"Because man is blind to those things he doesn't want to see."

Her answer impresses him. He doesn't allow his delight to show upon his face. Flatly he asks her, "And where do you stand?"

"I believe in the Almighty, and his anointed son as my Savior. I may not know much more, but I stand on that."

A brief pause of silence fills the room, as the couple looks upon one another, as if telepathically they're probing one another's mind.

"Where do we go from here, Victoria?"

"Where would you want to go?" She asked tenderly.

Instantly his mind produces a picture of a life in progress with Victoria Owens. The mental snapshot, captures a joyful moment, with children playing about broad grassy fields, and the ills of the World far, far from this peace.

Armstrong stands, and hugs the desk sitting woman. She wraps her arms around his solid build and closes her eyes while engulfed in the rapture. Armstrong recoils his neck slightly so his mouth is at her ear. Then in a whisper asks, "Victoria . . ."

"Yes baby." She answered in a subdued tone.

"Will you marry me?"

Armstrong feels her body tense up as if her body has just turned to stone. She then gently, but firmly pushes away from him, until she is able to look him in the eye.

"What did you say?" She asked automatically while still stunned by his proposal.

Armstrong looks upon her and studies her expression of puzzlement.

"Marry me, Beloved."

The impact of Armstrong's question was as electrifying as their first shared kiss. The still speechless woman Agent causes wonderment about her response. Will she utter no? Will she now fade from my life, Armstrong wonders. This woman has satisfied a barren segment within my spirit. My dear God, . . . a rejection from this woman will be like a breath blowing out my final candle for life. He then concludes his silent prayer with a plead, oh please God, don't make that so.

"Yes." She answered, with her eyes filling with tears, and a warm smile spreading across her youthful face.

"Pardon?" Armstrong fires back.

He is unsure of what he heard for her response. She had answered him just as he completed his silent prayer, which he was conducting so loudly within himself, that it veiled her reply.

"Yes." She repeated with a bright smile.

They both kiss while chuckling in happiness. Armstrong breaks off the oral display of attention, and places his mouth at her ear and whispers, I love you. Victoria returns the emotional phrase. Armstrong then hugs her, as he begins, "You know, our lives may be a little hectic."

"Yes baby."

"But I want you to remember something, . . ." He now speaks in a firm tone, ". . . The minute the pressure becomes too intense . . ."

Victoria interrupts him.

"Hey, . . ." Her bright smile has transformed into a solemn expression, ". . . Don't worry about me."

"You're much too precious to me. Your happiness is much too important." He ended firmly.

Victoria looks away from him for a beat. She then looks back upon him. Her eyes look over his entire face, before they look into his chestnut brown eyes.

"As your wife, . . . I will not stand in the way of your decisions or your destiny. As my husband, . . . you lead and I will follow, . . . whether you're the President or not. I will be right beside you."

As their embrace tightens, their lips meet and passionately kiss. Such intimate contact with Armstrong cause Victoria's body to tingle. She stops the action and warns in jest, "You excite me every time we do this. Keep it up, and I won't be responsible for my actions."

"Hold that thought." He said.

Armstrong gives her a quick smack on the lips, and delicately removes himself from the embrace. He then begins in a business like tone. "There are a few matters we must resolve right away."

"Like what?"

He hesitates a beat, and then flatly answers, "Your position with the F.B.I. What do you plan to do, once your leave of absence is up?"

Victoria smiles at him. She already possesses the ability to sense his feelings. His strong solid tough exterior, seems to be transparent to her now.

"Well, . . ." She starts off casually. ". . . Up until a few minutes ago, I planned to return to my job after the election, . . . but now, I guess that is no longer my plan." She ended still smiling.

Still maintaining a stern businesslike manner, Armstrong replies, "You guess? That sounds pretty iffy to me."

"Then, that plan IS history. Now, . . . what would you like for me to do about my gig, . . . resign?"

"Absolutely."

"Then it is done." She returned instantly with a tone of conviction, and then adds, "I'm telling you now, . . . it's gonna be hard for me to sit still."

"You won't be, . . . I'm still going to need you to watch my back."

"That's automatic."

"Now, . . ." He started.

His voice is indicating an uneasiness. He looks at Victoria directly into her eyes, and continues, ". . . Just listen to what I am about to say. I know it might seem a little hasty, and unfeeling, but the bottom line is that we might not have ample courting time."

Victoria nods in agreement.

"How do you feel about short engagements?"

Victoria breaks eye contact, briefly. Her intuition senses where he is heading. Trying to suppress her excitement is like sitting on a volcano about to erupt. She returns her eyes to his, and the states. "You asked me to marry you, and I have accepted. I don't need any probationary periods to qualify my answer."

Her response makes a grin spread across his face like sunshine emerging in the aftermath of a storm.

"I spoke with Pastor Nagee this morning. He's going to be here for a social visit tomorrow, . . ." He pauses for a beat, swallowing hard, ". . . Would you object if he performs a very private ceremony for us, while he's here?"

She stumbles her words, "You mean, marriage? Us, . . . you and me, tomorrow?"

"Yes."

"Are you crazy!" She exclaimed, and then moved toward him.

Armstrong drops his smile, just as Victoria's face explodes with a grin. "Why didn't you tell him to come today?"

She throws her arms around his neck, as he wraps his arms around her waist. As they break into joyous laughter.

At sunset, on the 21st day of September, 2012, in a simple, private ceremony, Pastor Nagee, Duke, Mrs. Johnson and the loving couple, stand on a grassy knoll encircled by trees overlooking a gentle brook. Jonathan Taylor Armstrong, and Victoria Gail Owens, pledged publicly their love devotion to one another. Later that night, the couple retired into seclusion, and will not be seen until the day Armstrong is due to begin he 10 city tour.

Victoria doesn't like the fact that she is not accompanying Armstrong on his tour. Deep down, the fact makes her slightly ill. The past couple of days with him were much too short. Time, when in company with the man the would be President, seemed to accelerate beyond belief. Days seem like minutes, and weeks like hours.

As her plane starts it's final approach to National Airport, Victoria continues to reflect her unforgettable last few moments with the General. Her eyes begin to swell with tears as the desire to be with him engulfs her completely. She then consoles herself with the fact that in 2 weeks, they will be together again. As the small jetliner approaches the runway, it waddles and bounces along with the mile turbulence. Victoria commits herself to submerge herself in her affairs here in Washington with the hope that these 2 weeks will pass with haste.

While Victoria walks within the shadow of the terrorist resistant J. Edgar Hoover Building, she looks to her watch. As she continues to walk, she calculates Armstrong's arrival in Mississippi within the next hour. Her stomach churns like a vat containing oil and vinegar. The thought of him so vulnerable, leads to thoughts of the intentions of men that want to see him dead. Though, his voice of wisdom, echoes throughout her head to trust in the Almighty. With that she resigns herself of the thoughts, but as she now enters headquarters, she maintains her opinion that a wife should be with her husband.

A small army of reporters, camped out in the outer lobby, explode into action as Victoria enters. Stunned momentarily by the hordes of reporters descending upon her like a pack of wild animals on cornered prey. Questions are shouted at her like machine gunfire. Space violating mini-cameras are thrusted at her along with both handheld and extended microphones on poles. A microphone strikes her on her lip, just under her nose. The thump sparks her temper. She bulldozes her way through the wall of reporters as if she was exiting a subway train at rush hour.

The mob of reporters swarm around Victoria like bees around a hive. At the security check point, the incensed Agent presents her identification to the trio of security guards. After a momentary examination of her credentials, she is allowed to pass. As Victoria continues on, the shouting of questions from the reporters suddenly come to a hush. While she curses the existence of reporters, a clear distinct unnoble voice fills the corridor.

"Why were you arrested and locked in a jail cell in Madison, North Carolina?"

As if she had just blindly walked into a brick wall, the surprising question causes her to freeze in her stride. Immediately the informed reporter fires another question.

"What is the real story behind the deaths of 4 Police Officers in Madison, Agent Owens, and where do you fit into all of this?"

Victoria now figures the reporter to be from a tabloid media service with loose information from Madison. Perhaps one of the broken men in the jail cell is trying to sell a story. She dismisses the idea that this reporter has any solid information concerning the assassination plot to kill Armstrong, along with a large portion of the Mid-Atlantic United States. Without turning and facing the questioning reporter, Victoria continues her walk towards the elevators. The dead silence that had engulfed the corridor has begun to depart, as the other reporters begin to question what happened in Madison.

When Victoria stepped into her Office of Counter Terrorism and Intelligence, the scene reminded her of Times Square on New Year's Eve. She takes a few steps inward, walking in amazement at the frantic stirring of Agents appearing, as if the World was minutes away from termination.

Through a momentary break in the scrambled bodies of frenzied Agents, Victoria's eyes lock onto her partner's. Michael Peterson, while standing among unrecognized Agents, blinks his eyes several times before the realization of Victoria's person is standing only a few feet away. Victoria smiles, and starts walking towards him. A wave of Agents begin to cross and fill her now obstructed path. Though blocked from her view, Victoria continues onward in the direction she last saw her partner standing.

As she politely makes her way through the sea of Agents, she unexpectantly, and suddenly meets Peterson, who has made his way from his end, towards her. The two co-workers momentarily look upon each other, as smiles of happiness brighten their faces. Simultaneously they hug briefly and then separate. Full of smiles, Mike asks cheerfully, "What in the Hell are you doin' here?"

Victoria draws in a deep breath, and flatly reports, "I'm here to resign."

She could not believe she heard herself say that. She never imagined saying those words. She now immediately reflects that she never thought she would have uttered the words, I do, either.

"So, you're really going through with it, huh?" He started with a smile, though not as illuminating as moments ago. As he allowed the realization of her leaving to settle in, he sincerely says, "Good."

Victoria can see the disappointment in his eyes. She is going to miss him as well. To avoid a tearful scene, Victoria quickly asks, "Mikey, . . . what's going on?"

Peterson facial expression changes instantly. His serious expression precedes a tone of despair. "Vicki, . . . the shit has finally hit the fan."

Victoria's heart sinks to the lowest depths of her stomach. With her mouth now as dry as desert sand, she fears what has this office in such a state of madness. "What's happened?"

"Attacks upon the U.S. Government have just become

full scale, and organized. We have formed Task Forces to go after groups and or individuals opposed to the U.S. Government. A state of war, if you will, has been declared upon the government, and it's law enforcement body. The C.I.A. and the N.S.A. are advising that these domestic groups have ties with governments hostile to the U.S."

"Domestic groups?"

"Yeah, the militias, and other so called anti-government groups."

Victoria lightly quips, "You mean to tell me that a bunch of guys with semi automatics, and a few hand grenades have this place goin' nuts?" She ended as she looks around at the fevered activity.

"The bastards have acquired a biological device." Peterson informs flatly.

Snapping head back to him she unconsciously squints her eyes, and in a tone of disbelief responds, "What?"

"One, maybe even two." He answered grimly. "They have threatened Houston and El Paso."

"What?" She repeated still not grasping the unthinkable news.

"They want the President to surrender the government to the people of the United States, or . . . they are going to detonate their bombs." He now looks over to the gathered men in suits he parted from, and signals them him momentary return. "Vicki, I have to get back over there. Those guys are from the Homeland Security. Skinnermen wants me to go out to Texas where they, . . ." he motions with his head towards the Homeland Security Agents, ". . . Think they have one of the devices located."

Victoria looks over to the Agents automatically, as she tries to digest all the information Peterson has presented.

"Mike, I don't understand. Homeland Security located the Suspects and the illegal weapon of mass destruction? Since when—"

"That's the other latest development. Come January, the Bureau will be absorb by Security."

"Absorb?"

Peterson explains patiently, "Actually, it will be disbanded and restructured under the Homeland Security umbella."

In an upbeat tone, he begins as he starts to step away from her, "I'll see you before I go."

"Mickey wait, . . . this is not making any sense. Bio-chem weapons make lousy weapons on open air targets like cities."

Stopping his movement he questions, "What?"

She steps up to him, and in a soft voice, begins, "Something just isn't right with all this."

"What are you talking' about?"

"The Militias, . . . they aren't at war with the American people, so why would they put them in harms way with such an act?"

Sharply he answers, "What about Oklahoma City, years back?"

"Exactly, . . . everyone was screaming about the Militias being responsible then, so if they do have such a device to cause massive civilian casualties why wave a flag about it. Why don't they just use them? To alert us to the fact that they have them is so stupid. They know we would respond making Waco look like a Boy Scout Wiener Roast." She glances over towards the suited men, and then says grimly, "There is something wrong here. Something is just not right."

"Look, I have to go."

Victoria watches him as he returns to the trio of Security men. She then turns on her heels, and in a trans like state, autopilots herself out of the office. Her mind is occupied by the overwhelming information Peterson has told her. As she steps out into the corridor, heading towards the bank of elevators, she wonders what on Earth can possibly be next. Instantly Armstrong comes to her thoughts. Immediately sadness begins to descend over her like a dark cloud. We will not see each other grow old, the prophetically thought announces. Everything is out of control. All of these things are happening at an unprecedented rate. Sooner, more than later, it's all going to give way. I can't ignore the feeling that I have, she thinks to herself, time is running out!

As if cued, Assistant Director Walter B. Skinnermen steps from his office out into his reception area, just as Victoria enters. In his usual authoritative tone he begins, "Agent Owens, . . ." He walks over towards her, while extending his hand.

As they shake he continues, ". . . It's nice to see you again." He ended with a warm smile.

"It's nice to see you too, Sir." She returned respectfully.

"You've picked on Hell of a day to visit."

"I see. I just saw Peterson, and he clued me in. I just can't believe it."

Motioning toward his office, he says, "Come in to my office a minute, will you."

She nods in approval. Skinnermen leads her to his office door, and stands aside to allow her to enter first. As Victoria steps in, Skinnermen closes the hand designed oak double doors, while he invites the woman Agent to have a seat.

Victoria sits in one of the two black leather chairs, that faces the Assistant's large rectangle desk. While enroute to his desk he informs, "Agent Owens, when you return to work, you will have to prepare for a medal ceremony."

Now standing at his desk, smiling at the surprised Agent, he adds, "Though your actions in North Carolina is classified, your remarkable accomplishment cannot be ignored." He ended solemnly, and sits down.

Wowed by the recognition due to be bestowed upon her, Victoria beams brightly, as she adjusts her seating, moving towards the forward edge of the chair.

"Sir, . . ." She begins awkwardly, ". . . as to the matter of me returning to work, . . ." She pauses purposely, allowing the A.D. to catch her hint.

"Am I going to lose you Owens?"

"Yes." She returned flatly.

"In two weeks?"

"Yes." She said without emotion.

Skinnermen pauses momentarily, and then probes, "You found a position with Armstrong?"

Straining to compose herself from bursting with the news of her marriage, she quickly answers, "Yes."

"Well, . . . congratulations, . . . though in two weeks will be an unhappy day for the Bureau, . . . as well as for me personally. I wish you all the best."

Displaying a blushing smile, she says, "Thank you, Sir."

"It's been a true pleasure having you assigned here." He now paused momentarily for the sentimental moment to pass, and then begins in his usual no nonsense tone, "Well, . . . I called you in here to tell you about the recognition ceremony, and then to give you my personal at-a-boy pat on the back, concerning your effectiveness in the North Carolina incident. Now, I have to find something for you to do for the next two weeks."

"What's the deal with Texas?"

"Well, . . ." He starts flatly, ". . . A rather decent sized Militia group down in Texas, have acquired a biological device. We have information that shows this particular group with connections to hostile governments toward the United States. This group in Texas, and all of the so-called Militia groups have gotten out of hand. They are too large, and have become too strong."

"Yes, so it seems." She said flippantly.

"Well, . . ." He begins sternly, ". . . They won't be for long. The President is taking off the kid gloves. She's moving to abolish all of such groups in America, using her power under the National Securities Act, and the Patriot Acts."

Alarmed by this, Victoria states with concern, "My God Sir, . . . these people look upon the government as the enemy. They feel they are protecting the American way of life from foreign influence, and or control. Force, could spark a civil war."

"Just what is the President supposed to do, Owens?" He sharply asked. "These people now have weapons of mass destruction."

"Sir, does that make any sense?"

Skinnermen looks upon her as if she spouted another head. She sees his dumbfounded expression, and then she continues her thought. "Sir, . . . if they have such weapons, then what are *they* waiting for?"

"They want the President to surrender the government over to them."

"But Sir, that is what doesn't make any sense."

"Well it's no secret that these people are a little too far out in left field."

"No Sir, I mean the fact that they know, we know, that they have weapons of mass destruction."

"Agent Owens, just what are you talking about?"

"Sir, . . . why would they announce such a demand, backing it with such a threat?"

"You're losing me quick, Owens." He said with his jaws becoming tight.

"Sir, . . ." She starts firmly, ". . . If I had weapons of mass destruction, knowing damn well that this government will come down on me with all of it's hardware, the last thing I would do is tell Uncle Sam I have one."

Skinnermen pauses before he responds to her logic. His mind quickly processed her thoughts on the situation. He looks her straight in the eye, and says, "Well, . . . it's a good thing they aren't as smart as you." He adjusts his seated position, and then adds, "We will know exactly what the situation is once Peterson gets out there."

Victoria's mind starts to spin like a gyro, as she plots a way to join her partner.

"He's going to be my direct link. There is a Strike Force

already out there in position around the Freedom Compound."

Still suspicious of the entire matter, Victoria probes, "What the Hell, . . . if they do have weapons which threatens the well being of the United States, then why don't we just allow the Air Force some target practice?"

"It is not that quite simple. There is a problem with confirmation." He admitted.

"Confirmation?"

Skinnermen draws a breath and begins apprise, "There is great concern that my action taken, will not result in disaster for the Administration. Domestically, as well as internationally."

"Since when? We *all* know the drill by now. False evidence gets presented. The 'spin doctors' will spin, and the Media will make sure the deception sticks." She said flatly.

"Even more the reason that our Operations in Texas produces a 'smoking gun' on scene and on live TV." he pulls open a desk drawer, "There's no need for you to get all wrapped up in this." He now pulls out a 8"x5" sized form, "I'm assigning you to an administrative post."

Interrupting him, Victoria politely calls to him, "Sir, . . ."

She pauses until his eyes make contact with hers, ". . . Allow me to go along with Peterson."

Skinnermen sits silently, looking at the Agent blankly. Victoria now explains, "We probably would have been assigned the task as a team anyway, . . . besides, . . ." she displays a weak smile, ". . . I would probably foul up the Bureau for centuries if you put me in Admin."

Skinnermen pauses in thought. He then picks up his pen, as he firmly says, "I'm putting you in administration anyway."

"Sir, . . ."

Interrupting her, skinner sharply states, "Agent Owens, . . . you have only two weeks to give to the Bureau, and then you are out of it to do what you please, alive and in one pieced. Why do you wish to jeopardize that?"

"Well, sitting in *this* building will not be exactly the safest place on Earth. Not only is this place on the top 5 of the international terrorist hit parade, but there are some domestic terrorists that would love to see this place blown to bits as well. I would much rather take my chances out there."

Now in a softer, but dire tone she reveals, "I have to keep busy, stay moving. If I stand still long enough, my fears will catch up to me, and beat me to death."

The seasoned F.B.I. man has heard that tone before. As he slowly lowers he eyes from the woman Agent, he instantly recalls being in the position such as this young Marine Corps Captain in Vietnam. Many missions had to be completed, and the likelihood of return was not likely. He never had to pick the men for the task, and Skinnermen thanks his god for that. He thanks God that he was in the company of such brave men. Men that stood up, and knowing the score, requested the task. A lot of them never did come back.

SEMPI FIDLES

His eyes return to Victoria's. As he looks at her sitting across from him, he sees the same bravery in Agent Owens. He personally opposes Victoria going out into the field, but he respects her too much not to allow her, her destiny. She possesses the look he has seen before in her eyes. The tone of her voice spoke the same inevitable fate, which seemingly is preordained.

A lump the size of a softball feels lodged in her throat. Skinnermen's piercing stare is nerve tensing. His unrevealing expression is without emotion. Now, after weighing the matter, Skinnermen lifts the receiver of his telephone, while he presses a button on the keypad. He pauses momentarily, . . . and then sharply speaks into the phone, "I need you in here on the double."

He returns the receiver to its cradle, and looks upon Agent Owens.

"Alright Agent Owens, . . . I'm giving you what you want." He said in a defeated tone.

With a gleaming smile, she says, "Thank you Sir."

Sharply the Assistant Director says, "Don't thank me."

He then turns away from her. Victoria saw the concern on his stone etched face.

Michael Peterson enters the office. The partners look upon one another, and smile in acknowledgment. Peterson then directs his question to A.D. Skinnermen.

"Yes Sir?"

With his back to the standing Agent, Skinnermen firmly announces, "I'm sending you out there with a partner."

Surprised by the announcement, Peterson automatically says, "Why what happened?"

"An equally qualified Agent has just become available."

Peterson dumbfoundedly looks from Skinnermen to his seated, long time partner. Victoria glances up at him, with a shy smile. It takes only a moment for Peterson to gather and process the information, as Skinnermen continues, "Agent Owens is now your right hand."

"Owens!?"

Swinging around in his chair, Skinnermen calmly asks, "Is there a problem here, Agent Peterson?"

"Yes Sir." He answered strongly, and then directs himself to the woman Agent, "What in the Hell is wrong with you? You're short. You're so short that you would need a parachute to jump off the curb. In two lousy weeks, you're outa here."

"I'm sure she's aware of that Agent Peterson."

Turning to the boss, Peterson sounds a plea, "Sir, you can't let her in on this, . . . not with only two weeks left."

"In two weeks, WE could have this situation in hand." Victoria said with an upbeat tone.

Snapping at her, Peterson says, "Just take it easy, Jane Wayne!" He now steps up closer to Skinnermen's desk, and confesses, "Skipper, . . . this mission really scares the Hell outa me. This thing can blow right up in our faces. . . ." He now turns slightly towards Victoria, and changes his tone as he continues through clenched teeth. ". . . Therefore it will not be a place for a short timer!"

Firmly she says, "I want in."

In disgust, Peterson faces Skinnermen and says, "See Sir, she's crazy. I think she should be relieved for her own damn good!"

Skinnermen calmly says, "Peterson, . . . she's in."

The A.D.'s word was delivered with a thud of closure. He then looks to his watch, and then looks Peterson directly into his eyes and adds, "Brief her on your way, it's time for you two to get underway."

Peterson turns to her. Victoria stands, while silence descends upon the office. Peterson motions towards the door with his head. Victoria looks towards the door, and then starts for it. Peterson turns about, and looks to Skinnermen. Skinnermen looks upon the eyes of the concerned Agent. Both men pause momentarily in thought before Skinnermen slowly turns his back to him. Peterson leaves the office, and joins the waiting Victoria in the outer office.

As he approaches, Victoria can see his unhappy expression upon his face. The large, solid built man steps right up to Victoria, and in a low voice, angrily states, "I want you to go back in there, and tell him you've changed your mind!"

"What?"

"Damn it Victoria!! . . ." He then clams down, and explains, ". . . Things have changed. It's not what it used to be." He continues with concern, "You don't have to be here now."

"I know."

"Then go back in there, and tell Skinnermen you've changed your mind. Stay here and hold down the fort." He ended with persuasion.

"I can't."

"Why not?!!" He fired back in anger.

With fire in her eyes, she responds, "What in the Hell do YOU care anyway?!"

"I just don't want to see you blown to bits!"

"WE, aren't going to get blown to bits! We have dealt with madmen before!"

They both take a step toward one another, closing any space between them.

"You just don't understand do ya?" He asked with a frown.

"Well Einstein, . . . explain it to me!"

"Damn you Owens, if you don't go back in there, I'm going to bust you up so bad, your ass won't walk for two weeks!" He ended through clenched teeth.

Victoria snatches him by his lapels. Her speed is blinding. Before he has time to react, she kisses him on his lips, just as Bugs Bunny does when he gets the best of Elmer. She releases him, and smiles. Peterson stands in complete surprise, while she sincerely says, "Thanks, for caring THAT damn much."

Now with his anger totally defused, all he can do is smile, and mumble, "You are one stubborn ass."

Victoria motions with her head and then gently says, "Let's go to work."

Peterson looks to his watch and says, "We have 30 minutes to get out to Andrews."

"30 minutes, . . . I have to stop by my place and pick up some, . . ."

Interrupting her, Peterson says, "No time Vicki. What we need, we'll have to pick up in Texas."

Chapter Eleven

An hour later, Special Agents Owens and Peterson are sitting in an Air Force Leer jet, traveling near 800 miles an hour, at 38,000 feet, rocketing towards the Lone Start State. Victoria Owens and Michael Peterson are sitting isolated from the rest of the jet's Flight Crew. The F.B.I. duo is speaking quietly while facing one another in a rear corner of the streaking jet.

". . . Bottom line, . . ." Peterson pauses momentarily before he continues with a dramatic flare, ". . . An Air Force Bomber is waiting with the biggest non-nuclear payload in the war chest, and is waiting in New Mexico. In a few minutes, it will be taking off, and orbit high above the Freedom Compound. If we cannot obtain control over the compound, . . ." He now points upward with his index finger, ". . . They will make it disappear."

Not believing her ears, she confirms.

"They're planning to drop that damn thing on that site?" she asked in an astonished tone.

"I hear it's the next generation. Hiroshima 1945, but without the nasty fallout."

In an alarmed tone, she asks, "And what about the surrounding areas?"

"The compound is an old farm some 40 to 50 acres in size. It lays 75 clicks, south of San Antonio. The compound is out in the middle of nowhere. A press release will disclose a medium quake had struck the area."

"My God."

"Vicki, . . . this matter is much too serious for search warrants, and Miranda warnings. This situation has apparently caught us with our pants down. We are now eyeball to eyeball, with terrorism IN the United States."

"Damn!!" Vicki then restrains her anger. "The handwriting has been on the wall for years. Now we're supposed to pull a rabbit out of our hats, huh? Those SOB politicians sit on their thumbs, delay countermeasures, and now look at us. We're, damn near, dropping nukes on our own soil, and on Americans." She takes a breath, and a quick glance at the uninterested personnel. She then looks back to Peterson, and then angrily growls, "Just how in the Hell did they obtain such a weapon anyway?"

Flatly he answers, "Homeland Security claims all the information necessary for this group or any other group is available on the Internet or public library."

"So what now. Book bans? Unplug the 'Net'?"

"The White House wants all Militia groups shut down. As we speak, the President is drafting a new anti-terrorism bill, that is directly aimed towards combating anti-government groups."

"You mean, they left that out of Patriot Acts One and Two?" she asked perspicaciously.

"Let me guess, . . . domestic terrorism is probably worded in there, and the definition is a broad description, which also includes the banning of private ownership of firearms in the U.S."

"What was attempted in 1994 is nothing compared to

what is being pushed for now. Vicki, . . . this issue is now on the global stage. The President is supporting the Japanese push to disarm the citizens of the World."

"Do they really believe Americans will surrender their arms?" She fired back in a bark. "And just who in the Hell is supposed to enforce such a ban?"

In a calmer tone, Peterson begins, "I imagine local and state police agencies, Homeland Security supported by U.S. Troops, or even perhaps U.N. Forces."

"My God, . . ." She now looks to him solemnly, ". . . There WILL be bloodshed. Civil war, revolution, . . ." She thinks further and then utters, ". . . It could be the beginning of the end for this United States."

"It IS the beginning of the end." He stated firmly, and continues, "The Russian Bear has awakened, and is more dangerous than ever. U.N. Troops are already being allowed to police the border between Mexico and the U.S. They are even, . . ." He uses his fingers to indicate quotation marks, ". . . 'Helping out', in crime torn cities like Atlanta, Chicago and San Diego. The North Koreans are steadying massing troops on the DMZ. There is absolutely no doubt that invasion is in the air." He then slowly begins to shake his head no, and then grimly states, "It IS the End of the Beginning. We, as a species have finally come of age. We as a species have wrecked a paradise. Hydrogen bombs, germ warfare and genetically modified foods." He looks sadly upon Victoria and painfully adds, "This madness has to stop, . . . or we as a species are going to die."

A pause of silent thought passes between the duo. Peterson peers out of a distant window, as his thoughts focuses on the World being like a huge balloon. His mind pictures this balloon being filled with air. The balloon continues to fill, until the rubber becomes so stretched, that the balloon seems almost transparent.

Victoria has absorbed all of the pervious information, and is now furious. To satisfy the egos of a minute few, they would allow the destruction of the Planet. In five years, we will be eating one another, . . . in ten, . . . it will be the planet of the apes, for real. We have to turn things around. This present course must be altered.

"Why does Armstrong want to be President?" Peterson asked in a whisper.

His voice snaps her out of her deep thought. She answers without emotion. "He believes he can turn the tide. He believes he can save America before it's damned."

Slowly shaking his head, Peterson responds coldly, "I'm afraid he's 40 years too late."

The statement causes a cold chill to engulf the woman Agent. Her thoughts now render her silent. She stares off wondering what will happen next.

Shortly before noon, Central Standard Time, the Air Force jet touches down at Randolph Air Force Base. An all black unmarked military Blackhawk helicopter sits nearby. With it's crew on board, and rotors spinning, the jet copter is ready for immediate lift off. As the Leer jet taxies to a stop a few yards away, a Blackhawk crewmember runs over to the now stopped jet. The F.B.I. Agents are hustled off the jet aircraft, and rushed by the crewmember to the awaiting helicopter. They are helped aboard, and as soon as they are strapped into their seats, the pilot takes off, and thunders southwestward.

41 minutes later, in a remote region of unpopulated land, the jet-powered helicopter suddenly slows, and begins to land. As the helicopter descends, dust and dirt form a blinding cloud. As soon as the unarmed Blackhawk settles down upon the ground, a crewmember shouts to the Agents to deplane.

Victoria Owens hesitates, for she cannot see anything but a swirling dirt cloud all around the aircraft. Peterson jumps off the craft, as it's twirling rotors above are causing an artificial hurricane like environment. Peterson then holds his arms out toward Victoria. She releases her seat belt, and grabs a hold of one of his hands, and then jumps to the unseen ground. The crewmember motions for them to get clear, as the pilot applies additional power for lift off.

Huddled together, the duo trots away from the helicopter in a reflective hunch, in order to avoid the chopping overhead blades. The helicopter rises only to a height of 10 feet before it engages in a forward motion. Within a moment, it is gone. Only the air beating rotating blades can be heard, like a giant rapid pounding heartbeat.

Suddenly the rumble of a fast approaching AM General's Hummer, causes the Agent to turn automatically in its direction. As soon as the pair responds to the approaching noise, the vehicle tears through waist high bush, and stops about 20 feet from them.

"You two are to come with me!" The lone enlisted man shouted firmly from behind the wheel, as he and his vehicle becomes encircled by a brownish cloud of dirt and dust.

Victoria pauses momentarily as she desires to allow the dirty cloud to disperse. Peterson quickly steps to the military vehicle. Victoria pacifies herself with the thought, that this could be worse, and treks off in Peterson's wake.

The 5-mile journey to the Army's staging area was very bone jarring. Victoria is sure that her ovaries have been knocked out of place. She instantly likened the ride to traveling along the Cross Bronx Expressway, between the George Washington Bridge and the Bruckner Expressway merge.

The driver drops the duo in front of the command tent. As Owens and Peterson step away from the all terrain vehicle, the driver accelerates, causing all four wheels to spin. A cloud of dust kicks up as he speeds away. As the dust settles, Special Agent in Charge, Willard B. Halagen emerges from the tent. Special Agent Halagen is the 'top' F.B.I. man in the State of Texas. A distinguished looking middle-aged 50 year old, tanned, clean cut, 6'4" tight-bodied man seems to have materialized amidst the settling dust.

Halagen stands at the mouth of the tent in silence. Both Agents simultaneously look upon him. Though they have never met the Supervising Agent before, they instantly detected his identity. Agent Halagen's body language projects authority. His form fitting, powder blue polo shirt, has the F.B.I. seal, just over his left nipple line. With a slight southern twang in his speech, Halagen peevishly says, "Now, . . . I told Washington that I DIDN'T need any so-called experts out here."

Provoked by his hostility, Victoria flippantly begins, "Hi, . . ." Now motioning towards her partner, ". . . This is Agent Peterson, and I'm Agent Owens, F.B.I." Then she adds to insult, "Who might you be?"

In a huff, the 'top' man begins, "I am Special Agent in Charge Halagen. W.B. Halagen. Now, . . ." He starts as his neck and face becomes red. ". . . Why don't you and your friend there, turn around and get on back to Washington."

Just then, an Army Colonel emerges from the tent, shadowed by a Major, and a dark suited black man. The Colonel takes a look at the duo through his squinting eyes, and stops his movement. He then sternly asks for their identity.

"Peterson and Owens, F.B.I." Peterson fired at the camouflaged Colonel, while peering at the unpleasant S.A.C.

Facing the inquiring Colonel, Halagen announces, "There's no need for introductions, these two were about to leave."

". . . 'Fraid not." Peterson starts, as he looks directly upon the Agent in charge. "We are under direct orders of the Director." He ended strongly.

Becoming angry, Halagen sharply says, "I'm afraid son, that I have just given you a direct order to return to D.C.! You and your friend here, are not needed!"

"I'm afraid that they are!" The black man said flatly, as

he steps towards the Agents, while passing the flaming hot Halagen.

In a huff the senior F.B.I. man, spins on his heels and while placing his hands on his hips, whines, "Colonel, this operation is startin' to turn into a three ring circus!"

The Colonel coolly responds, "Sir, there's nothing amusing here today." He then directs his next statement towards the suited black man.

"Tatum, 15 minutes, and then we jump off. We're not waiting for anyone." He then turns to the ego crushed Halagen, and adds, "And my orders come from the President of the United States."

Tatum reaches the Agents, and extends his hand, shaking each of theirs as the Colonel and his Command walk off.

Halagen faces the Agents, and states, "That gives me enough time to call Washington, and get a few things understood."

He disappears into the large house sized tent, as Tatum introduces himself.

"I'm Tateum, Homeland Security."

Peterson responds, "I'm Peterson, and this is Owens." He now looks towards the tents' entrance, and then continues, "Tell me something, . . . is it us, or is he an asshole?"

Tatum looks Peterson in his eyes, and answers, "He's an asshole. Forget 'em. I've been waiting for you two to arrive, and it looks as if you made it just in time."

"Why, what's happening?" Victoria asked with concern.

"Hell, we still have no hardware confirmation of any weapons of mass destruction in there." Tateum said in frustration.

"What?" She said suspiciously.

Peterson asks, "Still nothing from the satellites?"

"Nothing and from their low orbits, despite the fact that they can count the hairs on a man's head while he walks around within his house, but tell you the color and measure length and width."

"Then call off that bomber." Victoria said firmly.

"Can't, and Washington won't until there's an absolute, no threat condition. A device might even be off site and planted at their targets."

Victoria pleads, "Does that make any sense?"

"No, but then we are dealing with a bunch of psychotics." He answered flippantly.

Victoria steps closer towards him, as she has become completely convinced of a Governmental conspiracy to create an excuse for Martial Law. "You have nothing here. Homeland Security has nothing on these people at all, Mmm?" she questioned sternly.

Dumbfounded by her demeanor, Tatum defensively responds, "What?"

Continuing in the same manner, Victoria says, "Homeland Security needs a great big feather in its cap, huh?"

"Watch it, Agent." Tatum warns without a smile.

"I won't watch these people murdered for any political agenda, nor for some BS agency's grubstaking."

Angrily, Tatum warns, "You better check that tongue, Agent Owens."

Victoria looks to Peterson, "These people are going to be wiped out to push some politician's agenda, Mike."

"Com'on Vicki."

"Tell me that has never happened before." She started sharply. "A bunch of cowboys in Texas."

Tatum directs himself to Victoria, and grimly explains.

"That might be true for some, but this Agency will strike first. It will not wait. It cannot afford to wait. The welfare of the Nation out weighs any possible error. Now, . . ." he begins gravely, '. . . unless you guys can pull a rabbit out of your hat, the Colonel has the authority to make that entire farm disappear from the face of the Earth."

"My God." She said in a whisper, as she begins to feel her blood run cold.

Responding to her remark, Tatum says flippantly to her, "Whichever god works for you."

"Despite it all, the order to vaporize this place is coming. Isn't it?" She asked flatly.

"What do you think?"

She steps closer to the suited Agent, and looks him in his eyes, and asks, "What do you know?"

Tatum looks upon the pretty Agent. He then swallows hard, and confesses, "Yeah, . . . kiss this place goodbye. This is not some jive time ATF raid on a bunch of cowboys with some AK's, and armor piercing bullets. These guys suppose a threat to the United States."

"But there's no clear evidence of . . . ."

Cutting her off, Tatum sharply says, "Don't you get it? This operation boils down to, *so what.*" He pauses while throwing his hands into the air. "Who is going to bitch? The Media is going to report what we *tell* them to. There is no longer any free press. *We control it all.* You see, . . . the America people are too emotionally subdued to face matters of this magnitude. They protest about their rights being taken away . . . ***bullshit***! They are surrendering them." Tatum continues in a mocking, unflattering tone of voice, "Enslave us, so long as we are safe in our little fantasy world." he motions towards the distant, unseen farm, and states, "There's the crisis, . . . and it doesn't matter if its real, or not, because the remedy awaits, circling above. America will soon have what it wants." He ended in a evocative tone.

"This is a trigger event, Tatum?" Peterson asked in a mumble.

Tatum looks to him.

"To totalitarianism, baby." He then humbly states, "You two better get a move on. Next stop, . . . ground zero."

"We, . . ." Victoria states directly her question to the Homeland Security man. ". . . Aren't *us*, . . ." She motions with her hand indicating herself, her partner as well as the Homeland Security man Tatum, ". . . Going up to ground zero?"

Tatum looks directly at the Agent and then flatly replies, "You two are suppose to be pretty damn good at what you do." He displays a phony three dollar bill smile and adds, "I'll probably just get in the way."

"But aren't you here to oversee F.B.I. operations?"

"Agent Owens, I am here to oversee all operations. As of this moment, the F.B.I. is still in business, therefore this scene is an F.B.I. matter, unless a higher authority says otherwise, or if they kill you." He ended flippantly.

As the suited man starts to walk off, Peterson begins to follow him. Victoria takes a hold of her partner's arm, stopping him. She then pauses momentarily as she watches Tatum walk out of earshot.

"What's up?" Peterson asked mystified.

In a low solemn voice, Victoria begins, "What if we all get up to the Freedom Compound, and then they burn us?"

"I don't think they want to die. I think they would of detonated their bomb by now, if that was the case."

In the same tone, she clarifies her question, "No not them, . . . THEM. Suppose the bomber gets the 'go' word?"

"What are you saying, . . . the General is also going to be at the scene. Why would he send, . . ."

Interrupting him, she interjects, "No, . . . not the General."

"Then who?"

"Perhaps Washington." She replied firmly.

Discounting her statement as nonsense, Peterson exclaims, "Com'on Victoria, why? Why would they kill us all?"

"Because THEY would then be BLAMLESS!" She fired back.

Peterson looks away from her, as he looks out towards the horizon. Victoria witnesses his expression transform into one of horror. She then gently speaks, "You know to cover your ass. They know how to do that as well, in Washington."

Facing her, Peterson weakly states, "They would not kill us."

"Oh no? . . . Are you willing to bet your life on it?" She ended coldly.

Angrily Peterson snaps at her, "So what in the Hell do YOU propose we do?!"

"It just might be too late for us." She said in a macabre tone, as she begins to walk in the Homeland Security man's wake.

The Freedom Militia for a Free America, has been active in south Texas for 3 years. They have a local active membership of about 150 people. They had got national attention when they began protesting U.S. government policies, which were in conflict with the U.S. Constitution. Lately the Militia has been responsible for the examination of the records to determine if the State of Texas is legally apart of the United States.

Today, now surrounded by a small detachment of U.S. Army soldiers, and various battle ready pieces of equipment and vehicles, the Freedom Movement holds the 46 acre site with less than 100 men and women armed well enough to give the Army a fight.

A simple chicken wire gate stretches across the unpaved road that leads to the large wood framed farmhouse inside the Freedom Compound. Manning the gate are two fortified positions, one on each side of the gate, just inside the property. Some 20 yards behind them, in a crater like hole in the middle of the road, are three men. They serve as the Freedom's welcome committee. In the crater is a M-60 machine gun, and two RPG anti-tank rockets launchers. The third man is the eyes and ears for the Freedom Command

Post, which is beneath the farmhouse. He's in direct contact with the Freedom's Commander. If the Army begins an attack, these 5 members have vowed to die before a soldier passes by them.

On the road, only some 50 yards from the gate, are elements of the Army's assault forces. The Freedom Forces peer through their gun sights at their cameo green targets. The scene is very tense. Presently a negotiating team is continuously attempting to defuse the uneasy standoff.

As the Colonel, and the Federal Agents arrive at the Army's front line, the Army leader is briefed with the news, that the negotiation team has just become successful with terms for a meeting between the Colonel, and the Freedom Leadership, at the chicken wired gate.

"Colonel, Sir, . . ." Peterson began as he moved toward him, ". . . Would you mind if we tagged along?"

The Colonel looked upon Peterson as if he was able to look through the man, and examine his soul.

"I don't see why not."

As the Colonel starts walking beyond the Army's line, Peterson looks to Victoria. She approves with a slight nod, and then together they step smartly to catch the long striding Colonel.

The Army's line became silent, as all eyes watch the trio walk along the dry dirt road, including the two well hidden Army Snipers, providing the Colonel with long range cover. The walk to the well-guarded gate was completed in silence. As the trio nears the gate, they can now clearly see the heavily armed positions, as well as an additional six men, now standing at the gate.

The tension is clearly visible now.

Victoria smoothly reaches nonchalantly to unsnap the weapon retention strap holding her pistol in its holster. Peterson in entertaining the thought, that this scene is the O.K. Corral. The Colonel's stress level is too high to be concerned with the tension of the scene. He prays that he would not have to give the order to incinerate this site, . . . and these people along with it.

As the trio steps into spitting distance, one of the men standing at the gate with a semi-automatic rifle disrespectfully says, “Ooooh-wee, lookie here, . . . a full bird” As he turns towards the Leader, he adds, “. . . Shit, I guess next, it will be the Joint Chief.”

“Knock it off.” The stone faced, heavy set man snapped, as he kept his eyes on the trio.

The middle aged, clean-shaven, portly man, looks to the military leader, and executes a hand salute with the sharpness of a bullwhip. Taken back by the action, the General pauses a beat, and then returns the salute, and then immediately informs in a no nonsense manner.

“Sir, . . . I stand before you with a personal pleas this one and final time, . . . surrender your weapons and yourselves, to Federal authority, . . . now.”

The portly leader, is a former military officer, and is unimpressed by the Colonel’s Patton-like manner. He looks from the Colonel, to Peterson, and then over to Victoria. As he looks upon Victoria, he flatly asks, “Feds?”

Victoria nods in confirmation.

The Leader then firmly probes, “Well, . . . just who in the Hell are ya? NSA, CIA, ATF or perhaps the FBI?”

Victoria nods again.

“They are here to take you and your Forces formally into custody.” The General said.

“Well, here we are, so come and get us, but first let me advise y’all of somethin’ first, . . . y’all gonna need some more Agents, and second, . . .” His voice now becomes sinister, “. . . If’n any of you F.B.I. types set a foot upon this here land, we will shoot you for trespassing, . . .” And now he looks to the General, “. . . And Colonel, . . .” He spits on the ground, causing it to strike the ground on the trio’s side of the gate, “. . . That’s my answer to a surrender. But let me tell you somethin', we here are Americans. We were born in free country, but what we're seein' here now is a dictatorship forming in this country. We tried to effect a change, as the right of an American, . . . but that sell out in the White House sic'ed her storm troopers upon us, and here they are now, ready to kill us. Well Sir, . . . we're ready to die."

The Colonel looks each man at the gate, square in the eye. He then raises his walkie-talkie up to his mouth, and sharply orders, "Demonstrate force."

In the sun dried, waist high brush behind the Colonel, suddenly comes alive with well camouflaged Army Troops, while thunderous noise from half a dozen helicopter gunships fly very low overhead. As the battle veteran Colonel watches the overwhelming scene in the eyes of the defiant men before him, he grimly announces, "And if this isn't enough to change your mind, . . . two, M-2-A battle tanks are just over that hill. So now Sir, . . . are you still ready to die?"

Maintaining his defiant stand, the Leader responds, "We are not afraid to die."

Recognizing that this present situation is about to unfold into senseless bloodshed, Peterson suddenly steps forward, and addresses himself to the Leader.

"Just what in the Hell, are you gonna die for?"

The Leader's blue eyes narrow, as he firmly answers, "Freedom."

Sincerely Peterson stresses, "Damn it man, we are not here to rob you of your freedom. We aren't the FSB."

"Russian FSB or American FBI, . . . you are all the same shit, it doesn't matter if YOU are Americans."

"Bullshit!" Peterson shouts at him, and then explains, "I'm here because some smart asses have acquired weapons of mass destruction, and there is strong reason to believe that said weapons are on these premises."

"Bullshit!"

"No, real shit!!" Peterson snapped back.

"Hey, . . ." Victoria quickly adds in a softer tone, ". . . Let us search. Prove us wrong."

One of the men standing next to the Leader responds to Victoria's plea.

"You people are settin' us up. You people are here to take us out, . . . weapons of mass destruction, . . ." He now turns and addresses himself to Peterson. ". . . Shit, . . . who in the Hell do you think we are?"

"Dead men, . . ." The Colonel answers flatly. ". . . Unless you allow us entry."

"Colonel, . . ." The Leader starts in a calm tone. ". . . Our freedom is guaranteed by our weapons." He now charges his weapon for firing. He continues to speak, as the other men do the same. "We cannot, nor will not allow that guarantee seized by anyone."

"Very well." The Colonel hauntedly said.

Peterson knows that the next breath from the Colonel will set a small series of events into motion, which will eventually result in this farmhouse being a lifeless testament to domestic terrorism.

"Then take me." The F.B.I. man said aloud.

As everyone stands stunned by his statement, he adds, "I'll be your hostage as they search. I'm telling you, we are ONLY here to look for bombs."

"There ain't no bombs here!!"

"Then there won't be a problem."

The Leader looks to the Colonel, who is looking upon the F.B.I. man with a dumbfounded expression.

"Listen to me, . . ." Peterson starts as he steps closer to the rifle toting Leader. ". . . Keep your weapons. Tell your men to keep their weapons shouldered." He looks to the Colonel and adds, ". . . The Army will do the same."

The Colonel explodes back to life.

"Now just one damn minute!! Just what in the Hell do you think you're doing?!!"

"Saving lives, . . ." Victoria answers firmly, as she steps in front of the Colonel. ". . . Perhaps ALL of our lives."

The Colonel looks harshly into Victoria's eyes. She unmistakably reads the contempt in his winter blue eyes, but notices them begin to soften slightly just before he looked away from her. As the Colonel focuses his eyes upon the Leader's, he holds his breath.

Suddenly, without a word, the Leader slings his rifle onto his shoulder. Peterson now presents his sidearm to the Leader. As the Leader takes the semi-automatic pistol, and slips it into his waistband, he looks upon Peterson, and says in admiration, "You've got a set of solid steel balls, G-man."

At this very same moment, half a dozen Militia members escaped from the Army's encirclement, and made their way into town. There they began notifying all the news agencies about the events unfolding at the Freedom Ranch. The news of Waco II caught on faster than dried brush.

The Army, along with their searching equipment, are moving freely within the compound. Tension is high as the Army, and the Militia members are only a few feet from one another. In the farmhouse, the Colonel has stepped up his command post. He has informed the Pentagon, that he has gained entry to the compound without resistance, and Operation: Lost Dog, is under way. Victoria sits with the Leader on the opposite side of the room, while Peterson under Militia guard, sits in the kitchen.

The Colonel is presently being informed by the staging area, that a number of town's people, and a local reporter, have arrived, demanding answers to the reports of WMD searches. The Leader continues to disavow any knowledge or association with international terrorism.

"Missy, . . ." The Leader begins solemnly, ". . . Somebody has given all of yous' a bunch of shit. There aren't any mass destruction devices here. That IS bullshit!! We're being set up, or y'alls being set up, to set us up. Now, . . . just which is it?"

"Vicki!"

Peterson shouts for her from the kitchen. The distress in his voice, causes the tense woman to rush to his placement. She stops at the threshold between the hallway, and the large country kitchen, and scans the scene.

Peterson is sitting at the head of a long rectangular table, with an old 13-inch TV, sitting at the opposite end. His two guards are sitting behind the man on a countertop, with their guns resting across their laps.

"I think you need to take a look at this." Peterson said flatly, as he motions towards the TV.

Victoria enters the rundown, faded yellow kitchen. As she approaches Peterson, she looks over the two Militia guards with distrusting eyes. Uneasy about turning her back on the heavily armed men, she stands to view the television in a manner in which she can also view the two guards.

The Pentagon, as well as Texas Air Force Bases and Army Units, have become besieged with calls, as the media has begun reporting military action upon the Freedom Compound. Scores of news helicopters are now approaching the compound, but are being chased away by military helicopters.

"Leroy!!" One of the guards shouts out, startling Victoria.

Leroy, the Leader of this organization, steps into the kitchen, with his walkie-talkie baring about civilians arriving and media helicopters above. The guard happily reports, "The whole World knows what's happening here."

Suddenly a clear message rips from the portable radio, *'The Army is pulling out!'*

Now standing in the doorway, Colonel Fox announces that his forces have been ordered out immediately. A cold chill of fear engulfs Victoria, as she moves towards the Colonel.

"What about the search?"

Not making eye contact with her, the Colonel mechanically speaks, "There is no longer evidence of illegal weapons of mass destruction. All detection devices, including satellites, are now positively reporting, 'no joy'."

She now steps closer and in a low but firm tone asks, "And THAT bomber?"

"It's been ordered to stand down."

"Are you sure?"

"I gave the order myself!" He answered sharply.

With her teeth locked together she returns sharply, "So what, . . . that damn thing could still be up there, about to wipe us all out!"

The Colonel smiles, and flippantly responds, "Tell me Agent Owens, . . . do you also believe that this government conspired in the assassination of President John F. Kennedy? My God child, . . . this is America."

Overhearing their conversation, the Leader responds, "Yeah, . . . but these days we spell it with a 'K'."

The Colonel looks to the Leader, offended by his statement, responds politely. "Good day Sir."

"Same to you."

The Colonel looks into Victoria's eyes momentarily, and then turns and departs from the room. Victoria turns and faces her still sitting partner. The Leader turns to his guards and orders, "I want you men to do two things. One, . . . make sure all continues to go smoothly, as the Army withdraws, and second, . . . go over every inch they covered. Make sure no booby traps have been left behind."

As the guards hurried out of the room, Victoria begins to slowly approach the table. The Leader now turns his attention to Victoria.

"I got a funny feeling you don't trust 'em soldier boys."

Victoria looks from the Leader to her partner. Peterson can read the question in her eyes. He cannot allow himself to entertain Victoria's thoughts of Air Force bombs being dropped regardless, but he is aware of history. He know well of atrocities by this country.

"It's just like the man said, . . . no supportive evidence to continue on." He said, not believing the statement himself.

"Or, there are just too many eyes about now." She responds coldly.

"Is it safe for me to assume that your business is finished here as well?" The Leader asked as he presented Peterson with his pistol.

Taking his gun, Peterson answers, "For now."

"Mister, . . ." Victoria begins as Peterson checks his gun, ". . . You don't know how lucky you really are."

"Lucky?"

"Yeah, lucky." Peterson reinforces, as he walks towards his partner.

"What is that, . . . some sort of threat?"

"No threat intended, . . ." Victoria says sincerely, ". . . It's only an observation."

Owens and Peterson leave the unkempt farmhouse. Under the distrusting eyes of heavily armed Militia members, the duo begins walking the same dusty trail toward the now open gate, making the Freedom property line. With the last few soldiers yards in front of them, Peterson lightly quips, "Well that was fun."

"Oh really?"

"Yes, job well done." He said with a smile.

Not as light hearted, Victoria says, "Oh, . . . surrendering yourself as a hostage to a bunch of government hating, heavily armed whackos, is just another day at the office, huh?"

"It just might have prevented a bloodbath."

"Hey, I've got a bulletin for ya. They were going to burn this location, . . . device or no device."

A pause of silence descends, as Victoria's thought provoking statement settles in. Suddenly, after mentally acknowledging that she is correct, Peterson painfully mumbles, "I believe you're right."

"These people didn't have any biological or chemical weapons."

"Well, we know that now."

"These people NEVER had such weapons."

Suddenly, Peterson's portable phone chirps. He didn't realize it until the 3rd ring, for his mind was consumed by Victoria's devastating conspiratorial allegation.

"Peterson." He said into the mouthpiece, automatically, still reeling from Victoria's opinion.

A woman's voice, unrecognizable to Peterson's ear, begins in a professionally clear mechanically voice, "One moment please, for A.D. Skinnermen."

As Peterson awaits the connection, Victoria is silently deducing the circumstances involving the Freedom seize. There's no doubt that someone's plans have now been derailed. That someone has gone to a lot of trouble. The whys are now so very clear. The devil has only so little time remaining.

"Yes Sir." Peterson's sharp reply interrupts Victoria's thoughts.

Sitting at his desk in Washington, Skinnermen informs Peterson of a new assignment.

"I'm informed that the Freedom matter is now a closed issue, and now I need you and Owens to get over to New Mexico. The Carlsbad office is tracking a vicious, murderous bank robbing crew, which we believe consists of former Soviet Intelligence Operatives. Our expertise is needed in Carlsbad. You are the Agent in charge, understand?"

"Yes Sir."

"Now arrangements have been made with the Air Force. They will transport you from Texas to New Mexico, so leave there and get to Randolph right away."

"Yes Sir."

"Good luck."

"Thank you Sir."

Skinnermen terminates his call.

As Peterson returns his cellular phone to his hip pocket, Victoria questions him.

"Skinnermen?"

"Yeah, we've been ordered to New Mexico." He said flatly.

Surprised by the location, she responds, "New Mexico?"

"The Carlsbad office has some bank robbers in their sights, and Skinnermen wants us there."

Again, surprised by the assignment, she questions, "Bank robbers?"

He explains, "These are no ordinary bank robbers. They are supposed to be some bad ass former KGB types."

"KGB?"

"Yes Polly Parrot. The KGB is robbing banks in the American Southwest." He said sarcastically. "Com'on, we have to get out there on the double."

"What's next? An invasion form outer space?"

Smartly he says, "That will be handled by the MIB."

Chapter Twelve

By 5:30 p.m. Owens and Peterson were sitting in the small Carlsbad, New Mexico F.B.I. office. The fourth floor office view provided a commanding overview of the downtown Carlsbad business district. For the next six hours, Owens and Peterson are briefed on the activities of the murderous bank robbers.

By midnight, the duo are on their way to a nearby motel, for some rest before their 7 a.m. assemblage, with the rest of the surveillance teams. As soon as Victoria got settled in her motel room, she placed a call to her Husband. For nearly two hours they spoke. Upon hanging up, her eyes filled with tears. She misses him. The two weeks they will be apart will feel like two months.

An unseasonably brisk morning meets the Agents, as they emerge from their separate motel rooms, and climb into their specially equipped F.B.I. Chevy Tahoe. The Blazer is an all wheel drive, gunmetal grey vehicle with dark tinted windows. Cosmetically, it is a typical non-descript SUV. Inside the Tahoe is basically standard equipment, except for the F.B.I. radio with state, county and local police department frequencies, night vision optics, .40 caliber handgun ammunition, as well as .9 millimeter armor piercing ammo for the two dashboard mounted Heckler and Koch, MP-5's. Completing the list of F.B.I. add ons, is a 5.7 litered Corvette V-8, under the hood.

Shivering, Victoria tells Peterson to turn on the heat. Remarking that her blood is too thin, Peterson ignores her request, and asks with artificial concern, as he pulls away from the motel, "How did you sleep?"

"Not long enough." She said as she looks upon the instrument panel, and visually scans for the climate controls. Matter of factly she asks, "Do you know where to meet these guys?"

"Yes, I know where I'm going."

He then reaches for the radio power button, and punched it with his index finger.

Observing his movement, Victoria warns, "If you turn to that idiot shock-jock, I'm going to hurt you."

'. . . WE STILL AT THIS HOUR, . . .' the frantic voice of the news reporter blasts from the radio, '. . . THE EXTENT OF THE DESTRUCTION!'

"What happened now?" Peterson mumbles.

A calmer voice now emits from the broadcast, 'THAT WAS WAYNE ROBBINS, FLYING OVER DOWNTOWN BUFFALO, NEW YORK WHERE A MAJOR EARTHQUAKE STRUCK THE CITY THIS MORNING AT 6:45, EASTERN STANDARD TIME.'

"Is that near Brooklyn?"

Stunned by the report, Victoria answers robotically, "No, . . . Buffalo is clear across the state."

Suddenly the F.B.I. radio comes to life.

'ABLE-NAN, . . . ABLE-NAN, . . . ON THE AIR?'

"That's us." Peterson excitedly said.

"I know. Give me a chance to get to the radio." She snaps back, while she reaches for the microphone.

"Able-nan, standing by."

'YOUR E.T.A.?'

Victoria looks to Peterson. He quickly figures their arrival time, and responds, “Tell them, in about 5 minutes.”

“About five.” She reported into the microphone, and then, while looking over at her partner adds, “That’s if we don’t get lost.”

‘10-4’

“Com’on Vicki, don’t let these guys think we’re jerks.”

She smiles, and then reaches for the car radio. As she attempts to tune in another radio station, she reveals, “Relax, . . . I didn’t say that over the air.”

‘AT 6:30 A.M. NEW YORK TIME, THE STATE’S WESTERN CITY OF BUFFALO WAS ROCKED BY A MAGNITUDE 7.4 EARTHQUAKE. RESCUE UNITS FROM SOME 100 MILES AWAY, ARE NOW CONVERGING ON THE DEVASTATED CITY. AFTER SHOCKS ARE BEING FELT AS FAR AWAY AS TORONTO . . . .’

Seven minutes later, Owens and Peterson arrive in an alley, two blocks from New Mexico Savings and Trust. Awaiting their arrival are the members of the Carlsbad office. The members are huddling around together, drinking coffee. One of the two vehicles in the alley is a city of Carlsbad maintenance truck, which contains a bucket. The other is a dirty white Blazer equipped exactly like the one Owens and Peterson are stepping out of.

The Senior Agent, of the Carlsbad office, meets the two Agents, as they approach the others. After greetings are exchanged, Special Agent Wybeck, a 12-year veteran, confidently says, “Today, we’re putting some real bad guys out of business.” The senior Agent ends with a smile.

“You sound very confident this morning, Agent Wybeck.” Peterson said flatly.

Smiling, Wybeck proudly explains, “We figured out why they are going to hit the N.M.S.T.”

“Why’s that?”

“The fact is that they don’t intend to hit the bank at all.” He paused momentarily, allowing the Agents to become dumbfounded. "This morning an armored truck, with 8.5 million dollars, in new counterfeit proof 20 dollar bills on board, will be stopping at the N.M.S.T. this morning. And, . . . the N.M.S.T. is the truck's first stop." He ended with a large grin.

As Owens and Peterson look to each other, the tanned, salt and peppered hared Senior Agent, calls over two other Agents. While the Agents approach, Wybeck continues, "This is Nelson, and Simon, . . . you didn't meet them last night because they were babysitting the bank." He turns to the uniting Agents, and then states, "Guys, . . ." He now returned to the duo, ". . . Victoria Owens, and Michael Peterson is the A.I.C. for this takedown."

Once the polite hailings are completed, Peterson immediately looks to his watch, and firmly asks, "Are we all here?"

Wybeck instantly reports, "Landol is keeping an eye on the location."

He then turns towards the maintenance truck, and whistles. Agent Jose Rivera exits the truck, and as he approaches the gathered, he joylessly says, "Man that earthquake in New York is unbelievable. They still can't get any ground rescue equipment in. They say, any great number of survivors will be a miracle. Half the city is on fire, and the other half is flattened."

A pause of silence falls over the group, as each wonders about the nightmare the people of Buffalo must have experienced.

Snapping everyone's mind back to business, Peterson's stern tone suddenly booms, "People, . . . I want to allude once again what we might be dealing with, if our perps show up." He now pauses momentarily, as he looks upon them to ensure their attention. "The perps are known to be armed with high tech military grade weapons, and these maniacs are very good with them. They attack without mercy and kill, . . . anybody for any reason. Our orders are direct, and simple, . . . engage these maniacs, and take them down." He stopped coldly.

Simon, a Ken Doll look alike, promptly speaks, "Where is everybody else? HRT, or local PD SWAT?"

Peterson looks the Agent in his sparkling blue eyes and unemotionally explains, "We, . . ." He motions towards himself, and Victoria, ". . . Are all the back up available. With all the turmoil in progress throughout the country, the Bureau's resources are stretched beyond its limits. I do assure you that if these maniacs weren't murdering cops, and civilians, we all wouldn't be here. These days, there are more important Federal matters than bank robbery. So, . . . since it is up to us, and only us, we better not fuck up, huh?" He now becomes stern in speech, as his Marine bearing begins emerging. "We have the equipment and more so, we have the element of surprise. These bastards are not home grown pussies, out on a robbin' and murderous spree, that will surrender at the first sight of law enforcement firepower. These maniacs are hardcore. They are not going to go peaceably, nor will they go alive. Now, if you give them the opportunity, they will blow you right outa your socks! I do strongly suggest, that you line 'em up in your sights, and drop them as soon as possible."

A death-like hush follows in the wake of Peterson's words. Special Agent in charge Peterson stands silently, allowing his statement time to absorb into their minds, while he psychologically begins to smell the distinct odor of blood in the air. Perhaps he has developed this sixth sense from many bloodletting exposures, as an embattled U.S. Marine Recon Team Leader engaged in many covert, highly secret missions for the U.S. government.

He glances over to Victoria. While in a moment of thought, he wonders if the smell of HER blood will fill the air this day. Angered by the thought, he looks to Wybeck, and unconsciously snaps, "Wybeck, let's review the battle plan once again!"

"Right, . . ." Wybeck said flatly. He then turns to Nelson and Simon, "You two are high in the maintenance bucket. Nelson, you're on the sniper rifle, and Simon, . . . you're high cover with the semi-auto." He now directs himself to Agent Rivera, and continues, "Jose, . . . it's me and you in the Blazer. Landol is going to be out on the sidewalk, where he is now, . . . across the street from the bank." He faces the Agents from Washington and informs, "Landol is dressed as a homeless man, and that leaves you two, manning the other Blazer, and will approach from the north, when the party begins."

"Now remember one thing, . . ." Peterson starts firmly, ". . . We have to hit them hard, fast, and decisively. We have to protect each other's positions as well. We cannot afford for them to concentrate their firepower on us on the ground or the guys in the bucket. We cannot loose the momentum the element of surprise will give us."

"What if we lose it? What if they really got their shit wired? What if THEY have back up?" Simon rattled off with passionate concern.

Peterson immediately answers in a callous tone, "We die, and they win." He then looks to his watch, and asks Wybeck, "What do you think, . . . is it about time that we get into place?"

With the dread of this assignment mounting within him, Wybeck could now only nod in agreement.

8:03 A.M.

Agents Simon and Nelson are now high in the maintenance truck's repair bucket. They have lined the bucket with a few heavy-duty ceramic, bulletproof vests. Agent Landol is now sitting on the curb, across the street from the bank, with a junk filled shopping cart beside him. Under his long raincoat is a Beretta M-12, with two twenty round magazines taped together. Special Agent Wybeck, and Agent Rivera sit quietly parked in a scarcely populated municipal parking lot, a half a block away from the bank. Victoria and Peterson are sitting in their idling Blazer, a block from the bank. The vehicles' radio is continually reporting the news and updates, concerning the Buffalo quake.

"You know, . . . all this amazes me." Victoria began.

Peterson turns, and looks to her. She takes his non-verbal response as an acknowledgement of interest, and continues. "We're sitting out here about to pounce on some unexpecting bad guys, all because a DEA wiretap, picks up the 'hype' in the crew trying to score. They trace it, . . . put two and two together, . . . press the supplier, . . . and now here WE are."

Harshly Peterson replies, "The miracles of modern law enforcement."

Sensing his irritation, Victoria gently probes, "Are you okay?"

His body now swells as if it is about to explode.

"No damn it, I'm not okay!!" He snapped at her like a junkyard dog. "I've got a major problem with your stupid ass thinking!"

Peterson's words had the same effect, as if Victoria was struck by a lightening bolt. Stunned by his sudden rage, she could only manage to muster a pitiful response, "What did I do?"

Recovering from his momentarily out of controlled emotion, Peterson adjusts he tone. His concern for his partner now emerges.

"You're short. Too short to be out here, playing G-Men verse the Gangsters."

Defending herself, Victoria says, "I rather be out here, than back in Washington behind a desk."

"Vicki, you're getting' married soon. You're gonna be startin' a whole new life. Hell, . . . you might just be the wife of the next President of the United States." He now sits back in the driver's seat thinking about what he has just said.

Victoria remains silent. She looks upon him, and views his agitated state, and fails to imagine his reaction, if she informs him that she is already married to the popular Presidential Candidate.

The F.B.I. radio is silent. No transmissions for fear the robbers might be monitoring all police frequencies. Victoria sighs, and then flatly states, "Look, . . . that won't be for another 12 days, . . ." She now continues in an upbeat tone, ". . . We can even have the terrorist matter resolved by then."

While turning towards her, Peterson sits straight up in his seat, and barks, "What the Hell's the matter with you? THAT shit is NOT, repeat, NOT going to be resolved by US! What, just because you got lucky in North Carolina, you think the good guys will always come through?!" He now continues sternly. "You better stop acting like a first year rookie, and wake the fuck up!"

As he turns away from her, and eases back into his cloth-covered seat, Victoria's fury begins to rise within her. She feels as if she's five years old, and has just been chastised. Now resisting the urge to choke him out, she composes herself. Through clenched teeth, she asks, "What in the Hell is wrong with you? Are you and Mary having problems?"

"My marriage in just fine, thank you." He snapped.

He now looks to her. His eyes meet her seething gazes. He then takes a breath, and then sincerely apologizes.

". . . I guess I'm letting things get to me." He ended in grief.

Like hot air released from a balloon, Victoria's fury subsided.

"Perhaps it's time for you to take a vacation."

Peterson looks out the side window, and sits motionless. Victoria watches him as he sits in deep thought. She has never seen Peterson act in such an uneasy, emotional fashion. Perhaps he's just getting tired, she thinks. The seemingly inability to obtain a foothold upon the criminal element has perhaps begun to take it's toll, she ponders. Right before his eyes, as well as mine, this country, . . . in fact, the World, has transformed itself into one very dangerous place to live. It seems like to some people that the famous light at the end of the tunnel is no longer there. To them, . . . only death and destruction lie at the end of the tunnel. The Godless masses believe man will survive despite nature's retaliation, and his will to make war and destroy. The New Agers not only accept some sort of impending cleansing, but also look forward to it, with the hope that man will be able to begin anew, minus the evil which now occupies the planet. The Bible's promises salvation for believers, before the Heavenly Father's wrath is unleashed upon the inhabitants of the Earth.

"I don't mind tellin' you Victoria, . . ." Peterson started, interrupting Victoria's thoughts, as he continues to look out of the window. "I'm fuckin' scared."

She remains quiet, as she immediately asks herself if she was afraid. No, . . . a little apprehensive perhaps about all of the unprecedented events that are taking place throughout the World, but she is not afraid. She now recalls her Bible studies with her Husband. He explained Matthew 24, and now she knows why such unrecorded events are occurring. As a believer, 1 Thessalonias, chapter 4 verse 16 through 18 calms her fears about any approaching doom. This is the light at the end of HER tunnel. She has attempted to discuss the Savior as an answer with her troubled partner, but he had quickly rejected any participation in such a conversation.

"I've been offered 125 grand, for all the dirt I can muster up on you." Peterson revealed flatly, as he continues to stare out of the window.

"What?"

He now turns to her, and unemotionally reports, "1.3 million if I pen a novel disclosing our exploits."

In disbelief, Victoria repeats, "What?"

"And if Armstrong does get elected, and then really screws up and marries you, . . . I will pocket 3 million dollars!

So, you better watch your ass, 'cause if you so much as fart, I'm writin' in down!" Peterson said, seemingly recharged from his burn out phase, "And then I can say, to Hell with all this!"

"IT'S GOING DOWN!!" The shrieking, unrecognizable voice, shouted suddenly over the F.B.I. radio shattering Peterson's, and Victoria's detached atmosphere.

Instinctively Peterson slams the steering wheel mounted gear selector, into the drive gear. He stomps on the accelerator, and pulls out of the parking space, with tires smoking. Victoria unlocks an MP-5 from the dashboard, and then looks to her hard driving, virtually orgasmic partner and remarks, "Man, YOU ARE Federal F.B.I. Three million dollars or not, . . . don't kid yourself!"

Before Agent Landol, who is disguised as a homeless man screamed excitedly into his hidden portable radio, that the robbery was going down, he was carefully watching the armored truck routinely pull up across from him, in front of the bank. Then suddenly a white cargo van pulls up and stops against the curb, in front of the armored truck. As the unmarked Ford van's rear doors flew open, another van stops hard in the street, at the truck's rear.

While all attention was directed to the tire screeching van, the floor mounted 20-millimeter cannon, in the rear of the white ford van, crackled like a thunderclap. A second shot reported, as the first, impacts on the armored trucks front end, thus destroying its engine. The second shot, which was followed by a third, and then immediately by a forth, were directed into the driver's compartment. As the thunderous roar of the cannon fire echoed through the early morning stillness, four men dressed in black, and totting rifles, jumped from the van stopped behind the armored truck's rear doors, a third van charges up, and stopped abreast of the burning truck.

All of this happened within three beats of a human heart.

Agent Landol, now having made his alerting broadcast just before the cannon fire, takes cover behind the borrowed city maintenance truck. Special Agent Wybeck and partner screech up in their white Blazer, blocking the street.

As the hard charging 5.7 liter Corvette powered Tahoe of Peterson and Owens approaches the scene, a flash of disbelief causes the robbers to freeze their actions. The pause was the F.B.I.'s opportunity to engage the surprised robbers, as they stand frozen like statues. Failing to take immediate action will now cost the F.B.I. their one of only tow elements of success. Now only their combat skills taught at Quantio, will determine their survival.

The robbers now open fire on the one obstacle blocking the roadway. Wybeck's Blazer took the full firepower of the criminals devastating ferocity. The Agents in the bucket, as well as Agent Landol, now open fire on the heavily armed robbers. Agent Nelson manning the M-21 scoped sniper rifle, kills a robber with his first shot, while Simon sprays the rear of the cannon firing van.

Peterson stops his Tahoe hard in the street, cutting off the rear of the robbers. On the opposite end of the scene, Wybeck and Rivera, who is armed with a compact Browning automatic rifle, are now unleashing their combined firepower upon the robbers positions of fire, as well. A pair of robbers attempt to flee in the cannon carrying van, but Rivera's BAR quickly terminates that attempt, before they could get the van in gear.

Between the intense fire from Peterson and Owens, and Simon's high up assistance, the four men dressed in black, who are using their vehicle as cover, fall dead succumbing to the armor piercing rounds of F.B.I. gunfire. Suddenly the third van, which was sitting idling next to the armored truck, spins it's tires as it drives off. The getaway van manages to get past Wybeck, despite his and Rivera's heavily concentrated gunfire upon the fleeing van. Wybeck and

Rivera are unable to give chase, since their Blazer is defuncted by massive amounts of effective military grade bullets.

Peterson calls out to his partner, as he rushes to get into the undamaged Tahoe. Reflectively, Victoria responds to his calls, and jumps into the Tahoe, as Peterson stomps on the accelerator, causing the modified all wheel drive to launch after the bullet riddled escaping van like an a cheetah after its prey on an African plain.

With morning commuters starting to fill the streets, the disrupted robbers drive without regard. As Peterson maneuvers through the traffic, in the robbers wake, Victoria reloads both her's as well as Peterson's MP-5's with fresh 30 round, armor piercing, mercury tipped bullets. The Russian natives are running, and definitely aren't stopping for anyone, such as people in the crosswalk, or anything, such as red traffic lights. Peterson is pursuing skillfully two or three car lengths behind.

The criminal van makes a high-speed right turn, side swiping a few cars, waiting for the light. Peterson follows through. Victoria looks back at the damaged vehicles, and evaluates the scene.

"Damn, . . ." She started in frustration. "I don't even know our direction, or location."

Suddenly, the pulse quickening electronic whistling of a siren, causes Victoria to look rearward once again.

A Carlsbad police car has now joined the chase. The police band scanning radio inside the Tahoe picks up the Carlsbad police officer, as he transmits the location and direction of the pursuit. The dispatcher acknowledges the pursuit, and then advises that the vehicles are connected with the robbery and shooting at the New Mexico Savings and Trust. Then the sound of helicopter blades, beating against the air is heard, as a loud transmission immediately follows the dispatcher, 'COUNTY TO AIR CARLSBAD, . . . ADVISE THT UNIT THAT WE ARE PRESENTLY ENROUTE TO HIS LOCATION. ETA 2 MINUTES'

'ROGER THAT!'

Victoria picks up the microphone on the police band radio, and firmly announces, "Carlsbad be advised, Federal Agents are in pursuit of heavily armed, wanted bank robbery subjects at this time. Advise your units that WE are in the sliver Tahoe, copy?"

'10-4' the dispatcher acknowledged, and then proceeded to advise all units on all frequencies of the F.B.I.'s involvement in the chase.

The pursuit continues to weave in and out of traffic. The getaway van turns onto another main roadway, where about a half a mile away lies railroad tracks. As the van straightens out from it's high-speed turn, the railroad crossing gates come down, and the warning lights begin flashing. The van's driver continues to race towards the crossing. Peterson releases the Tahoe, and closes to a car length behind the van on the wide four-lane roadway. The Carlsbad police sedan continues onward even though the Tahoe has distanced itself effortlessly.

The police radio begins to chatter about the impending apprehension of the robbers, due to the imminent road-crossing freight train. Victoria heard the chatter, but wasn't listening. She was studying the getaway vehicle in front of her. She judged the rapidly closing distance of the flash lit road gates, and the speed of the van. She now realizes, "He's not going to stop!"

Peterson doesn't respond to her deduction. He does not begin to slow the high performance Tahoe either. The van now moves over, crossing the double yellow pavement markings. Now on the wrong side of the road, the van is clear of the cars stopped at the crossing gate. Peterson follows. With oncoming traffic stopped at the gate on the opposite side of the tracks, the speeding vehicles won't be stopped by a head on collision.

As the train nears the intersecting roadway, so too does the chase. The trains loud electric horns blow, as if to cry out in a desperate plea for caution. The getaway van smashes through the road guarding gates, like a bullet smashing through a toothpick. Peterson continues through, as bits of gate, and plastic warning lights, showers the scene. As the Tahoe rockets through, Victoria glances to her right. Though the very near locomotive seems to be as mammoth as a mountain, her eyes lock on the expression of the terrified engineer, who is now close enough for Victoria to notice his gold front tooth. As the Carlsbad police car approaches the crossing the 200-ton diesel locomotive begins crossing the roadway. The Officer immediately applies the brakes, bringing the car to a stop, inches away from the crossing train.

At speeds reaching 100 miles an hour, it isn't long before the city's scenes are transformed into a densely populated rural environment.

"I think it's time for us to bring this to an end." Victoria stated, as she chambers a round in the MP-5.

It seems that the fleeing robbers have also decided to take action. They have figured that the madman driving the Tahoe will never give up, therefore he will have to be killed. As Victoria braces herself for the windblast, when she electronically slides down the window, the van's rear doors suddenly are kicked open. Peterson's eyes lock on the activity of a figure in the shadows of the van. Peterson's keen eyes see the figure tossing out a bunch of small, . . . dark, . . . round, ...

"Grenades!!" Peterson shouts, as he abruptly yanks the wheel to the right. The G-forces would have snatched her into his lap if it weren't for her safety belt.

The Tahoe violently changes directions in a 90-degree turn, leaving the road. It lands hard into a dry creek bed as the baseball sized explosives detonate sounding like a chorus of the 1812 Overture. The robbers look in their wake convinced that the madman in the Tahoe is no more. Now they direct their attention to the helicopter overhead.

Peterson feverishly wrestles with the steering wheel to keep the bouncing SUV on all fours. The Tahoe appears to have the characteristics of an angry, bucking wild horse. Victoria sees through split second openings in the dust cloud, trees along the creek bed rapidly coming closer.

Cursing in every combination known, Peterson is expressing his determination to regain control and get the fleeing bad guys.

"You gotta stop this thing, or we're gonna be sucking wood!" Victoria shouts, as she continues to watch, as the thick wall of trees nearing are so dense, that they might as well be a solid brick wall.

Like a cowboy riding a buck, Peterson contains the sliding and skidding vehicle finally. Seeing the bend to the right in the dry stone creek bed, he feeds the Tahoe additional power causing the rugged vehicle to power slide around the 90 degree bend. The creek bed now gently turns to the left, descending slightly downward. Trees are now forming on both sides. The trees squeeze the creek bed to a width just wide enough for the speeding Tahoe to travel through.

"This is no good!!" Victoria begins in despair. "We're getting further away from the road!"

"Have faith." He gently returns.

'YOU GUYS MUST DRIVE WITH THE ANGELS!' the Deputy says over the radio. 'WE THOUGHT YOU GUYS WERE DONE FOR!'

Victoria snatches the microphone and firmly says, "Are you guys still tracking the perps!?"

'IN FACT WE CAN SEE YOU BOTH!' the Deputy responded. 'WE HAD TO CLIMB HIGH. AFTER YOU LEFT THE ROAD THEY BEGAN TO OPEN UP ON US!'

Peterson shouts, "Where are they!!?"

Into the 'mic', Victoria asks the helicopter Deputies for the perps whereabouts.

'THEY ARE ABOUT, . . . 11 O'CLOCK, AND ABOUT A MILE FROM YOUR PRESENT LOCATION!'

The creek bed in now becoming littered with small fencepost sized trees, brush and a group of hikers.

"Shit!!!!!" Peterson shouted, as he suddenly spots the cluster of strolling naturalists. Victoria shuts her eyes and grabs the dashboard, bracing herself for the impacting bodies against the front end.

Suddenly Peterson shouts to her, "Com'on! Pay attention, this is no time for napping!"

Victoria's eyes open as if an ice cold popsicle has been inserted in her.

What the Hell, she ponders as she looks into her side view mirror. She is just in time to see the hikers, arising from the banks of the creek bed. She smiles at their apparent uninjured condition.

'F.B.I. BE ADVISED, . . .' the Deputy excitedly began, '. . . THAT TRAIL YOU'RE ON WILL ONCE AGAIN PARALLEL THE BLACKTOP IN ABOUT FIVE MILES! THE SUBJECTS HAVE A BANKING LEFT TURN, THEN A LONG SWEEPING RIGHT. WE FIGURE AT Y'ALL'S CURRENT SPEED, . . . WAIT A MINUTE!!' His voice has suddenly filled with concern.

A beat of silence from the radio, then suddenly the Deputy's voice returns with a tone of panic. 'F.B.I. BE ADVISED THAT A STREAM CROSSES YOUR PATH DEAD AHEAD. DEPTH IS UNKNOWN, BUT IT LOOKS TO BE ABOUT TWENTY FEET WIDE!! DO YOU COPY?!! REPEAT, . . . DO YOU COPY?!!'

The instant Peterson sees the flowing waterway, he decides to attempt to cross it, at speed, though he hasn't informed his partner of his intent. Victoria slowly looks from the view ahead to her partner. She sees his failure to reduce speed, or any preparation to stop.

"You've got to be kidding!"

"Afraid of getting a little wet?!"

"Mike, this isn't a boat!" She informs sharply.

"Better batten down the hatches!"

'F.B.I. STOP!!! WATER AHEAD OF YOU! DO YOU READ!!!?' The Deputy's voice boomed over the radio.

Victoria brings the microphone to her mouth, and smoothly says, "We're going for it."

'BE ADVISED, THAT WATER COULD BE VERY DEEP, VERY DEEP!!'

"Well, . . . we'll know for sure in a few seconds." She responded with a slight ring of anxiety, as Peterson stomps on the accelerator.

No further words are spoken, or transmissions broadcasted, as the Tahoe charges towards the flowing water. The creek bed is now becoming muddy, which quickly becomes shallow standing water, as the creek bed begins to descend towards the stream. The steering has now become very light. Peterson doubts that he possesses any steering control at all. The Tahoe plunged through the water, and across the stream like a champion swamp competitor on ESPN 2.

Seconds later the Tahoe is back on dry ground. The momentary blindness from the water, seemed as if the Tahoe became a submarine.

'OOOOOOH, WEE, . . .' the Deputy started in an approving tone, 'DOES THAT RIG TALK TOO?'

"Where are they!?" Peterson shouts out.

Automatically, Victoria relays the inquiry.

'BETTER BACK IT DOWN F.B.I. OR Y'ALL GONNA RUN RIGHT INTO THEM!'

Peterson, with determination mumbles, "And won't they be surprised."

Victoria witnesses a sinister grin forming across his face. She knows this look. She knows what he is thinking now.

"Michael, . . ." She started collected, ". . . If we broadside 'em at this speed, . . . we are ALL going to die."

Composed, he responds, "It has to happen one day."

"Michael!!!" She yells at him, losing her composure.

Meanwhile, high above in the Sheriff Department's

helicopter, the Deputies have a bird's eye view of the two vehicles. Though they are unseen by one another, they are on an unmistakable collision course.

"Oh man, this is gonna be messy."

The pilot reviews the trek of the vehicles and grievously says, "Better get on the horn, and get some medical personnel rolling out this way."

Tightening her seatbelt, she looks to Peterson displeasingly, as he tries to lock his safety belt. She moves in, swatting his hand away from the male end of the shoulder belt. She tugs firmly, and upon hearing the metallic click, locking the belt into the female portion, she settles in her seat and says, "Michael, this Rambo shit isn't cool!"

"No, . . . this is F.B.I. shit." He proudly states.

Through clenched teeth she leans over to him, with her erect index finger pointing at his face, she seriously warns, "If I get hurt, I'm going to kick your ass."

"Alright listen, . . ." He began decisively. ". . . You gotta nail those bastards. It is all gonna be up to you."

The heavily armed robbers continue to travel at a high rate of speed, along the traffic free two laned blacktop. As the sweeping right turn begins to straighten out, leading into an endless straightaway, they are completely unaware of the imminent return of the F.B.I. Peterson power slides the Tahoe around the right handed bend. The Tahoe is now parallel to the roadway. Traveling below the line of sight of the roadway, the fleeing robbers do not notice their pursuers. The flying Deputies advise the F.B.I. that the wanted van is just slightly ahead of them.

Suddenly, Peterson guides the Tahoe on a 45-degree angle up a 15-foot embankment, causing the vehicle to leap onto the roadway. Now traveling only a few yards behind the unsuspecting van, Peterson steers the Tahoe to the left of the van. With her MP-5 at the ready, Victoria electronically drops her window. She then leans partially out of the window while taking aim at the van. She then open fires upon it, unloading half the 30 rounds in the magazine.

The armor piercing bullets tear through the rear of the van, as if it was made out of paper. Victoria's effective firing pattern kills the passenger robber, and wounds the driver. The driver, now dying form his wounds attempts to keep the van on the road. Victoria remains prepared to deliver another burst, if any attempt to fight from the van.

After a few silent, tense moments, the van now swerves off the road. Peterson follows it. The van plows through some brush, and then finally rams into a tree. Peterson stops the Tahoe directly behind the smashed up van with a thud. He purposely rear-ends the vehicle, in order to prevent the usage of the rear doors.

Victoria and Peterson bail out of the Tahoe with guns drawn. Victoria begins to approach the van with her 9-millimeter carbine, at the ready. Peterson with his .40 caliber, pointing at the driver's door, advances cautiously. The Sheriff helicopter descends, and prepares to land on the blacktop. Peterson is now at the driver's door. He sees the driver slumped over the steering wheel, which is now lodged against his chest due to the frontal impact. The Agent sticks his gun in the dead man's ear, as he checks for a life sign.

Victoria did not need to check for any vital signs on the passenger. Brain matter, along with bits of skull surrounded in an ocean of blood, covers the interior.

"These would have been some famous bastards." Peterson said from the opposite side of the totaled van.

As he walks around the sturdy tree, which stopped the van, he coldly adds, "Nailed by the next First Lady of the United States of America." He looks over the passenger, as Victoria leans against the side of the van. While looking over the two dead men, Peterson says, "You assholes should of surrendered, . . . y'all woulda' made some money."

Without a word, Victoria begins to walk away from the

scene. She comes to a stool sized rock some 10-yards away. She sits upon it, facing the scene of the wreck. Her adrenalin high is eroding now. As she places the deadly weapon across her lap, she feels that the barrel is still warm. She watches quietly as Peterson confers with the Deputies. As she watches, she thinks. The violence now sickens her. She no longer hears the call of the Bureau. She is now a wife.

She recalls Peterson's referral to her, as the next First Lady. Victoria, for the first time, accepts the possibility. Her passion is no longer consumed with catching the bad guys. Her passion is now totally consumed with the man who has captured her heart. Her Husband, Jonathon Taylor Armstrong, . . . the man who would be President.

As she sits upon the rock, she feels as if her soul has left her body. She acknowledges that she had doubts about leaving the Bureau, but as of this day, sitting here on this rock out in the middle of nowhere, that regard no longer exists. Though she has spent all of her adult life in law enforcement, she has experienced more death and destruction, that would be psychologically sound. She admittedly loves her job, and believes in its mission. But now she has a deeper love, and it is for a man. J.T. Armstrong has touched her, and now she realizes, that life means much more than a rewarding secured appointment.

The passionate embrace and compassionate touch of her Husband, fans a fire which was buried deep within her soul. Afraid to love, and not permitting to be loved, Victoria's encounters with men were few, distant and filled with turmoil. The former U.S. Army General, and now Presidential Candidate, has conquered a well fortified and heavily defended position, Victoria's heart.

After their first tender kiss, she knew that to resist this man would be useless. Her mind instantly recalls the way he makes her feel. She feels the honesty of his emotion, when he makes love to her. Being without him, or his touch has been painful. Victoria is love sick, and she wants very much to leave this place. She wants to be with her beloved.

She now looks to the robber's van. Her mind details its damage, and it's two dead occupants. Her mind flashes on the battlefield intensity of the earlier shootout. A cold chill runs up her back, as if a cold February wind engulfs her.

"My time is finished her." She mumbles to herself.

She senses time is running short. She passionately wants to spend these days with her Husband. Her soul now reunites with her body. Feeling at peace with herself, she stands. A small pleasant voice, from the depths of her mind says for her to go and rejoin the General.

Chapter Thirteen

The aftermath of the confrontation with the Russian bank robbery team, put Carlsbad in the national news. The handful of Agents survived the deadly firefight, but two of the armored truck guards were killed. It's been a little more than eight hours since Victoria has been able to put her feet up. The Carlsbad F.B.I. office, has finally settled down to a tranquil atmosphere. Most of the office's Agents began to leave an hour ago. Special Agent Wybeck has just departed, smiling from ear to ear, after receiving a big 'at-a-boy' from Washington.

Victoria now glances over towards her partner, who is still on the phone at Wybeck's desk over in a corner. She returns her attention to the small 9-inch color T.V. on the desk in front of her. A news helicopter, flying over what was once Buffalo, New York, is now on the screen.

'WHAT YOU ARE SEEING IS WHAT REMAINS OF DOWNTOWN BUFFALO, WHERE WE ARE TOLD, WAS THE EPICENTER OF THE MAGNITUTE SEVEN QUAKE, WHICH STRUCK THE SLEEPING CITY, SOME NEAR 12 HOURS AGO.' The newscaster stated flatly. 'AS WE CAN SEE, . . . IT IS TOTAL DESTRUCTION. WE CANNOT SEE RIGHT NOW,

BUT WE UNDERSTAND THAT THE DESTRUCTION IS MUCH LIKE WHAT WE ARE SEEING, THROUGHOUT THE CITY. MOST OF THE CITY HAS BURNED DUE TO THE FACT, THAT THE FIRE DEPARTMENT PERSONNEL WERE SIMPLY UNABLE TO GET THEIR EQUIPMENT WHERE IT WAS NEEDED. AT THIS HOUR, POLICE AND RESCUE PERSONNEL HAVE TO PERFORM THEIR DUTIES ON FOOT, . . . AND INSOME AREAS, . . . THAT TOO IS NEARING IMPOSSIBLE.' He ended on a solemn note, pausing only for a breath, and then continuing, 'IN THE PAST HOURS, TREMORS, ...'

"The earthquake?" Peterson asked as he stood behind her.

Startled by his undetected presence behind her, Victoria relaxes back in her chair, and turns to him. In a compassionate tone she reports, "Yeah, . . . Buffalo is gone." She faces back towards the T.V. and adds, "It looks like a bomb hit it."

"Well, . . . get used to that image. You might be seeing them again." He said grimly.

She turns to him. "What do you mean?"

"This afternoon, a nuke note was delivered to headquarters."

"What's a nuke note?" She asked dumbfoundedly.

"You know, . . . a threat, with nuclear consequences."

"What in the Hell happened to the simple bomb threats? A car bomb here, a pipe bomb there."

"Welcome to the 21st century. Anyway, . . . the demand is for the President to surrender to the people, and answer to the charge of treason. She has until November 1st, or Washington, D.C. goes boom. The message further states that she has taken the government away from the people."

"You're makin' that up." She said flatly.

"Nope, that's the straight scoop, and oh yeah, . . . we got a job well done from Washington."

She stands to her feet and states, "Well, that was my last

well done job." She looks at him in his eyes, and announces, "I'm finished."

As he looks upon her, she then sighs.

"Mikey, . . ." She started sincerely, ". . . Take the money and run."

"That won't be enough."

"Then tell them we've slept together. That should be worth another one hundred grand, at least." She said now smiling.

He chuckles briefly, and then solemnly says, "No, . . . I mean, . . . I can't leave this shit. You were right, . . . this shit IS in my blood. I'm F.B.I. all the way. I'm going to die F.B.I."

Victoria drops her smile, and gently returns, "Don't let them kill ya."

Changing the subject, Peterson announces, "We depart for Washington in the morning, on a 9 o'clock flight."

"Hey, . . . do you want to stop and get a drink, before we turn in?"

Peterson smiles, "Hey, that's right, . . . since you're going to be quitting as soon as we get back, this may be the last time that I'm going to get to do that with you."

"Oh sure you will, before I leave Washington."

"I doubt it. Orders are now being cut for us, . . . I mean me. The group that sent the note has the Bureau on its feet."

"Just who are they, anyway?" She asked with her curiosity aroused.

"The People." Peterson answered, and then pauses for a beat, and adds, "Com'on, . . . let's get outa here."

Victoria switches off the T.V. and as she prepares to leave, she speaks. "The People? What in the Hell's going on here? Our office monitors, investigates and is responsible for all domestic terrorist threats to the country. Why is it that we know less than anyone else, or are the last to know?"

As the two Agents leave the dimly lit office, and stroll

through the hallways, outward to the street, they discuss the peculiar circumstances. Peterson speaks with an unconcerned tone. "Well since the C.I.A. has determined that the sponsor of the threat source is from outside the United States, our office, ..."

She interrupts, "But that source has supposedly matted with a rooted domestic source."

"Yeah."

"Then why is it that, we don't know squat?" Her tone now reflects a dubious sound. "Mikey, YOU don't miss these things. Just what in the Hell's going on?"

Wearied and mystified by the strange events, he himself is witnessing, he answers her sternly, with a macabre spirit. "What's going on? Some damn maniacs got their vile little hands on the ultimate terror weapon, . . . but their actions might be all for nothing." He added with a hint of gloom.

"Why do you say that?"

"Because I now believe that if the North Koreans, or the Chinese, . . . hell even the Russians for that matter, don't sneak us with a tactical first strike, . . . or some crippling plague-like disease doesn't wipe us out, . . . we could be on the dawn of domestic warfare here in this country. From what I've heard from Washington tonight, . . . I think civil war may not be too far away."

"Have you been around me too long?"

"The President is about to ensure control of America. The word is, that in 48 hours, the Bureau is going to be suiting up. All deemed renegade Militias, will be quelled, . . . by deadly force if necessary."

"All Militias groups are deemed renegades." She said flatly.

"Listen!" He began sharply, but now adjusts his tone, "A presidential order, to ban all firearms is about to be signed in a matter of hours. Citizens will then have 24 hours to surrender their hardware. Then afterwards, all possessions, and ownerships of firearms will become a Federal felony, and that is where the Bureau will come in." He stops, to take a breath.

"You're on a roll, don't stop now."

The two Agents have now stepped out onto the sidewalk. They begin to stroll towards their parked rental car. Peterson continues, "As I understand it, . . . the Bureau's function will be sort of a mop up detail, under the Department of Homeland Security."

"No more F.B.I. as we know it?"

"No."

"That's nuts."

"We will become a branch of Homeland Security. No more Department of Justice. Under the new umbrella we will engage and quell domestic terror."

"Behind U.S. Military Forces, no doubt." She said with hopelessness.

"What U.S. Military Forces?" Peterson returned bitterly. "They are all over the World providing snipers with live targets. We *will* be with military forces, but they will *not* be U.S. Did you know 250,000 troops of foreign countries, including Russians are here in America, on a so-called joint training operation?"

"No."

"Well, . . . it's the White House's plan to use THOSE forces. You see, . . . civilian registrants will be located, I assume by the F.B.I., and their weapons confiscated. Whatever resistance we encounter, military force will be applied."

"They can't do that."

"Did you know that in 1998, that President signed a pact with the U.N. allowing them to step in and assist with enforcement of Global Laws, even without the invitation of the President?"

"The Constitution, . . ."

Instantly cutting her off, Peterson interjects. "The

Constitution has become as worthless, as Affirmative Action back in the nineties."

Two mini-vans pull up and stop, just ahead of the strolling Agents.

"But the election, . . ."

Again, he cuts in.

"Vicky, . . . the question is now, will there still be a United States of America, by election day."

With this thought, Victoria is now more positive than ever that she is making the right decision about her early departure from the Bureau. She then looks at her partner, and decides, what the Hell.

"Mikey, I have to tell you something. I'm quitting the Bureau because I believe a Wife should be with her Husband, . . . especially now."

"What?" He responded dumbfoundedly.

"Mikey, . . . I married Armstrong."

Suddenly, from the lead mini-van, an authoritative voice heralds, "Agents Peterson and Owens, . . ." The voice pauses momentarily, awaiting their attention.

Instinctively, the duo looks to the direction of the query. Their eyes immediately focus on the pair of min-vans, as a suited clean-shaven man presents his official looking identification. Then as the second van's sliding door begins to slide open, the unknown man politely adds, "Would you two come with us?"

"What is this all about?" Victoria asked automatically, in order to buy some time to think of a tactical solution.

As she prepares to draw her pistol, Peterson has already assessed the scene. He's determined that if harm was intended, implementation would of happened already. With that, he now concerns himself with Victoria's previous statement to him.

"You did what?!"

"Agents please, . . ." The man still seated in the van says, ". . . This way."

Two men from the second van walk over to the first, while Victoria replies, "Can't this wait till morning?" She stalls.

Peterson, pursuing his questioning firmly asks, "When?"

One of the two men slides open the van's door, while the other, motions for the Agents to enter.

"Your presences are requested, . . ." The smooth, polite man begins, but now firmly adds, ". . . I must now, insist."

Knowing his partner as well as he does, Peterson knows Victoria is now about to reach for her pistol, and start shooting. Taking a firm hold on her forearm, and stepping slightly forward, Peterson asks in a booming voice, "Who wants to see us!?"

Still in a polite tone, the sandy haired man answers, "Congressman Casey. William T. Casey. Now, . . . will you please." He motions towards the open door.

"Casey?" Victoria questions her partner.

As he steps towards the van, he still holds onto her arm. It stretches outward as he moves. Noticing Victoria is standing firm, as if anchored to the sidewalk. He stops, and then turns to her, and explains, "Casey is a member of the National Security Counsel."

Looking at him with worried eyes, she gently utters, "Mickey?"

"It's okay." He said in a comforting tone.

Victoria releases her brakes, and follows only because her trusted partner said it was okay. Once inside the van, the door is slid closes behind them. The non-descript vehicle then drives off, gently into the night.

The Agents are rapidly transported to McArthur's Field. The small private airport sits 15 miles from Carlsbad. The solitary field, is now closed for the night, to air traffic and travelers. During the 20 minute ride, no words were spoken within the mini-van containing Owens and Peterson.

Peterson continues to wonder about the connection

between Congressman Casey, and himself. Agent Peterson has never personally met the Congressman. He only knows of the man's, no nonsense approach to circumstances. He's an exceptional man, of a caliber unseen widely in Congress today. Congressman Casey is a true American. Peterson remembers seeing him passionately speaking on C-Span, swearing that he would die, before he pledges any allegiance to any Global Union. The recalled patriotic stance Casey took, causes Peterson to smile.

Victoria wasn't smiling. She is very frightened. Inconspicuously, she has her mind on her pistol, as it rests in its unlocked hip holster. She doesn't know Congressman Casey, like Peterson does. She really doesn't believe that the Congressman wants to see them. The only reason she's present is because, her trusted partner said it was okay, but she is poised for battle.

As the mini-van drives up to the road blocking chain linked, ten-foot high barbed wire gate, a suited man slides the gate from across the airports isolated entrance. Without braking, the vehicle enters, and then turns immediately to the left. They proceed to an awaiting medium sized jet, with Unites States of America graphics upon it. The jet sits in the distance, in a dimly lit corner of the field.

As the vans come to a stop abreast of the jet, the man in the van carrying the Agents, exits and then opens the sliding door.

"Agents, will you please step aboard the jet. The Congressman is waiting." He informs politely.

Victoria steps out, and immediately looks to the other van. Peterson follows her out, and as he starts towards the transportable flight of plane boarding steps, he nudges the 'on guard' Victoria. She follows the relaxed Peterson, but continues to watch the suited men, as she ascends the aluminum stairway.

Standing alone in the plane's lounge, is a barrel chested man of medium height. His full head of silver and white hair, sparkles in the jet planes' interior lighting. As he stands with his hands behind his back in silence, he appears as tough as an overcooked pork chop. When Victoria looks upon him, she immediately notices his eyes. She sees they're fatigued and in bloodshot condition, as well as despair.

"Congressman Casey, . . ." Peterson started, humbly, as he approached the rigid man. ". . . It is quite an honor to meet you Sir." He ended with his hand now extended.

While shaking Peterson's hand, Casey sincerely replies, "Agent Peterson, I am very happy you came."

Victoria apprehensively approaches the pair. Congressman Casey, steps towards the cautious woman with his hand extended. As Victoria reaches for his hand, she watches his eyes. She sees them soften, just before he speaks. "Agent Owens, . . ." He begins in admiration, ". . . This is a pleasure."

"Congressman." She returned simply.

Addressing himself to the duo, Casey invitingly states, "Please sit down. Refreshment, snacks."

Victoria sternly interrupts, "With all due respect Sir, . . . why were we brought here, with all this cloak and dagger jive?"

With her anxiety displaying itself like a flashing neon sign, the wise Congressman firmly addresses her. "Stand down Victoria, . . . you are standing with a friend!"

"So you say." She said sharply.

"Vicky!" Peterson said in a threatening tone.

Raising his hand toward Peterson in a gesture of interruption, the Congressman says, "You're quite right Agent Owens. We all have been deceived. Just whom we can trust are all but a distant few. One of the few I trust is J.T. Armstrong. Another man I trust, though I have just met him, is this man." He motions to Peterson. "Do you know why that is Agent Owens?" He continues before she could reply. "It is because of his record. His loyalty is genuine. Agent Peterson is a solid family man, and a solid American. I know this man WILL die for these United States, if he had to. This is why I sent for him. I also know that he trusts you, Agent Owens, and I know you trust him. There is another man I respect, that trusts you as well, . . . J.T. Armstrong. This is why you are here." He takes a breath, and flatly states, "My time is short, and so I must be brief."

The Congressman takes a seat, and then addresses himself to Peterson, "Laddie, . . . fix us up a round, . . . anything will be fine for me." He looks up to the still standing Victoria, and in a grim tone, he begins, "You have learned a lot since the North Carolina incident, haven't you?"

"That's an understatement."

Casey motions for her to take the seat across from him.

"Have you progressed to the realization that this country's doctrine is being undermined from within? Slavery is soon to return to the U.S., but this time an alien power will be holding the whip."

"Well perhaps, if our domestic problems don't beat 'em to it." Peterson revealed.

"What domestic problems? Oh you mean the ones being effectuated." Peterson returns a not understanding, "What?"

Coldly he replies, "You heard me. There is a great deception in effect right his very second, and has been, for hundreds of years. Our forefathers recognized the threat, and warned of such things, as the New World Order, the Federal Reserve, and unchecked power. Now it's all coming together, but along came a monkey wrench.

"The monkey wrench is Armstrong, right?" Peterson asked sure he was correct.

"No, it's not him. Though his success is a complete surprise thus far and it is so only because the powers that be have been preoccupied." The Congressman ended as if it was an afterthought. He continues now back on track in an authoritative tone. "You see, . . . the monkey wrench is a power these people who control every blasted thing, fear and have since day one.

"I can't imagine what that could be." Victoria confessed.

"Truth is one." The Congressman returned. "That truth that he, and that does not imply that there aren't any women involved, is only a child in a vast universe which screams intelligent design. That means someone or something, older and smarter, . . . perhaps even responsible for even man."

"Most do not or will not believe that." Victoria said.

Chuckling briefly while recognizing Victoria's commentary, the Congressman responds to her in an enlightening tone.

"Yes, I know. Millions have been indoctrinated to believe we all come from a rock."

Interrupting, Peterson interjects, "I thought it was from some sort of prehistoric soup."

Clarifying the Congressman states, "Rain is supposed to have worn away the mountains to cause some sort of soup."

"So what are you saying, . . . they fear God?" Peterson asked.

"Then the question is which God?"

"Congressman, . . ." Victoria starts sincerely. "Are you saying that despite the fact that these people could be considered the offspring of evil, why would they be so fearful with what the Bible says?"

"Let me put it this way, . . ." He pauses momentarily in order to draw in a lung full of air. ". . . It appears we will presently sit on the dawn of Armageddon. Not the fairy tale of total life ending in nuclear exchange showcased in the movies, but one involving a power, . . . a force, . . . not of this Earth."

"Wait a minute." Victoria interrupts. "Are you trying to tell me we are about to face a hostile alien invasion?"

In a flat, unemotional tone, the Congressman answers, "Yes."

"Oh com'on!!" Victoria erupts.

"Agent Owens please, . . . !" Congressman Casey firmly thunders.

Victoria yields to the statesman's serious tone. Casey

continues passionately, "What I am going to share with you is fact. I know because I have sat among them. I have seen the data. I have been party to the plans of action. This is no fairy tale. These people, . . . the powers that be, World Governments, Intelligence Agencies, Defense Agencies, whatever or whomever anyone feels possessing the real power do possess great abilities. The knowledge in the hands of these people is frightening. Even as I now believe, . . . supernatural." He lowers his head and in a remorseful tone adds, "Mankind may be guilty of acts of horror against his brother but the evil that exists cannot be manmade. It must have been interjected from the womb of pure demonic existence."

Victoria glances over to her partner. She observes his blank expression. Peterson has been listening to the respected man, and desires to hear him out. Peterson sees Victoria's uneasiness and knows she is about to regard the Congressman as one nut the squirrels forgot to collect.

Congressman Casey stares at his drink in hand, and continues humbly.

"They have their hydrogen bombs, germ warfare stockpiles and the ability to change weather patterns as well as earthquakes and volcanic eruptions, . . . and those are just a few. They have massed such a power to the point to where no single power could ever threaten them." He chuckles and faces the duo. "Americans think they are free because they possess firearms. So what. What they don't realize is their beloved guns will be completely useless for what FEMA has in store for them." He ended and now drinks from his glass.

While he drinks, Victoria gently informs, "Congressman Casey, . . . you are starting to lose me here."

The Congressman drains his glass, and moves to prepare himself another drink.

"Very well Agent Owens." He answered firmly as he prepares his drink.

Casey returns to his seat. He looks Victoria directly into her questioning eyes and explains with abandoned conviction.

"Though they do not fear the well armed American Patriot, they do fear Planet X."

"That passing comet?" Peterson asked.

Before Casey can answer him, Victoria fires, "That thing is going to hit us after all?"

"Congressman Casey looks up at Peterson and replies in a tone of seriousness that would make a snowman shiver. "It is quite possible it is not a comet." He then looks into Victoria's softening eyes and continues, "And no, it is not going to hit the Earth. From what my NASA sources tell me, the fear is what this barely visible sphere many times the size of Earth represents." He ended.

Silence engulfs the trio as the Congressman drinks from his glass.

Victoria, feeling as if she is sitting on a hot plate impatiently asks, "And that is?"

The Congressman slides back in his leather chair with his drink in hand and states, "Well, that would depend on what one believes."

Frustrated, Victoria pushes herself back into her leather-covered seat and looks to Peterson with disgust.

"You see, . . ." Congressman Casey begins to patiently explain, ". . . It doesn't matter what we believe. We have no power, therefore we must understand the philosophy of those empowered over us all. In this case, they fear Planet X. They are preparing for it."

"Preparing for what?" Peterson asked. "If it is not going to hit us, then what's to fear?"

Victoria looks to Peterson and states, "But if it is not a comet, . . ." She looks back at the Congressman, ". . . As you said, . . . then what is it?"

Smiling, Congressman Casey says, "Okay, . . . let's connect the dots. We have been at war with E.T.'s since 1962. NORAD beneath Cheyane Mountain was built not for Russian sneak attacks but a space observation command, to monitor any space traffic out to 30,000 miles of the planet. There are advanced weapons the likes that would make lasers primitive on satellites. Secret launch facilities in the South Pacific to supply and re-man the three space stations in high orbit. Pine Gap I Australia is a massive military installation designed to fire upon any unidentified flying object entering Earth's inner space. So that answers an age-old question. UFO's are real, and they all are not black projects of the United States or any other governments of this World. How can one believe that this government is spending billions and billions to build Buck Rogers equipment to fight the Russians or the Chinese, or terrorism? Ronald Reagan wondered if we had to fight an alien force. General MacArthur wrote a report concerning UFO's. Even the Bible tells of aliens, . . . beings not of this Earth, visiting the Earth."

"So again, you are telling us Planet X is some sort of alien invasion?"

"Planet X could be a controlled object. It could be what the Sumerians wrote thousands of years ago, or in order for evil to respond so, it could be because the Creator is returning to eliminate the wicked from the creation?" Casey said.

Immediately Peterson snaps, "Or perhaps this is all nonsense. Perhaps this is all just some sort of 'psy-op', tricking everyone into the New World Order. The one World government. Full control, a 'Borg-like' state but without the tubes and wires sticking out of all our collective asses."

"That very well may be son, but whether anyone chooses to believe, the fact remains. Something terrible is soon to make itself known to all of us." Casey said grimly.

With unbelief Peterson balks, "Not more of this end of the World hype."

Disregarding her partner's emotional comment, Victoria directs her question to the Congressman, referring to his last statement.

"Like what Congressman, war?"

The Congressman looks away from her and focuses his eyes upon the carpeted floor.

"I just feel so sorry for the young ones." He said hauntingly.

The Congressman's sorrow filled face and repentative speech causes Victoria to feel goose bumps the size of marbles sprout from her skin as her blood seemed to suddenly turn as cold as an icy stream.

She slides slightly forward toward Casey and gently whispers, "Just what do you know?"

Casey takes his glass and raises it to his thin pale lips. Without hesitation he consumes the entire contents in one swallow. He looks to Peterson and then extends his arm with the now empty glass toward the Agent.

Peterson understands the nonverbal request and silently takes the Congressman's glass and proceeds to refill it.

"Agent Owens, . . ." Casey starts unemotionally. ". . . As we speak select members of the private elite and this government are preparing for the end of the World as we know it, by fleeing the United States."

"If Doomsday is just around the corner, just where on Earth do these people think they are going?"

"When I said they are fleeing the country, I mean this planet as well. They are not consigned to the planet as the rest of us are."

Peterson interjects as he hands Casey his highball glass of whiskey.

"I have heard of some plan to off world the big wigs in the event of nuclear war, especially if we start it, or some other World threatening event. They have Moon bases, maybe even Mars too by now."

"Mike." Victoria called to him.

Peterson familiar with her tone, addresses her. "No hear me out. Billions spent on a space program only to recover a few rocks from the Moon and a live video of a rocky Martian surface, Bull! These bastards have had this sort of an escape plan since the 1960's."

He now looks to the Congressman and adds, "Isn't that right?"

The Congressman while keeping eye contact with the F.B.I. Agent, sips his drink.

Victoria in an anxious tone says to her partner, "Mike, what in the Hell are you talking about?"

"He is somewhat correct, Agent Owens."

He looks to the Agent and explains, "We never stood on the Moon nor Mars. That was said in order to keep the funds available for this present day event. The Russians have three space stations orbiting the Earth. China has one, we, . . . two as well as the European Union. They are positioned in high stationary orbits above the poles, but are low enough so the radiation from the Van Allen Belt will not pose a problem. That is the major reason they aren't going to the Moon. The radiation will eventually kill them. The task could be done, but the large enough ships to be built with hulls thick enough to withstand the radiation have to be built off the Earth or they would never get out of the pull of Earth's gravitation field." He takes a breath and adds, "Being on the NASA / N.S.A. committees taught me a thing or two."

"So when do you check in to your high orbiting room?"

He chuckles and answers, "Like I said before, I am Earthbound. I am not even going to report to my assigned FEMA bunker. I figure what would be the point?"

Peterson protests, "You're a United States Congressman. You know continuity of government."

"That is Bull, as well. Martial Law and Executive Orders will be the next government. If any form of government is to survive you can rest assured it will not be a civilian one."

"Then tell me something, . . ." Victoria tenderly begins, ". . . If all this is true. If some sort of threat is upon us that will change everything, . . . maybe even wipe us all out, then why in the Hell was Armstrong such a threat?"

"He is a threat. Like I have said before, not all of these globalists believe that there is an end time threat. The so-called Third World War, U.S., the British and Israel on one side, Russia, China and the Arab World on the other is a certainty. The powers that be could care less for they have their underground cities and their space stations. As to Planet X or whatever they are calling it, . . . whether it is a space vessel or a wayward hunk of rock, they believe it can be dealt with. Their plan is to deal with Planet X out in space. You see X is not advancing normally. Sometimes it stalls hence the idea it is a controlled object. Since *they* believe *they* can deal with X, Armstrong also must be dealt with, hence the plot to assassinate him. With one stroke they can kill Armstrong, freedom and then bring forth their demonic New World Order, and the voters will never know, what hit them. Therefore, Election Day cometh. Despite the fact voting is now all electronic, and *they* can simply program the machines to elect whomever *they* want. Though 32 states are fighting to have these machines thrown out completely, or supply a paper trail. See, . . . eliminating Armstrong in this manner would be too risky. A landslide re-election of this current President would never be believed nor would a close count much like what happened back in the year 2000 contest.

Then there is his creditability. Armstrong has more than anybody in this present administration. He is a true war hero with the respect and admiration of Leaders Worldwide. Also, . . . he is not aligned with the Globalists. No plans of World domination, endless wars and the rest of the 'good ole boy' agenda.

The powers that be have sought to discredit him, but he is solid. No emotional buttons for the media to expose. They would have killed him, . . . you know, . . . the old plane crash bit, but I suspect *they* know such an act would cause massive queries. So this brings us to the reason why I summoned you here. The President needs a dramatic event to plunge the

American people into a state of fear and compliance. Remember that radiological bomb discovered in New York's Central Park a few years ago? Yes, well that my friends was to be *the* event. Martial Law was supposed to be declared. Congress would have been escorted from Washington and FEMA was to be Lord and Master over the land.

They were dealt another blow when you, Agent Owens derailed their latest diabolical plan, . . . but I have information that a re-attempt of said plan is to be activated.

A gathering is to take place in a mountain retreat in upstate New York. Green Country. The agenda is 'Planet X' and the terrorist attack involving a weapon of mass destruction, which would of course kill the General in the process. The emotion filled flag waving citizens of America will rally around the President and demand the spilled blood of the victims to be avenged at any cost, as well as blinding, allowing this administration to do whatever it decrees necessary to make them feel safe. These emotionally filled people will provide the matches for the burning of the Constitution and Bill of Rights.

You two have the skill to get close enough and eavesdrop on these traitors of the people. That is one thing they can't stand, light. Shine the exposing light of truth upon them and they will whither like a fresh cut rose in the Texas summer sun."

The Congressman swallows the contents of this glass in one gulp, as the two Agents remain silent as their thoughts inundates them.

Casey breaks the silence when he begins candidly. "So you see, . . . Armstrong must be eliminated. *They* know he is a man smart enough and strong enough to undo all *they* have done. Armstrong is presently the only man in position to bring American back from it's Hell bound course, . . . and they know the people will follow him."

Victoria has listened to all the Congressman has said. Fear now grips her like a pair of strangling hands around her neck. Her fear is not of the discussed doom and gloom, but for her love. He does not belong to the country, nor the entire World. He is mine! He belongs to me! Her thoughts cry out in a boiling anger.

"He is only a man Congressman." Peterson started. "He is not a God."

Casey sincerely returns, "He may not be a God, but the Almighty's hand is surely upon him."

Victoria's fear for her husband has been overwhelmed by anger. She has mentally drawn a line in the sand. Enough is enough. If these people won't stop coming for him, then they must be stopped.

"I cannot waste any further time here." She said sharply as she begins to rise from her seat, with her still filled glass of alcohol in her hand.

The Congressman motions to stop her. When their eyes meet, he sharply states, "Your feeling is correct, Agent Owens."

A cold chill, causes her body to quake. He now turns to the briefcase that has been sitting beside him.

Victoria takes a sip from her glass. The potency of the distilled spirit disrupts her ability to breath momentarily. While she coughs, and struggles to regain her breath, she looks to Peterson with a mystified expression.

Peterson catches her look, and defends, "That's premo sippin' brandy." He then immediately hoists his glass to his lips, and deposits the shot of liquor, and smile at the now recovered woman.

This nut will drink anything, so long as it's flammable, she thinks to herself. As she sits the glass into the recessed beverage holder on the table, Congressman Casey hands her a folder. She takes it, and opens the vanilla colored folder, while Casey explains, "Pictured there, are the key participants of tomorrow nights meeting. I'm sure some of these very same individuals were involved in the Armstrong assassination plot. Their names, titles and current government affiliations are listed on the back. The Agent who supplied these photos, and pointed us in the direction of the Catskill meeting, was found dead just a few days ago. He was stripped naked, and tortured slowly to death. It is doubtful that he talked, for their meeting is still on. I do hope that these bastards all burn in Hell."

His emotion is felt by Victoria. She looks to him and sees the pain in his eyes. She then looks over to her partner. His eyes meet hers for a moment. He slowly lowers his downward, towards his empty glass. He now starts over towards the bar and flatly asks, "Sir, . . . are you sure Agent Owens and myself are your best choice?"

Not looking towards the inquiring Agent, but peering into his own still full glass, the Congressman starts speaking in a lifeless voice, "Agent Peterson, . . . you are without a doubt, a patriot. For all your adult life, you have stood by this country. You bled for our flag. You truly believe in what our forefathers envisioned for this country." He takes a breath, and now looks to the fully attentive man. "Not only are you a battle veteran Marine, . . . but you also have associations with Black Projects. According to your resume, . . . you being in the F.B.I. is like this remarkable woman being a security guard in a fast food restaurant."

Now the older gentleman directs his attention to Victoria. He now speaks with a strong tone of conviction. "You just might of changed the face of history in North Carolina. Now, I want to present you with a task that will permanently ensure that change."

Peterson flatly says, "I think I can guess what you might want us to do."

Snapping his head to the drinking man, Casey sternly says, "No, no, no Agent Peterson. If that dirty little deed was done, then their cause would continue. But, . . . to expose them, . . . to turn the light onto them, . . . is what they fear most."

"This evidence you have."

Interrupting him, the Congressman says, "The evidence is weak, but capturing the meeting on tape will clinch it all. Getting those men conspiring to overthrow this government, will kill them all!!" He ended strongly.

"And you would like for us to record that meeting?" Victoria asked lightly.

"Yes."

"Why? I mean, there must be a bunch of guys who, . . ."

Stopping her, Casey firmly informs, "Yes, there are other sources, but during these trying, and deadly times, trust and loyalty are at a premium. Presently, . . . there aren't any spotlights upon you two. Look, you two aren't due in Washington until late afternoon, D.C. time. No one is really going to miss you both until the next morning. You can get to New York, and be back in Washington by day break, with the tape that'll stop these Godless, Globalists!" He ended intensely.

In almost a whisper, Peterson asks, "And if we fail?"

Coldly Casey answers, "Failing is not an option, Agent Peterson."

"What if we don't do this?" Victoria began, probing, "I mean, what if we pass on this?"

Facing her, Casey sincerely answers, "Do you really believe Armstrong will ever command this Nation, with these people out there?"

She swallows hard, and answers, "I'll get him to quit."

"My dear, . . . your emotions are showing." Casey compassionately said to her. "Now use logic. He won't quit, . . . he can't quit." He now leans slightly forward, and personalizes his message. "Before he went to North Carolina, I pleaded for him to withdraw from the race. He simply smiled and said, "Billy, . . . it's gonna be alright. You see, he's on a mission. His destiny has been written in stone. Perhaps what I am asking from you and Peterson is futile, . . . but God help me, . . . I must do something." He pauses momentarily to detour a heart wrenching display, "Pardon me, . . . now my emotions are showing." He confided. "I respect that man. I love him and I would surely die for him." His voice now changes to a sincere tone of veraciousness, "If I was 30 years younger or possessed either of the skills you guys possess, . . . I would not enlist you two. I would embark on the task myself."

Peterson walks over to the sitting Congressman, and reveals, "I received word tonight from Washington that disturbed me, and after conferring with my partner here, the news now scares me to death. If going to New York will stop this madness, . . . then I am in."

"So am I." Victoria said softly.

"No way!" Peterson objects strongly, and adds, "Sir, someone else will have to accompany me."

"I'm a big girl." She stated firmly.

Turning to her, and in a hearty tone Peterson insists, "Vicki, . . . go to your man."

She shakes her head no as she looks into her partner's eyes.

"I can't, . . ." She started in a soft tone. ". . . I see this entire matter as if there was a poisonous snake lying in wait, out there in the grass. Now, I can go and stand by his side, and help him to watch for it, before it strikes. Or, . . . I can venture out and hunt the snake, and cut its vicious head. You might not understand this, . . . but I am in." She now looks past the Congressman to Peterson, to enforce her statement. She releases her over protective partner from her stare, looks to Casey, and continues. "I too questioned why I have been driven to the field, when I could have been back in D.C. counting paperclips. Now I clearly see my purpose." Her eyes wonder off Casey, and then she adds, "It's all crystal clear now."

A pause of silence descends. Casey looks to Peterson. As the eyes of the two men meet, Victoria continues, sounding sharp, and direct.

"I do agree with you Congressman. I believe they will

attempt to assassinate my Husband. If I must die, so he can live, and the United States can once again be a country of liberty and freedom, . . . then so be it."

"The General's wisdom is evident in choosing you for a wife." He ends smiling tenderly.

"Just for the record Congressman, . . ." Victoria started matter of factly, ". . . He did the asking, but I did the choosing."

Congressman Casey lifts his glass towards the woman Agent, and in a toasting gesture smiles warmly.

Chapter Fourteen

Twenty minutes later Owens and Peterson were being driven back to their rental car. Prior to leaving the congressman, the elder Representative supplied them with vital information in order for them to complete their task. He gave Victoria an oversized vanilla envelope containing photographs of the farmhouse in the Catskill Mountain. Along with the photos is a detailed map of the entire area of operation.

Peterson was given a smaller business sized white envelope. Their pickup vehicle, which has already been parked at the airport is equipped with the items needed to fulfill their task. Inside Peterson's envelope are the keys to the non-descript sedan. Also enclosed are two photos of the midsized car, and it's exact whereabouts in the parking lot.

Now in Victoria's motel room, they sit with only the bedside lamp on. They are examining all of the information supplied by the Congressman. Peterson sits on the bed, up against the headboard, with his feet just off the floor. Victoria is sitting in the bright orange armchair nearby. She looks to him, and flatly asks, "So, . . . what do you think?"

"It reads like a simple recon mission. Almost too simple."

"You sound unsure about this."

"I don't know, . . . maybe I'm just getting too damn paranoid."

Tenderly Victoria replies, "Well, . . . anyone not paranoid these days, is just not paying attention."

"I just can't believe all these things that are happening. We were promised that the year 2000 would be the ushering in of Paradise. Oh, we have animal rights, and have boycotted products produced from trees of the World's Rain Forests. We wear crystals, chant to the Moon, caged man and returned the land to Nature, and things are worse now than ever." He ended bitterly.

In the same endearing tone, she says, "That's because, all you have said, were nothing more than doctrines of deception. You know, the Humanist kill me with all that crap. They think THEY can fix all the ills of Nature. No one person, . . . not even a thousand, or millions can fix the environment, . . . or bring the fish back to the sea, . . . or seal the holes in the Ozone Layer." Her tone now becomes filled with conviction, "Only a Superman can do that. Only a Superman can provide human rights for everyone. Only he can heal this sick World, and put an end to our slow, but sure destruction."

"Superman, huh?" He said cracking a smile.

"No not Clark Kent."

Beaming a smile, he proudly responds, "Oh, then you must mean the United States Marines."

She shakes her head with a smile, and then earnestly says, "No I mean the ONE, true Superman sitting the Heavenlies. He now sits at the right hand of the Father. He and only He, can fix all of these things. He is about to return shortly. All these things that are happening all around us are proof, that He stands at the door."

"If He has enough sense, He won't come in."

"Yes He will. Soon, when the trumpets sound in the clouds, the command will be given to the Believers to come forth, to meet the Savior in the air."

"Yeah, right." He said in a disbelieving tone.

His response sparks her to continue her speech with a warning. "Those that will remain on the Earth, will witness the instantaneous, and simultaneous disappearance of people, Worldwide. The Rapture has just occurred. The Almighty has just ordered the evacuation of His People, and now the commencement of Hell on Earth begins."

"Oh that's just an old story, written a long time ago for weak people. It's a fairy tale! Like civil rights, and affirmative action!" He now stands, and bitterly says, "What's with all this holy talk, anyway? What are you now, a Sunday school teacher?"

"Something comes this way soon. The World's state is approaching a climax. This course we're on has been pre-selected. All that comes has to be, this cannot be altered, because the Savior is about to return."

"For what, . . . this World is going straight to Hell." He said sharply.

"Not the whole World, Mike."

In an agitated tone, he snaps, "Hey, look around you will ya. There ain't no escaping this shit! So wake up, and get a grip. Your prayers are falling on deaf ears!" He ended.

He turns and starts for the door. As he lets himself out, he mumbles, "I'll see you in the morning."

The door closes behind him with a thump. Victoria sits quietly within her room. Peterson's objectionable tone reverberates throughout her steadfast mind. She begins to mumble a prayer for her hardhearted partner, as well as for herself, and for her Husband, and for all of Mankind.

During that night, hundreds of thousands of people Worldwide report sighting UFO's. Official statements respond stating the sightings are nothing but a meteor shower burning up in the Earth's atmosphere.

The next morning, Agents Owens and Peterson board a reserved chartered flight, for Steward Airport, New York. General Armstrong will be enjoying some spicy San Antonio BBQ this day, as he campaigns in the Lone Star State. Calm has seen another day throughout the strife torn streets of Paris. A CNN poll this morning reveals, that 2 out of every 5 Americans are Satanists. 98 percent of Americans believe in a higher spiritual power. 64 percent believe in the God of the Bible. 56 percent of Americans will be willing to surrender constitutional liberties, in order for law enforcement to make the streets of the U.S. safe. President Norge is leading in the polls by 2 percent, but her performance rating is less than 30.

Owens and Peterson's charted flight lands at Steward Airport, at 5:00 p.m. E.S.T. They immediately depart from the terminal enroute to the parking lot. They locate their prepared sedan, just where the instructions indicated where it would be. They open the trunk, and inventory the pre-loaded equipment. Peterson recognizes most of the high tech surveillance items instantly. 1120 to 1 zoom video camera, with night eyes capability. A nap-sack, containing a laser guided receiver, which has the capability to eavesdrop on distant subjects, without distortion or interference. Attached to each of the devices are simplified instructions. As Victoria eyes the Beretta M-12 submachine guns, Peterson rips the instructions from the items, and then hands them to Victoria.

"You study, I'll drive."

The duo, with Peterson behind the wheel, starts out of the parking lot. Victoria, with the precise map in hand, navigates the pre-plotted course to the Catskills Mountain farmhouse, which sits near the Roundout Reservoir.

Just as the brilliance of the sun's rays dim to dusk, the Agents arrive at the designated spot on the map. Peterson pulls the car over, onto the grassy shoulder along the deserted two laned roadway.

"17 point, 3." He reported while he looked upon the odometer.

Victoria opens the glove box, and withdraws the Global Positioning Device, and hands it to Peterson, while she tells him to remotely open the trunk. As she leaves the car, Peterson presses the trunk button, causing the trunk to pop open, and silently lift. Victoria takes out the knapsack, and begins securing it to her back. Peterson joins her at the auto's rear, and remarks, "It looks as is someone has already blazed us a trail to the house." He said as he looked at the positioning device.

He now looks to her and says, "It's gonna get pretty damn dark out here soon. This little baby will get us back to the car."

"Check." She says flatly, as she pulls the powerful, full sized video cameral from the trunk, and immediately begins to examine it for it's readiness.

Peterson slips the G.P.S. into his pocket, and reaches into the trunk and withdraws a M-12. He inserts a fully loaded 40 round magazine into the SMG, and chambers a round for firing. As Victoria examines the video camera, Peterson begins to attempt to attach the M-12 to the knapsack on her back.

"No." She said firmly, stopping his action. "I have the equipment. You're the security."

Peterson silently agrees to the arrangement, as he moves the weapon away from her. He then reaches into the trunk, and withdraws two additional 40 round magazines. He places the extra ammunition in his pockets, and then withdraws a non-commercial, compact pair of forward-looking night vision glasses with 'heat seeker' capability. A selector switch on the glasses allows the viewer to detect body heat or illuminate the moonless night as well lit as if it was a sunlit day.

He looks to her and asks, “Are you ready?”

She nods. Peterson closes the trunk, and then looks to his watch.

With concern, she asks, “Do you think we should hide the car?”

“We’re three miles from the house. They’re not going to have security out this far. It’ll be okay here.”

“What about the car keys?”

Snapping his fingers, indicating that she raised a good point, he produces the keys from his pocket. He then kneels behind the rear of the sedan, and says, “How about just inside the exhaust pipe?”

Victoria nods in agreement. He stands and then asks, “Are you ready?”

“Always.”

She then motions for him to take the lead. As he passes the woman Agent, Peterson stops, and festively says, “You know, if we pull this off, . . . we’ll be heroes.”

He then smiles at her, and then begins to trek the way. Victoria doesn’t smile, nor does she reply. As she steps into the thick forest of trees, she can’t help but to rationalize that a hero is nothing but a sandwich.

Some of the participants of the meeting have already started to arrive, by the time the Agents began their approach. As the duo marches deep into the trackless forest, they instinctively, fall back on their military training. Stepping deeper into the thick company of the trees, darkness has already seized the light of the day.

Peterson has been here many times before. Though, not in such a scenic setting, as among the trees of New York’s Catskills Mountains. He reflects on how indifferent this scene is, compared to those in other parts of the World. This walk through these stateside woods on this day has the potential to be as deadly as many of walks he has taken on hostile foreign lands.

This former U.S. Marine Corps Recon Ranger Leader figures, this mission will be a piece of cake. Simply avoid any contacts, get the video, and then 'd.d' out, and then get some grub. He's holding a craving for liver and onions, so the sooner they get this over with, the sooner he can eat.

Victoria has no desire for food, at this time. While she trails her partner, her thoughts are soley on this mission. She doesn't fear the dangers that could be upon them if they are discovered. She has accepted the fact, that she and her partner are committing the last attempt to, quite possibly, save the United States. All of the chips are riding on them, and with that, she has also accepted the possibility of death. She has concluded, she rather die, that to live in a Godless society.

There is no room within her spirit for fear. Rage has seized all available space. As she walks, she repeatedly recites to herself, yea though I walk through the valley of shadows and death, I fear no evil. For thou art with me, thy rod and thy's staff comforts me.

The Agents have made it to within 50 yards of the farmhouse, undetected by roaming security patrols. They have positioned themselves on a 45 degree angle, enabling them to see, both the front, as well as the side of the house. They lie prone upon the ground, and silently observe.

The night's sky is breathtaking. The full moon, hanging in a crystal black sky, dominates the millions of visible stars. The sky reminds Victoria of her nights in Madison with the General. The General, she begins to reminisce fondly, about him when suddenly Peterson speaks in a whisper, "So, you believe in God, huh?"

"Yes, I do."

In a belittling tone, he responds, "But you are suffering here, right along side of us non believers, . . . hello?"

"The suffering hasn't really begun, but when it does, I believe I won't experience it."

"What, you have a ticket to somewhere?"

"No, just a word of promise."

Dumbfounded by her answer, he questions her with curiosity. "What promise?"

"The Heavenly Father's promise. He has promised evacuation for his people, . . . and he will evacuate."

"Oh, here we go again with the Rapture jazz. Well, if that is what helps you make it through, then fine, . . . when it doesn't happen, I won't say, I told you so."

Hauntingly, she replies, "When the trumpets sound, and the command is given, pray that you are found worthy to be raptured. Pray Michael, while there's still time."

Harshly he responds, "Pray to whom, . . . God? There is no God. There is no Jesus gonna help you, and no Rapture is gonna save you." He now becomes indignant, and continues straining to remain hushed. "Get a grip Vicki, . . . we are in control of our own destiny. Just where is your God, huh? The World is falling apart. Earthquakes in Buffalo, crazy storms, floods, food shortages, riots, murder, death and destruction, . . . and you believe in God??! Since when have you become so religious?" He ended matter of factly.

"No, . . . my Mother was so religious. I on the other hand, have had what was a flame within me re-ignited, and now the flame of faith burns white hot. I am not a fool. A fool says, there is no Creator, as they partake in their play now, pray later, secular humanist narrow minded, egotistical agenda."

"Armstrong filled your head with all of this didn't he. You see, . . . that's the problem I have in voting for him. If he gets in, he's gonna try and jam that religious crap down everybody's throats."

Grimly she returns, "I don't think you have to worry about

that, my friend. I* personally think it's too late. This country is too far gone. I believe we, as a nation, have lost our favor with the Father in Heaven."

Silence falls over the duo, as they withdraw to their thoughts.

An hour and a half later, Victoria looks to her partner, and points to her watch. Peterson sees the signal, and looks over the scene once more before he replies. It's been an hour since the last car dropped off its occupants. He's satisfied that they are positioned well outside the dozen or so security team's patrol area. He now nods to her, and then scans the entire area with his 'night eyes'.

In a very quiet tone, he asks, "So, who do we have in attendance?"

With the photos in hand, Victoria answers, as she files through them, "Attorney General Christopher Rickman. Jack Van Kimple, the E.U.'s man. Kelly, retired CIA Chief, and Atkins, the current Deputy CIA Director . . . ."

"That's enough." He said, cutting her off.

"There are other odds and ends of government officials in there as well, Military, Cabinet Members, as well as other CIA Department Heads."

"Get that gismo fired up. I want to hear what they're saying."

"You know, . . . it was once said, that the CIA has total unaccountability, and it's tremendous power knows no limits. If a plot was to arise to overthrow this government, it would be borne, and executed by the 'community'."

"Com'on, get that thing together." He said flatly.

Victoria strips off the knapsack containing the laser receiver. She skillfully begins to place its folding, non-reflective, 8-inch collector dish towards the house. She connects the coaxial cable to the receiver. She then attaches the earplug's stereo wire, to the six-paced sized unit. Victoria places the ear canal filling plugs, in her ears. She now activates the unit. The built in battery immediately brings the high tech spy device to life. She applies her index finger, and thumb gently to the rotary search knob. She gingerly begins twisting the knob. Suddenly voices from the house, fill her ears, as clear, as any powerful F.M. radio station. The Agent now picks up a monoscope sized device, and looks through it, aiming it at the house.

Now she can see the unsuspecting guards from 50-yards away, as if they were standing within10-feet of her. Their conversation of desired breast sizes comes in loud and clear. Victoria now aims the optical sight on the front windows of the house. She pauses momentarily. There is no conversation going on in that room. She now concentrates her attention along the side of the house. She slowly drags the optical extension of the listening device across the distant windows until suddenly,

". . . rid of the Militias, then we can effectively disarm the American People." The unidentified man's voiced firmly.

"Showtime." She whispered, as she activates the mini 'night-eyes' camcorder.

Another voice, accented by an European intonation begins, "Within a week, gentlemen, . . . the Euro-Core Army WILL be deployed satisfactory throughout the United States, with another 100,000 troops here in 14 days. In a month's time, this country will be incorporated into the ranks of the New World Order."

Victoria nudges her partner. She hands him an earplug, and sarcastically says, "Do you want to listen to history in the making?"

Peterson takes the earplug, and places it in his ear. Victoria ensures that the powerful camera is on target. The thermograph imagery is working flawlessly, as the European man turns and says, "But my dear friends, all of this hinges on the removal of Mister Armstrong."

Both Agents snap their heads toward one another.

"Well, . . ." An American speaks, ". . . like I have said

before. The current plan to remove Armstrong is fail proof. Now, we are aware that his candidacy has gotten stronger, since the failure of the first attempt. He has a very good chance of winning. Therefore, there cannot be any further delays, regarding this matter. His mere existence in this race threatens all of our endeavors."

The European man speaks with a heavy heart, "I never thought, I would live to see the day when America would elect a Blackman, to her highest, and most powerful office."

Grimly the American, the former CIA Director explains, "That present possibility will end with tomorrow's sunset. As Armstrong's plane takes off from Dallas, it will be shot down by a surface to air missile. We will then see to it that factions of the Middle Eastern Alliance are to blame for this terror attack. The order will immediately be given to ground all air traffic within the United States. At the same time we will leak rumors to the effect that factions of Neo-Nazi groups in America may be responsible for the shoot down as well, thus causing the illusion of a unprecedented international and domestic link of terrorism within these United States."

Victoria looks away from the camera, and fights to keep herself in control, as the man continues.

"With provoked violence in New York City, L.A., Atlanta, New Orleans and other minority population centers, will begin to unfold with furor. The Media will hype the rumors, thus sparking a race war. U.S. Military Forces will be needed, but they will be found ineffective. A mourning, disrupted, and chaotic Congress, will grant sweeping powers to enlist the Euro-Core Forces, to restore order, even at the sake of Constitutional Guarantees. Goodbye Militias. Goodbye armed citizens."

Slowly becoming unglued at the seams, like a snowman melting in the sun, Victoria frantically withdraws her cellular phone, and begins punching in the number to Armstrong. The electronic tones reporting from the palm-sized phone, sound as loud as the gongs on a church tower. Peterson worries that a patrol might hear them. He scans the area quickly, with his 'night eyes', as the men inside continue.

". . . and what of the Agent that saved his ass in North Carolina? I mean, . . . in the aftermath of Armstrong's death, she might become a problem."

The frantic high low beeping from Victoria's phone indicates, that her call cannot be completed.

"By noon, . . . the emotionally unhinged woman will have committed suicide. It is known that they are romantically linked."

Chuckling, a man says, "This is like 1963, all over again."

Victoria snatches her pistol from it's hip holster, and starts for the house. Peterson grabs her by the arm, stopping the wrathful woman.

"Get your hand off me." She said in a low Hell-borne tone.

Victoria's utterance causes Peterson to shiver, as if he's just stepped from a shower, and into the cool air.

"What are you fucking crazy? You won't make it anywhere near that house."

Unbeknown to the duo, a pair of security men, have since spotted them, and are creeping up on them.

"These bastards are just too dangerous to live." She said.

"Then we'll kill them with a weapon they fear most, . . ." He pauses for dramatic effect.

She looks to him, but the seemingly sudden appearance of the two silhouettes, only a few feet away, catches her eye.

". . . exposure. They hate that the most, and I believe we got them by the short hairs now."

"Freeze!!!!"

Two beams of light projecting from the flashlights attached to the men's semi automatic rifles, shine into Victoria's eyes.

As the two men rush to close, the last few remaining feet that separates them from the couple, Peterson turns to face the direction of the startling voices. Though particularly blinded by the lights, he takes a quick look to his M-12 lying nearby on the ground. Victoria remains still and silent. Her hand gripping her pistol is at her far side, unseen by the advancing security men.

"What in the Hell are you people do'in here!!?" A voice from behind the light said, as another radios the discovery of the couple.

Out of character, Peterson voices a nervous, non-threatening young man. "Oh Officer, . . . we just came up here for a little privacy."

"We ain't cops asshole, now shut up!"

Victoria now politely asks, "Sir, would you please take your light out of my eyes, . . . I can't see."

Mocking her, the second man says, "I can't see, . . ." He then smartly takes his weapon and shines the light upon himself, and says, ". . . is this better?"

The face illuminating man's light is also providing enough light to highlight the other man as well. In a stern low voice, Victoria answers, "Yes."

Faster than the two unsuspecting men could react, Victoria fires once, striking the shadow man in the face, and then she fires again, hitting the man illuminating himself in the throat.

"Shit." Peterson mumbles in amazement, as he looks to the dead men.

Victoria turns and starts towards the house. She then stops, as she sees in the moonlit darkness, a dozen or so figures running towards her. She continues to stand, and watch them approach. She debates to fight them her, or take the battle to them.

Peterson picks up his submachine gun, and sees the advancing numbers. With his free hand he snatches Victoria by her collar, causing her to swing around 180 degrees. With her back now towards the house, and the charging security men, Peterson firmly gets her attention. "You better be listening to me damn it!! This is not the time, or the place! We're NOT going to die here, do you read me!! Now, get your ass in gear lady! Get that camera, and follow me right now!!" He ended sharply, and then pulling her by the collar downward, towards the camera.

Peterson's forceful tug carries enough momentum to cause the woman to fall to her knees. Now, with her senses jolted, she quickly reasons that to die here with all of this evidence at hand would be truly stupid.

"Com'on!!" He said, as he watched the men close to within stone throwing distance.

Victoria snatches all of the wires from the camera. As she stands with the camera, Peterson takes off through the woods, towards the car. He doesn't know if their pursuers are equipped with night vision aids, so he leads their retreat through as much natural concealment as possible.

As the duo runs, the security men begin firing upon them as they give chase. While they run for their lives, Peterson checks the GPS periodically, to ensure they are on the proper course. He keeps the pace at an all out run. He figures that they are going to need every second their lead grants them.

Peterson now recalls all the missions like this, he was on while he was in the Marines. He had never had to withdraw under fire. Now, he thinks about all the money he has been offered. Fuck this, he thinks, and now decides that he will take the money offered for his accounts, working with Victoria. He will then take his family, and leave to perhaps a nice piece of land in the Montana Plains.

All Victoria can think about is her Husband. She continually calms herself with the fact that it is still early. Armstrong is not in any real danger until morning. She figures, dust these bastards behind us, make a call, save him, and then he'll drop from the race, or I'll kill him. She recalls instantly the words of the late, German born leader of the men, who tried to kill the General in Madison. Mister Smith did make a point. Why be so loyal to a country that lies, mistreats, and disrespects Black Americans. That's right, J.T. and I should leave this country. Armstrong is too good for them. I won't allow America and her evil intendancies to destroy my Husband. We'll catch fish and make love all day. From our shores, we will witness America sink into damnation. Forgive me Father.

Victoria and Peterson's break out from the trees is sudden. Peterson stops at the tree line, and says under labored breathing, "Get the car squared away, I'll cover."

Victoria runs off to the car, as Peterson, using a tree for cover, begins firing into the forest. The former Marine's cycle of fire is fierce. By the time Victoria recovers the keys from the exhaust pipe, and gets the car started, Peterson has expelled the 40 rounds, and changed magazines. He hears the car start. Victoria gets out of the car, and begins a slow rate of cover fire for her partner. Upon hearing the pistol fire, Peterson fires another burst, and runs to the awaiting sedan.

Both duck into the car simultaneously. Victoria slams the gear selector downward, and stomps on the accelerator. The engine roars to life, as the front wheels spin wildly, chewing up the roadside grass. As the car pulls away without any illumination, the pursuing security men, break through the woods and prepare to fire upon the departing vehicle. They hold their fire as the car becomes absorbed into the shadows of the night.

As they watch the car fade from view, a message comes over their radio.

'SIR, THIS IS SEARCH THREE, INTRUDES WERE NOT MEDIA SPIES. I HAVE DISCOVERED TWO OF OUR MEN. D.O.A. AND SOME SORT OF A LISTENING POST HERE!'

The leader of the men raises his portable two-way digital radio to his mouth, and then calmly states, "Alright listen up, the intruders fled south on 46 in a light colored sedan. I want a full search for this vehicle. I want them found, and

I want them dead. Get me a vehicle over here, out." He said, terminating his transmission.

Victoria has activated the car's bright lights. She is currently holding the car at 90 miles an hour on the unlit, two laned roadway. Peterson is steadily watching behind them, through the rear window. With one hand on the steering wheel, and the other, holding her cellular phone, Victoria is using her thumbnail to punch in the numbers. With her eyes alternating from the road to the keypad, she finally completes her task.

The display on the phone immediately flashes, 'NO SERVICE', as the frustrating high, low signal cries out. Peterson now relieves himself from the rearward observance. He turns and faces forward in his seat. Victoria ends her attempt to phone, and drops the telephone in her lap, between her legs.

"I think we got away clean." Peterson said, as he looked to his partner.

He sees the tension on her face. In a comforting tone, he says, "Take it easy, . . . we got the bastards."

"I still have to reach J.T. before he gets on that plane!"

"Is the phone still out?"

"Yes."

"It's probably the mountains. Once we get outa them, we'll call Congressman Casey, he'll know what to do."

Snapping at him she responds, "I know what to do! I'm going to get my Husband, and then we are getting the Hell outa here! We are history! Goodbye!"

Recalling that he has made the same decision, Peterson humbly agrees, "Yeah, I hear ya."

A pause of silence floods the car momentarily, as the duo think to themselves.

"I just can't believe what I heard back there." He said flatly.

"You weren't dreamin'."

Peterson then asks, "So all the trouble that's going on, is the work of theirs? The Militia Groups aren't uprising, and they never did pose a threat to the American People?"

"Nope."

"But why? Power?"

"The ultimate power baby. GOD like power."

A short pause of silence follows, and the Peterson asks, "Did you ever see that movie, 'Seven Days in May' with Burt Lancaster?"

Victoria replies, "Movies!? You want to discuss movie trivia now!?"

Out of the corner of his eye, Peterson sees a car's silhouette, sitting in a small clearing, just off the side of the road. He snaps his head rearward, as Victoria flies by. He witnesses the car's headlights come on, as it pulls onto the roadway.

"Oh man." He said as he faces forward again.

"What?" She asked as she looks into the rearview mirror, just as an array of flashing red lights burst from the trailing car.

"You done woke up the 'man'. Doin' 90 in a 55 zone, man he's gonna bust your ass." He ended teasing.

"Bite me." She answered as she begins to decelerate.

While she starts to brake, and pull off onto the grassy shoulder, with the State Police car following, she places the M-12 on Peterson's lap.

"Do something with that, will ya. I don't want to get shot to pieces by a nervous Trooper."

Peterson places the SMG on the floor, while he reaches for his I.D. As Victoria comes to a stop, Peterson says, "I'll get you out of this." He ended with a smile, as he starts to exit the car.

She picks up her cellular phone, and as she starts to exit the car, she again attempts to make her call to Armstrong. When Peterson faced the stopped State Police car, he was immediately blinded by the brilliant, twin high powered, take down lights, as well as the two door mounted spotlights on the side of the patrol car. As he walks toward the seemingly ball of multi-colored lights, he displays his Federal I.D.

"F.B.I. guys, . . . we need your help!"

Victoria is now out of the car. The blinding light causes her to hold her head downward, as she starts to wander towards the patrol car, while she continues to enter the series of numbers to complete her long distant call. Peterson has now reached the rear of their sedan, when the two unseen Troopers, emerge from their car. Victoria's call goes through, and the ringing tones begin to emit. She cheerfully puts the phone to her ear, just as Peterson is gunned down.

She is now standing at the rear of their sedan, and sees Peterson falling to the ground. Taken totally by surprise, her mind does not process the data of the rapidly occurring facts quick enough. With the gunfire still echoing through the isolated woods, and the gunpowder lingering like a thin cloud among the powerful lights, her eyes remain fixed on Peterson. He lies on the ground face up, with multiple bloody holes in his dead body.

A voice repeating, 'hello, hello', breaches the stillness of silence from her cellular phone. The long distance voice snaps her mind back to the obvious deadly encounter she faces. Her first impulses are to go to Peterson, as well as responding to the voice on the phone, engaging the police, and running for cover. She knows she stands checkmated. Despite the fact she is unable to see beyond the bedazzling source of light, she drops her phone, and reaches for her pistol.

The shooters allow her the effort. They then open fire upon the woman Agent. Victoria screams out as the first bullet tears through her abdomen. Another bullet smashes into her hip, causing her to begin to spiral along the rear end of the sedan. Bullet number three, strikes her in the chest, right through her right nipple. Another strikes her forehead, but her twirling motion causes the bullet to deflect. The next three impact on her back. They pass through her, causing massive internal damage.

They now stop shooting. Victoria slides off the car's rear, and drops onto her bloody back. Her body, now settled upon the ground, is dying. She is experiencing severe difficulty in breathing, but not much of anything else. She reasoned at first that she was dead, but she can see the now clouding sky above, as well as hear the idling engine of her sedan. She hears someone walk past her, towards the sedan. One of the shooters picks up her cellular, and throws it into the woods. He then continues onward to the car.

The other shooter steps up to Victoria, and then stands over her. She figures, since she is still alive, it's now one to the head time. As she continues looking skyward, she begins to silently pray. Suddenly out of the stillness, the sound of an approaching car, racing toward the scene is heard.

The figure standing over her steps away. Victoria now feels very sleepy, and relaxed, as if she has just stepped from a soothing bath, and is now lying upon a very comfortable bed. She looks upon the fading star filled crystal clear sky. She finds the billowing thick, white cloud blanketing the sky, to be quite unusual. It appears if someone had a smoke machine, and was producing cottony white puffs of clouds. Actually, it is one big, continuous fluffy cloud.

The sound of a trumpet seems to come from everywhere. As one of the shooters returns from her sedan with the video camera, he delivers it to the occupants of the newly arrived vehicle. The leader of the security force, takes the video camera, and coldly asks, "And the intruders?"

The shooter, dressed in a complete New York State Trooper uniform reports, "Dead."

"Dying." The other uniformed shooter stated, as he looks upon Victoria.

Victoria has now heard a third chorus of trumpets, and now, like thunder from Heaven, a voice commands, 'COME UP HITHER!!'.

The leader firmly instructs, "Then finish him, and let's get the Hell outa here."

Coldly, the shooter above Victoria informs, "It's a her, . . ." He then adds sinisterly, ". . . I never watched anybody die before."

Victoria now sees her Mother's smiling face amongst the clouds.

"Mommy?" She called out weakly.

The shooter stands over her, with Victoria's dying body positioned, between his legs. He pulls out his pistol, and aims it at the center of her forehead. Victoria no longer sees him above her. She no longer hears the idling engines about her. She now sees her Mother. Victoria strains to lift her hand, raising her arm, as if she was reaching out to someone.

"Mommy." She mumbled with a smile.

The shooter looks towards his cohorts and humorously says, "Hey!! This bitch keeps calling me mommy!!"

"Shoot her damn it!!" The leader returned sternly.

The shooter looks downward, ready to pull the trigger, but then pauses. The leader sees the shooter standing frozen in place. Now enraged, he exits his car, and storms over to the shocked shooter. As he approaches, the leader angrily states, "What, you just found out that you don't have the balls, ..." He stops in mid-sentence, as he stands with the shooter, looking down upon the ground.

"She's gone." The shooter said in a chilling tone, and then repeats himself, but this time his voice rings with panic, "She's gone!!"

The other men rush over to the scene, as the shooter begins to hysterically rant, "She disappeared man! She fuckin disappeared!!"

The leader kneels down and examines where Victoria's body once laid, just moments before.

Now becoming defensive, the shooter begins, "There's no way, she coulda moved! She was shot to pieces! Look at all that blood!!" He ended, and then starts to look beneath the idling vehicles.

One of the leader's men walks up to him, and asks, "Sir, . . . there must be a blood trail. Should we commence a search?"

The leader nods robotically, as he stands to his feet. He senses deep down, that a search will discover nothing. He looks over to Peterson's still present body, and wonders.

The shooter that was standing over her continues his ranting, "I'm tellin' ya, she disappeared! She just fuckin vanished! One second she was there between my legs, bleeding and dying then, . . ." He snaps his fingers, ". . . she disappeared!!"

The leader looks to the ranting man, and then up to a crystal clear star filled sky, while dumbfounded by this bizarre scene. His man approaches him, and in amazement, the man reports, "Sir, . . . there isn't a drop of blood anywhere else but here. It's like someone has picked her up from right here."

"People just don't disappear!!" The excited shooter shouted in fright.

'For the Lord himself shall descend from Heaven with a shout, with the voice of the Archangel, and with the trump of God, and the dead in Christ shall rise first. Then we, which are alive, and remain, shall be caught up together with them, in the clouds, to meet the Lord in the air. And so shall we be with the Lord.

1 Thessalonians 4:16 & 17
K.J.V.

THE END

Printed in the United States
25583LVS00002B/200

9 781413 462951